HOW I LOST
YOU

Jenny Blackhurst was born in Shropshire where she still lives with her husband and children. Growing up she spent hours reading and talking about crime novels – writing her own seemed like a natural progression. Inspired by the emotions she felt around her own son's birth, HOW I LOST YOU is Jenny's thrilling debut crime novel.

Praise for **HOW I LOST YOU**:

'As twisted as a mountain road, Blackhurst's fast-moving and unputdownable debut will keep you glued to your seat'
Alex Marwood

'A thrill' *Shropshire Star*

'Utterly gripping – brilliant debut!' Clare Mackintosh, author of *I Let You Go*

HOW I LOST YOU

JENNY BLACKHURST

headline

First published in paperback in 2015 by
HEADLINE PUBLISHING GROUP

1

Cataloguing in Publication Data is available from the British Library

ISBN 978 1 4722 1896 4

Typeset in Meridien by Palimpsest Book Production Limited,
Falkirk, Stirlingshire

Printed and bound in Great Britain by
Clays Ltd, St Ives plc

HEADLINE PUBLISHING GROUP
An Hachette UK Company
338 Euston Road
London NW1 3BH

www.headline.co.uk
www.hachette.co.uk

To Ash, and to Connor, who never gives up and always finds a way. Love you chicken nugget.

Acknowledgements

Thank you, first, to my wonderful agent Laetitia Rutherford. Without your passion for Susan's story and your unwavering support I wouldn't be writing these thank yous now – you have truly made my dreams come true.

To Vicki and Darcy and the entire team at Headline. You've taken a stone and polished it into a diamond and I'm very privileged to have been welcomed into your world. Thanks for all the advice, for managing to treat me like I know what I'm doing whilst realising I don't and for every bit of hard work you do.

To the most supportive friends a little girl could have, for every time you've gotten excited for me when I was too scared to get excited for myself. For every time you've told me I could do it, and acted like without a doubt I would MAKE IT. To Sarah, my first ever reader, for telling me when I'd gotten it right, but more importantly when I'd gotten it wrong, Lorna, Jo and Laura for always being there – it's over seven years now girls, you're stuck with me. To Emma and the girls from JN who were there when I started this, and the ladies and gents at SFRS who were there when I finished. You probably don't realise how strange and totally awesome it is whenever one of you asks 'how's the book?'

To the dedicated reviewers at YWO – without your input this book would never have made it past the slush pile. Special thanks to Notley – everyone's first reviewer – not just for tearing it to pieces but for helping put it back together, Kay Leitch, Siobhan Daiko and Fred Hebbert for your continued support, and for making me believe I could be a 'real writer'.

And finally to the greatest family a little girl could wish for. To my mum and dad, who have always taught me I could do anything I set my mind to and have kept me going at it just by being there, and to my big little brother who I do love really. I hope I've made you all as proud of me as I am of you. I love you.

Ash. For all the words of encouragement, love and support; for my wonderful son and our unborn child; for the late night chats in the shed where you so matter of factly told me to 'give it a go' and for always being the man I married. I love you and the boy more than words can say.

To the honourable members of the board,

My name is Susan Webster. Nearly four years ago, on 23 July 2009, I killed my three-month-old baby boy. It has taken me this long to be able to say those words and accept that they are true, yet writing them still brings me unimaginable pain and grief.

During my time on remand and the subsequent two years eight months at Oakdale I have researched just about everything that exists about puerperal psychosis, the form of post-natal depression I suffered from after Dylan was born. Reading about it helps me understand and realise that I wasn't in control of my actions on that awful day. I also know now that my memories of those twelve amazing weeks with Dylan have been romanticised in my mind, created by denial of the terrible anger I felt towards him. I know this because that's what the doctors say. Harder to accept than the knowledge that I killed my little boy is the thought that my sacred memories – all I

1

have left of my beautiful son – are the product of my own warped mind. In my darker moments I find myself wishing that I could remember the hatred, the indifference towards the life I'd created. Maybe then I would have a moment's peace, some respite from the guilt and pain that clouds my every waking moment. I hate myself for feeling that way; my memories, real or imagined, are the only things that help me to cling to the person I used to be. The person I thought I was, at least. A wife, a mother, a little disorganised maybe, a terrible cook for sure, but never in my most hideous nightmares a murderer.

Whilst I have accepted what I did, I do not expect forgiveness. I know I will never be able to forgive myself. All I ask is that my remorse be taken into consideration during my parole hearing, so that I can try and rebuild my life, do some good in the world and begin to atone for the evil in my past.

Yours respectfully,

Susan Webster

1

24 April 2013

It's still there.

No matter how many times I leave the room and try to go about my normal life, every time I go into the kitchen, there it is.

It arrived this morning, hidden underneath the brightly coloured junk mail and ominous-looking bills. I dread receiving the post as it is. Sunday is my favourite day of the week.

No post on Sundays. Except today isn't Sunday. And today there is post.

I can only guess that my hatred of all things enveloped is down to the sheer volume of bills I receive every day. I've only been here four weeks and it seems every utilities company in the country is trying to bill me for something. Each and every 'To the Occupier' letter I receive reminds me of something I've forgotten to set up a direct debit for, depressing me about how disorganised I am, and how far my meagre funds need to stretch.

What arrived in the post today isn't a bill, though. I know

that by the handwritten envelope. It isn't a letter from a friend or pen pal. It's postcard size, and brown. The writing is small and cursive; it looks like it belongs to a woman but I can't be sure. None of these things are the reason it's still on my kitchen countertop, unopened.

I could just put it straight in the bin. I could wait until Cassie comes over and ask her to open it, like a student getting their mum to peek at their A-level results. Walking over to the envelope again, I see the words written on the front and my heart begins to race.

Susan Webster, 3 Oak Cottages, Ludlow, Shropshire.

But Susan Webster is dead now. I should know; I killed her four weeks ago.

No one in the world is supposed to know where I am, who I am. That was the idea of changing my name by deed poll. Even my parole officer calls me Emma. Sometimes I still forget to answer. My name, my new name, is Emma Cartwright. You won't know me by that, though. Four years ago I was still Susan Webster. I can picture you now, you're screwing up your nose a bit; maybe you recognise the name from somewhere, can't quite place it? Your eyes might flick up and to the left as you try to remember. If you live in the north, you might mutter something like 'Oh yeah, wasn't that the woman who killed her son? Such a shame.' More likely if you live in the rest of the country you won't remember me at all. The news broke at the same time as a major celebrity was caught dealing drugs. My son and I were only found on the inside pages of the nationals.

I'm going to do it. Hands trembling, I tear open the envelope, taking care not to rip what's inside. As the small piece of card falls into my hands, I wonder for a second if I should be wearing gloves, if it's some kind of threat and the police

will need it as evidence. It might sound strange to an ordinary person, worrying that my post might be filled with death threats. Believe me, it's a situation I would never have imagined myself in either.

It's too late to worry about forensics now. Anyway, it isn't a letter; it's a photograph. A young boy smiles widely at the camera, a warm, genuine, beautiful smile. My fear turns to confusion. *Who is he?* I don't know any children that age; he's around two or three, maybe. I have a niece but no nephew, and the few mums and babies I'd met at baby groups before . . . well, just before . . . have stayed away, probably blocking out what happened as though Dylan and I had never existed.

Why has this been sent to me? Scanning my memory for children I know, I throw it on to the worktop. It turns in mid-air, landing face down on the counter, and it's at that moment that my whole world narrows to the size of the 4x6-inch photograph in front of me. Written on the back, in the same neat handwriting, are just three words:

Dylan – January 2013.

2

'It's a prank,' Cassie announces, throwing the photograph back on to my kitchen counter. *That's it?* Twenty minutes of waiting while she stared in silence and all I get is *prank*? I take a deep breath.

'I know that, Cass, but who? Who but you knows I'm here? Is it a threat? Or does someone actually want me to think Dylan is still alive?'

She looks away, and I know who she thinks has done this.

'Mark,' I declare. 'You think it's Mark.'

Cassie grits her teeth at the mention of his name and fights not to say anything. Not easy for her. Her sharp chin juts out and I think she is literally biting her tongue. My best friend hates my ex-husband. She dislikes most men, but I think Mark tops the list. I know for a fact he wouldn't have liked her either, even though they have never even met.

I suppose I should explain about Cassie. She's the best friend I've ever had, the kind of friend I've always wanted, but we haven't known each other our whole lives. We didn't meet as shy schoolgirls on the first day of school and we weren't college roommates. When I met Cassie it was against a background of wailing voices and steel doors slamming

shut behind me. She was sitting on the top bunk, her bleached blonde hair piled in a heap on the top of her head and her thin black eyebrows narrowed. She threw herself off the bed and landed like a cat next to me – I found out afterwards she'd broken her ankle the first time she'd tried it. Loose ivy-green prison slacks hung from her protruding hip bones and her vest top could have come from the children's section, pulled up to show milky-white midriff. She looked like she could be knocked over by a strong wind, and yet she had the strongest physical presence I've ever known.

'Top's mine but I'm not a bed pisser like some here so you don't have to worry. Don't touch my stuff.'

I met Cassie on what was the loneliest day of my life. I didn't know it then, I wouldn't know it until much later on, but she saved it, saved me.

We met because she's a criminal. A murderer, like me. Cassie though, unlike me, remembers every second of her crime. She revels in the details, tells the story like Girl Guides tell horror stories around the campfire. She gets fed up of me telling her that her indifference is a 'defence mechanism against the memory of her crime'. She called me Freud for a week after I first suggested it, refusing to use my name until I promised to stop psychoanalysing her. It's the closest she's ever got to admitting I might actually be right.

'OK . . .' I'm willing to indulge her for a while. 'Let's assume it's Mark. How does he know where I am? And why would he want to make me think our son is still alive?'

Cassie rolls her blue eyes skyward in impatience. 'He works in IT . . . right?'

'Right.' I nod a confirmation. 'He's not a hacker.'

She just shrugs, as I get up to make yet another cup of tea. When my hands aren't busy, they're shaking.

'And the why? Why would my ex-husband-turned-computer-hacker send me a picture of a boy who we all know can't possibly be my dead son?'

'Maybe because he's an asshole? Or because he wants to add yet another layer of guilt to the emotional shitload you already carry? Or to mess with your head? Maybe "January 2013" isn't supposed to mean that the boy *is* Dylan, just that this is what he'd look like if you hadn't . . . well, if he wasn't, you know . . .'

'I know.'

'Do you still have your pictures of Dylan? In the album your dad gave you?'

'Somewhere,' I reply absently. I'm not getting those out. 'I don't think this would have been Mark.'

Mark was devastated by the loss of our son – any man would have been – but he tried his best to stand by me. He even visited me at Oakdale twice. Both times he was shaking like a shitting dog and could barely look at me, but it was good to know that he was trying to forgive me. Then the visits stopped, just like that. I received a letter a few weeks later informing me of the divorce proceedings, with just a handwritten note from Mark: *I'm sorry.* That was when Cassie crafted a dartboard from my pictures of him and took to throwing soggy paper towels at it to cheer me up. We weren't allowed darts in Oakdale. We weren't allowed sharpened pencils in Oakdale.

'So it's just a prank.' I'm trying to convince myself. 'Not a threat. Except the word "prank" suggests something's funny, which this is *not*.'

'Hoax, then, or, what do they call it, the fraud squad? A swindle.' This is what Cassie's like when she decides she's right about something. Her long blue gel nails strum a pattern on the table, her need for a cigarette clear. Those nails represent, for me, the complete transformation she's been through since leaving Oakdale. When I met her, it was bitten-to-the-quick nails covered in month-old chipped paint that tapped out their impatient pattern. Those are long gone, along with the short denim skirts and navel-skimming tank tops. These days her clothes cover her flesh and her nails are never chipped.

'Hoax, yeah, of course,' I reply absently. 'It's got to be a hoax. Definitely not a threat.'

I get rid of Cassie as fast as I can by pretending I've got errands to run. She knows I'm lying but takes the hint without question and kisses me, leaving a bright pink lip print on my cheek and an inconspicuous wet paper towel in the sink.

Turning the envelope over in my hands for the hundredth time, I notice something that sends a shiver down my arms. There's no postmark stamped on the envelope. It must have been on my mat before the post even arrived. Whoever did this was at my house, stood at my door and silently hand-delivered the photograph while I was in my kitchen. The thought makes me feel physically sick and I cover my mouth with my hand. *It's not a threat.* It makes no sense as a threat. If it's a threat, it's a rubbish one. There's no actual threat even implied. Except the subtle warning that someone knows my name. Someone knows who I am. What I did. Someone who was standing at my door.

I can't be strong any longer. The fight has melted out of me and I sink to my knees on the cold kitchen floor and begin to sob.

3

Jack: 23 September 1987

A foot connected with the boy's face, a heel slammed into his ribs. He curled tighter into a ball, let out a grunt, but not – Jack observed with grudging respect – tears. When they saw the blood, Riley stepped forward, but Jack grabbed his arm – it was too soon. Another minute or so, a couple more bruises, maybe a broken rib. From his position twenty feet away, leaning against the crap-coloured demountable huts, the beating almost looked choreographed, mesmerising. When he heard the crack, like a twig snapping, and the grunts stopped, he stood upright, wiped off the arm of his jumper and motioned for Riley to follow him towards the fun.

'Get the fuck off him.'

All three of the boys stopped, although one kept his foot on the fifteen-year-old's broken wrist – as if he was going anywhere otherwise.

'Fuck's it got to do with you two?' Boy one – Jack hadn't a clue who they were – made a gesture like he was headbutting an imaginary goat in front of him. Fucking moron.

10

'What's he done?'

'Grassed on Harris.' Boy two, the one with his foot on his victim's wrist, ground it into the floor. 'Didn't you, Shakespeare?'

'Wasn't me,' the pile of blood and clothes murmured from the floor.

'Who was it then?' demanded boy three – Harris, by the looks of it. He was the biggest of the three but from what Jack had seen he'd done the least amount of harm. Maybe he didn't like to get his clothes dirty. Made sense.

'Dunno. Not me.'

'Lying little snake.' Boy two made to start kicking again. In seconds, Jack was at his side, grabbing his claret-coloured blazer and shoving him away.

'I told you to get the fuck off him. He didn't grass your mate up. He's telling the truth, it wasn't him.'

'Oh yeah – how'd you know?'

'I know everything, you moron. You want to know who grassed you up, go and see Mike Peterson.'

Harris narrowed his eyes, and so did Riley at Jack's side. 'You sure?'

'I'm sure. And one more thing.' He gestured at the boy on the floor. 'He's with me now. You got any problems with him, you come and see me. If I ever catch you touching him again, I'll have your legs broken – all of you. See where your rugby career goes then, Harris, you fucking meathead.'

He held his breath, kept his jaw still. Harris turned back to his thugs and motioned with his head for them to leave. All three of them walked away as though they'd done nothing more than finish a game of football.

'You all right?' Riley pulled the boy to a crouch, kept his head forward and down. His shoulder-length brown hair was slick with a combination of grease, sweat and blood. He tried to turn his head to face Jack standing above him, then cringed and focused on the floor again.

'Why d'you tell them that?' The words were barely discernible through lips that were already beginning to swell. 'Peterson . . . didn't do it. I did.'

'I stopped them kicking the shit out of you, didn't I? Do you want me to call them back? Tell them I made a mistake?' He turned to face the direction the boys had retreated, knew they were well gone. 'Harris! Oi, Harris!'

'No, I'm sorry, didn't mean it.' The boy winced from the pain.

'Jesus, you're a mess. Come on, I'll get you back to mine – my mum and dad are never in and Lucy will be able to fix you up.'

'Who's Lucy?'

The housekeeper. I kicked off when they said she was coming to live with us 'cos I knew they were getting her to keep an eye on me but she's actually all right – she's only like eighteen and got massive knockers, and she makes wicked toasties. I'm Jack, this is Matt. Why did they call you Shakespeare? Is that your nickname?'

The boy tried to scowl through the blood. 'No. I hate it. I got a hundred per cent in an English test and Miss Bramall called me a little Shakespeare. Now that's what everyone calls me. I'm—'

'I like it,' Jack interrupted. 'Makes you sound smart, and I like smart people. I can call you Billy for short if you like, like our little joke. We are mates now, aren't we?'

'Why do you want to be mates with me? I'm not like you and your lot.'

'Oh yeah? And what are my lot like?'

'Rich. And well . . . good-looking and stuff.'

Jack looked at Matt and they both started to laugh. 'You queer, Shakespeare? Fancy my mates, do you?'

'No! I didn't mean like that. I just . . .'

Jack snorted. Jesus, was this guy really that square? He was going to have his uses, though.

'Come on, let's go and get you cleaned up.'

4

Like most Saturdays, the town is packed with teenagers,
couples, and mothers dragging their toddlers sullen-faced
and whingeing around the few shops we have left. 'The reces-
sion has hit the town hard,' Rosie Fairclough tells me as she
serves me a huge slab of sticky, warm chocolate cake. 'We need
more young blood like you to start bringing money back to
the place.'

I almost laugh out loud. Nosy Rosie would have a different
opinion if she had the first idea who had come to live in her
sleepy little town. *That* would be some gossip for the WI.

Digging into my chocolate cake a little too hungrily, I risk
a furtive glance out of the window. Nothing but cobbled
streets full of shoppers. I shake my head feeling ridiculous
and try to remind myself I'm not living in a low-budget spy
movie. No one is watching me. I need to try and forget all
about what happened this morning, the stupid *prank,* so I
switch my attention to the people around me.

Another woman sits near the counter, lost in thought and
nursing a slice of carrot cake without ploughing in the way
I have. She's about the same age as my mum would have
been but she doesn't look like she needs to worry about her

14

figure and I guess from her expression that something's wrong. Her long blonde hair falls into her face as she gazes at the newspaper in front of her and she doesn't bother to push it away. I find myself wondering what her story is. A fight with a lover? An errant husband? Or something much worse?

Almost as though I've called out to her, she abruptly looks up and catches me staring. Embarrassed, I move my gaze over to the door, hating the fact that I've been caught gawking at her. 'Don't stare, sweetie,' my mother used to tell me. 'It's rude.'

'Well that didn't last long.' Rosie sees my demolished chocolate cake and smiles. 'Can I get you another?'

Oh God yes.

'Oh God no.' I laugh a little too loudly. I've always had a struggle with my inner fat girl; food is my comfort. If ever I refused food, my mum would look at my dad and tut, 'Uh oh, I think we've got a problem on our hands, Len.' She'd tease me even though it was her fault we were a family of food lovers. Her home-made meals, especially her desserts, had my friends lining up to be invited for tea, and my lunchbox was the envy of my classmates. Roulades, lemon drizzle cake, raspberry meringue – I was like the primary school version of a crack dealer. Much to my husband's disappointment, my mother's culinary skills never quite reached me, and he had to settle for a bloody good Sunday lunch at the in-laws once a week. 'My hips would never forgive me,' I say. 'Rosie, do you mind if I ask you something?'

The older woman's eyes light up as though I've asked if she would mind if I gave her a winning lottery ticket. Being a fountain of information is what Rosie does.

'I was just wondering, what are people like round here? Do you get much trouble?'

15

Rosie shakes her head. 'Oh no, love, well, I mean you get the odd scuffle with the kids in town on a Saturday night, but not much else. Why, have you been having a problem with someone?'

Instantly I regret asking. I knew Rosie was a gossip but now I'm wondering if she has it in her to dig for her next snippet. Will she be on the net as soon as I leave looking for Emma Cartwright's secret past? Ah, paranoia, my old friend, I've missed you the last hour.

'It's nothing really,' I lie easily. 'I found an egg on my doorstep this morning; I just wondered if maybe the locals weren't keen on new people moving into town.'

Rosie looks disappointed. 'That'll be kids, love,' she tells me. 'This place isn't like some small towns, you know, where everyone knows everyone's business. We mainly keep to ourselves. I wouldn't let it worry you.'

'No, of course,' I reply, relieved my tiny fib hasn't raised any other questions. 'That's what I thought, just a prank.'

The slab of chocolate cake weighs heavily in my stomach as I leave, Rosie's words bouncing around my mind. *This place isn't like some small towns, you know, where everyone knows everyone's business.* They told me before I left Oakdale to be prepared for people to be hostile if they found out who I was. I was ready for torches and pitchforks; I didn't expect stalking and mind games. The fact remains, stupid joke or not – someone knows my old name. Which means they know what I did.

The bell above the door of Deli on the Square chimes loudly as I enter. The home of good food, Ludlow boasts some of the finest home-made and locally sourced cuisine in Shropshire and plays host to a food festival every September. The fat girl inside me *loves* Ludlow.

'Emma, lovely to see you.' Carole beams as she spots me in the doorway. 'How are you?'

'I'll be better for a box of your Camembert and some crusty bread.'

Carole disappears for a second and returns with a brown paper bag. As she hands it over it still feels warm, and I catch a waft of the freshly baked bread inside.

'I'll take a bottle of wine too.'

Carole raises her eyebrows. 'Something to celebrate?'

I force a smile. 'More like comfort eating. I might tell you about it sometime.'

She's polite enough not to push the issue. I've been on first-name terms with Carole since I first found the deli, but we are far from friends. I don't feel like I'll ever be able to get close to anyone who doesn't know my past. It's just too risky.

'Enjoy.' She takes my money and I venture back out on to the street. My mind is telling me to go home and destroy the photo, forget it ever came, but as I turn to make my way home, I catch a glimpse of something impossible. There is a woman in front of me, slim, with long straight dark hair. She is stooping slightly, bending to hold the hand of the young boy at her side. The young boy I saw beaming up at me from a photograph earlier today. My son.

I struggle to call out, my breath catches in my throat. Instead I take a few jerky steps forward, then break into a run.

'Dylan!' I manage to shout. It can't be him, this is totally impossible, but there he is. After all this time, the sight of him makes me want to drop to my knees. How can my son be so close to me after being so far away for all this time?

A few people turn around to look at me; my son and his kidnapper don't look back. It might be my imagination but it looks like she's upped her pace. Not enough, though; within a few seconds I'm upon them.

'Dylan.' I reach down to grab the little boy's arm and catch his navy coat. Adrenalin courses through my chest as the woman swings around to face me.

'What the hell do you think you're doing? Get your hands off my son!'

She grabs Dylan up into her arms and I lose my grip on his coat as she steps backwards. Her face is a mixture of fear and fury.

'That's my son, that's Dylan, he's my . . .' My words tail off as the realisation hits me. He's not my son. My son is dead, gone, and this little boy is clinging to his mother's neck, scared stiff of the crazy lady shouting at them. He suddenly looks nothing like the boy in the photograph; he doesn't resemble me, or Mark, or any of our family. This little boy belongs exactly where he is, in the arms of his mother. I falter, take a step back. I want to run but my legs are playing Judas. The woman, realising I'm no longer a threat to her or her little boy, launches towards me.

'Are you crazy? How dare you try and grab my son? I should call the police, you bloody lunatic!'

'I'm sorry, I . . .' Words fail me. I want to explain, but how? How do you describe arms that always feel empty? A heart that aches with loss? Eyes that see dead children on every street corner? How do you make anyone, let alone a stranger in the street, imagine the loss of someone you sheltered inside your body?

'So you bloody should be! You're crazy.' Until she shoves my arm away, I hadn't even realised I'd still been reaching out.

'She said she's sorry.' The words come from behind me, the voice strong and familiar. 'She made a mistake. Maybe you should accept her apology and go on with your day.'

Relief flows through me when I finally manage to turn and see my rescuer. Carole. I hear the woman behind me mutter once more about me being crazy, but footsteps follow and she's gone.

'Thank you.' I look around at the people who have stopped to watch the show. 'Oh God.'

'Forget them.' Carole takes my arm gently. She raises her voice, directing her next words at the bystanders. 'They have nothing better to do.'

A couple of them look ashamed; one woman shrugs and a group of teenagers snigger, but they all leave.

'Are you OK?' Carole asks me gently. I'm not, and my eyes fill with tears at her kindness. I sniff and nod.

'I'll be fine, it was just a silly misunderstanding. Why did you follow me out here?'

Carole holds out a piece of paper. 'You dropped this when you took out your purse.'

I don't recognise it, but automatically my hand reaches out. It's a newspaper clipping, and when I look closer, I realise. My baby son stares out at me from the black-and-white photo, one that was taken days after his birth. There's no headline, but I remember, after all these years, what it was. MOTHER GETS SIX YEARS FOR SON'S MURDER.

'I couldn't have . . .' I begin to deny that this photo could have been in my bag, but Carole's concerned look makes me stop. *Where else could it have come from?* 'I mean yes, it's mine. Thank you. Again.'

'Are you sure you're OK?'

I nod again, firmer this time. 'Yes. Thanks, Carole, but I have to go. Sorry.'

The other woman looks like she wants to say something but thinks better of it. Thank goodness.

'You know I'm only a few doors down if you need me, Emma.'

I nod again, then realise what she's just said. 'You're what, sorry?'

She looks embarrassed. 'Sorry, I thought you knew, we live on the same street.'

No, I didn't. How did I not know that? Have I walked around for four weeks without seeing anything or anyone around me? Well Carole's certainly seen me . . . . Who else has been watching?

'Emma? Are you sure you're OK? You look a bit ill.'

I've never needed someone more than I do right now, but this isn't the time or place to invite a stranger into my life. Even one who runs a cheese and wine shop. What do I say to my new friend? 'Actually, this morning someone found out I'm a murderer and now I'm having hallucinations about my dead son and carrying around photographs of him I never knew I had. So I could do with a cuppa really, your place or mine?'

'No, I'm fine,' I say instead. 'Thank you again.'

5

The library is deserted, even for a Saturday. I'd wandered aimlessly through the town and down the odd side street, clutching the newspaper clipping tight enough to leave the print on my fingers, and come face to face with the big stone building.

As I approach the desk, the stern-looking woman behind it doesn't even bother to glance up. Her name badge reads 'Evelyn'.

'Yes?' she asks, her head still buried in the huge library catalogue in front of her, leaving me staring at a mane of grey hair.

'Erm, I'd like a card, please.' The woman looks up in surprise at the sound of my voice.

'Oh, sorry, love,' she smiles, her fierce expression changing dramatically into a more welcoming one. She lowers her voice. 'I thought you were that fellow over there again.' She nods towards a rather odd-looking man in a green wax jacket and a trilby sitting in the corner staring purposefully at one of the computer screens. 'He keeps jabbering on about the bloody security restrictions on our internet. I'm afraid to go over and look at what he's trying to find. It's a library, for goodness' sake, not a flippin' porn convention.'

I can't stop myself and a short burst of laughter escapes my lips. This elderly, reserved-looking woman saying the word 'porn' out loud in the library just sounds so ridiculous. She grins again.

'Sorry, love, how can I help you, a library card was it?'

Ten minutes later I'm sitting in front of a computer screen – as far away from the trilby-wearing man as possible – and find my fingers typing the words 'Dylan Webster'.

I've always relied on research. The small room they called a library in Oakdale was nothing compared to this place. I hadn't even known it existed for the first couple of months. I'd spent weeks staring at the walls of my room, Cassie doing everything she could to engage the blank canvas she'd been roomed with in conversation. One afternoon she came to me after her shift in the canteen and took my wrist. This is it, I thought. She's lost her patience with me; finally she's going to attack me. Maybe I won't survive. Maybe I'll be with Dylan at last.

'Here,' she said, and prised open my fingers. 'Take these and come with me.'

I opened my hand to see what she'd pressed into my palm. Three shiny silver coins, no more useful in the real world than children's play money, but more valuable in Oakdale than gold bullion. Credits, our version of money, earned by hard work and good behaviour. Credits could buy you the finer things inside – cigarettes, new underwear, magazines – and access to the luxury areas like the gym. Or the library. She pulled me to my feet and I allowed myself to be guided out of our room and down the steel-floored corridors to the communal wing. A door to the left of the common room that I'd never even registered before bore a sign saying 'Library'. A rectangular hole to one side of the door was labelled 'Three credits, half-day access' and there was a slot for an access card. Cassie took my card from her pocket – God knows when she stole that; that's how much I guarded my property in the early days – put it in the slot and inserted the credits.

'There you go, half a day.' She pushed open the door and gave me a light shove. 'Go and do your research on that purple thing Dr Shaky keeps banging on about in therapy.'

'Puerperal,' I muttered, unable to say what I really meant to. 'Puerperal psychosis.'

'Yeah, that's what I said. When you come out, maybe you can teach me all about it.'

It was in that dark, silent cavern, with its total of thirty-three shelves and two computers with security so tight you'd be lucky to find more than pictures of fluffy bunnies, that I learnt everything I needed to know about the condition I'd been inflicted with. The more I talked with Cassie about what I'd learnt, the more it made sense: the effect of the IVF on my mental state, how C-sections could be traumatic enough to push a person into the depths of post-natal depression, the exhaustion and forgetfulness, my short temper I'd attributed to lack of sleep.

Images I've fought so hard to hide from myself seep through like water through rocks. Waking up in a hospital bed, not gradually but thrust awake, my eyes snapping open.

'The baby, help! My baby!' The room's empty, I'm alone, and when I try to sit up my stomach screams its heated refusal. What's happened to me? What's happened to my baby?

'Hey, hey, don't move.' Mark is at my side in seconds; his thumb hits the call button next to my bed. 'It's OK, love, don't sit up.'

'The baby, Mark, is the baby all right?' My hands press against the hard swell of my stomach and a small fluttering from inside tells me it's OK. It's warm and comforting and I let out the breath I've been holding.

The room smells of antibacterial handwash, a smell that

still reminds me of sickness and cancer, of watching my mother deteriorate. Mark is smiling, but before he can speak there's another person in the room, a woman. She has dirty blonde hair in a scruffy bun but the rest of her face eludes me.

'He's fine, the baby is fine,' Mark whispers. His smile spreads, as though there's something I should know, something I should understand, but I don't.

'He's doing well all things considered. You can see him when the doctor's seen you.'

'What are you talking about?' I press my hand against my stomach once more. 'Have I had another scan? Did they tell you it's a boy?' What was wrong?

Mark's words are soft and comforting. 'You went into labour, sweetheart, remember? There was a problem with the baby; they had to put you under. Don't you remember? You said it was OK, you gave your consent.'

You gave your consent. Why does my husband sound like a television lawyer? What is he saying? Why is that woman looking at me with such pity?

'It was touch and go, love. The baby wasn't responding well. We had to get him out as quickly as possible. He's fine, though, he's in recovery. Why don't I fetch the doctor?'

'He's beautiful, Susan, I'm so proud of you. Do you want to see a picture?' Mark pulls out his phone and hands me a picture of the tiniest baby I've ever seen. Why is he showing me this? Surely he isn't trying to say . . .?

'Mark.' My voice is harder now. I need him to stop messing around, showing me stupid photos and grinning like an idiot. 'What's going on? Whose baby is that?'

I see his face drop, the creases at the corners of his eyes – his happy lines, I call them – disappear. 'Susan, that's *our* baby. You had a Caesarean and our son was born. This is him.'

He pushes the phone at me again and I feel the wave of anger and confusion crash to the surface. I fling out my arm, batting his hand. I catch him off guard, his grip loose, and the phone skitters across the room, crashing against the wall.

'Stop showing me that! That's not my baby! It's in here, I can feel him in here!'

'Jesus, Susan.' Mark jumps up to retrieve his precious iPhone, turns on me, his face red and eyes narrow. 'What did you do that for? Can you hear yourself? That's our baby, *your* baby.'

He's lying. I'd know, I'd know if I'd given birth! He'd have held my hand while I pushed and screamed, I'd have heard my baby cry, felt him against my chest. *I would know.*

'You're wrong. That's not my baby. That's not my baby.'

It took three nurses, a doctor and a large dose of sedatives to calm me down, and it wasn't until four hours after I'd first woken that I saw the baby they claimed was mine. When I stared into the small plastic box they wheeled into my room, I felt no connection between the little boy in front of me and the life I'd grown so carefully inside me for the past eight months. I felt like I'd been robbed, the precious first moments with my son stolen from me by these people. I was allowed to hold him, the nurses took pictures and made encouraging noises and I began to feel it, the love I'd known since finding out we were having a baby, yet still that sense of unfairness didn't dissolve. I'd been cheated, first of a natural conception and now of a natural birth. I remember feeling then like maybe I wasn't meant to be a mother at all.

I'd thought that all new mums experienced the same as I had; research and the powers of Google helped me to understand. I worked rubbish runs and cleaned toilets after that, desperate to earn enough credits to spend whatever time I could in the library – and pay Cassie back for that first day – until one afternoon one of the warders came to my room to offer me a lifeline: a job, just a few hours a week, in the library, in return for unlimited access.

What I'd never done, however, was type my son's name into the search engine. I had no idea how difficult it would be to press enter, and wait the agonising few seconds it takes for the results to flash up.

My cursor hovers over the small cross in the corner of the screen, ready to close down the page if anyone comes too close. And then there it is. A whole page of references to Dylan's death, each time his name in bold indicating the search subject. The first few are stories about the trial, newspaper articles I saw at the time, but even now it's hard to face the fact that they're about me. Snippets of headlines like MOTHER WITH POST-NATAL DEPRESSION JAILED FOR SIX YEARS and MOTHER WHO KILLED BABY – 'I DON'T REMEMBER' stand out from the Facebook and LinkedIn profiles for other Dylan Websters. Every article bears the same photo, the photo that is in my hand. My heart pounds painfully against my chest as I scan the search results, each headline a reminder of a time I've tried so hard to push to a dark place in the recesses of my mind.

There are a few articles in there that don't look at all related to Dylan but his name must have come up somewhere. I send them all to the printer and promise myself I'll read them at home, where I can get upset in peace. All the time my mind is running over the clipping that Carole tells me fell from my handbag. *Who put it in there? Why? Was it me? Am I crazy?* I push the uncomfortable thought away.

On a whim, I type in my ex-husband's name, Mark Webster. All that comes up is a design service – not my Mark – and a professional darts player – *definitely* not my Mark. Then I come across an article I have seen before. Mark's photo stares proudly out at me from the screen as Durham University declares to the world how successful its alumni have been. I remember how pleased with himself he was the day this went out in the *Guardian*. A 'Where Are They Now?' piece that announced to the whole country that Mark Webster was a partner in a leading IT firm, the Mr Big of the IT scene. I'd smiled at how puffed up it made him; I always loved that he was ambitious and was fiercely proud of all he had achieved. The piece in the *Guardian* was like a stamp of approval, a sign that he'd made it.

Without even realising it, I've been in the library for two hours, and the warmth of the day has dropped away leaving a chill in the air. Back outside, I shiver, wrap my thick-knit cardigan around my chest and up my pace, eager to get back to where I've parked the car. I don't realise how little attention I've been paying to where I'm going until I hurry head first into a woman who has stepped out from the side of the library.

'Oh God, sorry.' I glance up and find myself looking at the blonde woman who caught me staring at her earlier in the café.

'My fault.' She looks unnerved at our surprise meeting and smiles uncertainly. I want to say something funny to lighten the mood – she seems very tense – but I'm aware that it might make me sound like a crazy stalker so I hold my tongue.

'No worries,' I reply instead. She looks for a second as though she's about to speak, but after a moment's awkward silence she simply tucks a strand of her wayward hair behind her ear and walks past me.

I'm bloody glad to get home and settle down in front of the fire with a mug of hot chocolate and the newspaper articles fanned out on the floor in front of me. The ones about the trial are still too hard to face, so I shuffle through to the last ones, the ones that just featured the name Dylan Webster somewhere in the text, and hope they aren't about some Olympic swimmer with the same name as my son.

They aren't. The first headline is useless, a random news piece about a university reunion. The second makes me sit up and pay attention.

FAMILY OF MISSING MEDICAL EXAMINER SPEAK OF CONCERN FOR WONDERFUL FATHER

By Nick Whitely. Published 20/11/10

Three days after Dr Matthew Riley was reported missing, his family have spoken of their frantic concern for a 'wonderfully reliable husband and father'.

Speaking from Dr Riley's home in Bradford, his cousin Jeff Atwater, 34, said, 'This is an incredibly difficult time for Matthew's family. Matty is a wonderfully reliable man, an amazing husband and loving father. He would never willingly abandon his wife or two lovely girls, so we are obviously very concerned. Everyone here is frantic.'

Kristy Riley, Matthew's wife, is expected to speak at a press conference later today.

Dr Riley, 36, has been in the spotlight recently for his part in the conviction of Susan Webster, the mother found guilty three weeks ago of smothering her son Dylan to death. He was last seen on 17 November coming out of Waitrose in Bradford with a carrier bag thought to contain wine and chocolates to celebrate his eighth wedding anniversary. Anyone who has any information on his whereabouts should contact West Yorkshire Police via the hotline number on their website.

Matthew Riley, do I remember him? My mind searches hazy images from a trial I attended in body only, and then I see him. A doctor who looked too young to be an expert on anything but according to the newspaper article was older than me. I remember struggling to focus as he took the stand, knowing this would be important. I didn't know if it was the stress, the lack of food and sleep, or the antidepressants the doctors at the hospital had prescribed me, but focusing on anything was a struggle after Dylan was gone. Grief, my father said; he'd been the same when Mum had died. I'd grieved the loss of my mother too, of course, but this was different, this was an all-consuming black hole, hovering just out of my line of vision but still I knew it was there, waiting for me to step too close and slip in. It took all of my energy not to just step in voluntarily.

The doctor was sworn in and the prosecutor stepped up to the box, a horrid little man who reminded me so much of the great and powerful Wizard of Oz that I had to try not to giggle and prove what they probably all thought anyway – that I was crazy. I tried to concentrate on what the doctor – Matthew Riley, I know now – was saying.

'. . . was unresponsive. I checked for a pulse, heartbeat, signs of breathing. I declared him dead at 16.06 but the post-mortem found the time of death to be approximately two hours previous.'

'And Susan Webster was . . .?'

He'd been looking at the jury throughout his initial testimony but at this question I saw him look at me and he cleared his throat uncomfortably.

'The emergency team had taken Mrs Webster through to the theatre room. From our encounter in the car park I had believed her to be deceased, however it was discovered fairly quickly that she was unconscious.'

The prosecution paused for a second, allowing time for this information to sink in, although, I thought, it was hardly news to the jury.

'What were your first impressions of how Dylan Webster had died?'

Dr Riley looked back at the jury once more and resumed his professional stance.

'It appeared that Dylan had been a victim of SIDS.' He glanced at the prosecutor, who nodded at him to continue. 'That's Sudden Infant Death Syndrome, otherwise known as cot death.'

My vision blurred. I had no clear memory of that day. Dylan was alive and then they told me he was dead. All I knew was that he was gone and I hated this man. I hated that he was talking about me and my son and saying the word 'death'.

'Could you tell us why you presumed this to be the case?'

'Well, unfortunately SIDS remains one of the biggest causes of death in children under one year of age and so it's natural to consider it a possibility when a baby has died in his crib with no outward signs of abuse or cause of death.'

'And what did the post-mortem evidence suggest?'

'During the post-mortem I found fibres from Mr and Mrs Webster's sofa cushion inside Dylan's mouth. There was acute emphysema and oedema of the lungs.'

You didn't have to be a medical expert to know what Dr Riley's testimony was building up to.

'And when you added up all this evidence, what did you determine to be the cause of death?' the prosecution asked with what I was certain was a perverse glee. Dr Riley didn't even look at me as he gave his damning evidence.

'It was my professional opinion that Dylan Webster died from homicidal smothering.'

'And in plain and simple English?'

'Dylan Webster was smothered to death with a cushion.'

Did they ever find Dr Riley? Does his disappearance relate to the picture at all? Sighing, I rub my hands across my face and sit back on my heels. That's when I hear the noise.

There's no denying that I heard it. It is a loud crashing sound from the back garden, like someone knocking into the outside bins. Jumping to my feet, I quickly scan the front room for something I can use to defend myself. The poker. Clichéd, I know, but probably for good reason, and it's got to be better than a rolled-up newspaper article.

After a good few minutes of waiting behind the living room door, I'm starting to feel a little foolish when I hear something else. A rattling, almost definitely the back door handle, and a scratching, like someone is trying to jemmy the lock. Oh shit. I've spent the last three years keeping out of trouble in a psychiatric institute and I'm about to meet a sticky end in a quaint Shropshire town. If I wasn't so scared I could probably have found the funny side of the situation.

The kitchen is in darkness and with the blinds closed I've got no chance of seeing who's outside the back door. Shit. My only hope is the element of surprise. Whoever is trying to break in is clearly no expert at it – they've been out there making a racket for about ten minutes and the door has remained firmly closed. I debate throwing it open and thrusting the poker at whoever's behind it, *Pirates of the Caribbean* style, but on reflection, the last thing I want is to end up on another murder charge for offing some confused drunk who's stumbled upon the wrong house and can't get his key in the door.

The rattling has stopped. Maybe they've given up and gone away. Poker still in hand, I creep over to the kitchen window and peer through the blinds. The darkness outside is thick, and I can see nothing more than my own reflection. A sudden thump against the glass makes me scream out in shock, and it takes me a full minute to realise what's caused it. My scream turns to a laugh of nervous relief. A huge black cat sits on the window ledge, pawing to be let in – none other than my resident stalker, and local stray, Joss. Taking a deep breath, I open the window and he stalks through.

'You bloody dumb animal,' I chastise affectionately, adrenalin giving way to the relief coursing through me. Joss purrs and rubs his face up against mine, unaware of the fuss he's caused. I lay out a bowl of Weetabix – his favourite – and, checking the back door is still locked, return to the comfort of my living room. Joss follows faithfully, curling up in front of the fire and promptly falling asleep.

I'm annoyed at myself for reacting so foolishly. The only thing creeping around my back garden in the middle of the night is a stray cat, desperate for his Weetabix fix and a warm place to sleep. What a fucking idiot. Still, I make a check of all the doors and windows: better safe than sorry.

6

'Yo, Shakespeare, catch.' Jack flung the chocolate through the air and laughed as it hit the other boy square in the chest. 'Too slow.'

'Cheers.' He frowned. 'What time are the others coming?' He'd looked at his watch three times since arriving at the house just fifteen minutes ago. The third time Jack had had to stop himself laughing out loud.

'Soon. Why, you nervous?'

'No.' He said it quickly but Jack could tell he was lying. He'd dressed for the occasion, wearing what Jack was sure were his coolest clothes, but still his ASICS trainers and unbranded navy joggers weren't going to cut it with the rest of the group. These were boys who, even at the age of twelve, were wearing Nike and Fred Perry – Billy probably thought Fred Perry was the bloke who ran the newsagent's.

'Just chill out. They don't bite. Well, not unless I tell them to.' Jack frowned as his Street Fighter lost yet another life. He threw the controller at the console, scowling. 'Fucking boring game. We need some new stuff to do.'

'You've got way more here than I've got at mine.' Billy was

gazing around Jack's room, soaking in every detail. Remnants of previous hobbies littered every available space: the guitar he'd pestered for weeks to learn only to give up after six sessions; last year's absolute must-have trainers caked in mud, lying on top of a jacket that probably cost more than the other boy's entire wardrobe. It was quite amusing to watch.

'Pile of junk. When Adam gets here he'll want to go out and play Tracker. You might get your nice new trainers dirty.'

Jack grinned as the boy tried his best to look unconcerned. Likelihood was he'd spend hours scrubbing them clean before going home. It must be absolute shit to have parents who were ever present, constantly asking you where you were going, who you were with. Then again, he'd seen Billy's house – from the outside, of course; he was certain he'd never be asked in – and in a place the size of a postage stamp he could imagine it would be hard to avoid each other.

When the doorbell rang, Billy flinched. Jack laughed and jumped up.

'I'll get it,' he yelled to whoever might be in the house. He hadn't seen Lucy since he woke up at eleven. She'd probably gone out to do the weekly shop and wouldn't be bothered if he wasn't here when she got back. His parents were the kind of people who thought teenagers should be given their freedom to grow – and who hoped he didn't notice when Lucy went through his school bag to check his homework diary.

Billy hung back in the bedroom as the others traipsed up the stairs. The first boy to enter was Riley. Jack watched Billy's shoulders sag with relief. He nodded towards Matt. 'All right?'

Matt grinned. 'All right.'

The second boy through the door screwed up his nose. 'Who're you?'

Jack shoved his arm. 'Don't be a twat. This is Shakespeare. He's hanging round with us.'

'What kind of a name's Shakespeare?' The second boy grinned. 'Your mum pissed when she gave you that name?'

'It's a nickname, dumbass. Because he's good at English. Shakes, this is Adam Harvey.'

The two boys nodded at one another but neither looked pleased about it.

'You look like shit, what happened to you?'

Jack spoke again before his new friend had a chance to answer. 'You shoulda seen the other guy. Shakes kicked the crap out of them.'

'Them?'

'Yeah, three of 'em, from Westlake. He kicked their asses, it was wicked. I got him back here before they could bring more of 'em round. Right, Riley?'

Matt nodded and Adam gave a look of grudging respect. 'Fair play. You coming with us for a game of Tracker?'

'Course he is. Where's Peterson?'

Matt shrugged. 'Dunno. Haven't seen him since yesterday.'

Jack raised his eyebrows as their new friend gave him a nervous look. He pulled him aside as the other two went down the stairs. 'Don't worry about it,' he whispered. 'I won't tell anyone you dropped Mike in it.'

HOW I LOST YOU

7

Cassie and I have volunteered the last three Sundays at the KIP Project for the homeless in Telford, twenty minutes from Bridgnorth, where Cass lives. I volunteer as a way to give something back, to atone for my sins. Cassie volunteers because I asked her to. Despite her insistence that she gets nothing out of the work we do and is only there 'to pass the time', I know that deep down she enjoys the thought that she's doing something good. Deep, deep down. This Sunday, however, she turns up looking a little sheepish.

'I want to apologise for the way I was yesterday,' she says straight away before I even have a chance to speak. 'I didn't mean to dismiss that photo; I just didn't know what to make of it.'

I look around me quickly; there's no one close enough to hear. The shelter is pretty empty today and until Cass turned up I'd been sorting through donations at a table in the corner of the large room by myself, my mind never straying far from the events of yesterday.

Should I tell her the rest? *And risk her thinking you're crazy?*

Quickly I fill her in on the newspaper article in my bag,

my findings at the library and my scare at the house later that night.

'Shiiiiit. I don't blame you for being jumpy. Do you want to come stay at mine?'

'Thanks, but I'm not sure it's that serious just yet. It was only Joss.'

'OK, but who the hell put that cutting in your bag? That's freakier than posting something through your door, right?'

I'm stupidly relieved that she doesn't think I might have put it there myself. I wouldn't blame her; the thought has crossed my mind. After all, I've had blackouts in the past and done worse.

We're interrupted by Bernie, the centre manager, who bustles over with a fresh batch of donations. Since I started volunteering two weeks ago, I've been amazed by how many people donate their unwanted belongings. The old Susan Webster would never have done that; she'd have thrown them out. I wouldn't say I didn't care, it just never occurred to me to help in that way. Bernie hangs around a bit longer than is comfortable and I can tell Cassie is itching for her to leave.

The minute she does – giving us a funny look in the process – Cassie begins to talk again.

'What if it isn't Mark?' she says. 'Who else would want to make you think you're going loopy? Maybe his friends? His mum?'

'Mark's mum lives in Spain; I never met her. As far as I know, Mark never even told her about Dylan. Something to do with the falling-out they had before his dad died.' I discard a pair of pants with three holes in them. There are some things even people in need don't need. 'And we're missing the obvious point. How would any of them know where I am?'

Cassie shakes her head. 'Anyone can find that out. All they need is the internet and half a brain.'

37

'What about the Dr Riley thing? Do you think it's relevant?'

'Probably not,' she concedes. My disappointment must show, because she hastily adds, 'It does look suspicious, though. I could be wrong. I'm always wrong when I try and guess whodunnit on *Midsomer Murders*.'

'Thanks.' Cute attempt to make me feel better about my amateur detective work. 'But you're probably right. So what do I do now? I'm jumping at my own shadow. And *someone* put that article in my bag.'

'Well if it is Mark, he'd probably be staying somewhere close, right? He's not going to drive three hours from Bradford just to post a photo and go home again.'

Ew. The thought of my ex-husband sneaking around Ludlow without me knowing freaks me out. I look quickly at the doorway of the shelter, half expecting to see him standing there watching me. It's empty, of course.

'So what are we going to do, call every B and B within a twenty-mile radius and ask if a Mark Webster is staying there?'

'Or . . .' Cassie replies, dragging the word out over three syllables, 'we could call his house and see if he answers. What's his number?' She pulls out her phone and out of the corner of my eye I notice Bernie watching suspiciously.

'Let's wait until we get back to mine.' I put my hand over the phone and motion with my head to the prying eyes in the room.

The next three hours seem like days, and even the appearance of my favourite regular, Larry, fails to take my mind off my ex and the photograph of the little boy. It doesn't seem like Mark's style to me, but it is a long time since we last spoke. People change.

'Thanks for today, ladies.' Bernie says her usual goodbyes as our shift ends. Something strikes me.

'You haven't seen any strange men hanging around the last week or so, have you, Bernie?'

She grins and jerks her head at Larry. 'You mean aside from the usual strange men we get here?' she teases. Larry bats her arm affectionately.

'Never mind strange men, what about all the crazy women?' he responds with a laugh. I join in, seriously doubting he knows how much truth is in those words.

8

While Cassie goes back to her house to change – with the
promise that it's not because she's been around homeless
people – I drive home on my own. When I arrive to an
empty mat, I'm relieved and disappointed in equal measure.
The house is too quiet, eerily so, and I head through to the
kitchen, put the kettle on to boil and pop the lid off the
coffee.

I don't know if it's the picture of Dylan scraping fingernails
over old wounds, but the smell of the coffee makes the fist-
sized scar on the top of my arm itch, and automatically I
reach up to scratch the puckered skin. A memory I've forced
into a steel box in my mind seeps back to me. I'm sitting in
a canteen, the tables like plastic park benches and the walls
such a dirty yellow that I don't think anyone knows what
colour they started out. Cassie sits opposite me, staring at
her cold cottage pie as though it might change into a Domino's
pizza if she wishes hard enough. I'm half aware of someone
behind me but I take no notice until the words are hissed
so close to my ear that to this day I can smell the stale cigarettes and dog-shit breath.

'Baby killer.'

The sharp pain spreads down my arm. At first I think I've been punched, my shock merging with horror as I realise the pain isn't fading, it's getting worse. Scalding water has moulded my uniform to my arm, the material trying to force itself into a second skin. Cassie's voice rings in my ears, a quick 'Oh shit,' then she's upon me, pouring ice-cold water on my arm and ripping the sleeve from my shirt. I hear the words 'Get a medic,' but they're far away like I'm hearing them underwater.

Days later, back in our room – they never called them cells in Oakdale; we were patients not prisoners – Cassie would tell me I was lucky that hulking Netty Vickers (at Oakdale for the attempted murder of the woman who'd slept with her boyfriend) had neglected to put sugar in the water. Sugar in the water, she said, made it impossible to wash off and caused much more damage. I never asked her how she knew that, just like I never asked her what had happened to Netty Vickers. She got transferred while I was still in the hospital wing. I heard the rumours, though. An accident with a kettle of boiling water, though no one could explain how the sugar got in there. I never heard the words 'baby killer' directed at me again.

The knock on the door is so gentle, and I'm so caught in that memory, that at first I think I'm hearing things. Nope, there it is again, a soft, almost apologetic padding. There are two reasons why such a simple thing as someone knocking on the door freaks me out. The first is obvious: yesterday morning I received a photograph claiming to be of a boy who has been dead for nearly four years. The second is that in the four weeks I've been here, I've yet to have a single visitor, except Cassie, who has a key. When you've lived with someone for as long as I lived with Cassie, it seems strange, somehow, to have to open the door for them, and the key that started out as 'for emergencies' has migrated into everyday use.

So I'm reluctant to open the door. Ignoring it would be easy – there's no one I want to see – but I've never been able to let a phone ring without answering it, and now I can't let whoever's out there walk away and have me wonder all day who it was. Best just to get it done with.

When I swing the door open, the man behind it takes a step back.

'Mrs Webster?'

It's the second time in two days that I've been reminded of that name, and I wonder for a second if I've heard him right or if I'm imagining that everyone everywhere knows who I am.

'Pardon? What did you call me?'

'Mrs Webster, I'm sorry, my name is—'

'My name is not Mrs Webster.' I spit the words through gritted teeth at the tall, dark-haired man on the doorstep. 'What are you doing here? Are you a journalist? You are, aren't you? Did you send me that photo? You people aren't supposed to be here, you know, can't you just let me get on with my life?' The words tumble from my mouth desperately, none of them fending off this stranger.

'I'm sorry, look, I shouldn't have called you that.' He's gone red and looks flustered; maybe it's his first day and he was sent here as a baptism of fire. First day or not, I'm not letting a frigging journalist anywhere near my home. 'I'm not—'

'I'll call the police!'

'No, please!' The man puts his hand up. 'I'll go, I'm sorry, I shouldn't have come.'

As he begins to do a quick run-walk down the path, a thought occurs to me. If I let him go, I'll have more questions than answers. Why is he here? Did he send the photograph? What does he want?

'Wait!' I shout the word before he can disappear into his car. 'Wait there.'

I'm not letting him back up the path so I hurry down to him, not thinking about how vulnerable that makes me, away from a door to slam. He looked so distraught at the idea of the police, I don't think he's going to attack me in full view on the street.

He gets in the car, and I've got more time to take a proper look at him. He's quite good-looking now that his face has gone back to a nice tan colour rather than postbox red. His eyes are a lovely blue and he looks around the same age as my husband. Ex-husband. I've got to stop doing that.

Before he can drive away, I bang on the window, hoping I don't look as crazy as this feels. He winds down the window a little bit – obviously not enough for me to attack him, though.

'Why did you come here? Did you post something through my door yesterday?'

He didn't; I can tell the confusion on his face is real.

'No, why would you think I did?'

'Because you called me Mrs Webster. You know who I am.'

'Someone sent you something?' Too late I realise I've revealed too much to a reporter. He doesn't – didn't – know anything about the photo and now he's got a whiff of a story.

'No. Forget it, it's none of your business. I'm not interested in interviews. Have I seen you before?'

'I was at your, erm, the trial.' So he's not new, he wrote about me when I was on trial. I wonder which side of the fence he fell on: the monster mother or the poor unfortunate soul camp.

'What paper do you work for?' Now I'm interested? Now I'm engaging in conversation with this man?

'I just want to talk to you. I knew—'

'What's your name?'

He hesitates, and I wonder if it's because I'm a criminal.

It's fine for him to know every detail of my life just as long as I don't find out who he is. 'Nick,' he answers eventually.

He looks harmless enough, all spiky black hair and very, very blue eyes, and for a second I have to remind myself how much I dislike reporters. How a simple 'just want to talk, that's all' can turn into a front-page scoop with an I HATE ALL BABIES headline the next morning.

'I'm sorry, I'm still not interested. Just leave me to get on with my life, please.'

He nods and for a few seconds looks like he feels sorry for me. Well, pity is better than hatred, by a hair's breadth.

'If you change your mind . . .' He pulls out a notebook and scribbles down a number. 'Here.'

'I won't,' I tell him, but I take the piece of paper anyway. When he winds up the window and drives away, a sharp, manly smell remains.

9

When Cassie arrives I'm still shaken, from both my encounter with the journalist and the memory of Netty Vickers. The noise of her key in the door makes my heart speed up a little until I hear her voice.

'Aloha, anyone home?' She pads through to the kitchen, where I'm sitting at the table. 'Hey, you OK? What is it, another photo?'

'No, worse, a reporter.' I quickly run through the last twenty minutes, and the more I speak the angrier her face gets. Cassie's such a pretty woman, but when her temper flares up it reminds me of the things she's been through, the physical and emotional scars she carries and how hardened she's had to become. The only time she ever let me catch a glimpse of her scars – an oversight when she thought I was asleep – I was reduced to silent tears and she was furious. She'd worked for years at becoming the hard-faced killer people thought she was, and I'm pretty sure I'm the only person who's seen the real Cassie, scars and all, for quite some time.

'If he comes back here he'll get more than he bargained for,' she warns, and I smile.

'I don't think he'll come back. He was pretty scared when

I threatened him with the police. Do you think it's a co-incidence? The letter yesterday, him today?'

She mulls it over, her nails, coral today, running their familiar pattern over the table. 'Yeah, probably. You said he looked confused when you mentioned the photo. Face it, you weren't given protection when you were released, you changed your own name. Finding you probably isn't that difficult, you're not Osama Bin Laden.'

'Great, cheers.'

'Shall we get a guard dog?' She's wanted me to have a dog since I got out. No hassle for her, instant pet when she comes to mine.

'Joss would be pissed off.'

She screws up her nose. 'Another good reason. What's that?' she asks as I throw the articles I found at the library on to the counter next to her.

'It's the stuff about Dr Riley and some bits on the trial,' I say. 'I was hoping you'd cast a fresh pair of eyes over them and see something I've missed.'

'Like Jonathan Creek,' she murmurs, her eyes skimming the pages. 'Except that I can't see anything at all. Family man . . . two beautiful daughters . . . I'd put money on it that his wife was about to leave him for the family accountant or something. I hate to say it, Suze, but it's probably a coincidence.'

I'm disappointed but I know she's right. I've just read too many crime novels.

'Another one? This weekend's full of 'em.'

She bites her bottom lip. 'I think I've found another. Here.' She passes back the article about Matthew Riley and points at the byline. Nick Whitely.

'Ah crap. Do you think it's him? Hell of a coincidence.'

'Do you think he knows something about Riley's disappearance? Maybe that's what he wanted to talk to you about.'

'Should I have spoken to him? He said he just wanted to talk but I kicked him out so fast he didn't have a chance.'

'And what are the three least trustworthy things on this earth?'

'Men, police and journalists.' I chant the mantra. 'But he didn't seem very scary. What if I just find out what he wanted, and don't say a word to him?'

She's pretending to consider it. 'OK, we'll call him. But if he can't help us, we're burying him under the patio.'

I'm pretty sure she's joking, but sometimes you can't tell.

'Shall I?' She picks up the scrawled mobile number from the counter and takes out her phone. 'It's ringing,' she whispers.

'Give it here.' I grab at the phone and she dances away.

'Hello, is that Mr Whitely?' Her phone voice is barely recognisable; she almost sounds professional. 'My name is Julie Williams, I'm calling on behalf of Susan Webster. She's got some questions for you and would like to know if you're available for a meeting.'

She frowns, then makes a face at the phone and holds it out to me. 'He wants to talk to you.' She covers the receiver. 'Just stick to the plan,' she hisses. I wasn't aware we had one.

'Mrs Webster, is that you?'

'Yes. Do we have a meeting, Mr Whitely?'

'That depends. What do you want from me?'

What's the plan for this bit? 'I want to know why you were at my house.'

'I can tell you that over the phone. I just wanted to talk to you, ask you some questions, how life is for you now, how you felt when your husband didn't stick by you. Call it human interest. Do you want to tell your side of the story?'

I close my eyes. 'Not in a million years.'

'Then what do you want from me?'

At least he's been honest. Maybe I should try it.

'I want information. I want your help.'

'I'm halfway to Doncaster, Mrs Webster. You're not asking me to come all the way back to Ludlow as a favour?'

'Of course not, we'll come to you, tomorrow if that's OK? Can you suggest somewhere?'

We arrange a restaurant half an hour from where he lives – a two-hour trip for us. When I get off the phone, Cassie is looking at me quizzically. I fill her in.

'You'd better get your best frock out, 'cause we've got to convince this guy that we're not the nutters the rest of the world thinks we are.'

Easier said than done. We sound pretty nutty right now. Cassie sticks to her end of the deal and after dialling 141 calls the number I've given her for Mark's house. He picks up, putting paid to my theory that he's skulking around Shropshire posting photographs through my door. I'm glad I didn't have to hear my ex-husband's voice. I'm excited about my meeting with Nick Whitely, but mostly I'm petrified that I've made the unconscious decision not to let this go and move on. I'm going to dig up the past and hope my spade doesn't hit too many skeletons.

10

Jack: 18 October 1987

'Look, this'll be the third time Ballbreaker's called my house for cutting class in the last month. It's not like I've got Lucy at mine to pretend to be my mum.'

'Jesus, Billy, lighten up. What's the worst that could happen? Tell them Adam's been pushing you around and if you didn't cut school he'd kick the shit out of you.'

'Hey!' Adam objected. 'Why me?'

Jack grinned. ''Cos his mum loves me too much to believe I'd do anything like that, and Mike . . .' he lowered his voice, 'is too much of a wimp to pull it off.'

Adam smiled back, willing to accept he was less charming than Jack but at least scarier than Mike. 'Well just make sure she doesn't call the school. My dad'll beat my ass if I'm accused of bullying again.'

'Right, fine,' Billy sighed. 'What's the plan, then?'

Jack rolled off the bed and pulled out a huge sheet of paper from underneath it.

'This is a plan of the shop. Here's where they keep the beers.' He drew a circle around a stand to the left of the counter. 'Walters, that's the guy who works the days 'cos he's too old to do nights, he

49

always *stands by the counter. He can't see great but he's close enough to catch you if you're not quick. We go in in twos. Me and you first, Adam: we read the magazines, mess around with the pick and mix, generally piss off Walters so he barely even notices when you two go in and take the booze. Get vodka, as much as you can carry.'*

'Remind me again why I've got to steal the booze?' Billy asked. 'I've never stolen anything in my life.'

'Yeah, you can tell.' Mike grinned, casting an eye over Billy's too long, slightly greasy mop and three-year-old shoes. 'We look the most innocent, mate. He won't even notice us when those two are twatting around in there. Plus it's usually Riley's job but he's not turned up. Don't worry; I do it all the time. You just hold the bag.'

Jack folded up the shop plan and slid it back under the bed. He pulled open the sliding doors of a double wardrobe, took out a large black jacket and threw it at Billy. 'Wear this. It's got extra big inside pockets, so you can fit some in there if you get a chance. We'll wait five minutes after you've left and follow on. Go home, get changed and meet back here at eight.' He looked at Mike and Adam. 'You two get a head start, we'll catch up.'

As soon as they were alone, he turned to Billy, who was studying his fingernails. 'Get this right for us and you can come back here and take your pick of my stuff to go to my cousin's party in.'

'Why would I want—' Billy started, but Jack cut him off with a shake of the head.

'Look, you don't have to pretend with us, we're your mates, OK? I know your family don't have money and I don't care. Do this and you can go to the party looking like the rest of us, and no one else there will know you're any different. There's gonna be girls there, Billy-boy, tons of girls. You ever got off with a girl before?'

The look on his friend's face told him the answer. 'Tonight's your night then, man. All you have to do is get the booze. You up for it?' He grinned as the other boy nodded. 'Yeeessss, nice one, mate. Come on, let's go.'

* * *

The take had gone as well as he could have expected really. Their new friend hadn't dropped any bottles or run up to the shopkeeper to confess, although he had shat himself when he'd walked in with Mike and seen that it wasn't Walters on the counter but some girl with perfectly good eyesight. It'd turned out to be for the best, though. Jack was ten times better with women than with old men. He looked years older than fifteen, and with his floppy brown hair and clear blue eyes there was even less chance that the girl, Tina, would notice what was going on elsewhere in the shop. It had been Mike who had surprised him the most: when Tina had glanced his way, he'd simply dropped his bag and walked out. Lucky for Billy that Matt Riley had arrived at that exact moment, realised what Jack and Adam were up to and seen Billy standing there like a deer in the headlights. He'd walked over to Billy, shoved the bottles into his bag and practically dragged him from the store. Peterson had been waiting as they came round the corner with three bottles of vodka clinking in Billy's bag, and greeted them as though fuck all had gone wrong.

'What the fuck happened to you?' Jack had demanded. 'You left poor Shakespeare on his own to bring out all the booze. I practically had to shag her on the counter to stop her looking to see why you'd stormed out. Lucky Riley showed up.'

'She was on to me,' Mike had protested. 'She probably recognised me – I thought I was better off leaving him to it. What did you get?'

Billy had gone to open the bag to show off his impressive haul, but Jack had thrust his hand over the top of it and shoved Mike hard on the shoulder.

'Fuck off. You dropped Billy right in it there. If you think you're coming tonight, you must be joking. Go on, fuck off home.'

'Aw, come on, man, I'm sorry, all right?'

'No, it's not all right. Piss off.'

'Fuck you then! Like you ever get your fucking hands dirty!' Mike yelled to their retreating backs. Jack snorted back a laugh.

'Thank God for that. Fucking mutant would've cramped our style

anyway. Back at mine at eight, Harvey?' Adam looked uncertain at the idea of returning without his friend, but eventually he nodded. Jack pumped the air with his fist.

'You coming?' Billy asked Matt Riley, who nodded.

'Yeah, may as well.'

'Thanks for your help in there.'

Riley grinned. 'Don't be gay. See you later.'

Jack slung an arm around Billy's shoulders and gave him a squeeze, then grabbed his arm and picked up his step. 'Come on, mate, we've got some work to do on you.'

11

Nick Whitely is a handsome man, now I can see properly through my anger. The less flustered look suits him, and as he stands to greet me I see he's got a noticeably good physique underneath his crisp white shirt. I don't know if he's noticed me looking but his electric blue eyes flash with amusement when he smiles and shakes my hand.

'Mrs Webster.' He turns to Cassie. 'And Cassie Reynolds, if I'm not mistaken?'

Cassie frowns. 'Sorry, I thought we were meeting a reporter, not a detective.'

My elbow shoots out reflexively, jabbing her in the side.

We take a seat at the table. Mr Whitely – I wonder if I should call him Nick? – has already ordered a bottle of Cabernet Sauvignon and a jug of iced water. For a small-time journalist from a local rag he knows how to conduct a meeting. It takes me a minute to realise he's been talking and I've been staring at his arms and trying to remember the last time arms like that were wrapped around me.

'Sorry, what?'

He's gesturing towards the wine. 'I said help yourselves.'

I take a glass of water while Cassie opts for wine.

'So, Mr Whitely,' I start.

'Please, call me Nick.'

'OK, Nick, you're probably wondering why I got in touch with you again after throwing you out so unceremoniously yesterday.'

Nick turns his blue eyes from his wine glass to meet mine. His gaze drifts over the rest of me briefly then returns to hold my own. 'What I'm wondering, Susan . . . if I may?' I nod in response and he continues. 'Is what you wanted from me so badly that you were suddenly willing to talk to a member of the press.'

'Is that why you're here?' I ask. 'Curiosity? You already had my new identity, address, probably a few photos. So what are you getting out of this?'

'I admit I was curious. I'm a journalist, so shoot me.' A grin passes quickly across his face, then he turns to Cassie. 'Not you.'

Cassie pulls her lips into a sarcastic smirk. I'm not sure Nick Whitely is joking.

'I'd better get on with it then.' I take out the article from my brown leather handbag and pass it over to him. He scans the sheet of paper and hands it back.

'I've already read it,' he informs me, his voice tinged with amusement. 'In fact I think you'll find I wrote it.'

'Exactly,' I reply, tense with the knowledge that I'm holding my trump card quite close to my chest. 'I'm wondering what you can tell me about Dr Riley's disappearance. I've searched and searched; according to Google he was never found.'

Nick faces me with an open look. 'Your Google-fu is strong. Matthew Riley was never found. A lot of people think he got in with the wrong kind of people and had to disappear. Others say he committed suicide over bad debts, but the police never found any evidence of that or foul play. Everything we turned up suggested he was happily married, beautiful wife and two young girls. No note.'

'What do you think?'

He shakes his head and is about to speak when an eager-looking waiter appears at the table with a pad and pen poised to scribble down our order. 'Can I get you something to eat?'

I look at the others.

'I'll have a chicken salad,' Cassie orders, 'no dressing.'

Nick looks over at me.

'Erm, I'll take the penne al pollo with a side of chips and some garlic dough balls.' *What? I'm hungry.*

Nick smiles. 'Sounds good. I'll have the same. I like a woman who knows how to eat. So what did you want to know about Matthew Riley?' His silky smooth voice forces me back to the matter in hand.

'What do you think happened? Why would someone with a good job and a loving family just disappear?'

'People do things out of character all the time,' he replies, taking a sip of his wine. Is he talking about me?

'I suppose they do,' I say carefully.

'So I guess my question is why do *you* want to know about it?'

Cassie is nodding furiously at my bag and I guess this is the moment she wants me to show him what's in there.

Reaching down, I pull out the photo and silently hand it to him. He takes it.

'I received this, two days ago. It was posted through my front door while I was in my kitchen. There was no postmark on the envelope. And then you turn up.'

Nick looks at the photo, studying it for any sign of what conclusion he should draw from the little boy with the beautiful smile. I watch the expression on his face change from a slightly bemused frown to one of surprise, then comprehension as he turns the photograph over and reads the words scrawled on the back.

'Do you see now what I'm getting at?' I lean forward in my chair, unable to mask my excitement. I can't explain why it is so important to me that this man believes my story. I hadn't realised until this moment how much I want *someone* to say they think it means the same as I secretly do. That my son might still be alive.

'I think so, yes,' Nick says slowly, placing the photograph down on the table. He's staring at it as though it might start talking to him if he looks at it hard enough. I've got no idea what he's thinking; those eyes may be beautiful but they are also completely unreadable. Maybe law would suit this man better than journalism. Or poker.

'Firstly, I want you to know I had nothing to do with this photograph, although I realise how it must look to you. Secondly, I find it hard to believe how from receiving this photo – which could be *any* little boy, *anywhere* – you've concluded that your son is still alive and that Dr Riley faked his death certificate in order to frame you for murder . . . *then* what, killed himself? Or maybe the Mafia killed him for you? Although he did return from the dead to hand-deliver you a picture of your little boy four years on.'

All right, when you put it like that, it *does* sound slightly far-fetched, but there's no way on this earth I am about to admit that to this smug bastard.

'I never said that,' I answer in my best defiant voice. 'And I don't appreciate the cocky little dig about returning from the dead you stuck in at the end there. I'm concerned it may be someone who knows my identity, someone who may have a vendetta against me. Why else go to all that trouble?'

Cassie has slumped down in her seat and is rubbing her face wearily. She obviously expected this to go better. Nick Whitely has made it clear he thinks we're idiots and I don't see the point in staying here much longer, but the food arrives so the three of us sit in silence while the waiter fannies around tucking napkins on to our laps and topping up our glasses. As soon as he's gone, I speak again.

'Someone put *this*,' I thrust the newspaper photo at him next, 'in my bag on the very same day. More questions, more unlikely answers.' He takes the second photo but his eyes don't leave mine. 'I don't deny I've considered what it might be like to find out that my son is still alive, as crazy as that sounds. But answer me this, Mr Whitely: if you had spent every day for the last one thousand and seven days wanting to die for what you'd been told you'd done to your little boy, then you found out there might be a chance, however slim, that you hadn't ever done it, that your little boy might be alive and happy, wouldn't you grab it with both hands? Someone out there put that thought in my head, even for the briefest second, to be cruel, or to scare me, I don't know which. But I want to find out who, and why.'

His fork freezes midway to his mouth and he looks at me in a way I realise he hasn't done before. Gone is the curiosity, that cat-playing-with-mouse smile and the cocky, self-assured twinkle in his eye; the man staring back at me looks like he knows exactly what it feels like to have something you wish so desperately had never happened. In his eyes now is a look of understanding. When he eventually speaks, I almost give in to the desire to reach over the table and kiss him.

'How do you think I can help?'

We stay at Dolce Vita until closing. When the waiters finally drop the pretence of good customer service and start stacking chairs on top of tables around us, we decide to give in and call it a day.

Before we leave, Cassie and I disappear to the ladies' for a long-awaited discussion about how we think the night has gone. Cassie doesn't look overly happy.

'It's a good job he fancies you,' she says, even her voice frowning. 'Otherwise we'd both be back in Oakdale.'

I try not to blush. 'He does not.'

'Oh shut up, he can't take his eyes off you. He's barely said a word to me since that wiseass remark about me shooting him. And it was a frigging picture frame, for his information.'

I shudder. 'I wish you wouldn't do that.'

We return to the table and find him hanging up his mobile phone. 'That was my boss. I've got a couple of days' holiday left, thought I'd take some time off.'

'Why?' Cassie asks, immediately looking suspicious. I know what she's thinking: it's one thing to spend an evening eating Italian food and indulging a strange woman's paranoid delusions, it's quite another to use up your hard-earned time off to chase imaginary criminal masterminds.

'You're welcome.' Nick laughs at her rudeness and I feel awful. I shoot Cassie a warning glare. If this gorgeous, intelligent man with his contacts and resources wants to help us, why is she pushing the issue?

'No, really, why?' she presses. 'Come on, Susan, don't look at me like that. I don't trust him. *Neither of us* were supposed to trust him. What's in it for you, Mr Whitely?'

Nick doesn't address Cassie's question right away. He just looks at me closely and says nothing for a full minute. I'm starting to feel uncomfortable under his intense scrutiny when he sits back in his seat.

'Let's just say it's not often that a case piques my interest like this one,' he replies, not moving his eyes from mine. 'I spend my days reporting on cases where the facts are clear. I'm a reporter, I'm not an investigative journalist. Press releases, court notes and police statements fall on my desk and I cobble them together into something people want to read. I'm bored.'

He holds out his hands in a take-it-or-leave-it gesture. I'm taking it and I don't care what Cassie has to say about it.

'In that case, thank you.' I get to my feet and Nick does the same. 'Where do you want to start?'

'I'll go home and get some stuff together, then I'll travel up tomorrow. Sound good?'

'His wife must be very trusting,' Cassie says evenly as we drive the ninety-mile trip home. 'Or maybe he's gay.'

'He's not gay. And he's not married. No ring.'

'That doesn't mean anything.' Cassie shakes her head. 'Slimeballs like him never wear their rings. Jim always said his was too tight. Too tight my ass.'

'Maybe not all men are like Jim,' I snap, and she says nothing more about Nick.

The journey home takes less time than expected. The roads are quiet and I don't always stick to the speed limit. Dropping Cassie off at home, I kiss her on both cheeks, thank her for all her help and promise to call her in the morning when I know what time Nick's arriving.

The car's too quiet without her constant chatter. On goes the radio and I turn it up as far as my ears will allow to try and drown out the thoughts buzzing through my head. Can I trust Nick Whitely? I know Cassie doesn't trust him just because he's so good-looking – if there's one thing she hates more than men, it's attractive men – but maybe she has a point.

I know something's not right as soon as I pull into my driveway, but it takes me a few seconds to figure out exactly what it is that's wrong. When my brain catches up with my eyes, my heart becomes a lead weight in my chest. My front door is ajar. I wouldn't have forgotten to close it, no matter how much of a rush I'd been in. Protecting your personal space and your belongings is a lesson that's drummed into you early on in Oakdale. What's more disturbing than the door, though, is the shiny red liquid I can see dripping slowly down the handle and on to the step below. My front porch is covered in blood.

12

Every instinct I have is screaming at me not to walk inside my house. So why do I find myself getting out of the car and heading towards the front door?

As I step closer to the blood-soaked porch, my heart hammering a fist-sized hole in my chest, I let out a small sigh of relief. The blood that looked so menacing dripping from the handle and pooling on to the cement slab below is slightly too thick and slightly too red. Paint. *Someone's been in there*, I warn myself, *and someone might still be in there*.

I know I should get back in the car, drive away and call the police, yet instead I cover my hand with my jumper and push open the front door.

'Hello?' I shout nervously. *There goes your element of surprise, Sherlock*. No one answers my shout, and encouraged by the fact that I haven't had my head bashed in with any of my own ornaments yet, I take a step inside.

My hallway has been trashed. There is no other word to describe the scene that greets me. The table where I keep my post has been smashed, the drawer and all its contents have spilt out on to the floor and everywhere is covered in red paint. The walls are smeared with it, droplets marking

61

a trail into the kitchen ahead. I'm perversely reminded of one of those demonstrations against women who wear fur. I know I shouldn't go in. No good can come of it. Edging forward, I push open the kitchen door.

The kitchen is, if possible, even more of a mess than the hall. Cutlery has been scattered all over the place, my juicer lies smashed across the kitchen counter and the toaster is in bits on the floor. Paint smears the walls, counter tops and floor; my house looks like a scene from *The Texas Chain Saw Massacre*.

A sudden thumping noise from upstairs makes me cry out in shock. It is unmistakably the sound of footsteps running across my landing, and before I can react, it's on the stairs. As whoever is in my house runs down the stairwell, I scan the mess for something I can protect myself with. My trendy designer knife block is empty, all six knives sticking menacingly out of the wall. They have been driven deep into the plasterboard and I can't wrestle any of them free. That's when the panic sets in.

Fumbling with my keys, I am trying desperately to open the back door when I hear the front door slam loudly. Breathing heavily and beginning to feel hot all over, I practically fall into the back garden, pulling my phone out of my pocket. I scan through my contacts with a shaky hand and press call. Cassie's phone rings and rings: no answer. I scroll down, and relief courses through me when the phone is picked up and I hear the deep voice at the other end.

'Nick? It's me, Susan.'

'And after you exited out of the back door, what did you do then, Ms Cartwright?'

I try to let out my sigh slowly so that the officer doesn't notice my impatience. I have been sitting in Ludlow police station for nearly three hours now and am going through my statement for the fourth time. They already know who I am – the probation service is obliged to keep them informed, in case of situations like this I suppose – and when they arrived it was almost as though they'd been waiting for something like this to happen.

'That was when I called Nick, um, Mr Whitely,' I repeat, knowing what the next question will be, and not really knowing how to answer it.

'And why is it that after finding your house and possessions trashed and a possible intruder in the property, instead of calling 999 you decided to call a reporter you met for the first time today? A reporter who lives almost *three hours* away?'

'The intruder wasn't still in the house,' I reply defensively. I realise that that isn't the point of what he's asking me, but I don't like what he's implying, and being obtuse – along with the sarcasm – is another one of my specialities when I'm pissed off at someone. 'I tried my best friend first. She didn't answer.'

'But you had no idea where the intruder was?' the officer presses. 'And yet you had a whole conversation with Mr Whitely before you called for help?'

He has a point, but I'll be damned if I'll let him know that. It's none of their business why I called Nick before the police, but it certainly wasn't to report a story, which is what he's insinuating. Him and the other three officers who have interviewed me since rescuing me from my back garden a quivering mess.

'I wouldn't say a whole conversation,' I reply, digging myself in deeper. 'And I don't see the relevance here. I called the person I'd been with that night, the first person that came to mind. He told me to ring the police and he'd get here as fast as he could. That's when I called the station. It was two minutes at the most.' I don't want to tell him why I was reluctant to

63

call the police, the panicked memories that even seeing the uniform brings back. The feeling of being led away in handcuffs has stayed with me for four years. The realisation that the police aren't always on the side of the good guys. That you don't always know if you're one of the good guys.

'Two minutes can cause a large delay in apprehending a potential criminal.' His eyes narrow. 'But I'm sure I don't have to tell *you* that.'

The meaning of his words slaps me in the face.

'I don't see what you're getting at—' I start, but he cuts me off.

'What we would usually do in a case like this is to narrow down people who might want to harm the alleged victim . . .'

I'm too stunned at this point to cut in, even to defend myself.

'. . . but in this case I think we'd have an easier time narrowing down the people who *wouldn't* want to harm a convicted child killer.' He leans in closer and fixes me with a stony look. 'We live in a small quiet town, *Ms Cartwright*. We don't take kindly to criminals on our doorstep.'

Before I can speak to defend myself, the door to the interview room opens and relief overtakes my anger. Another police officer who looks younger than the socks I'm wearing crosses the room without even glancing in my direction. He leans down and speaks quietly to my interrogator, who nods and looks up at me.

'It would seem your knight in shining armour has arrived.' I feel a jolt of nervousness – he's actually *come*? What am I supposed to say to him? Now that I've calmed down, I feel more than a little silly at having to face the man I've only met once and summoned a hundred and thirty miles to rescue me from an intruder. Better to get it over with, I tell myself, following the officer out into the reception area.

Nick is standing in the foyer, head down and hands shoved deep into the pockets of his light grey tracksuit bottoms. I don't know why I was expecting to see him still in his suit trousers and crisp white shirt; it's close to 3.30 a.m. and I've obviously dragged him from his bed. A fleeting image of Nick Whitely rising from his bed crosses my mind. Shaking my head to dislodge the picture before I have to face him, I cross the reception and am surprised when he hurries forward and takes me in his arms.

I wasn't expecting the embrace but it's exactly what I need. I don't care about the officers watching us with raised eyebrows, or the fact that I've known this man less than twelve hours; after my run-in with the intruder followed by the horrible police officer, all I need is some human contact, a little bit of compassion. The tears begin to flow and Nick holds me tighter, my head buried in the armpit of his navy blue hooded jumper, body racked with sobs. When the tears begin to subside, he holds me gently at arm's length and looks me square in the face. 'Susan, are you OK?'

Immediately I feel stupid. Of course I'm bloody OK, it's not like I've been attacked. 'I'm fine,' I mutter, wiping my eyes on the sleeve of my jumper. 'Sorry.' Nick smiles at me kindly, then looks over at the policemen behind the desk, who are making no effort to hide the fact that they're glued to the scene in front of them.

'Are we all right to go?' he asks them shortly. The officer who was so horrible to me only moments ago now nods as if butter wouldn't melt.

'We have everything we need, sir. The officers have secured your house, Miss Cartwright, but you can't stay there tonight I'm afraid. Is there somewhere else you can go?'

'I'll try Cassie again,' I say. 'I'll have to go and stay with her.'

'Not tonight you won't,' Nick tells me, taking me by the elbow and leading me out to the car park. 'I've already booked us in at a hotel down the road.' He opens the passenger door of his car and practically places me inside. 'We'll be in bed before you know it.' He cringes at the look that clouds my face. 'Not together,' he hastens to add. 'I mean separate beds, in separate rooms. I don't want to . . . well, not that I don't *want* to . . .' He sighs in defeat. 'Look, it's late and I've lost the ability to speak properly, so how about we head to the Travelodge and get some sleep.'

The Travelodge is closed but Nick has had the good sense to arrange for the night porter to let us in and book us into our rooms. It's with a huge sense of relief that I thank him again for his help, and after I manage to convince him that I'm not on the verge of a nervous breakdown, I settle into the comfortable bed and pull the covers up round my face, just like I used to do when I was a little girl. With the last couple of days' events running through my head, I don't expect to be able to sleep at all, but as I lay my head against the pillow my eyes close automatically and I drift away in an instant.

13

The room is cold.

Which room? Where am I? Is the room cold or am I cold? I don't open my eyes, I can't open them. For now my world is confined to my other four senses.

Smell. I can smell the fresh, citrusy scent of the shake and vac I regularly use on the carpet to cover the cloying smell of baby sick. There's something else: a male scent, a man that isn't my husband. An expensive scent that smells cheap, something one of my ex-boyfriends used to steal from his dad when I was a lot younger than I am now.

Touch. My body seems to melt into the carpet – my carpet judging by the smell – but when I try to spread my hands beneath me they won't work; almost like I've forgotten how to make them perform the simple function of opening and closing. What has this man done to me? Who is he and why is he in my home?

Focus, Susan, what else is there? Taste. Something acidic stings the back of my throat, almost a burning sensation but without the pain. My mouth is dry, like I've been asleep a while. I try to swallow to move some saliva around, but none comes, just that feeling I get when I've drunk too much the night before, like I've swallowed a mouldy sock.

Was I drinking last night? I can't grasp at the last thing I can remember, how I have come to be sleeping on my sitting room floor rather than in my bed with a funny taste in my mouth and another man's scent in my nostrils. I try to focus on sound but the room is silent, another sense that has betrayed me. Have I gone blind and deaf? No, it isn't an absolute silence – there's just nothing to hear – and my eyes are definitely closed, I'm not blind.

'She's dead. Shit, she's really dead.' It might have been a minute or an hour. I feel as though I'm drifting in and out of sleep, the way I do on a long car journey, never realising how we've got from A to B so quickly when I've been awake the whole time, honest. Just resting my eyes.

When I wake at the Travelodge the next morning, my head feels like I've gone ten rounds with Amir Khan and nearly every inch of me aches. I should be used to lack of sleep by now. My time with Dylan was punctuated with trips around the house in my pyjamas, rocking and shushing, praying to the gods of sleep for just one peaceful night. Afterwards, in hospital and Oakdale, my sleep was deep and dreamless – I took so many pills I hardly knew when night finished and day began – but I never woke up feeling rested. I don't remember the last time I felt rested.

I roll over in the luxurious king-sized bed and check the time on my phone: 9.20. I have three messages and four missed calls, which I ignore, deciding to tackle them later. I step into the spacious shower and my aching muscles welcome the hot spray like an old friend. I stay there longer than usual, hidden away from everything that awaits me outside these safe and secure walls. I know I'm simply trying to prolong the moment when I have to go downstairs and confront the complete stranger I dragged from sleep at midnight and who drove three hours just to escort me half a mile down the road and sleep twenty-eight rooms away. It's safe to say I feel a bit of a prat, which is probably why I spend half an hour showering and applying my make-up. The plus side of this is that I don't look half bad when I finally decide to head downstairs in search of Nick. Crossing the hallway and pressing for the lift, I pluck up the courage to check the messages and missed calls on my phone. The texts are all from Cassie, wanting to know what I was calling her for last night. Two of the four missed calls are from her too. The other two are from a withheld number. Nick? I find his number in my phone's address book and press call.

'Morning.' His voice is gravelly, the voice of someone who hasn't had much sleep. Immediately I feel guilty again, although it does sound a little sexy. 'How are you feeling today?'

'Like crap,' I admit. 'And starving. Did you call me? Where are you? Did you know when you booked this place that there's no restaurant?'

'My apologies,' Nick laughs. 'There aren't too many places willing to answer the phone at midnight, let alone take your breakfast order. I'm in the pub next door. Cracking food, are you coming?'

'You had me at pub. I'll be there in five; feel free to order me a full English.'

The pub is homely and welcoming, everything you would expect from a Shropshire country inn. Nick is sitting well away from the bar, presumably to avoid being overheard. To his right stands a huge log burner that looks like it could produce enough heat to keep the whole of Ludlow warm when it's lit. I sit down next to him and give him a weak smile, thank him for the mug of tea he's ordered and dig in when the food arrives. Nick's right, it tastes amazing, and to his credit he waits until I've finished shovelling huge forkfuls of beans, bacon, sausage and egg greedily into my mouth before attempting to broach the subject of last night.

'Before you start,' I interrupt as I see his mouth open to speak, 'I really am sorry for calling you last night. I have no idea why I didn't just ring the police. It really was so good of you to come all this way, especially as we've only just met. I feel like a prize—'

'For God's sake, woman, will you stop apologising?' Nick cuts in. 'I heard enough of it last night. I came because I wanted to make sure you were OK. I can't just leave someone who's in trouble, you know, even a person I've known less than twenty-four hours.'

'Well, thanks.' I swirl a piece of toast around my plate to soak up bean juice. *Of course he would have come*, I tell myself sharply. *What makes you think you're so special?*

'I think what happened last night confirms your suspicions that the photo was a threat,' Nick remarks, nicking the rest of the toast from my plate and devouring it. I look up at him and find those piercing eyes locked on to mine, watching.

'Why?' I ask, but I already know the answer even as my mouth forms the question, and I nod slowly.

'Whoever was in your house was trying to scare you.'

'Maybe it wasn't the same person. Maybe someone else knows I've been getting hassled. But then how would anyone know about the photo? You're the only person we've spoken to, and I'm presuming you haven't told anyone.' Nick raises his eyebrows in a pointed no. 'And I certainly haven't.'

'And are you sure . . .' He lets the sentence trail off and I shake my head firmly.

'Cassie hasn't told anyone,' I say in a tone that I hope warns him not to argue with me. 'She knows how to keep a secret.'

Nick doesn't look convinced. 'How much can you actually trust her? After all, she's a murderer, Susan.'

I try not to show my anger but my face flushes red, giving my fury away. 'As am I, or had you forgotten?'

Nick looks embarrassed. 'I'm sorry, I didn't mean to offend you.'

'Cassie has been there for me since the day I got to Oakdale. I trust her as much as I trust myself. I'm not justifying our friendship to you or anyone else. You need to accept that she has done what she's done, and it's more than likely that so have I. I'll understand if you don't want to get involved in this any more.'

Nick shakes his head. 'I'm sorry, I shouldn't have said what I did. I'll try and be nicer to Cassie, although it's pretty clear she doesn't trust me one bit.'

'She's used to it being just the two of us. She'll come round. She's very protective of me.'

'OK, I'll be nice.' Nick smiles. 'So if we're presuming that none of us told anyone else, then maybe you were overheard. Tell me again what you did after you got the photo.'

I repeat my exact movements from the minute I picked up the envelope until the time I met him yesterday. Nick listens intently, trying to figure out when someone might have discovered that I was poking around.

'Did you speak to anyone at the library?' he asks eventually.

'No. Well, just to apply for a library card in my new name. I spoke to the counter lady, Evelyn, but I didn't tell her what I was looking for.'

He looks thoughtful. 'In that case I'd say it's the same person who sent you the photo. Too many coincidences otherwise.'

'And the phone call.' The memory comes to me as though someone's handed me a Post-it. How had I forgotten? But it didn't seem like anything at the time; could it be something now?

'What phone call?'

'It was last week, right at the beginning, like Monday or

Tuesday. The house phone went and I straight away thought it was a sales call. No one else calls my house phone. I don't even know why I answered it.'

'And who was it?'

'No one. Well, almost no one. I thought it was a dead line, but then there was some house noise, like footsteps and a TV somewhere. Then there was a kid, I don't know if it was a boy or a girl, shouted "Nanny" and it went dead. I thought it was a wrong number.'

'Is that what you think now?'

'I don't know. What do *you* think?'

'I want to say coincidence, but how many coincidences can happen to one person in two weeks? The article in your bag, the photo, your house, now this? I don't know.'

I'm not too proud to admit that this scares me. When I received the photo, Cassie and I were quick to dismiss it as a prank; only for a minute did I consider it could be anything more sinister. Does someone really want to hurt me?

'Do you think my phone's been tapped?'

Nick looks impressed that I've thought of the possibility.

'It's something you have to think about. I mean, I don't want to be dramatic, but the photo is a relatively harmless – albeit unpleasant – trick to play. Trashing your house? That's escalated quickly. Maybe whoever it was knew you were meeting me.'

I sit back in my seat, the mug of tea warming my hands and providing a much-needed sugar kick. 'The police officer I spoke to suggested that people round here wouldn't want a child killer in their town. He's probably right.'

Nick purses his lips sympathetically. 'It does happen, I'm afraid. Some people hold grudges because they have nothing better to do with their lives. They might not know you from Adam, just what you did.'

My head is hurting again. It's all a bit surreal for me. I

don't live in a world where things like this happen. This is my life, not boredom relief for some desperate housewife. I sigh and rest my head in my hands, covering my tired eyes. When neither of us has spoken for five minutes, I look up to check Nick is still there. He's flipping through a notepad he already had out on the table when I arrived at the pub.

'What's that?' I ask, too curious to stay quiet any longer. Nick holds out the pad for me to take. It's a roughly scrawled chart, the word 'Evidence' written at the top of one column; another is headed 'Follow up'. In the evidence column are four points: the photograph I received, the newspaper in my handbag, the disappearance of Dr Riley and the break-in at my house.

'Wow, someone's organised,' I remark, unable to explain why this annoys me so much. 'Let's face it, it's much more likely I sent the photo to myself because I'm still as crazy as the doctors said I was.' I stop short at the look on his face. Guilt. Of course, how stupid am I? 'You've already thought of that.' It's a statement, not a question. It doesn't need to be a question; his face tells me all I need to know. 'You think I did this. You think I'm crazy.'

'It crossed my mind,' he admits. 'For about two seconds. I saw how upset you were about what happened at your house, Susan, and I know you didn't fake that.'

'How can you be so sure? You don't know me, you don't know anything about me.' I'm taunting him, daring him to deny that I could be unhinged.

'I just am.' His eyes don't leave mine for a second.

I'm too exhausted to argue. My mind is screaming for just one small white pill to take the edge off this feeling of help-lessness. Maybe I have some left at home; there's no way I can ask the doctor for more so early in my parole. I can't admit I might not be coping.

When breakfast is done, I don't think we can avoid going

back to my house any longer, so I'm happy to hear him suggest we have a coffee in the pub garden.

'Can I tell you something?'

He's trying not to look too eager. What does he think I'm about to confess?

'Of course, anything.'

Now I've said it, I can't refuse to tell him. 'I thought I saw Dylan yesterday.'

'What? Where? You didn't tell me this.'

'I was embarrassed. There was a boy in the street in front of me and he looked so much like the boy in the photograph, I just thought . . . Of course he didn't look anything like Dylan when I got up close, but from a distance, and I'd just seen the photo and . . .'

'Hey, hey, calm down.' My eyes are cast downwards and he dips his head to look into them. 'You'd just had a shock: people make mistakes like that all the time. I used to think I saw . . . Everyone's eyes play tricks on them.'

'Maybe, but not everyone chases kids down the street and grabs them. I honestly believed it was Dylan. If I was wrong about that, if I can't trust myself . . .' My words tail off.

Nick stays quiet for a long time, then looks at me like there's something he's dying to ask.

'Got any brothers or sisters?' I don't think that was it.

I smile. 'How come you get to know everything about me and I know zero about you? Apart from the dubious choice of vocation.'

He leans back in his chair looking amused. 'Well what do you want to know?'

'Married?' The question comes out too quickly and my cheeks burn. 'Sorry, too personal.'

He holds up his ring finger. 'Not married.'

'Hmm, Cassie said that doesn't mean anything.'

Nick frowns. He picks up a fork from the stone wall. It's

obviously been there a while; it's rusty and dirt-encrusted. He looks like he's studying it for the meaning of life, but I can't see what's so interesting. Finally he speaks. 'What's her problem anyway? Cassie, I mean. She's so bloody suspicious, it's like she thinks I'm going to run off with your life savings or something.'

That'd get you a bus ticket to Manchester.

'I told you before not to worry about it. Cassie just doesn't trust people. She's like that with everyone.'

'Wow, how flattering,' Nick remarks. 'Nothing special, eh?'

I grin despite my rotten mood. 'She might seem all brassy highlights and F words, but she's the best friend I've ever had. When you're in a place like Oakdale you have to accept that your life as you knew it, your old friends, your old house, it's all gone. You start to realise that the life you've been forced into doesn't have to be anything like your old one.' I let out a snort. 'I can just imagine Mark's face if I'd brought someone like Cassie home from mother and toddler group.'

He looks blank. Surely he doesn't need me to spell it out for him? The press were all over it, the have-it-all Stepford Wife who killed her baby son. The worst thing was, they were spot on in most of the things they said about us.

'Mark is loaded,' I explain, my cheeks reddening again. 'We ate at the best restaurants, I wore clothes once then threw them away – yes, I realise now how it sounds.' He's barely masking the disdain on his face but I don't hate him for it. I know the person I used to be. 'I wasn't used to mixing with people like Cassie, her angry tirades and her forty-a-day habit. Then I went to Oakdale and for the first time in my life I was the lowest of the low, not someone to be mollycoddled and looked after. I didn't have friends; no one wanted to be associated with a . . . with me.'

I've never spoken about my time at Oakdale with anyone,

but Nick's cool blue eyes have locked on to my face, and now I've started, I can't stop.

'Cassie was unlucky enough to be stuck in my room. She tried everything to make me talk. She lent me magazines and make-up – God knows why she was so keen to befriend me, but she wouldn't give in. It wasn't that I thought I was too good for her – that ship had long sailed. No, I didn't think I was good enough, for her or anyone. I actually just wanted to be left alone to die.'

'How did you get better?'

'She kept at it. When the magazines and make-up didn't work, she started smuggling me food. I wasn't on a hunger strike exactly, but I didn't have the energy or the inclination to get up to eat; I barely got up at all except to use the toilet. Every day Cassie would bring me food, but not from the cafeteria – chocolate bars, and sausage rolls. She always managed to get her hands on the best of everything. She had a deal going with the warders most of the time; sometimes other patients would help her out. One day the smell of a bacon sandwich was too much for me and while she wasn't looking I just started to eat. I hadn't even realised I was doing it until it was all gone. Cassie just winked at me. Ever since then, when the going gets tough, the tough get food.'

'I had wondered,' Nick laughed, 'about the monstrous appetite.'

As he checks his watch and indicates that it's time to leave, I realise that once again the conversation has switched around to me, and he's managed to answer a grand total of one question in the time we've been out here. Either he's deliberately avoiding talking about himself or he was an armchair psychologist in a past life.

14

Jack: 18 October 1987

He'd done a pretty good job, even if he did say so himself. Billy had finally emerged from his bathroom smelling like the aftershave counter at Boots and wearing an outfit that would have cost his own parents a week's wages.

'About fucking time. You want some of this?' He poured a shot of vodka and held it out. Billy screwed up his nose.

'Nah, I'm OK.'

'Seriously?' Jack laughed. 'You nicked it and you're not even going to drink it? Come on, don't be a pussy.' He shoved the drink towards his friend again, some of it sloshing on to his fingers. Billy took it, gave it a sniff.

'Just knock it back, it'll taste better the more you have,' Jack promised.

Billy swung his head back and threw the drink down his throat. Jack laughed as he put his hand to his mouth, coughing and retching.

'That's the way,' he said as there was a knock on the bedroom door. 'C'min.'

Lucy's face appeared in the doorway. From behind the door Billy made an obscene gesture that made Jack scoff. Poor lad wouldn't know what to do with a girl like Lucy. He was fifteen, for fuck's sake, and he'd never even kissed a girl. Ah well, maybe tonight was his night.

'Your friends are downstairs.' She eyed Jack suspiciously. 'Have you been drinking?'

'Yes. Do you want one?'

She moved further into the room, noticing Billy for the first time. 'Oh, hey.' Spotting the shot glass in his hand, she smiled. 'Well, I'm impressed. Even Jack won't shoot vodka.'

Billy widened his eyes at Jack, who shrugged unapologetically. 'Tastes like shit. Come on, Shakespeare, let's go.'

Jack moved to leave the room but Lucy stepped in front of him, blocking his way. She was close enough for him to smell her subtle flowery perfume. Even at three years younger he was at least two inches taller than her. 'Aren't you going to invite me to your party?'

'I don't need a chaperone, thanks.' He reached out to place his hands on her waist, pulled her slightly closer then moved her to the side. 'Come on, Bill.'

15

I hate the idea of seeing my house again, but I can't live out of the Travelodge indefinitely. We stop at the police station to collect my keys and they confirm I can go back into the house. When we get back, there's a figure sitting on the doorstep. Nick groans.

'What the fuck is going on?' Cassie's shrill Manchester accent hits me as soon as we get out of the car. 'What's he doing here? Why's there red paint all over your doorstep?'

I fill her in on the night before, her face darkening with every word she hears.

'You need to drop this,' she warns me, her finger close to my face. 'This is serious now, Suze. Being watched? Spied on? People in your house? Give. It. Up.'

I shake my head. 'I can't give up, I just can't. Even if it's some kind of hate campaign by locals, how can I live just waiting for the next person to break into my house, or attack me in the street?' We're still outside and I'm trying to keep my voice low. Cassie isn't.

'If this is some sicko out for revenge, you don't have to go through it on your own! You can come stay with me, or I'll stay here. Let's just forget that photograph and go back to normal.'

'What's normal? Normal for us is . . .' I can't say it. I can't say that normal for us is three square meals a day served on a plastic tray still encrusted with part of yesterday's meal. Normal is sharing a room the size of my old laundry room with a woman who talks about bodily functions as easily as my old friends compared Yankee Candles.

Now that I've started, I can't give up that easily. The part of me that has always wondered – that tiny inch of me that remembers making it all the way to the bus stop while my baby screamed relentlessly inside the house – *has* to know the truth. I have to wade back into my past, knee deep in crap, to see what's underneath. Do I deserve this? *Am I crazy?*

When I enter the front room with drinks, Cassie and Nick are sitting in silence. I hand Nick his mug of coffee and take my place on the sofa next to Cassie. I get the feeling they've been arguing.

'What?' I ask, looking between them. 'What?'

'The journalist wants to poke his nose in where it's not necessary.' Cassie's voice isn't so much tinged with venom as saturated with it. I look at Nick.

'I was just wondering if it would help if I were to, um, if I saw some, if you have any . . .'

'He wants photos of Dylan.'

My throat fills with bile. Photos? I have them, of course; they sit in the bottom of the pine dresser, encased in a brown leather album that has remained unopened for nearly three years. My father brought the album on one of his visits to Oakdale, but I have never had the courage to lift the cover. I took almost three hundred photographs of my newborn baby in the weeks following his birth: Dylan with his first teddy bear, Dylan's first windy smile, Dylan on a Wednesday. I guess from the size of the album that it doesn't hold all three hundred; I never wanted to find out which ones my dad had chosen to include.

'Why? They won't tell you anything; we know it can't be him. Besides, all babies look alike.'

That's a lie. My baby didn't look the same as other babies; other babies were screwed-up, wrinkly little things that barely resembled anything. My baby was beautiful, a perfectly smooth face and huge eyes that had changed from darkest blue to the deep brown I had fallen for in his father years before. A fine sprinkling of dark hair that grew so fast in those first few weeks that I'd had to brush it lightly with a soft-bristled white brush every morning, a present from my brother and sister-in-law. His tongue so adorable, even while it trilled its shrilling war cry deep, deep, deep into the night.

'You're right, I'm sorry, it wouldn't help anyway.'

But I know he thinks it will. Nick thinks it will help, and if I'm going to put myself through this ordeal, if I'm going to relive the twelve short weeks of Dylan's life one day, I may as well start here. I stand, Cassie takes in a sharp breath.

'You don't have to do this, Suze,' she warns. 'You've had enough shocks for this lifetime.'

'But if you do want to, it's better to do it when we're with you,' Nick presses.

'It's OK, Cassie, I want to.'

Both of them watch silently as I slide open the door at the bottom of the dresser and lift out the pristine album. I pass it over to Nick, but as he reaches out to take it I can't let it go.

'You don't have to.' Nick echoes Cassie's words gently.

I pull the book back towards me slowly and sit back down next to Cassie with it on my knee. She places a hand on mine and together we ease open the front cover.

On the first page, under the shiny transparent stick-down

paper, is a single photo. In it I am sitting in a hospital bed, pillows propping me upright, looking more exhausted than I have ever been in my entire life. I'm wearing not a scrap of make-up, my blonde hair is slicked back and my son – by the time this was taken, I'd at least admitted he *was* my son – lies wide awake in my arms. I remember it as though it was this morning: our first family photo. He wriggled so much, like a slick little fish unused to being handled, that we struggled to get a picture, Mark beaming and saying, 'That's my son,' over and over again. My eyes fill with fresh tears at the memory, and at the questions it causes. Was I already depressed when this photo was taken? The nurses told me not to worry about the baby blues – that was what they called it, but it felt so much worse. Shouldn't they have done something?

Cassie's hand squeezes mine. I don't have the strength to squeeze back.

After what feels like an hour, my hand reaches out and turns the page. The absence of a photograph shocks me almost as much as the photo on the first page did. A sheet of notepaper sits under the adhesive sheet. Printed on it, in my dad's spidery handwriting, are the words *I hope this will make you see*. I read them out loud and they don't make any more sense when they are floating in the air than they do in my mind.

'Make me see? What does that mean?' I ask no one in particular. 'What does it mean?' My voice rises to somewhere between hysterical and a pitch that only dogs can hear. 'Why would he say that?' I'm on my feet holding the album away from me as though it might burn me.

'Calm down.' I'm not too hysterical to see the look Cassie throws at Nick, a clear 'now look what you've done'. Three years of hard work in Oakdale and I'm right back to a volatile shaking mess again.

'He probably means see how much you loved Dylan,' Nick offers. My heart slows down slightly. That does sound like something my dad would say. Make me see how much I loved my son. That has to be it.

'You don't think he meant see what I'd done? See what I'd lost?' My voice is almost a whimper.

Cassie shakes her head vehemently. 'No. No way. It has to be what *he* said. Your dad stood by you all the way through the trial. He came every day to see you in the hospital before you were arrested. He adores you; why would he send you something malicious?'

I nod numbly. They're right. Cassie puts her hand on the page to turn it and looks at me to check that I'm ready. When I don't respond, she slowly flips it over.

On the next page is a photo of Dylan dressed in a pure white babygro and lying serenely in my arms, the only thing visible of me an elbow and a forearm. That's the way things go when you become a mother: you're always there in the background, a pair of legs or a hand, but you're not the focus any more. Did that bother me? Was it the fact that I wasn't the centre of attention in my husband's or my father's life any more? Mark had no family close by; all we'd ever wanted had been the two of us, until we'd made the decision to become three. Did I wish that Mark would stop staring at him sometimes and do the washing-up? Yes. Was I jealous of my baby? I never thought so.

'Do you still love me?' My words made Mark's eyebrows lift slowly, scared of being tricked into saying something wrong, no doubt.

'Of course I do, baby.' His words were slow and he reached out to pull me close. I flinched when his fingers found soft flesh where a taut, toned stomach used to live.

'More than Dylan?'

I felt his body stiffen. Was he wondering what kind of

mother could ask that question? All I'd wanted was to know I was still wanted, needed.

'I love you both the same, sweetie.'

Nick is still staring at the album, studying each photo so intently I wonder if he's looking for similarities between the recent photo and old ones, or if he's just trying to gauge my reaction to the pictures of my son. I turn the pages faster as the album goes on. A black and white picture of my baby's tiny hands against my giant fingers, a shot that took me seven attempts to get right. On the fifth page are the black ink footprints, no longer than two inches. A full-colour 7x5 picture of my little boy in his bouncer, Big Ted sitting at the side twice the size of the sleeping baby. One of the last pictures I ever took. If my dad chose these pictures to make me see how much I loved my son, then mission accomplished.

It is when we near the end of the album that we find it. After a page of photos showing Dylan being proudly held by my dad and Mark. Nick and Cassie have started to take turns turning the pages to save me the effort, and it's on Nick's turn when the photographs suddenly show a different subject. Lots of different subjects, in fact. Five different dark-haired toddlers stare up at me from the album, a space where one has been taken out. Taken out and posted through my door two days ago. And folded up in the pages is a newspaper article with the photograph carefully clipped out. The head-line: MOTHER GETS SIX YEARS FOR SON'S MURDER.

The blood drains from my whole body and bile rises in my throat. My head rushes as I struggle to make sense of what I'm staring at; the pictures swim in and out of focus. Confusion knits Cassie's brow, and when I look at Nick for answers or reassurance, he doesn't meet my eyes.

'I need air.' Somehow I make it to the back door, my knees shaking perilously. I rest one hand against the door jamb, holding myself steady. The cold, fine rain is a welcome antidote to the heat of my face.

'Susan?' Cassie's voice is low and calm. *Don't make any sudden movements or loud noises. Don't want to frighten the crazy lady.*

'I don't know how they got there, Cassie. I've never seen them before in my life.'

A hand rests lightly on my shoulder. 'I know that. Come inside, you'll get soaked.'

The front door opens and slams closed. The two of us freeze, waiting for the sound of Nick's car, but it doesn't come. Is he leaving? Running away from the mentally unstable woman in the back garden? Instead, his voice carries over the fence and I catch three words: 'more to it'. He's on the phone to someone, unaware that we're so close.

I make a move to walk inside. Whoever he's talking to, I have no interest in listening to him saying I've lost the plot. Cassie grabs my arm.

'Wait.'

His words float in and out, as though he's pacing the doorstep. All I catch is 'I promise', then a lower 'you too'. The front door opens again and there's silence.

'There you go.' I jerk my head towards the front room. 'He knows what it means. Those photographs are *in my house.* The picture I found on my doormat came from a photo album only I've had access to. How could I do that? Collect those photographs of little boys and send one to myself without remembering? I don't even remember killing my own son, Cassie! What makes you so sure I couldn't have done this?'

'Because I know you, Susan. You're better now, you're not crazy.'

I laugh without humour, a short, bitter sound. 'You never even knew me. You never saw me crying myself dry at three in the morning because I couldn't express enough milk to make my son's next feed. *I couldn't even feed him.* Do you know what that feels like? Do you know how alone you can feel, in the dark, the TV playing reruns of *Special Victims Unit* on silent so the rest of the house doesn't wake up? I'd finally get him back to sleep and I'd have to sit with my freezing naked tit stuck to a milking machine so that I had enough for two hours' time when he woke again. Sometimes it would take forty-five minutes to make an ounce and I would sleep on the sofa, not wanting the comfort of my own bed because it would kill me to have to drag myself out again in an hour. It's finally time for me to face what I did. I'm ill. It's not my fault I got ill, but I still have to live with the consequences. I killed my son and now I'm trying to convince myself that I'm innocent and Dylan's still alive. I've been so convincing that I've even persuaded myself it's true! I just wanted, I needed . . .'

I needed to believe I wasn't capable of harming a baby, my baby, even though deep down the most horrific thing has been knowing that that's exactly what I was capable of. The mind has funny ways of making you face up to things too hard to admit to.

I sigh, scared and defeated. 'That's not just the most probable explanation, Cassie, it's the only one. The sooner I come to terms with what I've done, the more likely it is I'll get better.'

But I don't believe myself. I don't believe I'll ever be better again.

16

Today, Wednesday, is parole day. I have to keep in regular contact with my parole officer, Tamara Green: a visit every two weeks, a phone call every other fortnight. This week is phone call week, a fact I'm very glad of given the fact that I've spent the last hour cleaning up after last night. I don't think I could face her today. I'm taking the call from the same position on my tatty brown sofa where I've been sitting all night, staring at the photographs in the album, pleading with myself to remember putting together that last page. I think I slept, for a short while at least, because I don't remember how the clock got from 2.45 to 3.52, but the rest of the time I just sat.

I thought of calling Tamara when I first received the photograph. She's nice and I felt sure she'd help me if she could. Now I'm relieved that I never got around to it; nice as she may be, I'm not sure she'd be able to overlook me putting together some sort of morbid album of current-day Dylans, taking one out, putting it in an envelope and printing my own name and address on the front. The kind doctors at Oakdale would be preparing my old room before I'd even hung up. The best thing I can do now is keep my head down, answer her questions and try not to scream.

'Emma, how are you?' Tamara's voice is warm and friendly. How can she sound so normal when my world is falling apart?

'I'm good, thanks.' I force myself to say the words but my voice betrays me. Tamara ignores this and carries on with her script.

'How's the job search going?'

We go around on the meaningless carousel of questions as usual, only this time I'm waiting. Waiting for her to announce that she knows what I've done, she knows what I'm capable of. But she doesn't. Is this what my life will be like from now on? Always waiting for someone to suddenly announce that they know my secret? Always wondering what I'm going to find I've done next?

Before I even realise it, I've answered all of Tamara's questions, obviously satisfactorily, because she tells me she'll see me next week and says goodbye.

I'm not going to do anything today. Cassie hasn't called and neither has Nick.

When they left last night, I barely spoke to either of them, just nodded my goodbye. Nick told me he was going back to the Travelodge to stay another night, and that he'd be in touch, but I know he won't. His story is gone, his interest in my plight over now that he knows the truth. *He felt sorry for you, that's the only reason he agreed to help in the first place. He knew all along you were the one responsible.*

And if I'm truthful with myself, so did I. My eyes may sting with tiredness and the burden of last night's tears, but my soul almost feels lighter. There's no worrying, no wondering, no lying to myself. In the last two days I've managed to face the memories of how difficult those early days with Dylan were for me, something even three years in Oakdale didn't force me to do, and I'm still alive, even if I do hate myself for it.

I can take that. Self-hatred is something I've lived with since the day my son died.

When the doorbell goes at 6 p.m., I expect it to be Cassie. Pulling aside my front room curtain, I'm surprised to see Carole from the Deli on the Square staring nervously at the door. She's got something in her hand; it looks like a brown paper bag. Has she brought me cheese? I can't even think about food right now. *Uh oh Len, I think we have a problem.*

Still, I can't leave her standing on my doorstep, so I swing open the door.

'Carole, hi, how are you?' I don't want to engage in conversation, today of all days, but I don't want to be rude either. I just hope that her witnessing my outburst in the street the other day doesn't make her think she can pop over whenever she likes. I feel a little tricked, really, that I never even knew she lived so close yet she must have. Why didn't she mention it one of the many times I've been in her shop? I step out on to the front step rather than invite her to come in. I know. Rude.

'Emma, I'm so sorry to just turn up on your doorstep. I don't want you to think I'm being pushy or anything . . .'

'Of course not.' That's exactly what I was thinking.

'It's just that this was left for you in my porch this morning.' She holds up a brown box. 'I was in a massive rush to work and I completely forgot to bring it round before I went. I hope it isn't important?'

She looks as if she's expecting me to explain, but my eyes haven't left the box. When I don't speak, she hands it to me awkwardly.

'Did you see who left it?' My tone is sharp; she's got her answer – yes, it is important. It's very important.

'No, it was inside the porch when I got up this morning,

bloody stupid deliveryman put it in 33 instead of 3 – I know it was early but how stupid can you be?'

I turn the box round and my heart stops.

'There must be some mistake. This isn't addressed to me.'

Carole looks at the box in my hands, at the name Susan Webster printed in black, and then back at me. There's pity in her eyes and she reaches out to touch my arm.

'But it is for you, isn't it?'

'I think you'd better come inside,' I say.

Carole is sitting on my ugly brown sofa, picking at the edge of the brightly coloured throw I put on there to cover up whatever dubious stains the previous tenants left behind. I'm standing, too agitated to take a seat. Neither of us has spoken for a few minutes.

'How do you know who I am?' She looks up at my tense words.

'When I saw the name on the parcel I did some Google searches and eventually I found pictures of you when you were Susan Webster.'

And that's how easy it is. I knew it would be possible for people to find out who I was, but I'd never imagined my neighbours trawling the internet to find grainy pictures of me. I've been so naive, so stupid to think people would be too busy with their own lives to care about mine.

'I'm not going to tell anyone, if that's what you're worried about. What is it?'

'I don't know.' The revelation that my cover has been blown has made me all but forget about the package Carole came to deliver.

'Sorry, I shouldn't be prying. I just want you to know that your secret is safe. I'm not going to take out a full-page ad in the paper or anything.' She makes to rise from her seat.

'Stay.' I realise I don't want to open the box yet, and I

don't want to be on my own. 'Let me make you a cup of tea.' She's not going to say yes. Now that she knows who I am, she's probably going to run as far and as fast as she can.

'That would be nice, thanks.'

She stays for almost an hour and we talk. I tell her how I still can't remember anything of the day Dylan died, although I don't tell her how it terrifies me to think that I can't remember because my mind is protecting me from the fact that I'm guilty. I do confide in her my fear that I might never get the truth about what happened to my son. I don't tell her about the photograph, or any of the other things that have happened to me since last Saturday. In return, she tells me a story of her own.

'I suffered from post-natal depression too.' I lift my eyes, but hers are averted. She's not talking to me; she's talking to the uplighter, the vase on the corner shelf, anything but me. 'When my daughter was born. I looked at her and I expected this rush of love, like you read about. She was sleeping, and she didn't look beautiful, she looked all wrinkled and her head was a cone shape from the suction cap. I didn't want to hold her, like a proper mother would. I thought she looked horrendous.' Finally she looks at me and there are tears in her eyes.

'I've never told anyone that. Even though I got help, and I got better, and I love my little girl so much, I still never told a soul that I thought she was the ugliest baby I'd ever seen.'

'Did anyone notice?' I whisper.

'My husband.' Her hands work furiously at a stray thread on the throw. 'But not at first. She was perfect for everyone else; they all said what a chilled-out baby she was. But for me . . . every time I picked her up, she just cried and cried. I found out afterwards that she could smell my milk; she wanted food whenever she was near me and that's why she cried. But at the time I just thought she must hate me. She'd look at me with her huge blue eyes and I felt so guilty that I couldn't just love her like everyone else did.'

'What happened?'

She looks away again, takes a sip of her tea. 'My husband left us on our own for the day, and from the minute he left, she just screamed. Nothing I could do would make her stop. I was so tired – I'd been up all night feeding her every two hours – and I couldn't take it. I put her in the nursery and just listened to her cry as I sat on the floor in a heap at the front door. When my husband got home he couldn't even get in; I was lying in a ball against the front door. He had to kick the back door down because I'd left the key in it. He took me straight to our GP, who diagnosed me with post-natal depression.'

Her eyes fix on mine. 'Was that how it was for you?'

'I can't really remember,' I admit, sitting down, careful to avoid looking at the box on the edge of the table. 'Afterwards the doctors asked me all sorts of questions: had I been tired, irritable, nervous? The answer to all of those questions was yes. I'd been exhausted and snappy a lot of the time. We had so many visitors after Dylan was born, my aunties and neighbours, that I felt like I was the first woman on earth to give birth. They would turn up at all hours, without calling, and I felt like screaming at them to fuck off, leave us alone. I felt like I hated everyone. But I never once remember feeling like I hated Dylan. It seems strange, because I said it a couple of times – "Won't you just shut up! I hate you!" – but I never really felt like I meant it, even as the words spilled out.' This is the first time I've told anyone this, maybe because Carole has just told me one of the worst things you can say about yourself. I feel like if anyone can understand, she will.

'It was one of those times when he wouldn't go to sleep. He'd sleep in my arms, so peaceful and angelic, but as soon as

I put him down he'd wake up screaming. All I wanted was a shower; I'd been up all night. I cried, I pleaded, nothing worked. That's when I said it: "I wish you'd never been born." But I don't feel like I ever really meant it. Does that sound silly?'

'No.' Carole shakes her head. 'I always felt like that afterwards too.'

'But then there were times, when we were playing together, or when he was sleeping soundly, I'd sit by his crib and stare at him like if I wasn't looking at him he might disappear like a dream. Those times I loved him so much I felt it might stop my heart.'

'Bipolar.'

'Yes, that's what they said. But not just bipolar,' I admit. 'Puerperal psychosis. An illness so bad that you start to hallucinate. You're high one minute, low the next; you feel paranoid, suspicious, as though you're in a dream world.' I sound like I'm quoting from a medical website, because I am. I can spout this stuff backwards.

'Did you feel any of that?'

'Not that I remember. But there's another symptom. You can believe your baby is the devil, evil and out to get you. You harm him because you believe you have no other choice; if you don't, he will harm you first.'

'And you felt like that?'

'I didn't think so. Not until afterwards. I remember all the stuff you talked about – wishing someone would just take him away, feeling guilty because I couldn't even make my own son love me, stupid, fat, inadequate, lazy . . . I felt all those things but I don't remember wanting him dead. Wanting him not born isn't the same as wanting him dead, is it?' *Is it?*

17

The box is the size of a shoebox, wrapped in brown paper. My heart speeds up, my chest tightens and my face gets hot.

I'm torn between wanting to rip the paper off as quickly as my fingers will allow and wanting to hurl the box on the fire and watch it burn. I do neither. Instead I walk into the kitchen and switch the kettle on.

My mother once told me that there was nothing that didn't look clearer after a cup of tea. I believe at the time I was nursing a broken heart; one of the few boyfriends I'd had before I met Mark had cheated on me with a girl in the year above who had bigger boobs and would put out. I'm just glad my mum isn't here to see me find out that there are some problems that can't be fixed by a cup of tea or a 'stop for a kiss'.

When I was little – I can first remember it at five or six, but Dad said it started much earlier than that – my mum and I would slide down the stairs together on our bums. After every step I would say to her, 'Stop for a kiss', and we'd have to freeze, have a kiss and bump down on to the next step. If we were in a rush, Mum would carry me quickly down the stairs then look at me in mock horror. 'But we forgot to stop for a kiss!' she'd exclaim, and smother my face in kisses, one for each step, while I laughed and squirmed and tried – not very hard – to escape.

It always amazed me how different my parents were to those of my friends. *My* mum and dad still kissed each other goodbye every morning, and held hands when we went to the park, me clinging on to my mum's other hand, swinging it back and forth. My dad still brought home flowers, even when he hadn't done anything wrong, and Mum got up – in the middle of the night, it seemed – to do Dad's sandwiches for work.

The day I told Mum that Mark and I were trying for a baby, we were sitting in the garden, flicking through the Sunday papers. She just smiled and said, 'Not a moment too soon, love.' It wasn't until much later that I found out she'd already known about the illness that would take her life.

We tried for two years before admitting that something might be wrong and going to see the doctor. By that time Mum had already had two rounds of treatment and seemed to be doing really well. She got out in the garden three times to tend her tomato plants and came shopping with me for a couple of new dresses for the trip they were planning. Dad took her away to Italy the weekend I went into hospital for my egg harvest. Three months later we found out I was pregnant, and the month after that we were back in the same GP's room to be told that Mum's cancer was back.

She fought harder than before, but I knew this time that she wouldn't live to see our baby born. The only thing I cling to now is that at least it meant that she never had to experience his death either. My father, on the other hand, has had to live through the loss of his only wife, his only grandson and his only daughter, all within a space of two years.

Dad sat in the dock every day of my trial. On the first day I made the mistake of glancing over, to try and catch a glimpse of him. The moment my eyes found him, sandwiched in between my brother and his wife, he looked up and saw me staring. His jaw was clenched and he was forcing himself not to cry, not to show how upset he was. For a moment I imagined him running down the steps from the gallery, gathering me up in a hug and refusing to leave my side until I was allowed home. This was the first time that he couldn't make everything better for me. I couldn't bear to look at him again for the entire four-week trial, not until the jury read out their guilty verdict. The eyes of the press were trained on me and my husband when the jury returned; mine were fixed on my father. The last time I saw my dad, he was sobbing like a child.

A quick check of the hallway: the package is still there, on the table where I left it. As I stand staring stupidly at the inanimate object, trying to decipher its exact contents by psychic energy, a pounding on the front door makes me cry out.

'Susan?' It's Nick. Even after everything, relief floods through me when I hear his voice. I cross the hall quickly, ignoring the package once more, and open the door. 'Are you OK?' he asks. I nod and point to the table, watching realisation cross his face.

I know immediately what he's thinking.

'I know what you're thinking,' I tell him. 'That the timing is perfect. That I put it there. Well I didn't.' I don't know why I'm so desperate for him to believe me. Maybe if he believes me, I can believe it myself.

'You don't know what I'm thinking,' Nick states. I get the feeling he doesn't know what he thinks himself. I push on.

'You think I put it there after yesterday, to make you take me seriously again. Well I didn't. Carole brought it round an hour ago. She came in, we talked. You can call her and ask her. Go on.' I fumble for my mobile phone, where I have Carole's number saved. 'Call her.'

Nick ignores my rambling. He doesn't even ask who Carole is.

'You haven't opened it?' It's a stupid question really, seeing as it's still wrapped in brown paper. Resisting sarcasm, I shake my head.

'Do you have any gloves?' he asks. For a fleeting moment I wonder if he's cold, then I realise he means to pick up the box. Thank God I didn't produce my woolly thermals.

'I have a pack of vinyl ones in the bathroom,' I tell him, then, feeling the need to explain myself, I add, 'For cleaning the toilet.'

Looking like a crime-scene investigator, Nick dons the gloves and hands me a pair. He picks up the box, carries it into the kitchen and places it on the counter. He takes a knife and positions it inside the fold of the brown paper. Shit, he's actually about to open it. I hold my breath, as though whatever is in there can't hurt me, can't affect me if I'm not breathing. The lid comes off and I exhale.

'It's a hairbrush,' I say stupidly, picking the small blue brush up out of the box. It's full of hairs, not baby hairs like my son's, but hairs belonging to a much older child. I've never seen it before in my life.

'What about this?' Nick asks, lifting a folded piece of cloth from the box. 'Does this mean something to you?'

I don't need to take it from him to see what it is. The piece of cloth is a baby's blanket, hand-stitched throughout a mother-to-be's pregnancy and given with love to her baby boy on the day he was born. I'd made it using pieces of material from my own baby blanket and squares of light blue and green cellular material. There's a patch that has toy soldiers marching along it I'd come across in a charity shop in Devon on our last weekend away before Dylan was born;

a square of beige with white spots left over from the material I'd had the nursery curtains made from; and a fleecy patch with a picture of a giraffe and an elephant. I'd trimmed the whole thing in light blue satin that had been so fiddly to attach I'd almost given up and thrown it in the bin. No, this is one of a kind and there's no getting away from that. And there's only one person in the world who knew where it was.

My mind goes into overdrive. Did he send this? Does he know about the photograph? Did he send that too? I know I have to call him, demand to know what the hell he's playing at, ask him why he sent this here, but I can't bring myself to do it. At least now I know the truth: Dylan isn't alive, he's been dead for four years just like everyone told me, just like the jury heard at the trial.

Does this mean my ordeal is over? Now all I have to do is glue together the newly shattered pieces of my life and try to forget – something I'm practically a professional at by now.

I haven't spoken since Nick lifted the blanket out of the box. To his credit, he doesn't push me, just waits for me to process the contents. The words stick in my throat; I don't want to say them out loud.

'It's Dylan's,' I manage to whisper. I'm stalling. Nick is a clever man; he's already figured that much for himself. 'I made it for him.' Another pause, then I push on. 'Dylan's things went to charity, things he'd never worn or used, but his real stuff went into storage. I couldn't expect Mark to keep it in our home, so I asked someone I trusted. Someone I knew wouldn't let me down.'

'Who?' Nick asks. He is speaking as gently as possible but there is urgency in his voice. He knows the revelation might bring us closure on all this, then he can return to his normal life. I realise I don't want it to be over, not just because of who has caused this or because I'm in denial of my son's death, but because I can't stand what I'm thinking. I can't just pretend I don't know, though, so I answer as strongly as my voice can manage.

'My father,' I tell him, breathing in deeply to stop the tears. 'I gave it to my dad.'

18

Jack: 18 October 1987

*Matt and Adam had met them at Jack's cousin's party. Her mum
and dad had gone away for the whole weekend and she was supposed
to be staying with their grandmother, which basically meant waiting
until their grandmother fell asleep at 8 p.m. and sneaking back
round to her own house to let them all in. She was the year below
him in school so her mates were no more than fourteen, but old
enough to want a bit more than jelly and ice cream at their parties.*

*'Jack!' His cousin greeted him by throwing her arms around his
neck and kissing him on the cheek. She'd already had a couple;
Granny must have gone for her lie-down early tonight. 'Come in.'*

*She led the way through to the front room, where several groups
of girls were sitting separately from the few boys in the room, giggling
and throwing them secretive looks. Adam and Matt carried the booze
through to the kitchen and Jack gestured for Billy to follow him.*

*'Hey, Shakespeare, nice to see you again.' She smiled. 'Can I get
you a vodka?'*

*Billy nodded. He's nervous, Jack thought fondly. Bless him. His
cousin disappeared into the kitchen and returned two minutes later
with Matt and drinks for all of them.*

'Come on, mate,' Jack nodded at the vodka she handed him. 'Get stuck in.'

Matt gave Billy a sideways look. 'Here,' he hissed. 'You can have this if you want.' Jack watched him swap Billy's vodka for his beer. 'Might be easier on you if you're not used to drinking.'

Jack scowled. 'He's not a baby, Riley. Let him drink what he wants.'

Matt shrugged. 'Whatever.'

'I'll just have this for now.' Billy nodded. 'Save the harder stuff for later, right?'

Jack screwed up his nose. 'Whatever.'

'Um, I think this one needs a lie-down.' Jack guided the young girl over to where Billy was still deep in conversation with his baby cousin. The girl – was it Vicky, Nicky? – clung to his waist but it didn't stop her wobbling dangerously. She'd been fine until five minutes ago, when Jack had suggested going outside for some fresh air. She'd hit the air and started to sway. Jack had just managed to catch her before she'd hit the floor. 'I'm going to take her upstairs.'

Billy jumped up. 'You're not going to . . . you know . . . are you? She's plastered.'

Jack laughed. 'What kind of person do you think I am? I'm just going to put her upstairs to sleep it off. If she's lucky, I might get her in the recovery position.'

His cousin smiled and put her hand on Billy's arm. 'Don't worry about it. Vicky's always like this. She'll sleep it off and be fine.'

Ah, so it was Vicky then. Would be best if he knew her name if he was going to screw her. And his cousin had the hots for Shakespeare! How had he not seen that before?

'Anyway, he's got his prick-tease housekeeper to go home to.' The little bitch smiled, a triumphant gleam in her eyes. How long had she known about Lucy?

'What?' Billy turned his narrowed eyes on Jack. 'Are you sleeping with Lucy?'

'Don't be fucking stupid, Billy.' He gestured to his cousin, who *was looking very pleased with herself. 'She's just winding you up. Lucy's too skinny for me. I like a girl who knows how to eat.' He grinned and pinched the flesh of the girl lounging on his arm. 'Isn't it about time you found yourself a little something, Billy?' He shifted the girl uncomfortably to one side and she giggled, her eyes still closed. He was desperate to get her up to one of the bedrooms – his auntie and uncle's preferably – but he wasn't leaving without ruining his cousin's evening in return for her dropping him in it. He turned to a group of three girls who were trying their best to smoke a cigarette between them without looking like they'd never done it before, and gestured one of them over.*

'Sally,' he started.

'Samantha.'

He gave his best winning smile. 'Sorry, yeah, Samantha. This is Billy, he hasn't seen the pond yet. Would you show him?'

Samantha grinned. 'Yeah, sure, Jack. C'mon, Billy, it's pretty cool.'

Billy didn't even have time to object before he was dragged off in the direction of the back door.

'Asshole,' his cousin hissed at him.

'Yeah, yeah, whatever. I'm busy. Keep your fucking mouth shut in future.' He walked off, but not too fast to miss her adding, 'I hope she gives you crabs.'

19

Nick recovers a lot quicker than I do, and before I even realise what I'm doing I'm standing in the back garden, my hands shaking as I struggle to light a cigarette with one hand and hold my coffee in the other. I smoked a lot at Oakdale, through boredom or as a way to get fresh air – I know, I know – and even though I quit when I left, I still keep a packet in the house just in case. Tea for problems, coffee and cigarettes for a crisis.

It's a full ten minutes before Nick speaks to me, and when he does it's tentatively, as though he's trying hard not to upset me further.

'When was the last time you saw your father?' he asks. I'd almost forgotten that we've only just met and he's got no idea of my family situation.

I take a deep breath. 'My dad tried several times to visit me in Oakdale.' I feel guilty just saying the words. 'But I turned down every request for a visit and refused to leave my room.'

Nick looks confused and I don't blame him. The evening has drawn in and it must be cold – I can see the goose bumps on his arms – but I can't feel it and he doesn't complain. Maybe my body is shutting down, switching off my senses one by one until one of these days I'll just stop, wherever I am.

'I thought you said he's supported you? Stood by you? Why didn't you want to see him again?'

'He did support me.' I see Dad's face again, the way it crumpled as the foreman said the word. Guilty. 'More than I deserved. And he refused to abandon me, even after I'd gone away. He sat outside the facility week in week out. Eventually, after about six weeks he gave up and stopped coming.' I was so relieved and so disappointed. He'd lasted longer than my husband but in the end he still did what I'd known he'd do, what everyone else from my old life had done. He gave in and left me, leaving the album behind with two warders.

I'm not telling Nick the whole story. I'm not telling him how the warder my father handed the album to refused to give it to me – I'd never been 'nice' enough to him to earn my privileges. It was a rock and a hard place: if I didn't complain, he knew he could treat me however he wanted, and without sexual favours I'd never see what my father had sent me. If I complained to the head warder I'd be branded a whinger and a snitch, and more than one of the officers would make my life unbearable. I'm not going to tell him how I got the album, how Cassie just walked in and handed it to me one morning without a word, and didn't once complain when I couldn't bring myself to open it for three years. Something else I've never asked about, something else I owe her more than I could ever repay her for.

I wanted Dad to forget about me, pretend he had never had a daughter or a grandson. I couldn't bear the thought of him visiting me each week, having to endure the searches by the warders – glorified prison guards and most of them bloody bullies. I imagined him having to deal with my situation at work, in the pub and at the golf club, daily reminders that his daughter was a murderer. It would be hard enough for him without the added shame of having to sit across from me and make small talk about the weather or what Jean next door had done with her begonias.

In the last four years I've thought about my dad at least twice a day. I've wondered what he's up to, how he's coping and whether he's keeping OK. I tried so hard to take care of him after Mum died, to make sure he didn't get depressed or too lonely. After I went away, did anyone do that for him? Or was he allowed to just fade into his own little world, where I was responsible for everything that was wrong in his life? Did he grow to hate me in my absence? It's no more than I deserve.

Nick listens to my story without interrupting and takes my hand when I begin to cry silent tears.

'But if your dad supported you through everything, why would he be tormenting you like this now?' he wonders, more to himself than to me.

'Don't know,' I admit, 'but I know that blanket is one of the things I asked him to pack away for me before the trial began. I couldn't bear the thought of it going to charity, or worse, being thrown away. No one else could have sent it to me, no one.'

'And your dad would know that,' Nick reasons. 'He would know that by sending it you would realise it was him. I don't know much about your family, but it doesn't sound like the work of a heartbroken old man. And how would he know where you live? He doesn't sound the type to skulk round in the bushes outside your home.'

'I don't know,' I repeat, sounding like a stuck record but not knowing what else to say.

'Is there anyone your father would have given the blanket to? This is really important, Susan; think, please.'

There is an urgency in his voice that I don't feel entirely

comfortable with, and I wonder if he's getting too close to the whole thing. This isn't his mess. Am I going to end up with another ruined life on my conscience? Another broken career, another man in tatters?

When I don't say anything, he pushes on. 'I think you need to see your father, Susie.'

I hear this and I know it's true, but the only thing I can think is that he called me Susie. Mark is the only person who has ever called me that, and hearing it coming from another man's lips feels strange. How can it feel like I'm cheating on my husband by speaking to another man? I haven't seen Mark in four years. I forced myself not to write to him or call him; it took so much willpower to cling on to the last bit of my self-respect when all I wanted to do was beg him to come and see me, to tell me that I wasn't completely alone. In a way it was like another bereavement, losing Mark; he was in a place where I couldn't ever see him, speak to him, lay my head in the crook of his arm and share my grief for Dylan. For all I know, he could be with another woman now, he could be remarried and – God knows I've thought this enough times – have another child. The problems we had conceiving were mine, not his, and I've tormented myself with visions of my ex-husband and his pregnant wife a hundred times. So why can't I move on and let myself be happy? Why is it such a crime for me to want this man to hold me, make me feel better?

'Now?' I realise Nick is looking at me expectantly. 'You want me to call him now?'

'Well you want this sorted, don't you? You want to know why he's done this?'

No, I don't really. The fact is, there can't be any *good* reason; there can't be anything in this that is for my benefit. What was it he wrote in my album? To make me see? To make me see what I've done to my life? To see what I've done to my family? Well congratulations, Dad. I see it more clearly now than ever.

I'm saved from an explanation by the front door opening. I know it must be Cassie – at least I hope it is – she's the only one with a key.

'Only meeee—' She stops short, the smile gliding off her face when she sees Nick. 'What are you doing here?' And to me, 'Has he been here all day?'

'Nice to see you too,' he replies, his face equally grim. 'I could ask you the same.'

'No you couldn't. You have no right to ask what I'm doing here. I've been here countless times, I have a key.' She produces it with a flourish. 'I'm supposed to be here. You're the one who's out of place.'

'Cassie, that's enough,' I warn. Like a dog defending her owner, she retracts her teeth, but only slightly.

'I thought he'd have gone back home by now, that's all.' Is it my imagination or does she sound a little sulky?

'There's been something new.'

Cassie looks confused. 'Another photo? But I thought . . .' I'm certain she stops short of saying she thought I was responsible for the first one. She *thought* it was all cleared up. She *thought* Nick would be back in Doncaster.

'Not another photo.' I retrieve the box from the table. 'Carole from the deli brought this round. It was addressed to Susan Webster but the delivery man let her sign for it because I wasn't in.'

'Oh shit. Is she going to tell anyone? What's inside it?'

I nod my head towards the sofa. 'You might want to sit down. This might take a while.'

Taking care not to agree with Nick in any way, Cassie insists I call my dad. I suppose if I'm going to do it I'd rather do it when they're both here with me, so when she hands me the phone I take it. I almost hang up on the first ring, and the second, and the third, but somehow I manage to keep the receiver clasped tightly in my hands and wait for my dad to answer, which he does on the fifth ring. At the sound of his voice, just a simple hello, I almost lose my nerve a fourth time. It isn't until he repeats himself that I remember that it's my turn to speak.

'Hello, Dad.'

There's silence at the other end while my father processes a voice he hasn't heard for four years. I wonder if he's hoped for this call, waited for those words that never came. Cassie smiles encouragingly, rubs my free hand.

'Susan,' he whispers finally, and I can't tell if he is pleased to hear from me or preparing to slam down the phone.

'Yes, Dad, it's me.' I suddenly realise I don't have a clue what I'm going to say next, and I end up saying stupidly, 'I'm out now.'

'I know, Rachael called me.'

Rachael called him? My lawyer Rachael? When? Have they kept in touch? Was it her who made him send me the blanket? My mind spins in confusion but I know now isn't the time to ask this.

'Can I come and see you, please?' I hold my breath, waiting for him to say no, sorry, it isn't a good time, and I'm surprised when he replies simply, 'Of course you can, Suze, I've missed you.'

Tears fill my eyes as I once again picture him stooping in the gallery as the jury delivered their verdict. The lives of the people I love most, ruined, all in that one day.

'Thank you,' I whisper, unable to say much more. 'I've missed you too.'

We're meeting tomorrow. I declined the offer to go to his house, refusing to give the neighbours something to talk about; instead I've arranged to meet him at a pub we both know somewhere outside Bradford. It's a two-hour drive but one I won't lament making. Nick looks proud of me, and when Cassie's not watching he squeezes my arm.

There's no point trying to convince Cassie to crash in my spare room; ever since Oakdale she's refused to sleep anywhere but her own bed, even if we've had a drink. Despite the ridiculous charge for the thirty-minute taxi ride, she always makes her way home no matter what the time. Luckily Oakdale never had that particular effect on me and I can fall into bed anywhere – which isn't as exciting as it sounds. I offer Nick the use of my spare room, I feel safer when he's around. I really want him to take me up on the offer. It's been so nice to just sit and chat, all three of us. Even Cassie forgot for a couple of hours that she can't stand Nick, although she still refuses to use his name and refers to him as 'the reporter', even to his face. Nick politely declines my offer and orders himself a taxi back to the hotel.

'Good night, sweetheart.' Cassie kisses me on the cheek and gives me a tight hug. 'It's all going to be OK, you know? Please call me as soon as you've seen your dad.'

I nod, wondering why on earth I'm beginning to well up. Cassie leaves my house all the time; I don't usually start crying. 'Thank you,' I whisper, wanting to tell her how truly grateful I am that she's trying to make sure I don't spiral back into the depression that gripped me when I first went to Oakdale, but the words don't materialise. Nick's taxi arrives at the same time, and I'm suddenly convinced that the hatred is just an act, that they're going to get into separate taxis just to go back to the same place. I picture Cassie running her hands through his hair and whispering how she may be a murderer but at least she isn't crazy. Now tell me I'm not paranoid.

Then the house is empty. It seems extra quiet now – my front room is so small that three people makes it feel like a village meeting – and my mind wanders to the place I've avoided all night. More than anything I know I didn't trash my own house and I didn't imagine the intruder. And I'm certain it wasn't my sixty-year-old dad breaking in to my house that night, so where does that leave my theory? Was it a coincidence? A vengeful neighbour who knows who I am? Or am I being watched? I shudder at the thought and cross the room to sit on the sofa furthest away from the door and windows, as if the short distance will save me from whoever might be outside. I turn the TV up louder so I can't imagine that every noise is someone coming to get me, to really make me pay for what I've done. Three years in Oakdale isn't enough, you see. I've always known it, that I got off too lightly for what I did. Now someone out there wants me to suffer, really suffer. My dad? I don't know. But what I do know is that this isn't over. It won't be over until I find out who's doing this to me.

20

When I wake, for the first few seconds I forget what happened the night before. Every day since Dylan left it's been heart-breaking to wake up. There's a few minutes, before I open my eyes, where I'm still in the dream I just had: my son is back in my arms, I'm giving him a bath or feeding him. Sometimes I swear when I wake my breasts still ache, heavy with milk that has long since dried up. When the truth dawns, my heart takes on that familiar heaviness, the constant ache that comes from remembering. Now I remember something else. The voice of my father, an image of Nick lifting Dylan's blanket from a brown shoebox. The intense dread in my stomach tells me this is just the beginning of what someone wants to put me through.

I want to close my eyes, roll over and sleep again, dream of my little boy, but I can't. Someone is outside; the doorbell's intrusive ringing is what pulled me from my dreams. I have to face the real world again.

'I wanted to be here when you got up.' It's Nick, and he looks concerned. 'I didn't want you to . . .' His words trail off but I know what he means. He doesn't want me to do anything stupid. I move to the side to let him in, my eyes sweeping the front step, the lawn and the bushes outside. He hands me a paper cup of steaming coffee.

'What time is it?'

'Nine thirty,' he replies, the concerned look still on his face. 'Are you OK?'

'Of course I'm OK.' I stiffen. 'Why, what's happened?'

'Nothing's happened, don't worry.' He sits down on the sofa, the uncomfortable look he gives me reminding me I'm still dressed in my flimsy cotton dressing gown, only a vest top and a pair of big pants underneath.

'Sorry, I'll just go and get dressed, give me a minute.'

He looks embarrassed and I hope he can't see through my dressing gown. They really are hideously big pants.

'Yes, of course, take your time. I shouldn't have come so early . . .'

Do I really look that bad? Seem so volatile that he felt the need to rush round here at the crack of dawn to check I'm not filling my water glass with pills? Christ, what must he think he's got himself into?

I pull on a pair of jeans, a vest top and a fitted jacket, drag a brush through my hair and slap on some mascara. The result is that I look slightly more together than I feel. Maybe if I make more of an effort to look sane, people will actually believe it. When I return downstairs, Nick is leafing through yesterday's newspaper. He smiles when he looks up at me.

'Hey, you look better. I mean, like you feel better. I mean . . .' He sighs. 'Will you be OK seeing your dad today?'

I nod reluctantly. 'I guess I'll have to. I mean, I want this to be over . . .' But I'm not sure I do. If this is over, Nick goes back to his life, back to Doncaster, and I have to deal with my father punishing me. Would I rather just not know?

Nick sighs again as he sees my face crumple. 'Shit, sorry.'

'Just hearing his voice . . .'

112

'Should I call Cassie?'

It must be bad for him to suggest that.

The sound of a mobile ringing saves him. 'I'd better get that.' He fumbles in his pocket.

I realise I have no idea who would be calling him, no clue of his life beyond my problems. Does he have family? Does he play football on Sunday or learn a language at community college? Does he prefer Facebook or Twitter, McDonald's or Burger King, *EastEnders* or *Coronation Street*? How crazy that I've leant on him as an emotional crutch and I don't even know where he grew up.

'It's just my colleague. I'd better call him back, check everything's all right at work. Are you OK?'

I nod because I can't trust my voice to lie for me. He leaves the room to take the call and I hear him go into the kitchen. I have to resist the urge to follow him, to listen in on what is probably an innocent conversation and definitely none of my business.

I've tried so hard to remind myself that Mark was right to walk away from my situation, and that I gave my dad no choice but to give in and leave me on my own, yet I don't think I've really ever forgiven either of them for actually doing it. I have to realise that I was the one who turned my back on them, and that if I'd just let them in, shared my pain, things could have been different. I have to learn to let people in, I have to learn to trust again, and for a split second I wonder if Nick could be the one to teach me.

21

I drive myself to the pub. Sitting in the car outside, it finally hits me just how big a deal the next few hours are going to be. I've avoided thinking about what I'll say and feel when I see Dad again after all this time, but now it's almost upon me, it's unavoidable. I'd always thought the bond between my dad and me was unbreakable; he was always my hero growing up, and after Mum died that bond only grew stronger. Mark and I had him over for lunch every Sunday; he was the first person we called when Dylan was born, and he was at my bedside within minutes of the call. I was both amused and touched to find that he had been sitting in the hospital car park whilst I'd been giving birth.

Dad fell head over heels for our little boy from the very first heart-wrenching moment that he held him in his arms. The clumsy, sometimes gruff man I knew transformed into a soppy, gooey mess right in front of my eyes, letting the tears roll unashamedly down his cheeks as Dylan grasped his pinkie finger with his tiny little hand, then fell instantly back to sleep in the arms of a man that he somehow knew would protect him against the world. Dylan's death devastated Dad every bit as much as it did Mark and me. I know why I made the decision not to let him come and visit me in Oakdale: I knew that every time my father walked through those doors I would see that vision, him holding tightly on to Dylan as though he might be snatched from him there in the hospital. Looking down into his little face and whispering that he would love him forever, not knowing that forever would be cut so short.

I swallow down the lump forming in my throat and blink furiously to push back the tears that threaten to spill down my cheeks. I'm grasping Dylan's blanket, partly to convince myself that I've not imagined all this. I picture my dad sitting at his kitchen table folding it into a neat square, then taking it down to the post office and handing it over at the counter, and I don't feel angry, just sad. I made this relationship what it is; the only question is, can I fix it? Is it too late to just be father and daughter again? I can forgive him for a few days of hell, but will he ever be able to forgive me for four years of it?

If I put this off any longer I'll never go in. Turning off the engine, I lock the car and head towards the doorway of the Talluah Arms in search of the answer.

The Talluah is busy and I don't spot him straight away. The long mahogany bar faces the doorway, and when I walk in, the young man standing behind it wiping the counter looks up briefly, then goes back to his task. I scan the tables of people: families enjoying their lunch and a few student types. My eyes eventually rest upon the table at which he sits nursing an untouched pint of Guinness.

Life has taken its toll. My father now looks every minute of his sixty-two years. He'd looked old ever since my mother's death, except those moments he spent with Dylan, but now he looks a different kind of worn: tired, crushed and – my mind searches for the word – defeated. When I was a child,

I used to climb on to my toy chest sometimes, after my parents thought I'd gone to bed, and sneak the curtains open just a tiny bit. My room faced the back garden, and if I heard the familiar crackling of the fire in the fire pit, I'd be there, at the window, watching. My mum and dad would be sitting on the swing seat, his big arms around her narrow shoulders, just gazing at the flames, folded up inside one another. They were so close it was like they were one person. She'd smile and I'd see her mouth form one word; Dad would laugh, a whole-face laugh that said they didn't even need full sentences to communicate. Once I dared to push open the back door and sleepily tell my mum I was hungry. Instead of sending me back to bed, she disappeared into the kitchen and returned clutching something in her hands, torn between exasperation and love. It was marshmallows; we stuck them on sticks and toasted them, the way she said she used to do with her own mum. My dad watched her, smiling like he always seemed to when he looked at my mother. He still smiled at her like that on the day she died, never letting anyone but me see his pain.

Taking a deep breath, I head over to the table.

'Hello, sweetheart,' Dad says as I stop opposite him. He was watching the door when I walked in and didn't take his eyes off me as I walked over. His face, his voice after all this time render me speechless for a second or two. I pull out the chair across from him and sit down, still stupidly mute.

'Aren't you going to say hello?' he asks when I don't speak.

'Hello, Dad,' I reply, careful not to let my voice break. 'How are you?'

It seems such an idiotic thing to say when so many other questions, explanations and apologies are running through my head at breakneck speed, but it is all my lips seemed to manage. We can't just sit here staring speechless at each other, wondering how it went so wrong.

'Let's get out of here,' says Dad.

We escape the stuffy confines of the pub and go for a walk along the river, something we did an awful lot in the early days following Mum's death, just to get away. As my pregnant belly got bigger, the walks got shorter, and the irony that I'd lost a best friend at the same time as gaining our coveted child became too much to bear. I shiver and automatically pull my jacket tighter around me to guard against the cold wind. Dad looks concerned.

'Not enough meat on you.'

'There's nothing wrong with my weight,' I assure him. 'I'm looking after myself, don't you worry. Can you say the same?'

'I'm doing my best, love,' he replies, and I feel guilty once more. I need to get this over with and get out of here. As much as I love seeing him again, this is slowly killing me.

'Dad,' I start, and I see the look on his face darken.

'And here it comes,' he says. 'The reason we're here.'

'We couldn't talk round it all day.'

'No, you're quite right.' His expression is serious. 'I've spent all night wondering why you called me when you did, Susan.'

'I got the photo you sent,' I tell him slowly, watching for the expression on his face. I expect guilt, not confusion.

'What photo?' he asks, looking like he genuinely has no idea what I am talking about. That throws me. My father never did do lying well; I thought all it would take was a mention of the photograph and he'd come clean. What if I'm wrong? I pull out the photo of the young boy and hand it to him. He turns it over, sees the writing on the back and his face drops. I know in that instant that I've made a huge mistake.

'Where did you get this?' he asks, then, without waiting for an answer, 'You think I sent this? Why would you think that?'

'I, um, someone put it through my door at my new address.' I stumble over my words, caught by the hurt in his voice. 'I *didn't* think it was you, not until the photo album, then I got the blanket . . .'

'The blanket?' My father rounds on me. 'What blanket? What are you talking about?'

I stop and my father follows suit. We stand side by side looking out across the river. Taking a deep breath, I start at the beginning, the day I received the photo, and tell him everything.

Dad doesn't interrupt, despite the thousands of questions that must be running through his head. His face grows darker and more concerned as I tell him about Nick being a journalist, and about the intruder in my house. Then I come to the part about the blanket. I pull it from my bag and hand it to him, watching his reaction as I explain how the box was posted to me but ended up with a neighbour. Realisation and understanding dawn on him slowly.

'You got this yesterday?' he asks. I nod. 'And that's when you called me. Because I'm the one you trusted with Dylan's things.'

'Yes. I'm so sorry, the last thing I wanted to think was that you had something to do with this whole thing. And then I rang you and you said you'd spoken to Rachael . . .'

'*She* called *me*. She said she felt obliged to let me know you were coming out of Oakdale. I thought you must have asked her to call me until she asked if I'd spoken to you.'

'Dad, about the blanket . . . If you didn't send it to me, who did?'

His face is pained. 'I never saw it, love. I packed up Dylan's things, like you asked, but the blanket wasn't one of them. I never even thought to look for it . . . I should have thought.'

I imagine my father silently putting away the memories of his beloved grandchild and pain pierces my chest. What made me think it would be any easier for him? I should never have asked him to do that so soon.

'It was the night before Dylan's funeral,' he continues quietly, his face scrunched up as though the memory causes him actual physical pain. He refuses to look my way but begins to walk slowly along the riverside once again. I stay by his side, hanging on his every word.

'I went to the funeral, you know?' He isn't waiting for a reply; I don't think he'd even notice if I turned and walked away. 'I wasn't sure I'd be welcome, but Mark made sure no one so much as *thought* a bad word. I really appreciated that.' He shoves his hands deep into his pockets.

'The night before, I went round to do as you'd asked me. I sat on the floor in his room, putting all his teddies and clothes into storage bags, but it never even crossed my mind to look for the one thing he was never without. I'm so sorry, Susan, I have no idea where that blanket came from.'

I link his arm to calm him down.

'It's OK, Dad. I shouldn't have asked you to do that,' I assure him, but he shakes his head.

'I wanted to do it. I wanted to feel like I was being some use to you. But I never saw that blanket, not in the house, not at the funeral. So where the hell did it go? And how did it end up back with you?'

22

'You are not going to fucking believe this.'

Jack hadn't seen Billy like this in ages, not since everyone started filling out their university applications. Maybe he'd got laid. 'What?'

'My dad, his business got a new investor. He's brought in these massive new contracts, four this month. He's going to be able to pay for me to go to uni.'

'Yes! Nice one!' Jack jumped up from the sofa and punched the air. He'd tried everything to get his friend to apply to Durham: offered to pay his rent, researched scholarship grants. He'd never admit it, but he hated the thought of going away without any of them: Adam, Matt, Billy, even Mike. With his grades Billy was the most likely to actually get in. 'You're applying for Durham, right?'

Billy's face dropped and he looked down at his hands, where he started picking at his fingernails – something he always did when nervous. 'Well my form tutor says with my grades I could try for Cambridge . . . Dad says he'll pay for wherever I want to go now that the business has taken off, so I thought . . .'

'You thought you were too good for the rest of us now. Clever and loaded, well haven't we done well for ourselves?' Jack's words were hard and his blue eyes flashed with anger.

'Don't be like that, mate . . .'

'Mate? I gave you everything you wanted, let you borrow my clothes so you didn't look like a bloody gyppo, introduced you to my friends – you had no one before you met me! Three years I've been the best mate you've ever had and what, now you just want to desert me? I offered to pay your fucking rent, for fuck's sake! Now look at you, a fancy haircut and a bit of money and you're off to Cambridge to try and outdo us all.'

Billy hung his head and Jack could see he knew how right he was. It was only through him that the square boy people called Shakespeare had become attractive and popular. His pimply skin had cleared up thanks to Lucy's various face creams; it had been Jack's mum who had taken him to get his mop of greasy hair cut into a half-decent style at the best barber's in town. He'd even had his first shag courtesy of Jack's wallet – not that he knew that Jack had paid the girls they had taken home that night. And now he was going to swan off to Cambridge and look down on the person who'd made him. Jack was clever, but he was too lazy to get the kind of grades Cambridge required, and even if his dad could pay his way in there, he wouldn't last long. And what was wrong with Durham? It was one of the best universities in the country.

'Look, I just thought you would be happy for me, I didn't think you'd take it personally. My dad said—'

'Fuck what your dad says. What, he gets a couple of contracts and he's Donald Trump? Just fuck off to Cambridge, go on.'

Billy opened his mouth to speak but thought better of it and got up to leave. Good fucking riddance. Who did he think he was?

Jack heard the front door slam, then stood up and made his way to his dad's study. So Billy thought he'd be leaving behind everyone *who'd made him what he was. Jack didn't fucking think so. His best friend was not going to Cambridge.*

He banged on the door to his father's study. 'Dad, I need a word.'

23

We wander along the river and talk for the next two hours. It's as though we've never spent a day apart. The fact that I refused his visits, effectively cutting him out of my life for four years, has fizzled and faded away, as though it was a tiff over who took control of the TV remote.

'I'm torn, Dad,' I confess to him when he asks in his most fatherly voice how I'm coping with the situation. 'I haven't told anyone else this, I've barely admitted it to myself, but a part of me so badly wants to believe that someone is trying to tell me that Dylan is still alive and the whole thing is a mistake, some cruel prank. Then I get this reality check, this nasty little voice telling me that real life doesn't work like that. But people do lash out at convicted killers. Human beings don't care about the truth, justice or rehabilitation, not really. They care about revenge, retribution and judgement.'

'Even if it was someone wanting to punish you, would it change things?' Dad asks. 'Would it make you feel you were any more capable of taking Dylan's life? If you want to find out the truth, you have to stop doubting yourself, Susan. Before you went to that place you knew who you were, and what you were and weren't capable of. I'm going to tell you this right now: I never for a minute believed you killed your son. Not just because I'm your dad and I raised you, but because I saw you with Dylan and you loved the bones of him. I'm not saying that I know whether that little lad is alive or not; all I know is that *you* didn't hurt him. I'd like to think that after thirty-two years of being your father I know you better than some doctor who met you days after you'd lost your son. You're as sane as I am and I'd have attested to that in any court of law if they had given a fig what I thought, but they didn't. I'd say it's about time you shared a bit of my faith in you. That's just what I think, if it matters.' He falls silent, looks embarrassed at his outburst.

'It matters, Dad,' I tell him, tears stinging my eyes. 'It matters a lot.'

I leave with the promise that I'll phone him every day to let him know I'm safe and sound. I feel like I've gained so much more than getting my dad back today. I have finally begun to remember how it feels to be Susan Webster again.

Dad's right. Before I went to Oakdale, I knew unequivocally that I hadn't killed my son, no matter who tried to convince me otherwise. I'd trusted in my own sanity, my own mind, and believed in my love for my son. Gradually my certainty had been chipped away by so-called 'experts', who'd decided that just because a jury of my peers had deemed me responsible for my son's death, then it was true, and eventually I began to believe it too. It's taken my father's faith in me to remind me that I once believed in my own innocence. Well now I believe. And if I'm innocent, then my son might still be alive.

24

I push open my front door, emotionally exhausted and ready for bed. It's only seven o'clock, but all I can think of is crawling under the covers and sleeping for a lifetime.

The house is too quiet, too empty without Cassie or Nick here. Throwing my bag on to the chair, I quickly fire off a message to both of them: Things went OK with Dad – no closer to truth. Call u 2moro. Then I make a cup of tea and grab a girlie book to take to bed. Reading takes my mind off everything; when I'm lost in the words on the page, I don't allow my mind to think of anything else.

I push the bedroom door open with my bum, careful not to spill the tea. The smell hits me before I see what's waiting on the bed. My cup hits the carpet, scalding tea spraying my trousers and feet. My scream pierces the silence like a siren.

The cold air hits my face, but it's not until my hands are in the mud that I even realise I'm kneeling on the grass outside my house. *How did I get here?*

On the bed, a voice in my head reminds me. *There's something on your bed.*

'Emma?' A voice I'm very familiar with cuts across my

thoughts. Oh God. What do I do? What can I say? Carole is at my side in moments; no time for me to think of a good reason why I might be hunched on my lawn at seven in the evening. I sure as hell don't look like I'm gardening.

'Are you OK? Shall I call a doctor? Are you hurt?'

The questions hit me like gunfire. Stunned, I recoil from her voice. 'I'm fine,' I manage to mumble. Unsurprisingly, she's not convinced.

'Come on, let me get you into the house.'

'No!' My shout shocks us both. 'No, sorry, Carole, I can't go back in there.'

Confusion and concern cloud her face. 'Has someone done something to you? Look, come to mine then. Come on, love, you can't stay here.'

Carole deposits me as carefully as she can manage on her sofa. 'Is this something to do with . . . you know, who you are? Does someone else know? What can I do? Can I call a friend, relative?'

I immediately think of Cassie. There's no way I can sit here for the half-hour it will take her to get here, no way I can go back into my house to wait.

'Can you call the Travelodge? There's a man staying there, a friend from back home. His name is Nick Whitely, he'll come and get me.'

Carole nods. 'Would you like a drink while you wait?'

I shake my head. Anything I put in my mouth right now is surely going to come back up. The image of what I saw lying on my bed brings bile into my mouth again and I don't trust myself to open it to speak. I can't risk being sick in this nice woman's front room.

'OK, I'll call now. I'll tell him there's been an emergency?'

'Yes,' I mutter. 'An emergency.'

* * *

I know I should have warned Nick what he was about to see, but the minute I saw him, words failed me. He thanked Carole, helped me up from the sofa and into his car outside. That's where I'm sitting now, waiting for him to come back, to explain what's in my room.

His face is deathly pale as he emerges from the house and crosses the grass. Once inside the car, he takes me in his arms. I let myself be held and try not to cry.

'What is it?' I whisper when I eventually let him go.

'It's a cat, what's left of it,' he replies, looking like he's going to be sick himself. 'It's been . . . it's been skinned.'

The image of the small animal lying on my blood-soaked sheets pushes itself uninvited into my mind. The smell of the poor thing lingers inside my nostrils and I wonder now why I didn't smell it as I came up the stairs.

'Oh God.' A sudden terrible thought crosses my mind. 'Did it have a collar?'

Nick looks as though he'd rather spend the night in bed next to the dead cat than answer my question. Eventually, though, he nods.

'Tartan?' I croak, wishing he could just make this easy for me and say no, knowing he will tell me the truth no matter how hard. He nods again. Oh no, please no. Not another casualty of this whole crazy mess, someone else I care about.

'Joss.' It's a statement not a question, and Nick knows I don't need an answer. Any energy I have left drains from my body and I fall back into his arms, a fresh wave of tears overcoming me. Stupid cat, stupid, stupid, dumb animal! Why couldn't he have just stayed away? Why did he have to be so nosy, so goddamn friendly? And why pick me of all people? Cats are supposed to be clever; surely he could sense the curse that follows me around, ripping apart the people crazy enough to care about me?

'You should go,' I whisper, pulling myself away. 'I'll take care of this, I'll check into a hotel.'

Nick looks confused. 'What are you talking about?' he asks sharply. 'We're calling the police and then you're coming back with me.'

'No, you don't understand.' I want to tell him how only bad things can come to anyone who gets themselves involved in my life. Mark, Dylan, Dad, even Joss the cat. I want to tell him that eventually his life will be ruined, just like the people on that list.

'What exactly is it you think I don't understand, Susan? That you did something four years ago that you've never come to terms with? That someone is using that against you to try and make you think that your son might still be alive? Or maybe I don't understand that this person has kept such a close watch on you since your release that the minute you contacted me they had your house broken into and vandalised, then killed your pet cat and put him on your bed? Do I sound unclear on any of that?'

'He wasn't my cat,' is all I can think to say. Nick's outburst has shocked the fight right out of me.

'Susan, this is a horrible thing to be happening to you, but it's about time you stopped feeling sorry for yourself and let me help you. I'm a big boy and I'm perfectly capable of deciding for myself whether you're cursed, or bad luck, or just plain crazy. Now if you can't stand to have me around any more, then tell me now and I'll drive you to your dad's and hand you over to what I'm sure are his capable hands.' His eyes fix on mine, look right into my head and it's as if he's running his fingers through my thoughts. 'Is that what this is about? Are you trying to get rid of me?' I shake my head numbly. I don't want to get rid of him. We've only just met, but he's one of only three people at the moment who I can be myself around, who know who 'myself' is.

'I'm not trying to get rid of you,' I whisper. 'I'm—'

'No,' Nick says roughly. 'Don't say sorry. Don't apologise to me again. Just stop it, Susan. I'm not going to bail on you; I'm here to help you. Stop acting as though I'm Mark.'

The shock of his words hit me like a slap in the face. Before I can speak, Nick opens the car door and gets out, pacing the lawn. He pulls his mobile from his pocket and dials what I presume to be the local police station. Was I comparing him to Mark? Were my attempts to push him away a defence against him doing exactly what my ex-husband had done – flee from me as soon as the going got tough?

His voice wafts through the closed window as I sit shaking. Oh God, oh God. Poor Joss.

The police take an hour to arrive and forty minutes to take my statement about what has happened at my house. The ever-so-polite officer nods in all the right places, promises to arrange for Joss to be taken away as evidence, and if there are any developments he will be in touch, thank you, ma'am.

'Am I OK to go in and get some of her things?' I hear Nick ask him. The police officer shakes his head: best not to go in there until Forensics have finished.

'I'll book a room at the Travelodge,' I suggest, car door open and my legs dangling out. 'I can buy new things for now. I don't really want anything he may have touched . . .'

Nick shakes his head. 'You don't need to be here, or anyway near here right now. I'm worried for you. I think you should come back to mine.'

'Oh no,' I object straight away. 'I can't let you . . .' *I don't know you . . .*

'Don't start that. I'm warning you.' He sounds serious. 'The officers can lock up; we'll pick up your keys from the station. Let's go.'

25

When we eventually pull up outside a semi-detached house in Doncaster and Nick parks his car on the drive, I'm shocked, in a good way. Far from the bachelor pad I was expecting, this is the type of house I would expect a married man with a very design-savvy wife to have. A fleeting vision of a woman in a power suit opening the door to greet Nick with a kiss crosses my mind and I have to shake my head to rid myself of it. What does it matter to me if he's married? He's only helping me in order to flex his journalistic muscles anyway. The garden is small but well manicured; despite the fact that he's been away for the last few days, the grass is still short and huge planters encase thriving flowers. *Who's been looking after all this, then?*

Nick gets out of the car and motions for me to do the same. I follow his lead, pulling my bags out after me. He isn't rushing me in; isn't he worried about people knowing who I am?

'Won't the neighbours talk?' I ask him, trying to sound casual as I haul my bag to the front door.

'I bloody hope so,' Nick replies cheekily. 'I know the nosy old biddies are starting to whisper about me being gay.'

'Stop parading me outside like some beacon declaring your heterosexuality and let me in.'

He pushes open the door obligingly and motions for me to enter ahead of him, which I do, soaking in every detail. The hallway is vast and open, plush cream carpet stretching out to greet a tiled kitchen floor in the distance. The walls are a pristine magnolia, antique pine furniture has been positioned perfectly and a huge ornate gold-framed mirror hangs behind the door. It looks a lot like the home I made for my family once upon a time, and I can't shake the thought that another woman is responsible for this one. I scan the walls for signs of where photographs might have been but see none.

The kitchen is no disappointment either. All sleek black worktops and chrome accessories that don't look like they've ever been used. Definitely not a woman's kitchen. There's not a cookbook or a cute kitten calendar in sight, and no spice rack either.

'Are you sure you're not gay?' I tease as Nick looks bashful at my amazement.

'Not my own work, I'm afraid,' he admits grudgingly. 'I had an interior designer come in when I bought the place.'

'Not bad for a journalist on a local rag,' I comment, then immediately feel rude for speculating about how he can afford such a place.

Nick doesn't baulk at my rudeness, however. 'I won some cash when I was younger and invested when house prices were low,' he explains. 'A stroke of pure luck really, given the way things are now.'

'Sorry,' I apologise. 'I didn't mean to imply you couldn't afford it here.'

Nick shrugs. 'It's OK, you're right, I'd never have been able to buy this place if it wasn't for luck. Anyway, I'll put the kettle on, then we can take your stuff upstairs.'

'Great, good, thanks.' I'll admit this all feels a bit strange, moving in with a man I barely know. *You're not moving in; just a stopover until you can sort yourself out. And Cassie knows where you are.*

Shit! Cassie.

'I didn't tell Cass I was coming here,' I realise suddenly. I'm so used to her being around all the time that I'd forgotten to actually tell her I wasn't at home. 'I'd better let her know, in case she goes to my house . . .' An image of her letting herself in and seeing the remains of what happened tonight makes my skin crawl. I don't add 'and in case you're an axe murderer'.

I pull out my phone and wince at the reply to my earlier text message. I don't care how tired ur. I want 2 no what happnd with ur dad. Call me!! <3

'She's not going to be happy you're here,' Nick says as I lift the phone to call her.

'Don't worry, she's too far away for any real violence.'

'Where the hell are you?' she demands the minute the call has connected. 'I've called your house, texts, you've disappeared! I've been worried! For Christ's sake, Susan!'

I'm sure the rant would have continued had I not cut her off quickly to explain what's happened. Her fury quickly turns to concern, until I tell her where I am now.

'Why didn't you come to me?' she replies a bit snottily.

'Nick was closer, he was only down the road at the hotel. I was petrified, Cass. Someone went into my house and left a dead cat on my bed! I just wanted out. Tell her I'm OK, Nick.'

I flip her on to speaker phone and he confirms I'm still in one piece. All he gets in reply is a grunt. I fill her in on what happened with my dad. 'And tomorrow I'm going to see Mark,' I surprise myself by announcing. I'm not sure when I made the decision, but now that I've said it out loud, it seems like the logical course of action. The only place to go now is home.

Cassie and Nick don't seem to share my confidence. They both begin to speak at once, Cassie's voice the loudest despite being over a hundred miles away, but nothing they say is going to deter me. It makes me feel better that I'm resolved in this decision; stubbornness is a trait the old Susan used to have in spades.

'Do you really think—'

'Suze, I don't think that's the best thing for you to do, hun. It's been four years; he's not going to want to see you. What if he calls the police? You could get yourself in trouble, or set yourself up for a fall.'

Since when does Cassie Reynolds care about trouble with the police? Not once in the three years I've known her has she shied away from a plan, no matter how hare-brained.

'Cassie's right,' Nick agrees. I can feel Cassie scowling despite the fact that he's agreeing with her, and it makes me smile. 'You could just make things worse. What if he doesn't know anything about this?'

'I'm going.' Part of me is just being stubborn because I feel like they're ganging up on me and my inner teenager is refusing to back down. 'This is my problem and I'm going.'

'Fine,' Cassie relents. 'I'm coming with you.'

'Not this time, Cass,' I reply. 'This is something I've got to do on my own. You can come here and help Nick.'

'No frigging way. I don't trust him as far as I can throw him.'

'Wow, thanks, coming from a murd—'

'Don't make me prove how far I can throw you.'

'As if I would be so stupid.' He turns to me. 'If she won't work with me, that's her prerogative. I'll dig up everything I can on your trial and Dr Riley and meet you back here.'

Cassie seems to realise that this leaves her sitting at home waiting. Alone.

'Fine. I'll help. I can keep an eye on the reporter. I'll drive down in the morning.'

I'm grateful they've given in so easily; now I don't have to lie to them. I'm nervous and more than slightly scared that in less than twenty-four hours I will be confronting the man whose life I shared. Whose life I ruined.

26

Jack: 13 January 1991

Predictably, when Billy had been rejected from Cambridge he'd been gutted – and Jack had been there to cheer him up. At least he'd been accepted for his second choice, and that meant they were all going to Durham together. Billy had apologised over and over for attempting to ditch them all but Jack told him not to worry – after all, they were mates, and mates forgave each other, right?

They'd been in Durham four months and already Billy had forgotten that he'd ever wanted to go to Cambridge. This was living. Every night was just drug-hazed memories of parties and shagging. Women threw themselves at all of them, it was fucking amazing. Even Shakes was getting laid left, right and centre; in fact he was beating Mike, Adam and Matty hands down. The change in Billy over the last year was ridiculous. His dad's business was turning over enough to fund the kind of lifestyle he'd always wanted: new designer gear and a monthly allowance to rival the foreign aid budget. Lately it was his name that got them into VIP. And that was fine; Jack was content to let his friend have his time in the sun, as long as he remembered who the real leader of the group was. The one who made decisions, the one who made things happen. The only concern he had was how close Billy and Matt were getting. He hadn't spent so much time on Shakespeare's complete transformation to hand him over to Riley to ruin.

It was in their third month that Billy brought Tanya back to their place. A pair of tits with legs, Tanya was tight in all the right places, but more amazingly, she could read and spell. Of course Shakespeare was hooked. She spent the next three weeks glued to his side; everywhere they went, there was Tanya. That was bad enough, but she'd walk around the place wearing shorts no bigger than a tea towel and vest tops so tight she looked like she'd been sprayed into them, her long dark curls skimming the bottom of her massive breasts. She'd be there every time Jack turned around, bending over for the remote, nipples looking like they could cut glass. He'd seen her around St Chad's a few times before but he'd never really noticed her until Billy brought her into their lives. Now all he wanted to do was touch her. Surely she could see the effect she had on him? Of course she could, and she liked it. He'd be doing Billy a favour if he showed him what this little prick tease was really like.

Ironically it was Friday the 13th when it all went wrong.

'Tanya.' Jack stood in the open doorway and frowned. 'What're you doing here?'

She smiled, held up a Waitrose bag that clinked with the sound of bottles and peered over his shoulder. 'It's a surprise. Is he in?' Tanya usually called Billy by his real name, another reason Jack didn't like having her around. She had a way of making it seem like the last four years hadn't even happened, like everything was year zero and she was the only person who mattered.

'No,' Jack said, without moving aside. 'He's studying, at Bill Bryson.'

Tanya looked puzzled. 'The library? On a Friday? That's weird. Maybe I'll go there and find him.'

'No,' Jack said quickly. 'Come in, wait here.' He guided Tanya through to the open-plan apartment, took the bag of alcohol and carried it to the kitchen area. 'Can I get you a drink while you wait?'

He uncorked the wine she had brought with her, poured a glass and – with his back still to her – added a shot of vodka for good measure. Wouldn't do her any harm. Then he poured half a glass for himself.

'Here. Hope you don't mind, I'm having a glass too.'

Tanya took the wine and smiled. 'Thanks, I'll just have the one then I'll go find him at the library. Maybe he could use a study buddy.'

'Look . . .' Jack sat down next to her and placed the bottle of wine on a side table. He ran his fingers through his short dark hair and gave her an apologetic look. 'I really wouldn't. It's best you just wait here.'

'Why shouldn't I . . . oh, I get it.' Tanya took a huge gulp of wine and pulled a face. 'God, that tastes like shit.' She finished the glass in two mouthfuls. 'So if he isn't really at the library, where is he?'

Jack leaned back and rubbed his face. 'I'm sorry, I don't know. If I did, I'd tell you, but . . .'

'For fuck's sake,' Tanya reached for the bottle. 'If he wanted to see other people, why didn't he just tell me?'

'Hey.' Jack raised both hands in defence. 'I didn't say he was seeing someone else. I mean, he really might be at the library . . .'

Tanya smiled as she slugged back another gulp. 'Thanks, but I'm not stupid, I can see it all over your face. Did anyone ever tell you you're a terrible liar?'

Jack looked bashful. 'I've never been much good, I'm afraid, not like Billy. He's the brains of the group. I'm just the good-time guy. I don't see the point of lying to women; what you see is what you get. Bit of a character flaw, I'm afraid. Here.' He reached past her to top up her wine again, his chest pressing against hers for a split second.

'I don't think that's a flaw, I commend your honesty.' Tanya took the glass from him – was it his imagination or did her fingers linger around his a little longer than before? – and raised it in a toast, her eyes glassy with tears. 'I mean, I never really expected a guy to want a relationship in his first few months as a fresher, but he seemed so keen. I should have known there'd be others. Why not just tell me? I mean, it's not like I've never had a one-night stand before, I could have coped.' She sniffed. 'I'd started to really like him, y'know?'

Jack reached out and placed a hand on her knee. 'I guess he just thought you were too beautiful to give up. Don't be too hard on him; you can't really blame him for wanting you around. I mean, when you're here . . . Sorry, I'm talking out of place. Must be the wine.'

'No.' Tanya moved so close her breasts were brushing against his shoulder and he wondered if she realised. Intentional or not, it was making him hard and he knew he had to get a move on. Even Billy didn't study too late on a Friday night. 'Go on.'

'I can see why Billy wanted you around, that's all. You're gorgeous and clever and funny. He's a lucky guy.'

Tanya screwed up her button nose. 'Was,' she corrected. 'I don't appreciate being lied to, Jack, and it was unfair of him to put you in this position. You've been so sweet but I really should be going.' She put down her glass, eyes widening at the empty bottle. 'Have I really . . . whoa.' She stumbled as she stood up and slammed straight back into the sofa. 'Head rush. Just stood up a bit quickly, I'm fine.'

'Here.' Jack held out his hand and helped her to her feet. 'Look, you don't have to rush off, Billy's probably not going to be back for ages.' He cringed. 'Shit, sorry.'

She stumbled forward and placed both hands on his chest to steady herself. 'I'm OK, I just drank a bit too fast. That was supposed to last all night! I just need to use the bathroom.'

'Sure.' Jack watched as she moved towards the bathroom in the deliberate way people do when they're trying to convince themselves they haven't had too much alcohol. When she was inside, he moved quickly, pouring his half-glass into hers and topping it up with a shot of vodka. No more, Jack, you need to be able to get her out again in one piece. Afterwards.

'You OK?' he asked as she emerged from the bathroom. Her floral chiffon blouse was untucked and she'd undone the top two buttons, revealing a glimpse of tanned breast. Her hair looked ruffled, as though in the absence of a brush she'd run her hand hastily through her loose waves. This was going to be good.

'I'm fine, thanks. You've been so nice, I'm sorry you got caught

up in this.' She stifled a sob and Jack took the opportunity to hand her her wine glass.

'Here, finish this and I'll walk you downstairs.'

Tanya looked crushed. 'Are you trying to get rid of me?'

Jack shook his head and moved closer to her. 'No,' he said, taking her free hand in his. 'I'm just worried about what might happen if you stay. Billy's my friend and . . .'

Tanya took a sip of her wine and placed it down again. 'And he's out right now having fun with some bimbo while you're left here looking after his girlfriend. That's not very fair, is it?'

She put her hand up to touch his face, trailed it down behind his neck and pulled his head gently downwards. He leaned forward and she placed her lips on his, gently at first and then, when she was sure he wasn't going to pull away, harder. As they kissed, they moved towards the bedroom, Tanya taking Jack's lead perfectly. He fumbled with the door knob behind him, pushing the door open and guiding her towards the bed, where she fell, all the while tugging at the bottom of his T-shirt, finally releasing it from the waistband of his jeans.

'I'm not doing this to get back at him,' she gasped when she pulled away for a moment. Her hands were exploring his body, working at the rough leather of his belt until she found the buckle. She released the clasp and yanked at the button of his jeans, then pulled down the zip and shoved the denim over his hips.

'We shouldn't be doing this at all,' Jack murmured, his fingers deftly unbuttoning the rest of her blouse, easing it open to reveal those amazing breasts. How he'd lasted this long with her flaunting her ass all over the flat he didn't know. It was Billy's fault really – did you put a crate of beer in front of an alcoholic? He slipped his thumb inside her flimsy bra, rolling it around her nipple and loving the way she groaned. He lowered his lips to her breast, taking the puckered nipple in his mouth and sucking gently at first, then pulling harder until she gasped.

'He deserves it, the bastard. Don't think about him, Jack.' Tanya undid her own jeans and pushed them to the floor. 'Do you know, he told me to watch out for you. Said you'd be jealous of what we have, that you'd try and ruin it. And all along he just wanted to keep you from seeing me so that you wouldn't let slip about his other whores.'

'That sly twat,' Jack swore. 'Well he's not going to get away with it.'

She pushed herself up on to her elbows. 'But doesn't this make us just as bad as him? Maybe this is a mistake . . .'

Oh for fuck's sake.

'Ssshhhhh.' He leant down and slipped off her lace knickers, threw them into the corner of the room. Shoving his boxer shorts down, he pulled her closer, placed one hand over her mouth and thrust himself into her, smiling as her eyes widened.

'Honey, I'm home.' Jack heard the door bang closed and Billy's voice drift in from the hallway.

'About time, darling. How was the library?'

Billy pushed the door open with his backside, his arms full of books. 'Fucking boring as. Remind me never to leave an assignment until the last minute again. What're you doing in on a Friday night?'

Jack shrugged, his feet up on the arm of the sofa. 'Fancied a quiet one. Get us a beer, will you?'

Billy threw his stack of books on to his bed and grabbed two beers from the never-ending stock in the fridge. Tossing one to Jack, he settled himself in his usual chair. 'So you're telling me you've done nothing tonight?'

Well, not exactly nothing.

Jack put his best concerned face on and turned to his friend. 'Look, mate, I needed to talk to you about something. It's Tanya.'

Billy sighed, shook his head. 'I knew this was coming. You're pissed off she's here all the time, right? Sorry, mate, I really like her. But we'll go to hers more, get out of your way . . .'

'It's not that.' Jack cut across him. 'It's just that, well, this is really embarrassing, but . . . well, she's been coming on to me.'

Billy looked like he'd been punched in the face. 'She's what? Tanya? When?'

Jack dropped his eyes to gaze at the floor. 'Ever since you first brought her back here. It's been pretty difficult keeping it from you, to be honest, mate, but I thought she'd have given up by now. She left these.' He held up the lace knickers Tanya had been wearing earlier that night. After they'd finished, she'd let him dress her and call her a taxi with very little argument – she'd seemed a little dazed, Jack thought; turned out she didn't like it as rough as he'd expected. 'Under my pillow the other night. I was going to just ignore it, but then she turns up here tonight . . .'

'What? Tanya was here?'

'Yeah, and she was smashed, mate, stinking of booze. I told her you weren't in and she said she knew, she'd seen you at the library. She practically threw herself at me, started taking her clothes off and ranting about how she knew you were seeing other people. I had to shove her out the door with her blouse half open. Don't worry, I called her a taxi first. I felt a bit harsh, you know, telling her where to go, but I didn't want you to get the wrong idea. I know you think I'm not the most trustworthy person . . .'

Billy's shoulders sagged; he looked crushed. 'No, thanks, mate, I'm really sorry. Fuck! What a bitch! I really liked her, you know? I even told her to . . . well, I thought maybe you . . . when all the time it was her that I should have been worrying about.'

Jack got up, slapped Billy's shoulder. 'Come on, mate, I know it's shit, but it's not like you were going to marry her, is it? Forget her; we've got the next three years to fuck our way through all the Tanyas in Durham. You know what I'd do if I were you? I wouldn't even call her. Go screw that little blonde in St John's that was all over you last weekend.'

'Yeah,' Billy replied. 'Yeah, you're right. Fuck her.'

Jack smiled. Things were back to how they should be.

27

In front of the full-length changing room mirror I turn on the spot, checking my reflection from the front and both sides. I'm quite pleased with what I see. Black jeans fit snugly over slim hips that have long lost the signs of pregnancy, and my buttons don't strain over a wobbly mummy-tummy. My once long blonde hair is shorter now and falls in a smooth dark sheet to my shoulders, feathered around a much slimmer face. It's only through my eyes, the so-called windows to my soul, that you might see how my life has changed for the worse – but only if you look very carefully. If you look very carefully you might notice that when I smile, the sparkle doesn't quite reach them the way it used to. You might notice how my nose doesn't crinkle either side of my nostrils when I laugh – if I ever laugh anymore – that sometimes those eyes glass over, as though I'm in another place, another time, which often I am. Usually I'm with Dylan, singing him songs from *The Jungle Book* as I change his nappy or splashing around with him in the bath, but sometimes, every now and then, I'm with Mark. We're honeymooning in Sorrento again, me lounging around by the pool while he plays water volleyball, or sitting at the bar sipping iced margaritas. Sometimes we're trekking around an old castle, me running ahead excitedly, climbing up hidden stairways and jumping out at him from dark alcoves. More often than not, though, in these daydreams of mine, we're just lounging on the sofa on a Sunday afternoon, me eight months pregnant, and struggling to stay on next to him while we watch some awful programme on TV. Then I picture that same sofa with a Moses basket next to it; waking up in a hospital bed scared and confused as two police officers look down at me, waiting to write down every word I say.

Yes. Mark knows – *knew* – me inside and out. He'll see the changes in me immediately. Every last one of them. And I suspect his eyes will look the same.

I've chosen a white vest top under a baggy grey off-the-shoulder jumper in the hope that I won't look as though I'm trying too hard. I don't want Mark thinking I'm attempting to get him back, or worse still that I'm crazy. *Still crazy.*

'Can I leave these on?' I ask the changing room attendant. She looks like she'd rather say no for the sake of being awkward, but clearly the thought of losing a sale changes her mind.

'Sure, just take the tags to the till. Don't forget to ask them to take the security tags off. Don't want to get yourself arrested.' She laughs at her own joke, oblivious of where her latest customer has spent the last few years. Damn straight I don't want to go back there.

Twenty minutes later I throw my handbag into the car and slide in after it, already planning what to say when Mark opens the door and finds his past on the doorstep.

Nick looked furious when he saw me first thing this morning. 'So you're actually going through with this?' he demanded. 'Aren't you the least bit scared of what he'll do?'

'He won't do anything stupid,' I replied. 'I know my

ex-husband.' I was only half convinced of this at the time. And now I'm fifty miles from his house, and not feeling so clever.

The house looks the same as it ever did, and as I approach I remember the feeling I used to get every single time I arrived home, a feeling of pride that this was where I lived, this was the life we had built for ourselves. Set slightly apart from the other houses surrounding it, it's beautifully modern and I fell in love with it the minute I saw it. It was the first home that was mine, so dramatically different from the small house we crowded into as children, and the grubby three-bedroom flat I shared with my university friends. I can still picture myself sitting on the front porch, Mark pruning the mini fir trees that line the small driveway that curls round to the right, trying to look like he knew what he was doing. I was never interested in tending the garden; I was always the one to put up photographs or do the painting – a job Mark never had the patience for. I notice, as I pull up, that his silver Merc is parked outside the garage. That's something he never did before, preferring to have his pride and joy tucked safely out of sight. It hasn't been cleaned for a few weeks, either. The first day he brought the car home he stayed out until gone ten shining the paintwork and applying Back To Black in the dark while I supplied him with cups of tea, amused at how much pride he took in his car when he could never be bothered to so much as wash up inside.

Without me noticing, my mouth has dried up and my tongue now resembles a piece of sandpaper. Swallowing hard doesn't help. It seems I've lost the ability to produce saliva altogether. My chest is tight, and I have the sudden aware-ness of my heart beating and heat in my face that I only get in situations like this.

A quick check of the mirror, and despite the heat in my

face I'm as white as a sheet. How bloody charming, I look like I've caught the plague. Mark's probably going to slam the door in my face and call the police.

The ten-metre walk to the front door feels like a mile, the ring of the doorbell as loud as the church bells tolling for a Sunday service. Or a funeral. The three minutes it takes Mark to open the door feels like an hour. And then there he is. The man I once loved more than I'd ever thought possible is standing in the doorway, and in the seconds it takes for him to recognise me, I realise with sickening clarity that I never really stopped loving him. How do you just fall out of love with someone who was once your everything? Even though he deserted me when I needed him most, I still have the image of the arms that are now folded across his chest holding me tight while I cried tears of loss for my mother, arms that were so absent for the loss of our son. The eyes that are now creased with anger used to smile at me in amusement when I uttered one of my 'blondeisms', as he called them. When he speaks, it's with the same voice that used to say 'I love you' daily. Now, though, the words and the tone have changed and I wonder if I've made a mistake coming here. I've tried so hard to hate this man, when all the time I was avoiding ever properly grieving for the loss of him.

'What are you doing here, Susan?'

I don't know exactly what I was expecting. In the hours since I decided to come and see Mark I've pictured our opening scene a dozen times, the apologies he'd make, how he'd tell me everything would be OK and he'd help me find out what happened to our little boy. Clearly this isn't going to be as easy as I allowed myself to imagine it.

'I, um, well I needed to see you . . . to speak to you.' My planned speech has been wiped clean from my mind at the mere sight of him.

The effect was much the same the first time I ever saw him. Roped Bridget Jones style into a dinner party by well-meaning smug couples, I was just about to invoke the 'emergency call' ploy when Mark walked in. Five hours later, glued to my chair, I was still listening enraptured to this beautiful, funny and warm man, the man I knew I was going to marry, or at least hoped to shag. That night, slightly tipsy and head over heels in love – well I was at least – we fell into bed together, and stayed there the entire weekend. Looking back, it still feels like the whole memory is a lie, a story I've told so many times I sometimes wonder if I could really have been that lucky or if I've romanticised our whole relationship, only choosing to remember the bits where I'm the centre of Mark's universe.

'I really don't think that's a good idea.' Mark moves to close the door and I know that my only chance is slipping away.

'Wait . . . It's about . . . um . . . Dylan.' I see him cringe when I say our son's name, but he doesn't close the door further. 'I was sent this.' I shove the photograph clumsily into his hands and watch his face as he looks down at it. Confusion clouds his beautiful brown eyes as he studies the photograph, then shock when he turns it over.

'Where did you get this?' he asks, his face noticeably paler than it was two minutes ago. 'Never mind, come inside; I don't want anyone seeing you here.'

He pulls the door open widely enough for me to enter and, feeling like a dirty secret, a mistress he doesn't want the neighbours to glimpse, I step into the hallway, trying not to physically recoil at the rush of emotion that overcomes me. The hallway, still a pristine cream with our expensive oak flooring and winding oak staircase, looks bare and cold without the huge black-framed photos that used to depict our whole relationship. I spent two days measuring the

146

distance between frames, displaying our proudest moments – our wedding day, our honeymoon in Sorrento, Dylan's first hospital photo – for the whole world to see. Now they're gone as if they never existed.

'You kept the mirror,' I comment, my voice dull and my words numb. It was the very first purchase I made on my own when we bought the house, and Mark took pains to remind me at every opportunity just how oversized and overpriced he thought it was.

'Cost almost as much as the bloody house,' he reminds me now. 'I wasn't about to just get rid of it, was I?' *Like you got rid of us.*

He walks through to the living room before I have a chance to say something stupid about the missing frames, and feeling decidedly awkward by now, I have no choice but to follow him. Before I can take in the room around me, he turns suddenly and thrusts the photo towards me.

'What the hell is this, Susan?' he demands. 'Some kind of joke?'

I step back into the hall, shocked by the anger in his face. 'Of course it's not a fucking joke,' I snap, beginning to feel pretty angry myself now. He cringes at my use of the F word. 'How sick do you think I am?'

The minute the words are out of my mouth I regret them, but it's too late. I've seen the look on his face and he knows it. As far as he – and the rest of the world – is concerned, I murdered his only son. Turning up on his doorstep with a photo of the boy I killed is probably close to the bottom of the 'how sick do you think I am' scale.

'Sit down,' he instructs, then walks through to the back of the room and out of the door to the kitchen. Too weary to argue, I step back in and oblige without thinking. As soon as I throw myself down on the cream armchair, my throat constricts. This is the exact same suite we had when I lived here. The three-seater sofa opposite me is the sofa I lay down on the last time I remember seeing my son alive. *My ex-husband is living with the very cushions I was accused of using to kill our son.*

I jump up, panic welling inside me. My thoughts spin around my head like a twister, dark and destructive. Why would he do that? *How* could he do that? At that moment Mark walks back into the room and sees me backed against the wall staring at the sofa. Realisation dawns on his face.

'God, Susan, I'm so sorry, that was bloody insensitive of me.' He places two mugs down on the end table next to the offending piece of furniture and crosses the room, putting his hands on my arms and pulling me close. I collapse into his embrace, my legs refusing to hold my weight. Mark lowers me to the floor and sits down in front of me, looking into my eyes and instructing me to breathe slowly. 'It's not the same sofa, Susie, it just looks the same. I replaced it when you left; I just didn't know what to replace it with. You were always the interior designer. I spent four hours wandering round DFS and ended up coming home with an almost exact replica of the bloody thing.'

His words sink in one by one. It isn't our sofa. Of course it isn't; ours was rounder, a little longer, it fitted better. Just like everything did when I was here.

When he's sure I'm not going to pass out or have some kind of nervous breakdown, Mark stands up, retrieves his cup of tea and passes me the other. I'm still not ready to sit on the sofa, replica or not, so I stay on the floor.

'So tell me,' he says, some of the coldness now gone from his voice, 'what is this supposed to mean?'

He picks up the photo from the table once more and I realise I don't want him to have it, I don't even want him touching it. I reach out protectively and he passes it back to me without comment.

'I don't know,' I reply truthfully. 'It was posted through my door just days ago, no letter, no explanation, nothing. I thought it might have been from you.' I can't meet his eyes when I say the last part, especially as I've omitted the bit about finding the other photos in my own album.

'Me?' He sounds disbelieving and I look up at him defiantly. *He kept the sofa,* that devilish voice inside my head tells me. No, not *the* sofa, just *a* sofa that happens to look quite similar. So there. 'That's crazy.' There's that word again, and Mark's realised it too. He rushes on. 'I mean, I know Susie, I know how much you punished yourself for what happened. I would never . . .' He trails off. Does he mean . . . has he forgiven me?

'So who?' I ask quietly. 'Who would do this to me?'

Mark looks tired all of a sudden, and for the first time since I arrived I see the change in him, I see what the years have done to my strong, strong husband. Creases surround his eyes; not the laughter lines I used to love, but signs of stress, old age creeping up before its time. His skin is paler than I remember; the perpetual tan that was the envy of every man and woman we knew has been replaced by a pallor that I initially attributed to the shock of seeing me, yet the healthy glow has yet to return. The cocksure look in his eyes, the one that dragged me under from the first glint in my direction, is gone. I see what I've done to the man who must once have felt like he had the world at his feet: a great job, a beautiful house, a glowing pregnant wife and then an adorable baby boy.

'I don't know. I do know there are some spiteful people out there. If someone is trying to hurt you, I don't know who and I don't know why, but I promise you it isn't me.'

I believe him. So I tell him everything. I tell him about Dr Riley, my meeting with Nick, Dylan's blanket, though I leave out the fact that I'm living with a virtual stranger. His expression is getting darker with every word. When I tell him about the break-in at my house, he looks like he's ready to explode.

'What the hell are you playing at?' he asks, pacing now, something I never saw him do when he was agitated before. 'Do you have any idea how much danger you could be putting yourself in?'

Well that's a shock. I might have been hoping for pity, sympathy, perhaps a little nostalgia. I even expected the anger, but not concern. I don't really know what to do with concern. I mean, he has a point, but he's about four years too late to be worrying about my safety.

'I didn't come here for a lecture,' I find myself snapping.

'Why did you come here then?' Mark is almost yelling now. 'What the bloody hell do you think you're playing at just turning up on my doorstep after four years? How did you think I'd feel, opening my front door and seeing your face again? I've spent years trying desperately to forget everything about you and yet here you are, looking like that and trying to drag up everything I've worked so hard to forget.'

'Well I'm sorry.' I stand up and cross the room, hand him my mug. 'I'll leave you to your cosy little life that you've managed to wipe us both from! If I find our son, would you like me to let you know?'

Mark's face falls and I know I've gone a step too far.

'Find our son?' he whispers. 'Susan, I already found our son. I found him with a cushion over his face, cold as ice, the breath sucked from him by the woman I thought was the love of my life. I don't have the luxury of clinging on to some hope that he's still alive. I remember holding him in my arms in the car park of the hospital begging him to breathe, screaming for someone to help, to save my beautiful little boy whose name you can barely say. His name was Dylan, Susan, Dylan Lucas Webster, and he's dead. He's dead because you killed him, and no amount of photographs of smiling little boys will change that. I think it's time you went.'

28

I drive away as fast as my shaking body allows and pull over
at the first opportunity. Leaning forward and resting my head
on the steering wheel, I give in to the racking sobs that have
threatened to overtake me since first seeing Mark. He knows
more than he's telling me. The conviction in his voice when
he spoke of finding Dylan's body certainly didn't seem faked,
but there is definitely something more, something I can't for
the life of me figure out yet.

When I manage to pull myself together, I take out my
phone and dial Nick's number.

'Susan?' He answers on the first ring. 'Is everything OK?
Did you speak to him?'

'I spoke to him.' I force back the tears and recount the
entire visit. When I finish, Nick is silent. 'Are you still there?'

'I'm here,' he answers. 'I just don't know what to make
of it all.'

'He knows something,' I tell him with certainty. 'And I
intend to find out what. I'm going back.'

'Do you think that's wise?' Nick sounds worried. It seems
to be becoming a habit for the men in my life to adopt a
concerned tone when they speak to me. 'It sounds like you

reopened some pretty raw wounds the first time. Maybe you should just let him be.'

'I have no intention of upsetting him again,' I reply, a bit stung that the concern this time is for my ex, not me. 'I'm going back when he's not there.'

'No way. No way, Susan, come back here now. Please.'

'What's the problem? I don't have to break in, I've got a key. I don't think he'll have thought to change the locks. Remember, the only danger in his life was behind bars.' I'm not sure if I manage to sound glib or just bitter.

'What if he catches you? You have no idea what he's capable of.'

Huh? 'What do you mean, what he's capable of? Mark's never done anything remotely scary in his life. He took back a belt once because the cashier forgot to put it through the till and he didn't want to be a criminal.'

'How much do you really know him, though, Susan? What do you know about his background?'

'What are you talking about? Mark doesn't have a *background*. You're being ridiculous. If I have any chance of finding out what he knows, it's now, before he remembers I still have a key to his house.'

'I can see I've got no chance of stopping you,' Nick concedes. Clearly he knows me better than I know him after such a short time. 'Will you wait until I can get to you?'

'No.' I am adamant. 'I need to do this on my own. I'll wait until I see his car pass, then I'll be in and out as fast as I can.'

'And if he doesn't leave?' Nick asks, probably already knowing the answer.

'Then I'll wait. He can't stay in there for ever.'

29

Maybe Nick was right. Mark could stay home for the rest of the night. What am I going to do, just sit here in the car? I can't even sleep, in case I miss him leaving and I'm waiting here like an idiot while the house is empty. This is the only way he could pass that leads anywhere, the town, the supermarket, so unless he goes for a drive in the countryside at least I'll definitely see him from here. If he leaves at all. What seemed like such a good idea ten minutes ago now seems ridiculous. What if Mark does catch me? And what did Nick mean about knowing his background? I wonder if he's found something out about Mark that he's not telling me, that he thinks I'd prefer not to know. I'm trying not to think about what the implications of that are, so I focus instead on the cars driving past the lay-by, making up stories about the people in them, what their lives might be like and where they might be on their way to.

It doesn't take as long as I expected for Mark to leave his house. Just forty minutes after I drove away, I watch his silver Mercedes pass the lay-by I am hidden in, drive to the end of the road and turn right into the town. I wait a few minutes just to be sure he isn't coming back, then start the car.

I park up in an industrial estate quarter of a mile from the house and walk the rest of the way in a nervous frenzy. If I'm found breaking into my ex-husband's home – although I'm not intending to damage anything – I will be in a lot of trouble. I might even be sent back to Oakdale to finish my sentence. Can they do that? I should have asked Cassie.

It takes me ten minutes to get back to the house, checking around furtively the whole way there. If I'm seen, someone will be sure to mention it at the next Neighbourhood Watch meeting. I fleetingly imagine Mrs Taylor next door pinning up Wanted posters on the lampposts in her winceyette nightdress.

Despite my confidence that Mark won't have changed the locks, I'm still slightly surprised when my key turns quite easily and the door swings open. I step inside quickly. That's it then, I'm a criminal. Well, again, I mean.

The kitchen has changed the most out of the rooms I've seen so far. The worktops are the same, but instead of the beautiful sage green I spent hours in B&Q having mixed just right, the walls have been painted a hideous sickly yellow colour. All that's missing are the chunks of carrot.

Now that the break-in part has gone so easily, I'm feeling overconfident. I'm going to infiltrate Mark's office, where a brown folder sitting on the desk marked TOP SECRET will obviously contain all the information I need to find my son. 'Wishful thinking,' I mutter, the noise out of place in the silent house.

The office has changed little since I left. The layout is the same, with the desk in the corner to my right as I walk in and a well-worn red armchair – the only bit of Mark's former life to seep through into ours – against the wall opposite. A few new pieces of art have replaced the family pictures, and for some reason he's taken down his degree certificates. That seems strange; those A4 sheets of paper bearing the Durham University crest were his pride and joy. He's probably having them specially cleaned or engraved or something.

The old locked filing cabinet still stands next to the desk, although where the key is I couldn't say. I have no idea where to start. The desk drawers are neat and ordered but yield nothing helpful.

It never really struck me when we lived together just how little I knew about my husband's work. Frankly, hearing about his job in IT bored the crap out of me, although I always managed to smile and nod politely at all his work parties. We were only there for the free drinks anyhow; Mark couldn't stand his workmates either. He was the complete opposite of most of them; they were so wrapped up in their own little worlds that anything as moronic as a joke bypassed them completely. I didn't understand any of it. In my world a cookie was something you ate with a cup of tea while you watched *Corrie*. I wish now I'd at least popped into his office occasionally, if only to see where everything was kept. The only time I remember coming in here was when Mark was working late and I wanted him to come to bed. I wandered in wearing his favourite negligee, which I casually let fall open as he stared at the computer screen. His resolve lasted all of three minutes and we ended up having sex right there on the desk. We laughed like teenagers when I kicked the cork board clean off the wall and Mark didn't even break his stride to clear it up. I can still picture it lying on the floor, a small key attached to the back with a strip of Sellotape . . .

No, that would be too easy. Pulling the board from the wall a little too vigorously, I turn it over, still expecting to find nothing, expecting my memory to be clouded by nostalgia and hope, but there it is, the small silver key still taped to the back of the board. I might not be Sherlock Holmes, but my husband is no Jim Moriarty either.

I shove the key into the top drawer of the cabinet and turn it sharply, letting out my breath as it clicks. I yank the drawer all the way open to find dozens of files arranged in alphabetical order by last name. A quick scan proves I don't recognise any of them; nothing as blatantly obvious as a Dylan file, or Dr Riley. My hopes of an easy find are looking bleaker. Taking out the first file, labelled 'Andrews', I hastily scan the contents. As expected, it is full of computer jargon and business details. I shove it back into its space, careful to leave nothing that might give away my presence. In the bottom of the drawer, underneath the files is a small blue leather book, the word 'addresses' printed across the front in gold. I shove it into my bag, certain it's disappearance won't give away my presence.

The second drawer down is clearly for accounts. Tabs marked 'Utilities' and 'Phone' contain little more than water bills and itemised phone bills. If I had all day I might be able to make use of the phone bills, but without knowing which numbers to look for, they're no use to me. I could just as easily spend my time jotting down numbers for the local takeaway and Domino's Pizza as anything helpful. I open up the file labelled 'Bank' and pull out a small brown ledger with 'Accounts' printed across it in black ink.

The book has three sections, one for bills, one for spending and one labelled 'Misc'. It's an account I've never heard of, not that that means a lot. Mark always took care of the money. He managed to train me well enough to balance my personal chequebook – my spending money – but beyond that I was clueless. Looking back now it seems pathetic; all I knew of our financial situation was what his lawyers offered me in the settlement, an offer I gladly took because in my eyes I deserved nothing. A fleeting look at the account book tells me I've been more than a little short-changed. I knew, of course, that my husband earned good money – we lived in a five-bedroomed house and I wore a different pair of designer shoes to every function we attended – but I had no idea he had these kinds of savings. Huge sums of money entered the account on a regular basis between 1990, when it appears Mark started keeping the ledger, and 1993. With what is stored away in there, Mark could have been living like a king. At the beginning of the ledger is a note of the money that was already in the account when the records began, and to all intents and purposes it looks like some kind of trust fund. I know Mark's father was a wealthy man who had died of a heart attack before we met. They hadn't spoken in years and Mark never wanted to discuss it, but I wonder now if the money was a legitimate inheritance, and why my husband never once mentioned it to me.

I don't have time to figure out if Mark's financial situation is important. I don't want any more of his money. I do, however, presume that Nick will want to see this, so I snap off a couple of photos of the pages, including account numbers, on my Blackberry and replace the book carefully. I need to hurry: Mark might be back any second.

The last drawer is a mess, and so out of character for Mark that it surprises me more than the discovery of the money. There are just piles of papers thrown in, one on top of the other. My heart steps up a beat. If I'm going to find anything, surely it will be in amongst this crap? Scraps of paper scrawled with phone numbers are shoved in between letters, junk mail and bills. I dip my hand in randomly, hoping that the luck that's got me this far won't fail me now. It lands on a photo. Hoping desperately for a picture of Dylan, preferably with an address and a full explanation of how he isn't dead written on the back, I pull it out.

What's that old saying? *Be careful what you wish for.* I am indeed holding a picture of my son. He looks safe and cosy in the arms of a beaming woman who appears to love him very much. A woman who will, within twelve weeks of this photo being taken, pick up a cushion and hold it over his face until he stops breathing. I want to scream at her, to yell at her to get help before it's too late, but maybe it was already too late. I can look at the past, I can hold it in my hands, but I can't change it. I turn over the photograph: no address, no amazing discovery, nothing I don't already know.

Susan and Dylan, 3 days old.

A lump in my throat threatens to choke me. It's been so long since I allowed myself to look at photographs of my son, and in the last few days I've been confronted with his image more times than I can bear. Not just on paper, but in my mind constantly. The love I felt for him for three months hasn't diminished, and I'd give anything I have now, or have ever had, to reach into this photo and brush my fingers across his soft skin, kiss his tiny lips.

I take a deep breath and tear my eyes away from the picture. Seeing it has drained the fight from me. I no longer want to find out what's going on; I just want to go home. I put the photo back where I found it, careful not to leave any sign of me being here, then, pushing those hurtful images to the back of my mind, I lock the drawer, taping the key back behind the cork board. Out on the landing I avoid looking at Dylan's door.

A noise from downstairs makes me freeze. Is Mark back so soon? No, there's no one down there, just house noises. I might not get another chance, so I decide to check the loft room. What had been a dusty loft hidden by a trapdoor in the ceiling when we'd moved in had been transformed by my fair hand – and an army of helpful builders – into a beautiful bedroom intended for Dylan when he was a teenager. The ladder had been replaced by a set of stairs and a skylight had been set into the roof. Any teenager would love it; it's so unfair that my little boy will never get the chance.

Now I move quickly up the stairs and my breath catches as I enter the room. It clearly hasn't been used as a bedroom since I left. It's filled with boxes, each one with labels such as 'Pictures' and 'Pregnancy Stuff', but there are other, less apparently painful boxes as well, two marked 'Magazines' and another four 'Uni Stuff'. I open the top of one of the 'Uni Stuff' boxes. Inside are three lever arch files, each full of lecture notes and essays. Seeing as I already know how much of a swot my ex-husband is, neither the copious amount of notes nor the highly graded assignments comes as a surprise. The second university box contains more files of lecture notes, and I'm about to give up when I see Mark's certificates lying in the top of the third one. They're still in their frames and they aren't damaged, so I can't see any reason for them not to be on the walls. I lift them out and put them to one side. Underneath are photographs: Mark with friends at bars, at various balls and festivals. More than a few are of a beautiful red-haired girl, fresh-faced and smiling. Her nose and cheeks are smattered with freckles and she doesn't appear to be wearing any make-up, but it's her eyes that have me captivated. They are a vivid emerald green and are full of such genuine happiness that I can't help but envy her, whoever she is. This feeling deepens the more photos I flick through. Now this girl has her arms around Mark, *my Mark*; now they are kissing, holding the camera at arm's length and taking the picture themselves, huge grins on their faces. The more photographs I see, the clearer it is that this is a couple deeply in love, and yet I have never even heard of her. Why would Mark have kept this from me? Between this and the mysterious money, it is looking like I didn't know my husband as well as I thought.

I turn each photo over but there's nothing written on the back. More and more pictures of the happy couple make my throat tighten and my heart ache, yet I can't stop. The girl on a beach, Mark wearing a backpack and walking gear, somewhere that looks hot. I have to get out of here. I manage to put the photos back in the box and replace the certificates, and I'm about ten seconds from leaving when I hear the key turn in the front door.

30

Jack: 27 November 1992

He hated getting mud on his shoes.

He hated mud on his shoes and he fucking hated the woods. Woods were for bears and tree-huggers, and he was neither. Bears, tree-huggers and dead bodies.

They'd left her on the edge where the newer trees had been planted, not thickening up for another hundred metres. Idiots! Further in and the animals might have got to her before the police did. She might not have been found for days. Weeks if that bitch Whitaker hadn't got her knickers in a twist and reported the girl missing already.

Well he sure as hell wasn't moving her. He was already going to have to burn these clothes and he hadn't even touched the body. What a waste of a fucking expensive suit.

He knew he shouldn't have come but he needed to see for himself. You couldn't rely on anyone in this world; he hadn't got to where he was without learning that. You did what needed doing and you didn't entrust the important stuff to weak-minded idiots who would never amount to anything.

The light had faded completely now but the moonlight here

among the sparse trees kissed the ground and slid over everything on it. There was no noise except the crunching of leaves under his feet. When he breathed out he saw his breath crystallise in front of him. In a few hours this mud would be rock hard, frosty and crunchy underfoot. She would be frozen like an ice pop.

He stepped as close as he dared to the body. Even in death the girl was breathtakingly beautiful. A random image of some girl gone to seed, a junkie dead from the cold, flashed through his mind. This one looked nothing like that sort of criminal scum. Despite the clumps of mud and leaves that clung to her long red hair, you could still see it had been in good condition. Her clothes were clean and good quality. She would have looked like any other nineteen-year-old girl were it not for the gaping blood-filled smile in her throat and the glassy lifelessness of those eyes.

He felt a small stab of regret. Things could have been so different for her, if only she hadn't tried to play games with him, hanging off Shakespeare every time she saw him enter a room, pretending she wasn't attracted to him. Billy was as bad, strutting around like Captain Big Balls spreading his feathers. Beth had had to find out what Jack was really like the hard way. She'd resisted his flowers, jewellery, even artwork, but she hadn't been able to resist the chloroform-covered rag clamped over her mouth. Finally he'd made her weak at the knees, although not in the way he'd planned.

They'd re-dressed her; he was a little disappointed at that but he'd expected it. There was still no way the police wouldn't know what had happened to her. It wouldn't be long before they found her here; he'd better be quick about what he needed to do.

His hand flicked to his pocket, where the girl's purse still sat, next to the syringe. Getting as close as he could without actually touching the body, he pressed the needle into the back of her knee and drew back. She hadn't been dead long enough for her blood to thin into water yet, or to dry up, so what he got was a beautiful claret-red syringe.

As much as he'd like to hang around and watch them find her, he had work to do.

31

I'm frozen to the spot, petrified to move in case I give myself away. Maybe I was mistaken – I'm two floors up after all – but then the front door opens and I hear the sound of keys being thrown on to the table in the hallway, followed by the rustling of carrier bags and footsteps carrying them into the kitchen. This is it then. Back to Oakdale for me. There isn't a chance I'm getting out of this; I mean I'm pretty sure 'I forgot my purse and went to look for it in your loft' isn't going to work.

Maybe I still have time. I have two choices: I can find a place to hide and hope Mark goes out again before he discovers me, or I can make my way back to the office and climb out of the window on to the extension and risk being seen. Or breaking my neck. It isn't really the best set of options I could hope for, but it's all I've got. As silently as I can, I push open the door and listen for any noise. The banging of cupboards tells me that whoever's down there is still putting away shopping, and it's only a short dash down the stairs to the office. I make it in seconds, and now instead of being trapped in the loft I'm trapped in the office. Not really much of an improvement, I know, but I'm slightly closer to the ground floor.

The jump from the office window to the extension doesn't look too bad, and I silently thank the con man at the conservatory place who convinced Mark to go for the expensive brick option, complete with foundations and planning permission, rather than the four pieces of glass I had in mind. That should take my weight quite comfortably, provided I don't bounce off the bloody roof.

As quietly as I can, I open the window and peer out. The extension is directly below, next to the kitchen. It was my laundry room and I loved it. It may seem slightly ridiculous to spend all that money on an extra room just to stick my washing machine and tumble drier in, but I'm bloody glad now that we did. Moving as quickly as my heeled boots will allow, I hitch myself up on to the desk and push the window open as far as possible. This would be a really bad time for Mark to decide to put out his washing.

The kitchen door opens – Mark is coming up the stairs. I have to get out fast. I hurl my handbag out of the window, hearing it land with a thump on the extension roof, and swing my leg over the windowsill. A huge heave and I am sitting on the sill, both legs dangling over, as I hear Mark at the top of the stairs. It isn't much of a drop – the real fall is from the extension to the ground – so I throw myself from the window, landing heavily. I can't chance a look at whether Mark has come into the study, gone into the bedroom or simply to the loo. I am standing on the roof of my former laundry room – thankfully all in one piece – and I have to get off before someone spots me.

Dropping to all fours, as low as possible, I make my way to the edge of the roof. The drop here is around ten foot, which is eight foot more than I am comfortable with, but once again my choice in the matter seems limited. I don't stop to think about how much the landing is going to hurt. I don't know how long Mark is going to stay upstairs, and his arrival back in the kitchen will cause me some problems. Wrapping the strap of my handbag around my wrist, I squat over the edge, lower my legs down slowly and let go.

I won't try and sound brave: the impact bloody hurts. As my knees try to recover from the shock, I manage to shuffle my way out of sight of the kitchen window. So far I haven't cried out in pain and I am feeling pretty pleased with myself when I hear a key turn in the back door. Bad knees or not, I run.

Gasping for breath, my vision slightly blurred, I'm forced to stop at the end of the street. I lean against the McKinleys' garden wall to steady myself and check the front room window for prying eyes. There is no one in and I haven't been followed.

I walk the rest of the way back to my car thanking God with every step for my new-found fitness. Four years ago I probably wouldn't have been able to pull my weight up on to the windowsill in the office, let alone drop from the laundry room roof and run for my life. I feel triumphant, more exhilarated than I have in years. The car's still parked where I left it, no parking ticket or wheel clamp. I let myself in and collapse in an exhausted heap against the steering wheel.

'How did it go? Did you get caught? Is this your "one phone call"?' Nick answers on the first ring and instantly begins a verbal assault.

'I haven't been arrested. And I'm not sure if I found anything. I'll leave you to work that out when I get back to yours. If that's still OK?'

'Sure.' Some of the anxiety in his voice has dissipated on

hearing I won't be needing him to post bail. How much does a journalist earn these days anyway? 'Drive safely,' he adds, and hangs up. Smiling wryly, I put away my phone and start the car. Feeling somewhat calmer and even smugger than before, I begin the drive back to Nick's house, both knees throbbing.

32

Forty minutes later, I pull into Nick's street. After the initial adrenalin rush of my daring robbery and resulting escape had worn off, Mark's words about finding our son had returned to hit me square in the stomach and I had to pull over twice on my journey to regain my breath.

'Thank God.' Nick's words are those of relief, but he doesn't look relieved. My euphoria subsides in an instant. He's holding an envelope.

'What's that? Where did you get it?'

'It was on the mat when I came to open the door. It wasn't there ten minutes ago.'

There's no child this time. The photographs that have been shoved through Nick's door show a much more familiar figure. Although my back is to the camera, I recognise myself immediately. Dressed in a loose grey jumper, my hair short and dark, I'm standing at the door of my former home, waiting for my former husband to open the door to me. This photo is recent. This photo is from this morning.

The next picture shows Mark opening the door to me; another shows me leaving. The fourth shows me returning to the house and the fifth is of me dangling from the laundry room roof. I would laugh if it wasn't so terrifying; I look ridiculous hanging there, suspended from the roof like a teenager climbing a tree. I thought myself so clever, escaping undetected like the Artful Dodger, but I'm not, am I? I was followed, caught on camera over and over again, then whoever followed me printed the photos and posted them through Nick's front door. For what? A warning? Are these photographs on the desk of some police station as I stand here congratulating myself on being a free woman?

A banging at the front door brings me screeching back to reality. The police, already? It's too late to run; for all I know they are at the back door waiting for another daring escape. I shove the photographs into my handbag and prepare to face the music. Nick opens the front door, both of us wearing our best 'please, officer, I'm innocent' look. Although that failed dismally for me the first time around, and I actually believed in my innocence that time.

Cassie stands on the front step, holding shopping bags and looking to anyone watching like the perfect Stepford Wife.

'Jesus, am I glad to see you.' I release the breath I've been holding and Nick lets her in. 'What are you doing here?'

'We've been looking into the trial,' Cassie reminds me. I'd forgotten that meant her coming here, to Nick's house, without me. 'I went to get some shopping. How did it go?'

'Not as well as I thought,' I answer darkly. I lamely hold out the photographs. 'These just arrived.'

Cassie looks through the photos and gasps, then passes them back to Nick, whose concerned look scares me even more. He leads the way into the sitting room, where he pulls the curtains closed and switches on the lights.

'What's that for?' Cassie asks. Even I agree it's overkill; we aren't Bond and Moneypenny, after all.

'They posted the photographs *here*. Before she even got here. Which means they knew she wasn't going home.'

Cassie immediately checks over her shoulder, as though someone might be standing behind her with a camera or a tape recorder.

'You didn't see anyone?'

'Do you see me waving at the camera?' The stress is making me snappy and sarcastic. 'Sorry.'

'Well whoever it is, we can't do anything about it now.' Nick affably ignores my barb. 'What did you get out of Mark?'

I tell them everything. Every detail of our conversation is etched into my brain and I repeat it practically word for word. I tell them about the money and the photos, even the sofa. Cassie is furious when I mention that my ex-husband is actually secretly loaded.

'What? How did he get away with not revealing that in the divorce?'

'I didn't ask,' I reply simply. 'His lawyer offered me a decent sum and I took it.'

'We'll contest it,' she continues, oblivious of what I'm even saying. I didn't fight the divorce; I didn't ask for anything. I was grateful for what I was given.

'I don't *want* to contest anything,' I insist. 'The money wasn't anything to do with me; the payments stopped long before we even met. I just want to know why he never told me about it. Or *her*.'

I won't admit it, but the photos of Mark and the girl have upset me far more than the hidden money. Granted, he never lied to me about her exactly; he just never told me about her. The fact that the mystery woman is absolutely gorgeous doesn't help, of course.

'The question is,' Nick muses, 'does any of it mean anything to us?'

He's used the word 'us', as though this is his problem as

much as mine, when we both know he could just walk away right now if he wanted to. I look from him to Cassie and wonder what they've been talking about all day, this odd pair who yesterday hated each other's guts. I hand Nick my phone with the pictures of the accounts, and an address book I took from the office. He frowns slightly at this, as though he doesn't approve of me stealing it, but he doesn't say anything.

'Did you guys find anything?' I ask Cassie while Nick's still deep in thought.

'We got these,' Cassie replies, excitedly pulling out her own sheaf of notes. I see the header 'ZBH Solicitors' emblazoned across the top – they've been sent from my lawyer's office. 'They're copies of the case files on your trial. ZDII blocked us every step of the way. Their bitch of a secretary only emailed them over when I pretended to be you on the phone and threatened legal action. Nick had me quoting all sorts of laws that entitle you to your own case notes.'

I start flicking through, my eyes falling on more and more that I don't understand.

'What do these tox results mean?' I ask, scanning the page. 'What's ketamine? Isn't that for horses?'

'It's a drug that was found in your system when they admitted you the day of Dylan's death,' Cassie explains.

That's news to me and I tell her so. Annoyingly, Nick is poring through the address book and says nothing.

'We figured as much,' Cassie says. 'It doesn't seem to have been brought up at the trial. Ketamine is used as a date rape drug, rendering the victim dizzy, disorientated and unaware of what's happening around them. It can also cause blackouts.' She sounds like a trainee pharmacist and looks proud of her investigative skills.

'What? How could I not know about this? Why did Rachael not mention it at the trial?' I thought Rachael Travis had

172

done a pretty good job as my defence lawyer. Mark had taken her on when the evidence against me had seemed watertight, but she had still fought my corner. Or so I'd thought. Maybe she hadn't had access to my medical records?

'Oh she had access all right.' Nick speaks at last when I suggest this. 'You signed a waiver when you took her on giving her full rights to all of your records. It's in there somewhere.'

'So she knew I had ketamine in my system and didn't think to bring it up in my defence? Would the police have seen these records?'

Nick shrugs. 'That's a good question. We only have the statements and details released to the press; we have no rights to the actual police notes, and short of hacking the system we have no way of finding out. Either someone on the case didn't do a very thorough job, or they knew about the drugs and they were left out of the investigation.'

My head is hurting. 'What does all this mean?'

'It could mean nothing,' Nick admits, 'Matthew Riley was a conscientious doctor and had no reason to lie. The ketamine I can't explain, but with such an open and shut case . . . Sorry,' he apologises quickly when he sees the look that crosses my face, 'but it did seem that way at the time. You were found next to Dylan's body, the cushion used to suffocate him was still in your hands with your skin cells and his saliva all over it—'

'I *was* at the trial, remember?' Immediately I feel terrible. Nick and Cassie are here helping me and I'm just being difficult. 'Sorry.' I lean forward and rub a hand over my face and eyes, suddenly tired again.

'Suze, are you sure you're up to this?' Cassie asks gently. She reaches over and puts a hand on my shoulder. 'You know, dragging up all this stuff over and over must be pretty upsetting for you.'

173

'No.' It's all getting a bit much and I'm not too proud to admit it. 'I'm not sure I am.' It's hard to hear details of the day I lost my son related so easily by an impartial observer. Much to my annoyance, I see Cassie shoot Nick a look. It's quick but not too quick for me to see what it means. They've clearly been expecting me to react like this. I decide I liked it better when they couldn't stand each other.

'We thought it might get too much for you,' she says, her tone still gentle, as though she might be dealing with a child. I think it's the final 'we' that tips me over the edge; what is it, the hundredth time since she walked in?

'Oh *we* did, did *we*?' I snap, rounding on my friend and conveniently forgetting that only seconds earlier I was admitting that I'm not coping.

'We just thought it might get difficult for you, you know, reliving what happened.'

'Quite the little couple these days, aren't we? When only yesterday you wanted to bash his head in with a picture frame. Any more thoughts about my mental state, Dr Reynolds?'

Cassie looks shocked and more than a little hurt. Nick just watches me with interest. His lack of reaction pisses me off even more. Which admittedly isn't too difficult at the moment.

'Don't get upset, Susan,' Cassie pleads. 'We . . . I mean *I'm* just concerned, you know, with your history . . .'

She knows me well enough to know instantly that she's said the wrong thing.

'My *history*?' I practically scream. 'What *history* is that then, Cassie? My depression? Or maybe it's the fact that I'm a murderer? Well you should know all about that, shouldn't you? If we're going to talk *history*, I mean. After all, I'm not the one who planned to murder my husband in cold blood because he slept with someone else.'

174

Cassie and Nick are stunned into silence. This should make me realise I'm being a bitch, and that Cassie doesn't deserve it. The knowledge of either of those facts doesn't deter me, though. Nope, I am on a big fat roll.

'So which is it, oh friend of mine? What is it that concerns you so much? Because there was me thinking we're trying to prove I *didn't* kill my son in a depressive rage. Or are you just humouring me?'

'That's enough, Susan.' Nick's deep voice cuts into the middle of my rant and I stop like a naughty schoolgirl chastised by the head teacher. When I see Cassie looking close to tears, I suddenly feel very ashamed of myself.

'Oh God, I'm sorry, Cass,' I apologise. 'I don't know what got into me. I'm sorry.'

Cassie reacts in true best friend form and smiles. It's hard to believe sometimes that this kind, loyal woman has done the thing she's done.

'No, I'm sorry,' she replies, coming across to the chair I've thrown myself in and putting her arms around me. 'It was a stupid thing to say. Would you like to carry on, or should we call it a day?'

'No,' I say firmly. 'You two have gone to a lot of trouble today and I'd like to know what else you found. God knows I'd prefer it to be over, but that's not an option, so the only thing to do is push forward.'

Cassie is relieved that I've calmed down and Nick remains silent. I wonder if he's finding it easier and easier to believe I'm a manic depressive. I'm certainly acting that way. He waits a second, probably to check that I'm not going to lose it again, then he leans over and turns a few of the pages until I'm looking at a report. A doctor's report.

'What does it say?' I ask, scanning the page. Nick doesn't answer, just waits for me to read it for myself.

It's a report written by my former GP, Dr Choudry. It's

dated 13 August 2009, three weeks after Dylan's death. Certain sentences leap out at me.

Mrs Webster showed typical concern with regard to her son's slow weight gain . . . no suggestion of any depressive symptoms . . . unlikely to be suffering from puerperal psychosis . . . no sign of hallucinations or disordered thought processes . . .

I look up at Nick. 'What does this mean? Why wasn't this used in court? He's saying I didn't have depression.'

Nick flicks a couple more pages, this time to another doctor's report, a name I don't know, Dr Ingrid Thompson. A scan of this one makes rather more disturbing reading.

Patient shows signs of severe post-natal depression . . . she is unresponsive, at times catatonic . . . the patient has no recollection of the incident . . . patient becomes agitated and upset at the mention of her son . . . the patient does not wish to discuss her child . . .

The date is 30 July, just seven days after the death of my son.

'What do you think?' Nick probes when I show no reaction.

'This was given in evidence at the trial,' I reply, remembering now. 'She, Dr Thompson, was there; she gave evidence for the prosecution. Why wasn't Dr Choudry called for his opinion? I don't remember seeing him.'

'Your solicitor's notes indicated that Dr Choudry was an unreliable witness, that the prosecution was likely to suggest his report was covering his own back, making excuses for the fact that he missed your depression at your post-natal checks. It was deemed more likely to hinder than help your case.'

'I suppose she had a point.' I speak slowly, rereading Dr Thompson's report. 'But these comments . . . I mean, of course I was in shock, I'd just lost my son. What was I supposed to be acting like?'

'It doesn't seem very in depth,' Cassie agrees. 'Those were our . . . I mean my thoughts too. And only one expert diagnosis after one interview. It all seems a bit rushed.'

'It's still very circumstantial, though,' Nick warns. 'Let's not get carried away with ourselves. We need to decide what we're going to do next.'

'Is there nothing else?' I ask, thumbing through more pages of notes.

'Not that I could see, but you'll need to go through it all and see if you can find anything. Wait, we got this too.' Cassie excitedly hands me a small file with the words 'Dr Riley' pencilled on the front. Inside are journalistic notes on Dr Riley's disappearance, interviews with friends and family, a statement from his wife and records of his finances. All come to the same conclusion: Dr Riley had no reason to run away, or to kill himself. He was a happy man with a good marriage, no apparent affairs they could uncover, two little girls and no financial problems. He had been quiet the last few weeks, his wife had told the journalist, but nothing to indicate what was to come. There had been no warning.

'I thought you were the reporter on this case?' I ask Nick, confused. 'These aren't your notes.'

'I just wrote the article,' Nick explains. 'I didn't do the legwork on that one. I think maybe it's time I did.' I look at him questioningly. 'I think we should go and see Mrs Riley.'

I shake my head. 'No way. I've dragged the past up for enough people already. The last thing Mrs Riley needs is us turning up on her doorstep with wild conspiracies about her husband's death.'

'I've already spoken to her,' Nick surprises me by saying. 'She's more than happy to see us. She says it's about time someone started asking more questions about her husband's disappearance.'

'Does she think there's more to it than suicide?' I ask. I'd not thought about that prospect. 'If he was murdered, surely we could be in some serious danger if we start poking around?'

'I think we're well beyond "poking around". But no, I think she's accepted it was suicide, she just never got a good enough reason why he would kill himself.'

'And she thinks we can provide her with that?'

'What I think,' Cassie cuts in, 'is that she's a lonely woman and your friend Mr Whitely here has a very good telephone manner.'

'Is that true?' I demand, noticing the use of 'your' rather than 'our'. 'Did you flirt an interview out of her?'

'By any means possible,' Nick replies, his right fist over his heart and making a three-fingered salute with his left hand. 'It's the journalist's motto.'

'So when do we go?'

'Tomorrow.'

No time like the present, I guess.

'That's not it, Susan.' Cassie takes my arm. 'There's something else. Something big.' She looks at Nick, who can't meet either of our eyes.

'What? What is it? What's happened?' Panic rises like bile in my throat.

'It was him. I told him you'd be mad, I was furious when he told me, but now I see it might be for the best, even though it meant going behind your back, which is not cool.'

'You're worrying me now – what the hell is going on here?'

'Cassie's right, it was me. Do you remember the hairbrush?'

'What hairbrush?'

'The one that was in the box with Dylan's blanket.'

I almost can't believe I'd forgotten. The small blue

178

hairbrush that had been placed on top of my son's blanket. I was so blindsided by the appearance of the blanket that I'd put it to one side, unconcerned with an item I'd never seen before. What use was a hairbrush to me when I'd thought my dad had been sending me vicious puzzles?

'What did you do?' My words are slow and measured, because I'm trying to breathe. I'm struggling not to panic, because I know what he's done. It's what I'd have done if my mind hadn't been so clouded over, if I hadn't been so bloody-minded about my father.

'Please stay calm. I took the hairbrush when I came over yesterday morning, along with one from your bathroom. I drove it to my cousin, he's a lab manager at an independent paternity testing company and he pulled an all nighter to get these results for me. I picked them up this afternoon.'

My breathing quickens and everything starts to swim. Nick's face, Cassie's face, both are a blur. I can feel heat rushing to my cheeks and I know I'm going to cry.

'How could you not tell me?' I manage to whisper. Cassie is holding my hand now, instructing me to breathe slowly. Nick is apologising but I barely hear him. I'm staring at yet another envelope that could change my entire life. This is it: if those results are negative, this is all over. If they are positive . . .

'Listen, Susan, listen to me.' Nick is speaking slowly and calmly and I try to focus on his words. 'You don't have to open the envelope. We can just throw it in the fire and forget I ever went. But if you do want to open it, there are some things you need to know.'

'OK,' I hear myself say. 'What do I need to know?'

Nick looks at Cassie, who nods. 'Right, firstly, the sample isn't a great one. There were only a couple of strands of hair that had roots, rather than just being broken. Plus they've been contaminated just by you taking the brush out of the box. So what I'm trying to say is that this wouldn't hold up as evidence in a court; this is just for you.'

I hear him, but I don't really care about what he's saying. Whether or not the contents of this envelope would hold up in court means nothing to me; I'm not in a court and I don't understand what contaminated evidence means. I want to open this envelope. And I really do *not* want to open it.

'Suze, are you going to do it?' Cassie strokes my arm gently and I realise I've been sitting here in silence for a few minutes.

It's false hope, a nasty little voice in my head taunts me. *What would Dr Nelson say?* Screw Dr Nelson, I reply, thinking back to one of the many psychiatrists at Oakdale, a podgy, bald little hypocrite in a tweed jacket, whose hand shook with the telltale signs of alcohol dependency as he told me I needed to accept *my* demons. I've made up my mind. What kind of mother would I be if I didn't search for the truth?

The kind that . . . No, I won't go there again.

I turn to Nick. 'Do you know?' I ask. 'Did your friend tell you what it says? Do you already know if those hairs belong to my son?'

Nick shakes his head.

'OK,' I say. 'I'm ready.'

Tears blur my eyes as I push my thumb under the envelope tab and rip upwards. My fingers are trembling as I pull out the piece of paper from inside and I have to squeeze my eyes closed to get rid of the tears. They spill down my cheeks silently, splashing on to the page. Slowly I unfold it and start to read.

It takes me a minute to understand what it says – there

is a lot of jargon and my eyes are working too fast to see what it all means. Then I spot it. In small black print, too small for the magnitude of what they convey, are the words 'Susan Webster is not excluded from being the biological parent of the child. This result is based on a 99.999% DNA match.'

So there it is, in black and white. My son is alive.

33

Over the next hour, Nick and Cassie have to stop me calling the police or Mark fourteen or fifteen times. My head is swimming; I'm swinging between anger, joy and devastation almost every few minutes. I can't stop the tears flowing down my face, running on to my T-shirt, into my hair.

My son is alive.

To say I've always known it would be a lie. Every person in any position of power who has looked at my life over the last four years has fitted it into the neat bracket of 'such a shame'; not once has it ever been suggested that there might have been a mistake, that I may have been innocent. I've dreamt of Dylan being alive, but even in my dreams I was imagining that I'd never been left alone with him that day, or that the doctors had given me enough pills to keep me sane – not that the whole thing had been a sick lie.

I'm not even in a place to think about who, or why. The only thing that keeps running through my head is *how*. How could this have happened? Is Dylan in danger?

'How old is it?'

Cassie's head snaps up and I realise it's the first time I've spoken in a while.

'The hair on the brush, does he know how old it is? Your friend?'

Nick shakes his head. 'Impossible to tell. All he could say is that it's not from a three-month-old baby, it's from a much older child.'

'So the brush could have been used what, six months, a year ago? Anything could've happened to him in that time. Anything could have happened to him in the last four years when he SHOULD HAVE BEEN WITH ME AND I'M HERE DRINKING FUCKING TEA!' Standing up, I hurl my half-finished mug of tea at the opposite wall and burst into tears as it smashes, splashing a milky brown stain in an arc across the paintwork. Cassie flies across the room and takes me in her arms, folding me into the soft cashmere of her jumper and holding me tight while I sob.

'What are we going to do, Susan?' It's the first time he's spoken in the hour we've been sitting at his kitchen table. He left me to it while I cried on Cassie's shoulder until I retched, brought us cups of coffee and said nothing about me chain-smoking in his spare room. Now it's past 2 a.m. and Cassie fell asleep on the floor of my room an hour ago, refusing even to go home to her own bed. I don't know whether I woke Nick when I came downstairs or if he'd been awake the whole time. Wordlessly he prepared me a mug of hot chocolate and took the chair opposite me in the kitchen, looking the whole time like there was a subject he'd rather punch himself in the face than broach.

I'm too tired to even shrug. 'I'm sorry about your wall.'

'You can repaint it another day. Stop avoiding the issue. We need to decide what to do about what's just happened.'

'About Mark?'

He nods. It feels like a lifetime ago that I pulled up at my old home, when I still thought Dylan was dead, when I still thought I had killed him.

'It all seems so different now,' I say. 'He couldn't get me in the house fast enough – I thought he was afraid one of the neighbours might see me on the doorstep, but now I wonder if he was worried about someone else seeing me.'

Nick doesn't stop watching me as I speak. He looks shattered; his eyes are puffier than usual and the skin underneath is dark and lined. 'Do you think he knows?' he asks eventually. 'Do you think Mark knows that you didn't kill Dylan? What do you think he's capable of, Susan?' His voice is intense; he's leaning towards me slightly and his hand is gripping his mug harder than it was before. What does he want me to say?

'It seems impossible.' I've thought of nothing since. 'He was so convincing when he made his speech about finding Dylan – but he couldn't have, could he? Not if Dylan's still alive.'

Nick doesn't remind me how shaky the DNA evidence is, how it's still possible the sample has been contaminated. And I don't mention it because I know my son is alive and I am innocent.

'Unless he was wrong about him not breathing,' he offers instead. 'It was a massively stressful situation; he might have believed Dylan was dead when he found him. I mean, he thought you were. What if something happened after you both went to hospital?'

I consider this for a minute. 'You mean like someone stole him and let us both believe he had died?' I'd much rather believe that than think for another second that Mark was involved in this. 'It seems crazy, but doesn't this all?'

'You still haven't answered my question, Susan. Do *you* think your husband was lying to you? What do you know about his past? His family?'

184

Everything, I'd thought. Until I found the pictures of him with the mystery woman, I'd thought I knew everything there was to know about Mark Webster. Does the fact that I didn't know about a university girlfriend change that?

I sigh. 'I can't think about this any more. I just need to speak to him, to ask him . . .' I still want Mark to hold me and tell me we'll get through this together.

'That's not a good idea,' Nick says firmly. Is there a note of urgency in his words? 'For all you know, he sent those photos to us today – it could be him having you followed in the first place. If you call the police they might—'

'They might think I've gone crazy again. I'll be committed.'

'I think we should still go and see Mrs Riley tomorrow; after all, her husband is the one who pronounced Dylan dead and who went missing four months later. But now we need rest.'

I don't think I can even consider sleep tonight, but as I lie down on my bed, Cassie still flat out on the floor at my feet, my eyes begin to droop. I can't remember what I was thinking about just a few minutes ago, so I know I'm falling asleep. Through the silence I hear a voice, as clear as if the woman speaking was standing next to me: 'I came to help you.'

In my mind I picture myself lunging forward, pushing something, someone. I'm defending myself, thrusting someone away, away from me and my baby. Hands reach out for me; I stumble backwards and scream. My mind switches view and I'm in the audience of a play. When I look at the person next to me, they're wearing a cycle helmet and clutching a camera. I look to my right; there they are again, and again in front. The whole theatre is full of faceless people taking my picture, and I wonder if I'll ever be free of them.

34

Jack: 1 December 1992

Three days since the body had been found and the police were still everywhere. The girls were getting annoyingly paranoid. On the first night after Beth went missing it had been fun, no one wanted to stop their lives ticking on. But they were careful, scared. The girls wanted someone to walk them home, see them to their rooms; they'd been so grateful to be in the company of someone safe. Now, though, now that the reality had kicked in, they were too terrified to go anywhere. Everyone was a suspect – well, apart from people like him.

The rumours were the best part. He'd heard it all: Beth had been sleeping with everyone from university lecturers to punters who had been paying her for sex. No one suspected the reality. He had a good idea that he could have gone to the police and told them exactly what had happened to Bethany Connors and they'd have laughed him out of the station.

Shakes had gone to pieces when he was told about the discovery of Beth's body. Jack hadn't been with him at the time – it was unlikely they'd kiss and make up just yet – but he'd watched from across the room as his face turned an ashen grey colour, seen tiny beads of sweat form on his forehead. Riley had had to hold him up – incredible really considering how much he'd been shaking too. Now Billy had run back to daddy's house, pathetic. Richard was a powerful man, sure, but even he couldn't bring murdered fiancées back from the dead.

Jack had to speak to Billy, make sure he wasn't going to be running to the police. Bad things happened all the time; he had to make sure Shakes knew this was nothing to get himself in a mess over. He would get over Beth, as he had got over Tanya; they'd find him a new piece and he'd be happy as a pig in shit again. This didn't have to be the end of everything.

35

Mrs Riley lives just outside Diudford in a stunning modern house with the kind of views that inspire poetry. The house doesn't stand alone; there are enough neighbours to make me nervous about our visit, even though I'm sure they're not psychic. I'm still waiting for someone to emerge from the bushes. The feeling of being followed has amplified since being at Nick's house, since my dream last night, and our new information. Now that I know about my son, I can feel determination radiating from me – I wonder if the person trying to scare me off can sense the change? Did they wake up this morning knowing that my first thought was that I am going to find them? That I am coming for my son?

Dr Riley had clearly earned a decent crust, or maybe they had inherited money. I'm pretty sure even a generous doctor's salary wouldn't stretch to such a beauty spot and the Range Rover that sits on the drive. I have no idea what Mrs Riley does for a living, of course. I could be selling the poor woman short – for all I know she could be a surgeon or a lawyer. One thing I do know is that I'm glad Cassie decided to go back home this morning. She would have hated this place.

'Nice house,' Nick comments under his breath. 'Wonder where they got their hands on this much cash?'

Always the investigative journalist, and now I'm thinking like him. Fighting the urge to take his hand as we walk towards the front door, scared of what we might find, I widen the distance between us just in case I automatically reach out and completely humiliate myself. I have to remind myself I have someone who believes in me enough to be here.

'Are you ready?' Nick asks. I nod in reply, hoping I won't be doing much of the talking. Before he has a chance to knock, the front door opens, surprising us both.

'Sorry,' Mrs Riley apologises immediately, seeing the startled look on both our faces, but it isn't the door opening that has surprised me, it is the person standing behind it.

Mrs Riley looks like nothing short of a movie star. The words 'doctor's wife' and 'deserted wife' conjure up visions of a poor elderly woman, not the stunning young *Footballers' Wives* extra who has opened the door to us. Silently I berate myself for failing to remember how old Dr Riley actually was – mid thirties according to the article – for being stupid enough not to realise that a frail elderly woman probably wouldn't be driving a Range Rover, and for not bothering to remove last night's make-up and reapply, preferring to just paste a fresh batch over it.

Following Mrs Riley inside, I quickly pull my fingers through my hair hoping to tame it slightly and run a finger under each eye to combat any eyeliner smudges. It never seemed to matter to Mark that I wasn't the most polished woman he'd ever met. The image of the beautiful redhead with her arms wrapped around my ex-husband dances in my head. She didn't look like someone who had to work at beauty. Such a contrast to the slightly chubby woman with the hair that wages war against brushes and straighteners that he ended up marrying. Was the contrast deliberate? Did he choose me because I didn't remind him of his former lover in any way? Did he take my son away to be with her?

'I thought we could eat in the conservatory,' Mrs Riley is saying, leading us through to a large glass extension where a beautiful spread of cucumber sandwiches, bagels, and jugs of iced water is laid out across a large table with a crisp white tablecloth.

'Really, Mrs Riley, you shouldn't have.' Nick looks slightly embarrassed and I wonder just how much flirting took place to warrant this kind of reception. Or what she's trying to distract us from.

'Please, call me Kristy.' She gestures for us both to sit down. 'What can I get you to drink?'

We sit around the table helping ourselves to sandwiches. As expected Kristy – which is probably short for Kristabelle or Krystal with a 'K' – barely touches the food and sits sipping water from an expensive-looking glass.

'So you said on the phone that you wanted to talk about Matthew?' she asks eventually, directing her question solely at Nick. I realise with some annoyance that she's barely glanced my way since we arrived, acting instead as though Nick has come alone. Her husband ruined my life; the least she could do is fucking look at me.

'We'd be very grateful.' Nick gives her his best look of sympathetic concern. 'But only if it isn't too difficult for you, of course.'

She doesn't answer him, but instead turns to fix her full attention on me for the first time.

'You're her, aren't you. Susan Webster.' It's a statement, not a question, and I suddenly think I liked it better when she was ignoring me. As far as I know, Nick used my new name when he arranged for us to see Kristy; he told her that we're researching an article on stress in the health profession and as far as he was aware, she'd bought that line. Looks like we aren't as clever as we think we are.

'Yes,' I reply truthfully. 'I'm sorry we lied to you.'

'Don't be,' she replies matter-of-factly. 'I knew it was you as soon as I opened the door. If I hadn't wanted to speak to you, I wouldn't have let you in.'

'So why did you?'

'I was curious,' she admits unashamedly, making me feel a bit like a sideshow act. 'The famous Susan Webster turns up with a reporter wanting to talk about Matty? Yours was the last trial my husband ever gave evidence at.' Kristy looks as though it hurts her to remember, which maybe it does. Maybe she has no idea what a lying bastard her husband was. 'I always wondered if the two were related. I've never forgotten your face; I saw it every time I closed my eyes. For years I blamed you for his disappearance.'

That's rich.

'But not any more?' Nick asks.

'No, not any more,' she replies, avoiding my eyes. 'The more I thought about it, the less sense it made to me. Matthew had had difficult and upsetting cases before and he'd never let them affect him. There must have been things going on I didn't know about. Maybe blaming you was a way of avoiding shouldering my own blame. I just didn't notice what was under my nose.'

'So you don't think your husband's disappearance had anything to do with Susan's trial? It happened so soon afterwards.'

'It couldn't have done, could it?' Kristy asks. 'I mean, he was just giving evidence, just telling the truth as he interpreted it. What happened to you, I mean your conviction, it wasn't his fault. But I still couldn't think for the life of me why he would leave us. The police looked into our finances, asked about our relationship but they found nothing. He had inherited a lot of money from a great-grandfather and made enough to keep us comfortable, as you can see. I knew they were barking up the wrong tree, but I was too shocked to ask questions and I still don't know now what those questions would be.'

'Did you ever get the impression your husband knew more than he was letting on about Dylan Webster's death?' Nick asks gently. Kristy's cheeks redden.

'How do you mean? Like he had something to do with the baby dying?'

'I didn't mean to imply that . . .'

'But that's exactly what you are implying! What's she said to you?' Her finger jabs accusingly towards my face. 'Whatever she thinks she knows, she's lying.'

Now it's my turn to go red. The heat rises in my cheeks and I can feel Nick's eyes boring into me, willing me not to explode. I never made him any promises. 'And what do you think *you* know, Kristy? You're telling me you don't have any idea why your husband might have done a runner?'

Kristy stands up. 'I still can't figure out why you're here, but if you're trying to insinuate that my husband was in some way involved in the death of your son, you may as well leave. I'm sorry about what happened to you, Mrs Webster. Post-natal depression is nothing to be ashamed of, and it's awful that you didn't get the help you needed, but if you think I'm going to sit here and have Matthew's name dragged through the dirt, you're both sadly mistaken.' She picks up my bag and shoves it at me, venom pouring from her. 'Get out, the pair of you.'

36

'Take us to Rachael's office,' I instruct when we're back on the road. 'It seems a shame to come all this way and miss an opportunity to speak to her.'

'Are you sure that's a good idea? The mood you're in?' Nick asks, once again adopting his concerned look. It was sweet at first, but if he keeps it up much longer, I think I might rip it off his face.

'Do you have any better ideas?' I ask instead. 'That was a bloody disaster back there! Did you think she was just going to come out and say that she knew what had happened to Dylan? Or were you hoping I was going to be bad cop to your good cop?'

He turns left without saying a word.

The office of ZBH Solicitors is a tall, old-fashioned building, but I know the inside is anything but. A large marbled reception holds a sleek white desk manned by a haughty blonde woman who looks as immaculate as the furniture.

'We're here to see Rachael Travis,' I tell her, approaching the desk. The woman recognises me immediately, despite us having never met. Were they expecting me?

'Mrs Webster, do you have an appointment?'

'It's Ms Cartwright,' I snap. 'And no, we were in the area and decided to stop by to visit an old friend. Will you tell her we're here, please?'

I expect her to argue, but she just picks up the phone and dials an extension. From the little conversation I can hear, it sounds like Rachael has been expecting a visit and puts up no fight. I presume Cassie's earlier phone call – as me – requesting my trial notes has put them on red alert, and the lack of resistance makes me certain I will get nothing from her. She's probably going to start reading from a pre-prepared statement, if I know Rachael.

'Ms Travis will see you,' Miss Stick-up-ass tells us, immediately going back to her paperwork.

Rachael's office is on the fourth floor of the building. When we get there, her personal secretary Tamsin smiles warmly at us.

'Emma.' She greets me using my new name, which endears me to her immediately. I've only ever spoken to her on the phone, but she's always been genuinely warm and friendly and never uses the judgemental tone so many members of the firm employ. 'It's nice to finally meet you in person. How are you?'

'I'm OK, thank you, Tamsin, and you?'

'I'm rolling along,' she replies affably. 'Ms Travis is waiting for you.'

'Thanks.'

Rachael's office is all polished wood and sleek lines. Immaculate law tomes, which I doubt are ever read, line the bookshelves and a comfy-looking armchair sits behind a heavy wooden desk. Rachael stands by the window, her back to the door although I know she's heard us enter. After a minute or so she turns to face us without smiling. Her face looks different from how I remember. The features are all still the same – sharp angles and high cheekbones, perfectly applied make-up and large almond-shaped brown eyes. Her haircut has changed – it looks sharper, more slanty and shorter – but the main difference is the expression on her face. I remember her bringing me packets of chocolate muffins and cigarettes when I was in Oakdale; new underwear and notebooks. I remember her smiling and taking my hand across the plastic visitors' table, with its fag burns and graffiti scrawl, and telling me how hopeful she was of my appeal, an appeal that went nowhere due to lack of fresh evidence. I remember her squeezing my arm and talking in low, comforting tones about how well I looked and how strong I was being, even in the early days when I wouldn't speak a word back to her.

'Susan, how's freedom treating you?' She doesn't sound like she cares now in the slightest; her words are short and clipped and she doesn't wait for an answer, instead turning to Nick and holding out a perfectly manicured hand. I wonder briefly how many other women are set to make me feel frumpy and unattractive today. 'Rachael Travis. And you are?'

'Nick Whitely.' Nick holds out his hand but doesn't return her false smile. I smugly spread my feathers.

'Whitely,' Rachael muses, 'I know that name. But I'm sure I'd recognise you if we'd met before.'

'I covered Susan's trial,' Nick replies. 'But I don't believe I interviewed you personally.'

'That must be it then.' Rachael turns to me sharply. 'What can I do for you, Susan? Surely you don't need the services of a criminal lawyer again this soon?' She smiles as if joking, but there is no humour in her voice.

'No, not yet.' I hope the threat is implicit in my words, but if she's caught one she doesn't let on, so I continue. 'I've been looking over my trial notes and there are a few things I wanted to discuss with you face to face.'

'Yes, Gemma told me you'd put in a request.' So it was the receptionist who dobbed me in. 'What is it that concerns you?'

She gestures for us to take a seat and perches herself on the edge of her desk, an act that may seem casual and relaxed to most people, but I know differently. This way she still towers above us, always trying to gain the upper hand, ever the criminal lawyer.

'There was a drug in my system at the time of my son's death.' I take a breath and look at Nick, who nods for me to continue. 'Ketamine. It could have rendered me helpless, according to my research, and yet its presence in my blood was never brought up at my trial.'

Rachael doesn't appear surprised by my revelation. Of course not: she already knew about the ketamine.

'Ketamine is a recreational drug, Susan. If I'd brought up the fact that it was in your system at the time of Dylan's death, there would be nothing stopping the prosecution saying you were high when you killed him.' I try not to visibly flinch at her words. 'You should thank your lucky stars they didn't spot it themselves; depressed child killer still sounds a hell of a lot better than drugged-up child killer.'

Keep calm. Count to ten. Don't cry. Don't hit her.

'But it might have proved that someone else was involved.'

Rachael takes a deep breath in. 'And so we come to the reason you're here. Susan, I know it's been hard to come to terms with what happened – God knows it would be difficult for anyone to accept that they had harmed their own child – but there was never anyone else implicated in Dylan's death.'

To think that I once considered this woman my ally. Seeing her standing so coolly in front of me, saying my son's name so offhandedly, anger begins to bubble up inside me. How dare she talk as if she knew Dylan? It's all I can do not to scream and throw the DNA results I have in my pocket in her face. I don't dare speak for a second. Rachael obviously takes this silence as an admission that what she's saying must be right and ploughs on with her armchair psychology.

'Lots of people who have experienced this kind of trauma go through intense denial. They search for someone to blame, anyone but themselves. It's perfectly natural for you to feel like I might have sabotaged your trial; you won't be the first. What you have to remember is that I've done this a thousand times, probably more, and anything I didn't include at your trial was for a reason.'

Her condescending, patronising 'I know best, you're the textbook criminal' tone does nothing to alleviate my anger. I take a couple of imperceptible breaths to calm myself down; losing my rag will not help the situation.

'And Dr Choudry's report?' I ask in a level tone. 'Did that not seem worth mentioning? When that woman stood there telling the whole courtroom how I had severe post-natal depression, did it not seem worth pointing out that my own doctor, who had known me since I was a little girl, said there was nothing wrong with me?'

Ms Travis has clearly been expecting this also. She looks at Nick imploringly, obviously thinking he might be a better bet when it comes to her female charms.

'Dr Choudry was in disgrace,' Rachael tells him softly. 'One of his patients had been suffering from puerperal psychosis and he had neither diagnosed nor successfully managed her condition, resulting in the most tragic of outcomes. It was expected that he would report that Susan had been fine merely to cover his own shortcomings. Putting him on the stand would not have helped her case, and if the prosecution had got hold of him it would have ended his career al-together.' She turns back to me. 'Would you have wanted that?'

'No,' I admit reluctantly. I had no idea how Dr Choudry's career had been affected by what I'd done. Mark, Dr Choudry, Dr Riley and his family – how many other lives has this ruined? I try to focus on why we are here. I know Dylan is still alive, that I never killed him in the first place and I'm not responsible for any of these lives being torn to shreds. *God how I want to believe that it is true.*

'Not only that,' Rachael continues, 'but we were trying to prove you *were* depressed. If we went around calling witnesses to say there was nothing wrong with you, you'd still have been found guilty but you'd have served twenty years.'

'It's a fair point, Ms Travis,' Nick relents, and I think for a second he is about to give up and leave. He's right, it is a fair point. Maybe I have just been looking for someone to blame. Before I received the photograph with my son's name on it I thought Rachael had done the best job she could do. Maybe she's just a crap lawyer. But Nick hasn't finished. 'So could you explain one last thing to us, as you've been so forthcoming thus far?'

This time Rachael does look surprised, and I try to hide the fact that so am I. We haven't discussed any other 'things'.

'Go on,' she says slowly.

'I'm wondering if you can tell me why you made seventeen phone calls to Mr and Mrs Webster's house in the week leading up to the trial, when Mrs Webster was being treated in hospital for her so-called depression? What exactly did you and Mr Webster have to discuss?'

My mouth falls open. Rachael blinks a couple of times and looks at me. *He's got her.*

'There was some trouble with the, um, the funding,' she replies eventually. My legal fees were paid from our joint account and I was never aware of any difficulties. 'Mr Webster thought it best that Susan wasn't troubled with anything to do with finances, so he dealt with me directly.'

'Really?' Nick asks, feigning surprise. 'It seems that Mr Webster has a different version. He told us you were gathering evidence to help Susan in any way you could.'

He's spoken to Mark? How did I not know about this? Rachael, to her credit, recovers well, but I can see her mentally kicking herself.

'Of course, that was another reason for my calls. I don't really see that this is any of your business. Who did you say you are again?'

Her tone suggests that this chat is over, and Nick, without losing an ounce of cool, gets to his feet and tells her so. I am too flabbergasted to say much except goodbye.

'Where the fuck did that come from?' I demand when we are outside, the door firmly closed behind us so Tamsin can't hear. Before Nick can answer, the door opposite us opens and a face to launch a thousand ships peers out from behind it.

'I thought I heard voices.' The man smiles and my heart steps up its beat.

'We weren't speaking,' Nick replies, quite rudely. Obviously he doesn't play well with other pretty boys. The man frowns.

'Weird. Wait a second, are you Susan Webster?' Before I can answer, Nick steps in front of me.

'Who are you?'

The man flicks his eyes to Nick briefly, then back to me. 'Rob Howe.' He puts out his hand, and when I give him mine to shake, he holds on to it a little longer than is usual. 'I'm the "H" in ZBH.' He gestures with his head towards the large letters on the wall.

'You're Rachael's boss?' He laughs at the surprise in my voice. 'I was expecting someone . . .'

'Less devastatingly handsome?'

Nick grunts. I feel my cheeks redden; Rob's don't. 'Older.'

'Susan, we have to go.' Nick nudges my arm.

'Do you have time for a quick word?' Rob asks. He moves his eyes pointedly to Nick. 'Alone?'

I can almost feel Nick opening his mouth to object. Before he does, I cut in. 'I'll meet you at the car,' I tell him.

'Are you sure?'

'Nick, seriously. What do you think is going to happen to me in the hallway of a law firm?'

He shrugs, like he could think of a million things but he knows none of them will be well received. 'Fine. See you at the car.'

As we both watch his retreating back, Rob says, 'He's overprotective. Who is he? Your brother? Boyfriend?'

I don't want to give too much away so I just shake my head. 'A friend. He's just looking out for me. Sorry.'

'Don't apologise.' Rob lowers his voice and I have to step closer to hear him. He smells expensive, and in a tailored Armani suit he looks it too. He must be under forty, well built, and his face has been chiselled by a steady hand. He's perfectly clean-shaven. 'I'm glad you have someone looking after you. Do you want to step in here? My PA is out for lunch.' His hand is on the door to his own office and he gestures with his head to Rachael's door, which we are still standing outside.

'Sure.'

The inside of his office looks a lot like Rachael's, expensive wood and leather tomes, although this one has certificates on the wall bearing the name 'Robert Lewis Howe, LLP'.

'I'm sorry I didn't get to meet you during your trial.' Despite all the space in the office, he's still standing just inches away from me. 'When your husband phoned the firm, I wanted to take your case on myself but Rachael insisted, and your husband agreed with her. I got the impression they knew each other.'

'If they did, they never mentioned it to me.'

He shakes his head. 'That's what I was afraid of. Look, I might be speaking out of turn here, but I always thought there was something we weren't being told about your case. Something Mr Webster was keeping from us. Now if I'm talking rubbish, just say . . .'

'No.' My answer might have been a bit quick. 'I mean, if there's something you think I should know, I'd rather you told me.'

'That's just it. I'm not quite sure what it was, more a feeling. I don't have any actual proof. If you wanted, I could take a look at your notes again, see if anything strikes me. Of course if you'd rather put it all behind you, I'd completely understand. Start afresh, forget it ever happened.'

How can I tell him that's impossible without telling him that I know Dylan is alive?

'Look,' I say instead. 'Look, and see what you think. If you find anything, this' – I pick up a pen from the desk and grab his hand, scrawl my number on the back of it – 'is my number.'

He's staring at the back of his hand and his face breaks into a huge grin. 'Did you just write on my hand? All this paper in the office and you write on my hand? No one's done that since school.'

I feel my cheeks redden. 'I'm so sorry. What a stupid thing—'

'It's fine.' He's laughing, thank goodness. 'Maybe we could go for a drink sometime? I'd understand if you didn't . . . I mean . . .'

My heart's pounding now. I don't know whether it's at the thought of going for a drink with Robert Howe, a real date where there's wine, small talk and perhaps a walk home – a kiss? – or at the knowledge that I'm going to say no. No matter how attractive he is, my life is too complicated at the moment for ordinary things like dates, a boyfriend. How would that even go? 'How was your day, darling?' 'Oh wonderful, thank you, sweetheart, I spent the morning chatting to a missing doctor's wife and the afternoon looking for my not dead son.'

No, it most definitely isn't going to work out.

'I'm sorry, Rob,' I say eventually, when I realise he's going to want an answer. 'I have so much going on, I'm just readjusting to being in the real world again – I'm not in the right place for dating at the moment.'

He doesn't allow his face to fall even a fraction. Or maybe he's just not that disappointed; maybe he asks out every woman he comes across, just in case.

'Of course.' He shrugs his shoulders easily. 'But just in case you change your mind . . .' He takes the pen that I'm still clutching and turns my hand over, writes a number on the back. 'That's me. Call me. Any time.'

My hand is tingling where he's touched it. Eek. It's time I was leaving.

'Thank you for saying you'll help. I'd better get back to the car, my friend, he's probably sealed off the building by now. But thanks. Thank you.'

I'm embarrassing myself, babbling, and Rob Howe is smiling again. I turn and practically fly from the room, along the corridor and down the stairs. I get the distinct impression he hasn't moved.

'What was all that about?' Nick asks when I sink into the seat beside him.

'He wants to help,' is all I can manage.

'You didn't tell him . . .'

'Nothing,' I reply a little too quickly for someone who's telling the truth. If he notices the number on my hand he doesn't mention it. 'Are you going to tell me how you knew about her phoning Mark?'

'I noticed her number in Mark's address book. I took a

swing at it and made up the number of calls, but she obviously contacted him quite a bit or she would have just said she didn't know what I was talking about. Bit of luck really.'

'So when did you speak to Mark about it?'

'I didn't, did I?' Nick looks at me as though I am a bit dense. Well forgive me if I'm not used to playing Inspector Morse. 'It was a bluff. I bet she's calling him now and kicking herself that she fell for it. Wish I could see her face.'

'Why do you think she was really ringing him? There were never any problems with my funding.' The excuse seems ridiculous in light of what I found in Mark's accounts ledger. 'And surely she shouldn't have been speaking to one of the main witnesses?'

'Definitely not,' Nick replies. 'This might be a bit of an awkward question, but do you think . . .'

'I don't know,' I answer unhappily, knowing what he's about to ask. 'You want to know if they were sleeping together and the answer is I don't know. I don't know anything any more, about anything.'

'Maybe your ex-husband isn't the saint you thought he was.'

I only allow myself a second to wonder what the hell that is supposed to mean. Nick knows nothing about Mark, or our life together. I know my ex-husband. I know Mark. I do.

37

We're back at Nick's house and I've known there has been something on his mind since we arrived. He's been fidgeting, tidying things that haven't needed tidying, and he's made three phone calls in the kitchen where I can't quite catch what he's saying. It's almost a relief when he says, 'Look, there's something I have to do.'

'OK, that's fine,' I say. 'Do you want me to go and do some shopping or something?' I'm trying to sound easygoing, but I want to know what it is that's so important. I selfishly want to keep him by me (what could be more important than what I'm going through?) but I know that's ridiculous and I don't want to sound like a petulant child. I have to remember how much of his life he's given up to help a complete stranger; he has other commitments too. Right? But why won't he tell me what they are?

'No, you stay here. If you'll be OK? You feel safe here, right?'

If I say no, will he stay? I don't want to test him so I just say yes. I don't want to sound like a wuss.

While he's away, I just walk around the house, feeling like I should be doing something, keeping busy, trying to avoid looking at my son's blanket, which has been in my handbag since Carole delivered it to me. I'm imagining him as a four-year-old child playing delightedly on a swing somewhere unknown to me. I try not to think of him being brought up by someone else, calling someone else Mummy, instead focusing on all the things we might do together when I find him. Because I'm certain now I *will* find him.

My phone rings. Cassie.

'Hey, how are you feeling after last night?'

I don't tell her that my eyes are aching, my face is tight with tears and my head hurts from thinking. I don't want to worry her so I don't say I feel like I'm a car cruising down a motorway in neutral. Instead I say, 'I'm OK, really. We saw Rachael today.'

'Oh yeah? And how did it go with Cruella?'

I smile. Never one to mince words. 'It went OK. Quite well, in a grim way. Not so good with Mrs Riley.'

Filling her in, I can sense her frustration that she's so far away, unable to help.

'I promise I'll keep you informed every step. I'll call you every day. It'll be like you're here.'

She sniffs. 'I guess you're not coming to the shelter tomorrow?'

Shit, is it Saturday again already? Part of me feels like it's been a lifetime since I received that small brown envelope; the other part feels like it happened just yesterday. The week has been a crazy blur, a snapshot out of a Hollywood blockbuster.

'Sorry, Cass, can you make me some excuse? You understand, right? I have to see this through now, I'm not coming home until I find Dylan. As soon as this is all over, I'll take you out for a Sunday roast, I promise.'

'Yeah, of course. It'd better be a carvery, though,' she

grumbles. 'And you'd better call me tomorrow. I really wish I could be there with you, but I kind of feel like I'm in the way.'

'Don't be stupid,' I say. 'You were amazing last night but I know you have a home to be at.'

As soon as she's gone, I grab a pen and paper. Lists have always been my lifeline – back when I had a life. Maybe they will rescue me now. I start writing down all the facts about my son's death. From the trial notes I can see exactly what my mind won't allow me to recall, exactly what happened that day in July 2009. Well, not exactly. Because nowhere in there tells me why my son's DNA was on that hairbrush, four years after his death.

I remember feeling so tired, so upset. Why? Why would I have been upset that day? Something that had happened with the health visitor . . . something she'd said had rattled me, made me feel like a bad mum, but I can't remember for the life of me what it was. I came home and settled down for a nap with my son. No, wait, first I made myself a cup of tea while Dylan lay on his play mat, kicking at the toy ladybird that dangled from the arch above him. I fed and winded him . . . That was it! The health visitor had asked why I'd switched to the bottle, completely insensitive considering the trouble we'd had breastfeeding. I fumed about it the whole time I was giving him his bottle that day . . . then I placed him in his Moses basket next to the sofa and . . . nothing. The next thing I remember is waking up in hospital, two police officers outside my room and a crowd of journalists outside the front doors.

Or is it? Hazy images from a dream I've had, more than once, swim in and out of focus in my mind, images of people talking, arguing. Are the images just dreams, or are they real memories of that day? It makes sense that they would be real: Mark was the one to find us; if he'd found his son dead in his Moses basket, a cushion covering his mouth and nose, he would be crying, and he would assume it was me who had killed him. Something about the scene doesn't seem right, although it's all written there in the trial notes in black and white, but I can't place what's wrong. Why can't I remember anything properly? It's so strange. I can remember other days with crystal clarity. Taking Dylan to see the diggers when they did up the local park; visiting my mother's grave to place a picture of Dylan and Dad on top. That was one of the main reasons why the doctors had diagnosed the psychosis: my complete lack of memory of Dylan's death. Although I could always sense Dr Thompson's frustration; the thought I might be acting, to lessen the impact of my crime.

I pull out the pack of aspirin I keep in my handbag to stave off the migraine that's threatening and swill a couple down with a glass of water. Without hesitation I grab a bottle of wine from Nick's never-ending stock and pour myself a glass of that as well. I figure I deserve it after what I've been through, and it might stop my hands shaking. Nick should be back soon; he can help me finish it off.

38

Jack: 16 December 1992

Keep it together, Jack. You've come this far, don't fuck it up now.

He could see things were getting worse and he'd had to do something. Shakes wasn't coming back to Durham – the situation with Beth had sent him completely over the edge and his father had pulled some strings to have him finish his degree from home. Now Jack was sitting in the police station, ready to be questioned about the murder, God, the filth really were clutching at straws.

I'm not here as a suspect. I'm here of my own accord.

The mantra made him feel calmer, more in control. The detective leading the case had offered to interview him at the university, given the family he came from, but he'd been insistent: no, he'd come to the station; he didn't want special treatment. Now he was sitting next to his father's best friend and lawyer – unnecessary, the detective had said, but his father would never allow him to cross the threshold of a police station without Jeremy present.

'So you knew Bethany Connors well?'

Jack looked at Jeremy, who nodded. 'Not really. I mean, she was my friend's girlfriend . . .'

'Fiancée,' the detective corrected. *Fucking imbecile, what difference did that make?*

'Yes.' Jack allowed a terse smile. 'Of course. But I'd only met her a very few times.'

The detective smiled back. His podgy stomach rubbed the edge of the table, pushing it closer to Jack every time he leaned forward slightly. His dark hair was slicked with the grease of a few days without washing and his face was darkened with stubble. *This man was working overtime, but he wasn't going to get anything more out of Jack. Jack would wager his own life on that.*

'Some of Beth's friends mentioned you had a crush on her.'

Jack sighed. *You could always rely on hysterical females to over-fucking-dramatise things.*

'I thought she was attractive, yes. I mean, you've seen her, right? She had that tiny little waist and tits you could balance a bowl of cereal . . .' Jeremy cleared his throat. 'Sorry,' Jack apologised, allowing himself to look chastised and trying not to grin at the detective's look of disgust. 'Yes, I found her attractive.'

'So it must have annoyed you when she began dating your best friend.'

Dating? Who did this guy think he was, the Fonz? Screwing was more appropriate; she was screwing Billy and it never would have lasted. Jack could see the look in those gold-digging green eyes whenever she looked at him; it was him she really wanted.

'Not really,' he said. 'Girls like Beth are commonplace at Durham. I'm hardly short of dates.' He emphasised the last word, mocking the detective for being so out of touch.

'So you didn't send her presents?'

There was no point in lying. Jennifer would have told the filth all about his gifts to Beth. 'Yes, when I first met her she mentioned she liked some artwork and I had it sent to her. Unbeknownst to me at the time she was already seeing my best friend; when I found out, I immediately apologised to Beth and suggested she keep the presents as a gesture of my sincere remorse. He's like a brother to

me; I would never knowingly pursue a girlfriend of his.' He hated
having to sound so pathetic, but it was working: this idiot was eating
up the 'my brother my friend' act. Jack glanced at Jeremy, who
nodded again. Jesus, how much was his father paying him to sit
there and nod?

'OK, so—' There was a knock at the door and a young police
officer entered the room. His eyes were wide, as though he still
couldn't believe someone had allowed him into a police station
unsupervised. His hands fidgeted as he addressed the detective at the
table.

'Sorry to interrupt, sir, it's just, well, we got him.'

The fat man at the table scowled. 'Fuck's sake, David, can you
not see we're in the middle of an interview?'

The young man at the door reddened at the dressing-down. 'Sorry,
sir, but Chief Inspector Barnes wants you in there now. He said—'

The detective turned back to Jack. 'I'm sorry, you're going to have
to excuse me. Can I just get you to wait here for a minute?'

Jack's heart began to pump. Had they found the tramp? The door
closed behind the detective, but not all the way. Jack got up and
opened it a crack more. He couldn't hear anything.

'I need the john,' he told Jeremy. 'I'll be back in a minute.'

Jeremy didn't have the balls to argue and Jack pushed open the
door and made his way in the direction of the two officers. Raised
voices made him stop short. Fuck, this was it. This could end it all.

39

After an hour Nick still hasn't made a reappearance, so I refill my wine glass and go back to my notes. According to the investigating officer's statement at the trial, Mark found me and Dylan and rushed us both to hospital. When the police got to our house, they found the offending cushion on the floor – where Mark had thrown it after finding it clutched in my hands – along with an empty bottle of aspirin and a pool of blood where I'd hit my head when I passed out. Mark accosted Dr Riley in the hospital car park and it was he who pronounced both me and my son dead. As they rushed us in, another paramedic noticed I was breathing, shocking the life out of them all. Once the police psychiatrist had confirmed that the blackout had probably been caused by puerperal psychosis as a direct result of the trauma of killing my son, it really was an open and shut case. I was admitted to hospital, where I woke up the next day.

I realise with some surprise that my glass is empty, and when I turn to refill it so is the bottle. How did that happen? I remember a time when you could get at least three glasses out of a bottle of wine. Uncorking a second bottle, I return to the sofa and put my feet up. I've only taken a couple of sips when I decide to lay my head down and rest my eyes, just for a second.

40

'Susan! Susan, wake up!' Something is wrong, someone is shouting, shaking my shoulders frantically. Where's Dylan? Is he OK? As I slowly take in my surroundings, I remember. Dylan is gone, I am not in my home, and the man shaking my shoulders isn't my husband, it's Nick.

'Nick, what the hell?' I sit up groggily, my head pounding and my mouth dry. 'Where's the fire?'

That's when I see what's wrong. The living room around me looks like a piñata has been battered to death above us. The floor is covered in ripped-up paper and it takes me a second to realise that every last page of jottings, trial minutes, medical notes and articles has been shredded.

'What have you done?' I shout, jumping to my feet. When Nick doesn't speak, I take in the rest of the scene. Three empty wine bottles lie on the floor next to an overturned glass, and my packet of aspirin sits on the arm of the sofa, empty but for two pills. 'Did you do this?'

The look on his face tells me he didn't.

'Well it wasn't me. Someone else—'

'How the hell did someone get in here while you were

asleep, drink three bottles of wine, empty out a packet of aspirin and rip up all this paper without you noticing?'

I know how. The wine. 'I drank some of the wine. One bottle, not three.'

'Well that explains a bit more,' Nick snorts. 'Like why on earth you left my front door unlocked while you went to sleep.'

'I thought you'd locked it when you left! And I didn't plan on sleeping, I only closed my eyes for a minute.'

Nick lets out a breath and sits down heavily on the sofa. 'For a second I thought you'd . . .' He lets the words trail off, but the end of the sentence is clear. He thought I'd overdosed on aspirin. He thought I'd killed myself.

'That's what they wanted you to think! That I'm a crazy drunk. Why else would they empty two bottles of wine and the aspirin? To make it look like I'm crazy. Do you think I should call the police?'

'And tell them someone came into my house while you were asleep . . .'

'Drank two bottles of wine, emptied out a packet of aspirin and ripped up all this paper without me noticing,' I finish dully. 'No, I don't suppose I will. They'll think the same as you did. But we've lost all our evidence, just when I thought we were getting somewhere.'

'I wouldn't worry about that,' Nick replies. 'I made copies of all this stuff before I gave it to you. Except . . .'

Except the DNA results, which I opened myself and had had on me ever since. Which had been on the table when I fell asleep.

'They're gone,' I confirm bleakly. 'Gone. My only evidence . . .'

'Don't worry.' Nick pulls me close into a hug. 'We can get copies from Tim at the lab. I'm just glad you're OK.'

'Am I? Are we safe here? Should we check into a hotel?'

Now that the initial shock and the urgency of having to assure him I haven't tried to top myself has worn off, I am feeling severely freaked out by the idea of someone being in the house again, this time while I'm asleep in it. I realise I'm pretty lucky it's just the paper shredded all over the floor.

'I don't really want to spend more time in a hotel.' Nick looks as though he's nervous enough to consider it, which freaks me out a bit more. 'I think as long as we keep the door locked,' a pointed look at me, 'and I stay by your side from now on, we should be OK.' He must see how much I disagree. 'At the first sign of any more trouble, I promise we'll ship out.'

I do feel safe with him. Despite the fact that whoever wants me to leave the past alone has followed me here to scare the spit out of me, I feel safe with Nick.

41

Sundays have long been my favourite day of the week, even before the days of dreading the postman. Back when I was married, we never worked weekends, so we'd spend a lazy morning in bed before dragging ourselves outside to go for a leisurely walk or a drive in the countryside. I was particularly fond of car-boot sales and could spend hours just strolling around surrounded by other people's junk. After we had Dylan, we'd often take him to the local park to feed what few ducks still found a home there. He was too young to appreciate it, but it cemented our belief in ourselves as a family, complete with family days out.

At Oakdale, Sundays meant an extra hour in bed – a real treat in a place where simple pleasures were rare – and then on to the chapel for service. I'd never been particularly religious, but it seemed such an ordinary, normal thing to do on a Sunday that I relished every visit, clung on to them as proof that I was still a real person. And the idea that God might grant me forgiveness for what I'd done kept me going week after week. Since my release I've swapped Sunday service for volunteering at the shelter and I figure God will be OK with that.

This Sunday the smell of breakfast pulls me downstairs. When Nick sees me standing in the doorway wearing his fluffy navy blue dressing gown, he grins.

'What?'

'Nothing. I made you breakfast.'

'Well I was kind of hoping it wasn't for the other woman you keep in the basement.' It's meant to be a funny remark but Nick doesn't smile; his eyes hit the floor and he quickly turns away. Something's wrong. I don't have the guts to ask what it is. I don't want bad news, I don't want to hear he's having second thoughts or he wants me out. I'd rather not ask; if he's going to say it, I'm not going to make it easy for him.

But he doesn't say anything.

Nick serves my breakfast and before I know it I'm tucking into the bacon like I haven't eaten for weeks. I laugh when Nick teasingly offers me a tablespoon instead of my fork. I haven't laughed properly in so long, the sound is alien to me.

'I've been thinking.'

Uh oh. Here it comes. He doesn't need me complicating his nice life, he has to get back to his job.

'Have you thought any more about Mark's involvement in all this?'

Oh. Paranoia, you little devil. Relieved, I swallow my pride and answer truthfully. Of course I've thought about it – practically every minute. 'I thought I knew everything about him. We talked about everything, not just at the start of the relationship either; sometimes when I was pregnant and I couldn't sleep he'd sit up with me and rub my back and we'd just talk for hours.' Nick is listening intently. 'He told me about his relationship with his father, which had always been strained, his childhood, and his fears that we'd never have a baby. He even told me how he thought God was punishing him for something he'd done in the past.'

Nick looks up from his forkful of beans at this revelation. Quickly I realise how it sounds and begin to backtrack.

'I don't think he actually meant he'd done something awful,' I explain. 'Just that all the bad things people do come back to haunt them.' I think of the girl in the photographs and the hidden money. 'Then again, it might be that I never really knew my husband at all, mightn't it?' The thought makes me sad, like everything we had together is spoiled with the bitter taste of lies.

'I've been thinking a lot about the girl in the photos,' I admit after a long silence. 'Who was she? Why didn't Mark ever mention her to me?'

'Maybe she didn't mean anything, just a university fling. Maybe she wasn't even worth mentioning.' It looks like the words leave an unwanted taste in his mouth.

That certainly wasn't the impression I had. Just the way they'd looked together, and the places they'd been. I'd heard millions of university stories but never met one of his university pals, or any of his friends from the past. It had never seemed strange before – they had probably all moved away to lead their grown-up lives – but now I desperately want to know what Mark's life was like before me. Even if this girl has nothing to do with Dylan's disappearance – and I don't see why she would have – I know I won't let this go until I find out why Mark 'forgot' to mention her to me. I tell Nick all this and I'm surprised to see him nodding.

'I expected you to want to find out who she is,' he admits. 'I was a bit surprised when you dropped it so easily. If she knew Mark at university, maybe she knows something about the money he hid from you too.'

'Shouldn't I just ask Mark who she is?' I know he still

cares about me, and there was a moment back at his house where I thought I might still be in love with him. If he isn't involved in this he deserves to know that Dylan is alive. Do I want to turn to him now?

Nick looks sceptical. 'He kicked you out of his home the first time you went there; I don't think he's going to welcome you back with open arms and answer all your questions about an ex-girlfriend from uni, do you?'

'But he should know . . .'

'Well when we find out what happened, you can tell him everything. Going to him now would just put him on the defensive.'

OK. 'So what do you suggest, Mr Journalist? Any handy hints and tips on stalking the general public?'

Nick grins. 'I thought you'd never ask.'

He stands up, goes to retrieve a laptop and pops it on the table in front of him. He types in a few words and after a few minutes he turns the screen around. The Durham University alumni page is open, plus another tab that links to Facebook.

'For an IT guy, Mark's a bit of a social network phobe,' he remarks. 'I've found his LinkedIn profile and there are a couple of alumni on there but no one who looks remotely like the girl you described. He doesn't have a Facebook profile.'

That doesn't surprise me. Mark always hated Facebook and used to rant on and on about how many lives it destroyed. It made me feel safe and secure that my husband didn't need to use social media; he had no interest in chasing the past, or in 'friending' or 'poking' random women. I presumed it was just an age thing; Mark said Facebook and Twitter were for teenagers to be able to moan about school and gatecrash each other's parties. Now I'm wondering if it's odd that a man who went to one of the best universities in the country wouldn't want to keep in touch with the people he shared the experience with.

'So where do we go from here?' I wonder out loud. Nick smiles as though he's happy I've asked.

'This is the number of the Durham alumni division,' he explains, showing me the web page he's navigated to. 'If we're going to find someone who went to the university, these are the people to help us.'

'That's assuming she went to Durham.'

'We better hope she did, then.'

Nick pulls out his mobile and dials the number.

'Hi, my name's Nick Whitely and I work for the *Star* in Bradford,' he tells the person on the other end. I'm a little surprised he's using his real name, but I guess we're not doing anything wrong, and the best lies are usually 90 per cent truth anyway. I listen to him as he explains how he's writing a story on social media and tracing long-lost friends and he'd like to compare the new technology to the old. He wants to know how he could find someone using only a photograph. He pauses to let the person on the end of the line speak, a woman I guess by the flirtatious tone his voice has taken on.

'Erm, just a second.' He covers the mouthpiece and asks me, 'When did Mark graduate?'

Five years before me . . . 'Nineteen ninety-three,' I reply.

Nick repeats the information and waits for an answer.

'Thank you, that's incredibly helpful. And where would one find that information? Great, Meredith, was it? I'll be sure to thank you in my story. And you.'

He puts his mobile down on the table and I make a face. '*Meredith* sounded helpful,' I remark.

'Now, now.' Nick grins. 'She was, as a matter of fact. Bill Bryson Library has yearbooks dating back to 1990 with matriculation photos from each college. And they open on a Sunday.'

'How long will it take us to get there?' I ask.

'A couple of hours.' Nick hits the keys on his laptop and a picture of the Durham University library fills the screen. 'We could be there by midday if you put some clothes on.'

It's hardly the occasion to pack a picnic, so we stop at a shop at the corner of the road appropriately named 'The Shop on the Corner' and pick up a couple of chocolate bars and a bottle of Coke. The silence in the car is charged with anticipation, but it's not uncomfortable.

'Did you go to university?' Nick asks after ten minutes. The distraction from the route my thoughts are going down is welcome.

'Yes, Nottingham,' I reply. 'I met Mark through friends when we'd both finished our degrees.'

'Did you keep in touch with any of your uni mates?'

I shake my head. 'Not really. I used to get the odd email telling me how they were getting on, but it became clear pretty quickly that they were all about careers in the City and my replies were all about wedding planning and house renovations. After the wedding, we pretty much lost touch completely.'

'Did you have many friends before you went to Oakdale?' He's trying to find out why I have no one in my life, why it's just me and Cassie. I presumed the answer was obvious, but maybe not.

'Most of our friends were mutual,' I tell him honestly. 'After what happened, it was easier to let them go than to try and drag things out and make it difficult for them.' I have no idea if Mark still sees our friends any more. I imagine him going to dinner parties at Fran and Chris's without me, a conspicuous empty seat where I used to be. Or worse still, a seat filled with my replacement.

'So Mark got the house, the car, the friends; what did you get?'

'I got Cassie,' I smile, only half joking. 'A couple of my girlfriends tried to keep in touch at first, but I did the same to them as I did to Dad. I had to approve all visits, but I just flushed away the orders. Cassie tried to sign one on my behalf but I tore that up too. At the time I told myself I was doing it for them, so they wouldn't be tied to a murderer, but looking back I guess I was just being selfish. I couldn't bear to hear how their lives were still carrying on when mine had been ripped apart. After Mark stopped coming, I convinced myself I didn't care about any of them.'

'Has anyone contacted you in the past month? Since you left Oakdale?'

I shake my head. 'It had been too long. I couldn't bear the thought of them pitying me, the uncomfortable "how have you beens" and the apologies every time they mentioned babies or a murder came on the news. I decided the best way forward was to meet new people, ones who don't know what's gone on in my life and aren't watching every word they say around me, or waiting for me to crack up again.'

'And how's that going for you?' he jokes. I let out a laugh.

'So far not so good. There are the people at the shelter, but I've kept my distance even from them. It's hard keeping a secret this big, you know?'

Nick's eyes are fixed firmly on the road when he replies a little too emphatically, 'Yeah, I know.'

I'm about to ask him what he means by that when a black saloon swings out of the junction ahead on to our side of the road and ploughs straight towards us.

I scream, Nick slams his foot on the brake, but it's no good, the car is still on the wrong side of the road and it isn't slowing down. Just as it's about to hit us, Nick jerks the wheel sideways and sends us screeching on to the pavement. We slam to a stop a metre short of a bus stop. I look up to see the black saloon straighten up on to its own side of the road and speed away.

isn't slowing down. Just as it's about to hit us, Nick jerks
the wheel sideways and sends us screeching on to the pavement. We slam to a stop, a metre short of a bus stop. I look

42

Nick looks across at me. Shock has drained the colour from
his face but he looks otherwise unharmed. There are six or
seven people stood round the front of the car peering in
through the front windscreen. One of them, an elderly woman,
raps on the window.

'Are you alright in there, Missy? Should someone get an
ambulance?'

I look at Nick who shakes his head. 'No, no, thank you,
we're fine. We'll be fine.'

She nods her head and steps back slightly but none of
them turn to leave.

'*Are* you OK?' I ask Nick and he slams his fist against the
steering wheel in anger.

'He tried to kill us,' I state eventually, unable to think of
anything else useful to say.

'Yes, he did.'

'Actually dead.'

'Yes, Susan, actually really dead.'

When I look at him again, he's shaking, and automatically
I reach out to put my hand on his shoulder. He pulls me

into his arms and we sit for a minute, stunned and scared, holding on to each other for dear life.

'Do *you* need to go to hospital?' Nick asks eventually, holding me at arm's length to check my face. 'Is your neck OK? Can you move it?'

I check for signs of whiplash, rolling my head forward and to the side.

'No, I think I'm fine.'

Nick reaches into the back of the car and pulls out the bottle of Coke. 'Here, have some of this, the sugar will help with the shock.'

'And the chocolate,' I reply. 'Chocolate helps with shock.'

Despite the seriousness of the situation, Nick laughs. 'Where did you hear that?'

I think for a moment and smile when I realise the answer. Dropping my eyes to the floor I mumble, '*Harry Potter.*'

Nick laughs as though this is the funniest thing he's heard in months, and I find myself joining in, the initial shock of what has happened beginning to dissipate.

'Are you ready to carry on before these people make our choice for us and someone calls the police?'

And that's it. No question of giving up on our journey or giving up altogether, like I know so many other people would have done. This is my fight and he doesn't have to accept the attack on his life so readily, but he has. Eventually he turns the key in the ignition and I let out a sigh of relief as the car starts up immediately. He pips his horn to move the crowd of people still gawking at us, and when they still don't move he rolls it towards them and they scatter.

'Should *we* call the police?'

Nick shakes his head. 'No. I mean we should, it's attempted murder, but the guy who did it will be long gone by now. And think of all the awkward questions we'd have to answer.'

'Nick, someone just tried to kill us. How often does that happen to you? And you think we should just let them get away with it to try again tomorrow? Or the next day?'

'It never happens to me, Susan. I'm a journalist, not a member of the CIA, or have you forgotten? I just thought you wanted to get to the bottom of what was going on here, not spend the rest of the day in a police station waiting room. And if it makes the papers, what of your new life then?'

'You're right.' God, I hadn't even thought of the newspapers. Lucky I'm travelling with a journalist. 'It just seems so surreal. Someone tries to kill us and we carry on as though it never happened.'

'You wanted proof you weren't going crazy, there it is. If whoever is following us realised it's Durham we're headed for they took a big risk to try and stop us. Maybe that means we're on the right track.'

Obviously I'm scared, I don't take attempted murder lightly, but I know now that we're going to find out what happened to my son, and I can't help but be excited by that. Either we find him, or I'll die trying. And although that's now a very real possibility, I don't care. I'm willing to die for my son. And if it's me or them, I'm willing to kill for him too.

Bill Bryson Library is a work of art. Glass-fronted, all sleek lines and curves, it sprawls itself out unapologetically. When I walk in, I feel like I'm stepping ten years into the future. It beats the old demountable hut we had in our school hands down.

The surly-looking young woman at the desk glances up at us as we approach, sees Nick and breaks into a wide smile. Apparently the face works on women everywhere, no matter how grumpy. This woman has a shock of murky blonde hair that fuzzes around her head like an 'after' shot in an electrical safety advert. She's thin, and her clothes hang off her frame like they're wearing her rather than the other way around. I instinctively want to give her a good meal. Her eyes are dark, making the paleness of her skin stand out even more. After an age, she turns to look at me.

There's a sudden pain in my head, so intense that I stop walking and close my eyes.

'Are you OK?' Nick places a hand on my arm.

'Migraine. I got them a lot . . . before.' I can't explain why, but my heart is racing. Panic overtakes me. I can't breathe, I should be able to breathe. I just want to run.

'Are you sure? You're . . .'

'Panic . . . attack,' I manage.

'What should I do? Can I get you anything? Is this because of the accident?'

I shake my head, lean it on his shoulder and he puts his arms around me. The panic begins to subside. I take deep breaths and my heart slows down. After a few minutes he holds me at arm's length.

'I'm fine now.' Only a small lie: my breathing is back to normal and I don't feel like I'm going to burst into tears. Looking around me, I remember we're in the library and people can see me. 'Sorry to scare you.'

'It's fine, really. Do you want to go?'

I force my voice not to tremble. 'No, we're here now. It's happened before, it's not a big deal.' Another lie. 'Can we get on with this?'

Nick frowns and studies my face for a few uncomfortable seconds, but eventually he nods and turns to the library assistant. She looks about my age, maybe older, but dark circles line her eyes. I'm glad I'm not the only one looking like I haven't slept in a week. After spending time with glamorous women like Kristy Riley and Rachael Travis, I'm happy to be the one who comes off better looks-wise.

Nick explains that we'd like to look at the university

yearbooks but carefully doesn't give away any more information. The woman promptly issues us with guest passes and shows us where the yearbooks are kept, scores of them, each labelled with different college names. I know Mark studied at St Chad's and we decide to start there. The woman informs us that the yearbooks are produced according to start date, not graduation.

'I came here myself once upon a time, so if I can help at all, you know where to find me. I hope you're OK now.' She gives us a parting smile and leaves us alone. The library is relatively quiet and this part is completely deserted.

'What was that all about?' Nick asks when we're alone.

'I don't know,' I reply truthfully. 'It's been a rough couple of days.'

He looks like he wants to say something but thinks better of it. He pulls down the class of '90 and opens it at the first page.

A familiar pang of nostalgia hits me when we find Mark's photograph. He looks fresh-faced and full of excitement, nothing like the man he was the last time I saw him.

'That's him,' I say, placing a finger on the photo. Nick raises his eyebrows.

'Nice-looking guy,' he remarks. It's the second time I've seen him act this way and it doesn't suit him. It's funny, because although he's right and Mark *is* a good-looking guy, he's not a patch on Clark Kent sat next to me.

'Looks aren't everything,' I say.

'Do any of these girls look like the one you saw in the photos?' he asks, ignoring my teasing. I shake my head.

'No, I'd definitely recognise her.' It's disappointing; there are sixteen colleges at Durham University and we have no idea which one our mystery girl is from. Not to mention the fact that she could have started any year between 1988 and 1992 to have crossed paths with Mark. More disturbing still

228

is the thought that she might not have been a student at all; she might have been a girlfriend from home or a waitress at the local pub for all we know.

Determined not to let our bad start put us off, we pull down book after book and study photographs from each one. It's nearly an hour before I see the familiar deep red hair and green eyes that I've been unable to put out of my mind for the last two days.

'That's her!' I exclaim a little too loudly. Looking around and seeing no one, I still lower my voice to a whisper. 'Sorry, but that's her.'

'Bethany Connors.' Nick runs his finger over the photograph and reads the name from underneath. 'History of art at Trevelyan College. She's . . . beautiful.'

The picture is the only mention of Beth in the yearbook, which is a little disappointing, but at least we have a name, a year and a degree subject, which is more than we had before. Seeing her photo makes me feel vindicated somehow: here is definite proof that I didn't imagine her. Nick is right, she really is beautiful, and I get a stab of jealousy when I think of her and my ex-husband, the man I loved, sharing intimate moments, walks around the college grounds and candlelit picnics in the park.

Nick photocopies the picture and pockets it. We spend some time browsing photos of Durham sporting events through the years and framed newspaper articles telling of the achievements of the university's alumni. When we find no other mention of Bethany Connors we decide to call it a day and head home to eat. It's already 3 p.m. and the two-hour drive back after our eventful journey here isn't particularly appealing.

'Feeling better?' the girl at the desk asks us as we go to sign out and hand back our passes. She looks like she's run a brush through her drab locks and applied some lipstick, but other than that she's still unremarkable. Her dark brown eyes look full of concern. I nod.

'Yes thanks.'

'Did you find what you were looking for?'

'Oh yes, thank you,' Nick responds with a smile.

'I didn't think to ask before, were you looking for anyone I might know?'

Nick takes the picture out of his pocket and hands it to the woman. 'Bethany Connors,' he replies. 'Did you know her?'

The woman's face changes abruptly. Her smile becomes a scowl and her busy eyebrows knit together. She looks at Nick as though she wants to strike him down.

'Is this some kind of joke?' she practically spits. 'Who are you? Are you reporters? Don't you think we had enough of this twenty-one years ago?'

Nick is as shocked as I am but tries not to show it.

'I'm sorry, I don't know what you mean,' he says, taking back the photo. I watch stunned as the woman points to the front doors.

'I'm going to have to ask you to leave,' she snaps at us. Funny how she's gone from addressing only Nick to suddenly acknowledging my presence. 'Or I'll call the police. You're here under false pretences and the university doesn't take kindly to liars *or* journalists.'

Despite the fact that we are both liars and one of us is a journalist, I feel more than a little insulted. Before I can object to her libellous outburst, however, Nick ushers me out of the library door, mutterings of 'dogs with a bone' ringing in my ears.

'What the hell was that about?' I explode as soon as we're outside.

Nick says nothing, just looks confused.

When we get back to the car, he immediately navigates us to a café that boasts free Wi-Fi and 'the best coffee in

Durham'. I test out the second claim while Nick boots up the laptop.

'Well I think I've found the reason Mrs Hyde switched her personality so quickly,' he announces after a few minutes.

'Why?'

He turns the laptop to face me, and a picture fills the screen.

'Because Bethany Connors was murdered in 1992.'

43

Carl: 16 December 1992

'What do you mean, got him? What the hell's going on?'

David was already making his way out of the door. If Carl wanted information, he had to follow, and quickly. He was reluctant to leave that jumped-up little prick Jack Bratbury, but he was getting nowhere with the kid, and none of it might matter now.

'Name's Lee Russon,' David read from a sheaf of papers as he walked. 'He's a known vagrant, got a record for petty theft, been moved on from sleeping on university grounds a coupla times. He was pulled in for pickpocketing a student, name of Harvey. They found him covered in blood and with Beth's purse hidden under his stuff and brought him in. He's waiting for us in room twelve.'

'This is bollocks and you know it.' Carl walked into the Chief's office without preamble. It had been three long weeks since the discovery of Bethany Connors' body and they still didn't have one single lead. The university had got fed up of the police hanging around, making the students uncomfortable, bringing their reputation down. Potential witnesses had clammed up, even the girl's friends were becoming hostile. Now, after all this time, they just had him?

232

The Chief Inspector stepped backwards.

'Carl, please, be reasonable. He confessed, for God's sake. I've got people in every direction demanding we wrap this one up, and a blood-soaked junkie found with the girl's purse confesses to killing her. What do you want me to do, say "Sorry, mate, there's a detective in Homicide who doesn't think you did it, so back off to the streets for you! Be a good chap and don't kill any more students." Come on.'

Carl gritted his teeth. 'Her name was Beth, Bethany Louise Connors, and most junkie tramps don't have the strength to wipe their own arses, let alone carry a body to the middle of nowhere and dump her.'

'He says he stole a car.'

'So where is it? Has he told you where she was killed? What he did with the murder weapon?'

'He says—'

'Oh fuck what he says!' Carl exploded. 'Do we have any evidence to back it up? You do remember evidence, *don't you, John? That stuff we used to use to prove a case?'*

'Look, Carl, I can see you're angry. For some reason this case has struck a chord with you. It's hard to accept that this girl, sorry, Beth, died for no reason. But sometimes that just happens. Sometimes there is no motive, no good explanation. Sometimes fucked-up people do fucked-up things. We just have to make sure those people go down for it. And he will, I promise. For a very long time.'

Chief Inspector John Barnes turned to walk out of his office, expecting Carl to follow him. 'And what if I'm right?' Carl called to his retreating back. 'What if you're putting away the wrong man?'

44

Bethany Connors was just twenty when she was abducted from outside her college, raped, murdered and her body dumped three miles away, sending shock waves through the entire university. She was a bright young talent, well on track for a first-class degree in art history, and had already been accepted by two prestigious art galleries for internship programmes. She had been due to meet her fiancé, Mark Webster, at St Chad's student bar, and when she hadn't arrived by 11.30 he had called her best friend, Jennifer Matthews, who alerted the supervisor at Trevelyan. Mrs Whitaker had called the police and a search had been mounted by fellow students. Bethany was found dead at 7 a.m. the next day – twelve hours after she had last been seen alive.

I now knew why my husband had never mentioned his relationship with Beth. According to the newspaper reports, he'd been questioned, but had never been made an official suspect owing to numerous corroborations to his alibi. Still, it was hardly a story one shared over dinner.

Trevelyan College campus is a short drive from the café, and we make it in silence. A group of giggling students direct us to the supervisor's office and confirm that Mrs Whitaker is still in charge. I have no idea what we're going to say to her and hope, as usual, that Nick has a plan and that we won't be threatened with the police again as soon as we mention Beth's name.

'Hello there, can I help you?' Mrs Whitaker is in her office. She is a small, homely-looking woman who I'm sure makes her students feel at ease in their scary new surroundings. I wonder if Beth felt safe here.

'Mrs Whitaker, my name is Nick Whitely, and this is Susan Webster.' We both shake her hand and I see no flicker of recognition at my name. 'We were wondering if we'd be able to speak to you regarding a former student of yours.'

Her eyes narrow slightly but her face doesn't lose its friendliness, yet. She motions for us to come in and closes the door behind us.

'Please, take a seat. What brings you to Durham?'

Nick sits down and so do I, hoping this will make it harder for her to kick us out. I let Nick do the talking.

'We're in the middle of an investigation of sorts,' he says, and I wait to see what story he is going to come up with this time.

'An investigation? Are you with the police?' She looks at me as though she seriously doubts I'm an officer of the law.

'No, we're not with the police; it's an investigation of a personal nature. We're here to ask about Bethany Connors.'

Her eyes narrow further and this time she looks distinctly less friendly.

'You're journalists,' she states flatly.

'Well yes, I am a journalist,' Nick admits to my surprise, 'but we're not here for a story.'

Mrs Whitaker stands up, but Nick stays seated and I follow his lead.

'I'm afraid I don't have anything to say about what happened to Beth. I can't help you.'

Nick nods. 'Yes, I thought you might say that. Perhaps you could just hear us out? Then if you still don't want to talk to us we'll go quietly and leave you to your work.' There is an open book on the table and it's clear she wasn't doing any work, but it's a nice touch. He's good at this.

After a pause, Mrs Whitaker shrugs. 'OK,' she replies. 'Go ahead.'

Nick turns to me. 'Perhaps you'd better take over. It is your story, after all.'

I'm shocked. Does he want me to tell the truth? I can't think fast enough to lie and I look beseechingly at him. Mrs Whitaker is waiting patiently and Nick gives me a small nod. He wants me to be honest, and so I take a deep breath.

'As Nick said, my name is Susan Webster,' I begin nervously. 'Four years ago I was married to a former Durham student, Mark Webster.'

Mrs Whitaker nods. 'I knew Mark Webster and I know who you are, dear.' There's no judgement in her eyes. 'I'd like to hear what you have to say, if you can manage it.'

I like her. She reminds me of my mother, a woman who always thought the best of people until they proved otherwise. I have a feeling her students rarely let her down; you can't help but try to please people like her. I nod in reply.

'Mark and I thought our family life was perfect,' I continue. 'Well, he seemed to, at least. I had no idea he had anything in his past he would want to hide from me, but I was hiding something from him. I wasn't coping as well as I thought I should. I doubted my ability as a mother and at times I thought they would both be better off without me. When Dylan was twelve weeks old, he was smothered in his sleep and I was accused of his murder.' Saying the words out loud hurts less now that I'm starting not to believe them, but it's still difficult to tell people how I was a less than perfect new mum.

'Go on.'

I take a deep breath. 'I spent almost a year on remand, awaiting trial and was diagnosed with puerperal psychosis then found guilty of second-degree manslaughter. I was sent to Oakdale Psychiatric Facility, where I spent two years and eight months. I was released almost five weeks ago. Last Saturday I received this.' I hand her the photograph with my son's name on the back and watch as she studies it, watch her eyes widen like everyone else's when she reads the words written on the back.

'Believe me, I was as surprised as you. I went to Mr Whitely for help. I believed that as a journalist he might have details of the trial that I wouldn't know where to begin to look for, and other knowledge that might have some bearing on my case – like the disappearance of the medical examiner who gave evidence at my trial. As it turns out, he's been more help than I could have imagined.' I glance fleetingly at Nick and plunge on.

'When I went to confront my ex-husband about it, he claimed to know nothing. That's when I found the photographs of Bethany Connors. I need to know whether what happened to Bethany has anything to do with what has happened to my son. I need to know whether my son is still alive.'

When I finish, I'm well aware that my eyes are glistening with tears and my hands are shaking. Mrs Whitaker gets to her feet again. It hasn't worked, I've blown it. Nick relied on my honesty and I've messed it up.

'I think we all need a drink and a more private setting. The students know where to find me if they need me. Why don't you both follow me to my house and we can talk in comfort?'

I let out a sigh of relief and Nick smiles encouragingly. As we follow Mrs Whitaker across the campus to her house, his eyes look distant and I wonder what he's thinking.

The college supervisor's bungalow is small but homely.

'Please, take a seat,' Mrs Whitaker instructs and offers us a hot drink, which we both accept. She leaves the room, and when she comes back a few minutes later it's with a tray of coffees and a plate of biscuits. Nick and I take a mug each.

'Mrs Whitaker,' Nick starts, but she waves her hand.

'Please, it's Jean.'

'Thank you, Jean. We realise that you may not want to go into what happened to Beth, but if there's anything you think we should know, we would really appreciate your help.'

She picks up the remaining coffee mug and sits down to join us. 'Susan, you have been honest with me and told me what must have been a difficult story for you. I'm going to extend you the same courtesy, but I must ask something of you first.'

I nod. 'Anything.'

There is fear in the small woman's eyes. 'If anything should come of this, if it is related to what happened to your son in any way, I must ask that my name is kept out of it altogether.'

I nod again, more emphatically this time. 'Of course.'

She nods and sits back in her chair. 'Beth was a lovely girl. I know as a supervisor we shouldn't have favourite students, but Beth was one of mine. Everyone who met her fell in love with her instantly; she had a very soft voice but her fellow students hung on her every word.' She looks upset but carries on talking. 'She was a bright and committed young girl and she had a brilliant future ahead of her. At the end of her first year she began dating Mark Webster.'

My heart speeds up at the mention of my ex-husband's name.

'Your husband was a very charismatic man, even at such a young age,' she tells me. I don't bother to correct the 'husband' part. 'He and Beth had a lot in common, people adored them both. I hope you don't mind me saying, but they made quite the couple.'

I do mind her saying.

'When they got engaged, she was over the moon. Not many people know this, but Beth had been offered a job in Sorrento after graduation and Mark had agreed to go with her.'

My heart drops and my throat constricts to the size of a pencil. Sorrento. The place Mark and I had taken our honeymoon. Had he been thinking of her even then?

Neither Jean nor Nick seem to notice my discomfort. Jean carries on but she has just ruined my memories of two of the best weeks of my life. 'In the days before her death Beth was a different person. She barely spoke to anyone and I hardly saw her with Mark at all. Her best friend Jennifer told me much later on that she had planned to break up with him. She said he wasn't the person she thought he was.'

'Was Mark ever a suspect?' Nick asks. Jean shakes her head.

'No, never. He had an alibi from around six p.m. until eight the next morning. He was drinking with friends until the early hours and passed out on a friend's sofa, where he woke the next day.'

'He was out drinking when his fiancée was missing?' It doesn't sound like the Mark I know.

'He told the police they'd had a fight and that he thought she'd stood him up to get back at him. He was devastated when her body was found, I honestly believe that. He'd called her best friend who was worried enough to call me and I alerted the police but they couldn't have cared less. Myself and some other students looked everywhere we could think of . . .'

So far I haven't heard anything helpful. Nick glances at me as though he's reading my mind. Again.

'When Bethany was found, the whole college was heart-broken. To lose a fellow student and a friend is bad enough, but the way it happened . . . When Beth's body was discovered, the police found evidence of a brutal sexual assault. She was completely naked, her wrists and ankles bruised from the ligatures that had held her, and her throat had been slashed—'

'Please, Mrs Whitaker,' I interrupt quietly. 'We know from what we've read what happened to Beth. Maybe you could tell us about what happened *after* she was found.'

She's visibly relieved and nods gratefully. 'Everyone was scared. Things like that just didn't happen in our little world. Parents demanded answers. Trevelyan and St Chad's are a twenty-minute walk apart and the easiest route is through the university grounds. It's mainly students around here and they feel safe. It was a couple of days later that the rumours started.' She takes a deep breath and I can tell this is hard for her. Neither Nick nor I speak. I feel bad that we're causing her pain, but I need to know what happened from her point of view, not just what we've read on the internet.

'One of Mark's friends made a statement to the police that he'd seen Beth in a less than reputable area of Durham, getting into a car with a strange man a few weeks before her death. The friend – I believe on Mark's insistence – retracted his statement, claiming it had been dark and he may have made a mistake about exactly what he'd seen, but the damage was done. Rumour spread like wildfire that Beth had been making money by having sex with strangers. It was presumed after that that she had got into trouble with a paying customer,' she blushes when she says this, 'and been killed when things turned nasty. With a complete lack of evidence the case went cold and the police all but gave up.' Jean looks angry, her hands are shaking and tears have filled her kind eyes. 'That's when they arrested that man, the drifter, Russon, his name was. They said he killed Beth because he didn't want to pay her.'

'You don't believe that's what happened?' I ask gently. She shakes her head emphatically.

'There's no way Beth would do a thing like that. Don't look at me like that, Mr Whitely, I'm not some naive senti-mental old fool and I'm no prude either. I know students do things that are less than savoury sometimes to make ends meet, although less so at Durham than other places, but not Beth. It was complete rubbish and the police knew it too. They were under pressure from some very important people to close the case and it was a convenient explanation at the time. I never believed a word of it.'

'But others did?'

She puts down her cup and looks at me. I've become so used to people ignoring me lately, preferring instead to direct their questions and answers to Nick, that this sudden shift of attention makes me uncomfortable.

'They believed what they wanted to believe. It's hard to convey just how scared these girls were. No one wanted to think badly of her, but the alternative was far more disturbing. The thought that another student or someone she knew might have done this to her was petrifying for them. They wanted to believe she had brought this on herself because it meant they weren't in danger. Everyone breathed a sigh of relief when the police went away, a true case of out of sight, out of mind. Life here went back to normal and sure enough, no one else got hurt. That settled it in the minds of the students; it became an unfortunate incident that no one mentioned again.'

'Did no one stand up for her?' Nick asks.

'Of course,' Jean replies. 'I and several of the tutors all begged the police to look closer to home. We were threatened with losing our places at the university if we continued to bring the college into disrepute. Her brother, Josh, was tenacious. In the end, though, even he gave in. However much we loved Beth, getting ourselves into trouble wasn't going to bring her back.'

'Do you know where her friends went after graduation? Do you think any of them would be willing to talk to us?'

'I don't know.' The supervisor gets up to take our cups and carries them out to the kitchen. When she comes back, she has a piece of paper. 'These are the names I can remember. Jennifer was Beth's best friend. She still lives close to here; as a matter of fact, she works a few shifts at the university library.'

Nick and I exchange a glance and suddenly it becomes clear why the young woman at the library reacted so violently to the photograph. She was Beth's best friend.

Somehow I don't think she will be as easy to talk to as Mrs Whitaker has been.

'You could speak to the police officer who dealt with Beth's, um, investigation. He never believed Russon was guilty, he resigned shortly after they convicted the homeless man. I don't remember his name, but I have a stack of old diaries here somewhere, I might be able to find it. And she had family, a sister as well as a brother. I don't know where they live, sorry, I never met them face to face.'

She gets to her feet again. 'I'm sorry I couldn't be of more help with regards to your son,' she says to me as she shows us to the door. I get the feeling she really means it.

'You've been more than helpful, thank you so much,' I reply genuinely. 'I'm sorry to have dragged this up for you.'

'It's no bother,' she assures us, but I can't help feeling she won't find sleep easy tonight. 'There's one more thing you could try . . .'

'Anything you think might help.'

'Well it's just I always did wonder about the boy who made the statement about Beth in the first place,' she says quietly. 'If it wasn't for him, the police wouldn't have thought so badly of her.'

'It's definitely worth looking into,' Nick says, pulling out a pen and his notepad. 'What was his name?'

'Let me see.' She looks thoughtful. 'He was Mark's best friend and neither of them came to me at Trevelyan. It was a common name, what was it?' She looks annoyed at her failing memory. 'That's it! I can't believe I forgot! He was a charming boy but I never trusted him after what he said about Beth. They called him Matty but his name was Matthew. Matthew Riley.'

We both thank her again and leave in stunned silence. In all the years Mark and I were together, he never once mentioned that Matt Riley was his best friend. They made no allusion to knowing each other during the trial, and he never told me that Riley had gone missing immediately after giving evidence.

'How do you feel about staying here tonight?' Nick asks me as we make our way back to the car. 'That way we can go and speak to Jennifer tomorrow, do a bit more asking around.'

I was thinking the same myself. I agree and pull my phone out of my handbag. I have five missed calls. Three are from Cassie, one is from my father and the other from an unknown number.

'Cass and Dad.' It's too late to call either of them now, so I send them both a text to say I'm still alive and I'll be in touch.

We check in to the Travelodge, managing to get rooms next to one another. Knowing he's only the other side of the wall makes me feel a bit more secure about being so far from home, especially after what happened on the drive up here, but that doesn't stop me from feeling a bit disappointed in myself – after my years in Oakdale, I didn't see myself relying on another man for safety quite so soon.

'I know that can't have been easy for you today,' he says as I stand in the doorway waiting to go into my room. 'Especially after . . . the library. But we're one step closer to finding out what happened to them.'

'Them?'

'Him, Dylan. Sorry, what did I say?'

'You said "them". I'm tired too. Like you said, we're so close now and I wouldn't have got anywhere near the truth if it hadn't been for you. I mean, I wouldn't even know Dylan was alive . . .'

'Susan, I'm not some kind of hero,' he starts to say, but I shush him.

'There's no need to be modest.'

'Susie, there's something I need to tell you . . .'

'You need to go back to work, don't you?' I've been waiting for days now for him to tell me, but I'm not prepared for how disappointed I am.

'No, it's not that. My boss has been really good, I haven't taken leave in years and he's told me to take what I want.'

'Then there's no problem. Unless you want to go now, unless you're fed up of running around after me. I wouldn't blame you, you know.'

'It's not that. I don't think I could stop now if I wanted to. I need to find out the truth as much as you do. I'm more involved in this than I should be because I . . .'

Oh God. Is he coming on to me? I should have seen it coming. Have I been leading him on? Does he think this is more than it is? I've been so wrapped up in finding out about my son that I hadn't stopped for more than two minutes to wonder why a good-looking, apparently single guy would want to drop everything in his life and go running around the country with someone who's spent the last three years in a psychiatric institute.

'Ssshh, tell me tomorrow. Tonight let's just forget. I don't want to talk.' I feel bad that I'm taking what I need emotionally and giving nothing in return, but he doesn't push it; maybe he feels the same. Maybe this is as innocent as it looks and he just wants to help me. Maybe I've pushed too far.

45

The sound of a telephone ringing pulls me from my sleep just after ten the next day. It's not my home phone and definitely not my mobile, I think as I wake gradually and begin to remember where I am. As I lie there, I run through yesterday's events in my head. Everything that has happened to me, everything I've seen and heard in the last twenty-four hours, still seems surreal. Eventually I throw a hand out of my warm bed and grab the receiver.

''Lo?'

'You awake?'

'Am now.'

'Do you think Mark had anything to do with what happened to us yesterday? In the car? Is he capable of something like that?'

'If you'd asked me that two weeks ago I'd have said there was no way, but two weeks ago I didn't think he'd had me framed for murder and lied to me about having a dead fiancée and a fortune in the bank. Now I don't know what the hell to believe. Should I be worried?'

'I don't know. Is there any way he might know where you are?'

'Not unless he asks Cassie.' If I wasn't so scared, I might laugh. The idea of my ex-husband and my best friend having a cup of tea together and discussing my whereabouts is ludicrous.

The banging in my head gets louder.

'I don't mean to worry you,' he says in a low, comforting voice. 'All we can do is try and get sufficient evidence to have the police reopen Dylan's case, and that means staying alive long enough to do that. I can't be sure, but I don't think we were followed after that guy ran the car at us, so it's possible whoever it was didn't know where we were going after all. We should go and speak to Jennifer Matthews, then get out of here. One step ahead and all that.'

'OK, but they saw me escaping from Mark's house, remember? Which means they followed me there without me knowing. I'd say we're not the ones who are one step ahead here.'

There's silence at the other end of the line, and for a minute I picture Nick Whitely the other side of our wall. Eventually he asks, 'Don't you feel safe with me?'

It's a stupid question and slightly petulant. It's a very teenage notion to believe that someone can keep you safe just because he's a big strong man. In the last week I've had my house broken into, been in danger while I was sleeping, been followed over a hundred miles, had my photograph taken climbing out of a window and been run off the road. And Joss. Whoever these people are, I think I'm justified in believing that a journalist from a local newspaper probably can't guarantee my absolute safety. In fact if I'm brutally honest, I'd be safer with Cassie, but I'm sure as hell not going to tell Nick that.

'Of course I do. Forget I said anything. I'm still freaked out about yesterday. I'll just be glad when we've spoken to Jennifer and gone home.'

'If she'll speak to us. She wasn't exactly inviting us around for tea when we mentioned Bethany yesterday,' Nick reminds me. He has a point, but we've still got to try.

'I'll go out and get breakfast while you drag yourself out of bed, I'll knock five times when I get back so you know it's me.'

Is he joking? Christ, I hope so.

Armed with a hefty breakfast order Nick hangs up, leaving me to make myself look half decent. While he's gone, I quickly phone my dad to assure him I'm OK. He's quiet throughout, and at the end of the conversation he tells me to be careful. I promise I will – fingers crossed – and jump in the shower.

I spend longer than necessary under the hot spray, the water that pounds on to my neck and shoulders feeling better than any massage I've ever had. I could stay here all day, but I know I'm just delaying the inevitable, so I drag myself out and wrap myself in one of the hotel's fluffy towels. Nick's made no mention of anything between us. Maybe that's not what he was going to say. I'm not ready to think about what might happen between us when all this is over – I'm not ready to think of anything other than getting my son back in my arms.

I've been out of the shower just minutes when my mobile rings. It's a number I don't recognise.

'Hello?'

'Susan?'

'Mark.'

'Where are you?' He sounds concerned.

'I can't talk now, Mark. How did you get this number? Why are you calling me?'

'I'm worried about you, Susie.' My old nickname. Seconds on the phone to him and I'm so close to tears it's unbelievable. 'Come home to me and we'll work something out. I want to help you.'

My heart pounds against my chest and my throat's almost closed. I want to do what he says. I want to turn around and go home, to the house where we were so happy. I want my husband to fix what's wrong in my life. That's why I surprise myself by what I say next.

'I'm not coming home, Mark. I need to find out what's going on here. I need to know what you've done.'

'I haven't done anything.'

He's lying. Dylan is alive, Mark's former fiancée is dead and I want to know who the hell I was married to. I stop myself telling him any of this; I can hear Nick's voice warning me not to show my hand, not to trust him, to *be careful.*

'Goodbye, Mark.' I hang up the phone and begin to cry. This is it. I've chosen to distrust the only man I've ever loved, the father of my child, and there's no turning back.

No questions have been asked, so I'm not forced to lie about Mark's phone call. When Nick gets back he either doesn't notice my puffy eyes or presumes that things have just got on top of me, which suits me fine, I don't like to lie.

The older woman behind the library desk today is friendly enough and doesn't pry when we enquire what time Jennifer will be here.

'She doesn't start until one,' she tells us as she issues us with another two guest passes. Clearly Jennifer hasn't had a chance to warn her to look out for a pair of evil journalists. 'But she usually gets here a bit early for a cigarette.'

When we go out to the front of the building, Jennifer is the first person we see. She stands out amongst the students mainly because she's a good twenty years older than them, but also because of the way she looks, the way she's dressed. Her bootcut jeans and plain black shoes aren't exactly dowdy, but they're a far cry from the black skinny jeans and suede ankle boots worn by the girls dotted around campus. Despite the fact that it's really not that cold, she wears a clunky green parka that might be fashionable on some but she manages to make it look, well, plain. Her hair, the colour of dishwater, is untouched by the GHDs used by half of the universe, me included when I can be bothered. She is holding her cigarette between her lips, fumbling in her bag with one hand and balancing a Styrofoam cup of steaming liquid in the other. When she looks up and sees us, an angry look crosses a face free of make-up.

'I'll call security,' she threatens as we reach her. I glance around but don't see anyone in uniform. I reach into my pocket and hold out the trusty lighter I've carried around since I started needing cigarettes again. She hesitates, then takes it.

'Hear us out first, then if you still want us to leave, you won't need security,' Nick promises. She shakes her head.

'No way,' she replies firmly. 'I had enough of your kind when it happened. Spinning your vile lies about Beth. You people make me sick.'

'I'm not a journalist,' I say quickly. 'I'm Mark Webster's ex-wife.'

Her bushy eyebrows lift in shock.

'Sit down,' she says at last, and gestures to the wall next to her. Relief floods through me: for a second I'd thought she was going to start shouting for security anyway.

'What do you want from me?'

'I want to know what happened to Beth,' I tell her honestly, gesturing for the lighter and pulling out my own cigarettes. 'What *really* happened, not what everyone said happened. I want to know, I *need* to know if Mark was involved.'

'You want me to tell you Mark Webster wasn't involved,' she states flatly. 'Well I can't. And if you're not here to hear some hard truths, you'd better take yourself back to wherever you came from.'

'I am. Well . . .' I falter and look at Nick. 'I'm not sure I'm ready, but I need to hear the truth. You were Beth's best friend; I need to know your side of things.'

'Why now?' she asks bitterly, and takes a long drag on her cigarette, savouring the taste of the smoke. She finally blows it out and continues. 'Why does it matter to you after all this time?'

I'm trying to be honest, but I don't want to tell this woman everything. I don't trust her.

'Mark never told me about Bethany during our marriage,' I reply. 'I only found out about her when I stumbled across some photographs of the two of them.' It's almost true.

'So you came to Trevelyan to look for an ex-girlfriend of your ex-husband, even though you knew nothing about her murder? Why would you give a toss who she was?' She tilts her head to one side and lifts her eyebrows again. They're thick and unruly; they've obviously never seen a pair of tweezers. Or hedge-clippers. She's not stupid, she knows I'm not telling her the whole story.

'I wanted to know why Mark never mentioned her,' I only half lie. 'It seemed strange that he would tell me about other former girlfriends but not this one. I know my ex-husband; I was suspicious and intrigued. I wish now I'd stayed away but I can't ignore what I found out.'

'So what do you want from me?' Her voice is softening; I think I'm winning her over. Well she hasn't called security yet, so that's a bonus.

'It's like Susan said,' Nick chips in. She looks almost surprised, like she'd forgotten he was there. 'We just want the truth.'

'And you are?'

251

I wonder if he's going to be as honest as I have been.

'I'm a journalist,' I'm surprised to hear him admit. 'But I'm not here for a story. Even if I wanted one, my boss would never let me stir up this much mud. I'm here as Susan's friend.'

I know better than to push her, but I'm not sure I can wait much longer. I'm about to say something when she begins to speak.

'You're right about Beth being my best friend at uni,' she says quietly. 'But she was more than that. She was like part of me. It was as though we'd known each other our whole lives. She was so amazing, and when I was with her I was a different person. She brought out the best in everyone around her; you couldn't be down when Beth was around.' She smiles fondly, memories lighting up her face. 'I felt so special that she'd chosen me. She could have been friends with the most popular, most affluent girls at Trevelyan, but she chose to spend her time with plain, square me. Purely and simply I worshipped her.

'In the middle of our first year, the Hill College Theatre Company put on a production of *A Midsummer Night's Dream*. As expected, Beth played Hermia. She was amazing, everyone in the audience was hanging on her every word. On the last night Mark and his friends came to watch the play. Afterwards we all met in the student bar.' Her face knits itself into a scowl. It's clear she loved Beth Connors and my ex-husband was a very unwelcome intrusion.

'Was that the first time they met?' Nick asks, gently trying to prompt her to carry on. She completely ignores him; right now she's in another place, a crowded, smoky student bar twenty-two years ago.

'Everyone was still in costume.' She smiles at the memory. 'It was the last night and no one wanted the run to end. David Thompson, from the props department, went mad the next

252

day: the university had rented the costumes from the Shakespeare Company, and Oberon – I can't remember his real name, isn't that funny? – got beer all over his tights. Lucas almost shit a brick when he found out.'

'What part did you play?' I ask. She looks up like she's only just remembered we're here.

'I wasn't in the play,' she replies, still looking bitter at the memory after all these years. 'My face was more suited to backstage.'

Always in the shadows, I think. On the outside looking in while her beautiful friend was the centre of attention. It's how I used to feel when Mark was around; he was the one people wanted to talk to, to be around. I'm no Bethany Connors. I've always been more like the woman sitting next to me, ordinary, nothing special. Not for the first time I wonder what Mark saw in me; if I was just a way of forgetting someone else.

'I didn't care,' she lies, as though she can read my thoughts. 'I enjoyed Beth's success. She had this amazing way of making me feel like her triumphs were mine too. She made everyone feel like that, that's why people loved her so much. We were all so wrapped up in her happiness. That old saying, "boys wanted to be with her, girls wanted to be her", that was Beth to a T. That night she was just radiant. Every boy in the bar wanted to be near her, but the minute Mark walked over, they didn't stand a chance.'

I understand that completely. Mark always had a way of making everyone else around him cease to exist. When he talked to you, you felt like the most special person in the room. It isn't just his looks; he has a confidence that sucks you towards him and makes you never want to be pushed out of his bubble. And outside Mark's bubble is a cold place indeed.

'I remember it so clearly. He walked over to her and said,

"What happened? Didn't they have any policewoman costumes left?" I thought she was going to punch him – no one had ever told her she looked like a stripper before – but she just cracked up and didn't leave his side all night. At the end of the evening he offered to walk her home, but she was having none of it. She turned him down so politely, then said to him, "I'll see you again though, funny man." When we got home, she spent hours talking about him like a lovestruck teenager.'

I try to hold back the feelings of jealousy. I imagine Mark going home that night, frustrated that his best efforts had been thwarted and vowing to get his girl no matter what, like some valiant fairy-tale prince. Memories of my slightly less classy and slightly more inebriated self falling drunkenly into bed with him the very first night we met come crashing to mind. How much of an easy disappointment I must have been.

What was it he saw in me? I was the complete opposite of what he was used to: I'd never been the centre of a man's world before, let alone a man like Mark. Was it because I was easy? Because I bore no resemblance to the love he'd lost? Did he love me, or was I a punishment for him, chosen because I wasn't even a close second to his first love?

'After that night they were inseparable,' she continues. 'Mark was a big man on campus, him and his friends used to strut around like they owned the place – which his father practically did, by the way. He was the last person I'd have expected Beth to fall for; she never could stand the rich list.'

'The rich list?'

Jennifer nods. 'The Durham elite. Mark was way up top, second really only to Jack Bratbury, the most affluent boy at the university. He was a nasty piece of work, the only one of Mark's friends Beth couldn't bear to be around. I think he used to hit on her in front of Mark, but Mark was too scared to say anything to him. One word from Jack and Mark would have been relegated to nothing. Beth hated the way it worked here, but Jack's father made some incredibly generous donations to the university. And didn't we all know it.' She pulls a face and finishes the last of her tea, which I'm guessing is probably stone cold by now. She doesn't seem to notice.

'Mark's best friend Matty was Durham elite and so were most of the boys he went around with. Beth said they weren't so bad really; she said she actually felt sorry for them, never knowing the true value of money. She thought Mark was different, though: he disliked the way the university worked as much as she did and hated that people thought he got in on his father's merits. The first real argument we ever had was about that. I remember saying, "God, my heart bleeds for him," and accusing her of selling out to the rich kids. I told her that before she knew it she'd be acting like she owned Trevelyan too. I was pretty harsh. She looked so hurt.' She shakes her head to remove the memory. 'I said I was sorry the very next day, but things weren't really the same after that. She kept her distance and her relationship with Mark seemed stronger than ever. That was until she turned up at my room, the week before she died, in floods of tears.'

My heart speeds up a little. This is more like it, this is what we've come to hear. I don't dare to speak in case I say something to change her mind.

'It was a Friday night, Mark's poker night with the boys. Beth turned up soaking wet and crying her eyes out. I immediately let her in, of course – it was the first time I'd actually seen her up close in a few weeks; before that I'd only spoken to her on the phone or seen her from a distance in the lecture theatre. She looked awful. She'd lost so much weight, she was pale and around her eyes was so black, I thought she was on drugs.'

'What did she say?' I ask, captivated.

'I couldn't get much sense out of her, just that she had to break up with Mark because of something that had happened. She kept saying something about how she shouldn't have gone there; she should have kept out of it. She kept talking about Ellie Toldot – I still have no idea who she is. I thought she meant Mark had been cheating on her but she said I'd got it all wrong, how I'd never understand. She wasn't just upset, she was scared.'

'What was she scared of?' Nick asks. Jennifer shakes her head.

'I don't know. Of Mark, I think, something she'd seen. She took off as quickly as she'd arrived, said she shouldn't be involving me in her problems, that she shouldn't have said anything at all.'

'Did you see her again before she died?'

'We had some classes together but she kept her distance. The week she went missing she'd barely been at class at all, and every time I saw her outside lectures Mark was glued to her side. It was like she was avoiding me completely. The night she died, I went over to her room to talk some sense into her.'

'And did you?'

Jennifer shakes her head again. 'No, and God knows ever since I've wished I'd tried harder. When I got there, I could hear through the door that she was on the phone. She said something like "What's he doing there?" and then "Oh God, Matty, fine, I'll be there as soon as I can." She sounded pissed off, and before I had a chance to knock she came rushing out of the door. She looked surprised to see me, and when I said we needed to talk, she told me she was in a bit of a rush and she'd come to my room the next day to chat. She apologised to me for how she'd been lately, said she'd had some stuff to sort out but things were going to be OK now.

I made her promise to come and find me the next day and she swore she would. She kissed me on the cheek and told me she'd missed me. I said me too. That was the last time I ever saw her.'

'Did you tell the police what you'd heard?'

'Of course I did. They didn't want to know.' Her face contorts in anger. 'I told them she'd been going to meet Matthew Riley somewhere, but they just said I had no proof it was Riley she'd been on the phone to, that it could have been her "client's" name. They pretty much called me a liar but I knew what I'd heard.'

'I thought Matthew Riley and Mark both had alibis for the time of Beth's murder?' Nick remarks. Jennifer gives him a derisive look.

'Haven't you heard anything I've said? The Mark Websters and Matthew Rileys of Durham could have found a room full of people who would swear they were on stage at Carnegie Hall if they'd wanted to.'

'What about the guy they arrested? They must have had some proof.'

Jennifer nods. 'He had Beth's purse and was covered in her blood. They said she'd gone to have sex with him.' She grimaces. 'There's not a chance in hell Beth would have slept with a guy like Lee Russon. Not for all the money in Durham.' She checks her watch. 'I'm sorry, but I have to start work. I hope you find what you came for.'

'Jennifer, wait.' Nick stands to stop her as she rises from the wall, squashes her cigarette butt under her toe and turns to walk away. 'Just one more thing.'

'What is it?'

'After Beth's body was found, how did Mark Webster react?'

She turns to look at me. 'He was devastated. To be honest, when I saw what he was like afterwards, it made me completely doubt his involvement. He was so crushed. He was ready to give up university altogether. If his father hadn't convinced the Dean to let him finish from home, he'd never have got his degree.'

'Thanks for all your help, Jennifer,' Nick says. 'We really appreciate it.'

'Doesn't make one bit of difference, though, does it? Beth's still dead,' she replies, turning to go once more. 'You want the truth? Well it won't bring Beth back.'

46

'Where the hell are you? Why haven't you called me? I thought you were bloody dead!' Cassie is shouting so loudly I have to hold the phone away from my ear until she's finished her rant.

'I texted you,' I try weakly.

'That could have been anyone! After everything we've been through, do you think I want to turn on the news and see you dead in a ditch?'

I almost laugh out loud but realise she's serious.

'Cass, the only time you've ever turned on the news is when you were on it,' I reply as seriously as I can. 'And why on earth would they show me dead in a ditch?'

'I don't think you're seeing the point I'm trying to make,' she practically hisses.

'I do, I'm sorry,' I say. 'I've been ridiculously selfish. I'm on my way back now, can I call you tomorrow?'

'You'd better.'

'Oh, could you do something for me?' I ask, before she can hang up.

'I don't know, I'll have to check my diary.' She pretends

to flick through pages. 'Ah, as expected, I've got a busy day of waiting for my best friend to call.'

'So is that a yes?' I reply impatiently.

'Fine, what is it?'

'I need you to try and find someone called Ellie Toldot.' I spell it for her. 'I'm guessing it's not an overly common name; can you google it for me? Maybe have a look on Facebook, et cetera.'

'OK, but you'll only find out if you *call me tomorrow.* Do you hear me? *Call me.*'

We both hang up and I sink lower in my seat, glad that that's over. She wasn't nearly as angry as I'd expected, considering how badly I've binned her the last few days. If I were her, I'd be furious at me.

My phone has an unread text message. Rob Howe from ZBH. Had a look at notes, nothing stands out yet. Changed your mind about that drink? If you can shake off your bodyguard long enough that is. X

I suppress a smile and fire off a quick Sorry, still minded 24/7. Worse than my dad. Is it a cliche to say it's complicated?

'She OK?' Nick asks.

'Furious. She'll be fine.'

My phone buzzes again. Total cliche. Is it unprofessional to say you make cliches sound cute? X

I reply with Totally unprofessional and end with an X. Then I delete the X and add a smiley face. See? This is why I don't date.

'Are you OK? You know, hearing all that about Mark . . .'

'I'm not sure what to think.' I don't want to talk to Nick about my relationship with Mark. I don't want to admit that I'm hurt and humiliated that I've had to hear more about my ex-husband's life from a librarian than I ever heard from him. I'm confused. I don't know if I was a distraction for him, fighting for his love with a ghost I never even knew about. Would I have tried harder if I'd known about Beth? Would I have been more graceful, more polished, more like a 'Durham elite' wife? More like Kristy Riley, more like Beth Connors? I search my mind for any hint that Mark was hiding this secret from me. Little things we did together now seem like they all lead back to his university sweetheart. Was he thinking of her when we went to see *A Midsummer Night's Dream* at the theatre? How could he not have been? Was he thinking of her when we spent a lazy Saturday at the National Gallery, or on our honeymoon? Was I just a cheap replacement?

I want to ask him all these things but I don't want to see his face when he lies to me. I just want to know what any of this has to do with my son, and how a twenty-one-year-old murder case could be linked to my baby boy.

47

Jack: 17 December 1992

'*You saw it all?*' *The voice was full of awe, the piece of ass with lip gloss attached so easy to impress. She edged closer to Jack, not even slightly mindful of the rest of his audience. Christ, any closer she'd be sat in his lap, not that he'd object. The girl – Sandy, Sammy? He didn't know and he didn't care – leaned in, her forearm resting on his chair. From this angle he caught a glimpse of a flimsy skin-coloured bra, imagined the small hard nipple that was pressing against its fabric. Jesus, he couldn't let himself get hard, not sitting with a group of people waiting to hear about the man arrested for Beth's murder.*

'*All of it.*' *He leaned back, inviting the rest of his audience to lean closer. People from other tables were listening now; Sandy/ Sammy hadn't been keeping her voice down.*

'*Like I said, I'd gone to the station with Jeremy to help the police with their inquiries. God knows, someone had to.*' *A few sniggers from around the table. The police hadn't made themselves popular in the university the last few weeks.*

'*Why did you go with a lawyer?*' *Graham someone asked, his nose wrinkled. Jack let out a short laugh.*

'*The old man would shit a brick if I set foot in a rozzer station without representation.*' *It was taken without another comment. Of course the son of George Bratbury should have a lawyer wherever he went.* '*Anyway, we'd only been there about fifteen minutes when there was a hell of a commotion outside.*'

His audience was hooked, exactly how he wanted them. He was loving this.

'*The fat idiot interviewing me went out to see what was going on, so I canned Jeremy and followed him.*' *The look on Lip Gloss's face was priceless.* '*There were two police officers, big knuckle-dragging things, both locked arms with a dirty stinking hobo. Hair down to his shoulders, so thick with grease you could have oiled the whole cast of* **Striptease** *with it. The smell in the corridor was fucking rancid.*'

He screwed up his nose at the imagined memory. These people didn't have to know it was all utter bullshit, that Russon had already been taken through to the interview room before Fat Man had been informed. They didn't need to know that the only time Jack had seen Russon was when he'd covered the filthy junkie in Beth's blood the morning after her death and buried her purse deep under the comatose hobo's possessions.

'*What was he like?*' *Lip Gloss's hand closed over his arm.*

'*He was a mess. High as a kite and throwing himself from side to side like a wild beast, trying to tear himself away from the gorillas holding him. But there was no chance. He was wailing, over and over again, not words at first, just noise. His jeans were so thick with filth you could barely see they were denim any more; he'd obviously been wearing them for weeks. And his T-shirt . . .*'

This was the best bit, the bit he'd been saving. Every breath he took drew the crowd in closer, like he was sucking them towards him with the force of his story. He paused, tried to look like he was composing himself. Jesus, he was going to come if this piece rubbed herself against him just once more. The power, the sexual high of

263

*having every person around him exactly where he wanted them,
the knowledge that he had the information every person on campus,
every police officer in Durham wanted to know . . .*

'His T-shirt was covered in blood. Beth's blood.'

48

I wake up to the smell of bacon cooking downstairs, that amazing sizzling aroma that permeates every inch of the house. I'm just about to throw on some clothes and go down when there's a knock at the door. Grabbing a dressing gown I shout, 'come in.'

'Sleep well?' The door opens and Nick walks in carrying a tray filled with food. Buttered crumpets, bacon, egg, sausage and tomatoes: everything looks amazing.

'Are you trying to fatten me up?' I ask. 'I haven't been for a run all week and all you do is feed me.'

'What would Cassie say if I let you stop eating again?' Nick grins. 'So where do we go next?' he asks as I shovel food into my mouth. 'We're still no closer to knowing what happened to Dylan.'

'I don't know,' I admit, wiping my mouth as discreetly as possible with my finger. 'I just can't believe that what happened to Beth Connors isn't related, but I can't for the life of me see how it can be. If Dylan had been murdered, or kidnapped for ransom, I'd think it was some kind of revenge for Beth's murder. But the photo I got shows a happy little boy, unharmed and smiling. That doesn't suggest revenge to me. We can't just turn up at Mark's house and ask him, "Oh, by the way, did you murder your fiancée twenty-one years ago?"'

Before Nick can reply, my mobile rings. *Shit.* Mark again? It's a number I don't know and before they have a chance to hang up I snatch it up and press the green button.

'Hello?'

'Is this Susan Webster?' A man's deep voice.

'Speaking.'

'Ms Webster, my name is Carl Weston, formerly Detective Carl Weston of the Durham Constabulary. I received a call from a Jean Whitaker, who said you might want to speak to me about Bethany Connors?'

Do I ever. I cover the phone and mouth *detective* to Nick.

'Would we be able to meet somewhere? In, say, two hours?'

I nod, then, realising he can't see me, say, 'Of course, where are you?'

'I'm coming from just outside Durham, I'll get the train.'

We arrange to meet at a café not too far from the train station. When I get off the phone, I expect Nick to be excited. Instead he looks apprehensive and suspicious.

'Who was that? Which detective?'

'Carl Weston. He's the guy who left the Durham police force because he didn't believe Russon was responsible for Beth's murder. We're meeting him in an hour.'

'I can't.' His voice is sharp. 'I have to go into work today to pick up some things. You go, you can tell me what he says.'

I can't hide my disappointment. 'You didn't mention work before. Can't you go in this afternoon?'

'Not everything revolves around you, you know.' His voice is cold and he gets up to walk away. 'Come back here when you're done. And be careful, you don't have a clue who this guy is.'

49

The cold air is biting and I decide to wait inside for Carl Weston. When he walks in, I have no doubt about who he is. He looks like a police officer, he walks like a police officer; when he sees me he deduces quickly who I am – like a police officer – and approaches the table.

'Ms Webster?'

I nod. 'Please, sit down.'

He takes a seat. He's older than I expected, I'd say in his sixties, and he's looking at me with caution, as though I might suddenly bite him.

'Did Mrs Whitaker tell you why we went to see her?'

Carl Weston nods. 'She said you wanted to know about Bethany Connors. You're Webster's ex-wife.'

'Did you meet Mark?'

Another nod. 'It was a good many years ago now, more than twenty, but I do remember your husband. We tried to interview him a few times.'

'Tried?'

Carl Weston looks up and smiles as a young waitress comes to take our order. He asks for two teas, then looks at me questioningly, as though he's forgotten what he was in the middle of. Or maybe he's forgotten why he's here at all.

'You say you tried to interview Mark?'

'Oh yes,' and he's back in the room. 'Not very successfully, mind you. The first time we saw him, he was a mess. His father had got him a hotshot lawyer – not that he needed one: his alibi was cast iron and there was no reason to believe he might have been involved. He just wouldn't stop crying. I had to stop the interview at one point for him to be sick. Anyone would have thought we were interviewing him as a suspect.'

'Is it unusual? For someone to be that upset?'

Carl shakes his head. 'Oh no. People react to loss in different ways, Mrs Webster.' He looks embarrassed. Of course, he knows.

'Of course they do.' My eyes drop to the table so he doesn't see them tear up. Thankfully the waitress arrives with our drinks, giving us both a reason to shake off the awkward moment.

'I'm afraid I can't be much help to you.' He throws me another embarrassed look. 'If I knew anything worth knowing, I'd have found a better explanation than Lee Russon.'

'So you definitely don't think he did it? Killed Beth, I mean.'

'There's just no way. After we brought him in, he was babbling incoherently. He claimed to have stolen a car to take Beth's body to the wasteland, but he couldn't remember where he'd left the car.'

'Was he mentally ill?'

Carl nods his head. 'He couldn't afford a decent lawyer and the courts accepted his confession. The thing is, Russon had nowhere to sleep and no way of getting his next meal. Inside he had a bed, a roof over his head and three meals a day. We see it all the time, vagrants confessing to just about anything to get themselves taken care of. We never usually take them seriously which is why it boiled my piss to see Russon go down for Beth's murder.'

'Jennifer Matthews said something about him having Beth's purse? And blood on his T-shirt?'

Carl blows through his teeth; he looks disgusted. 'He could have got the purse from anywhere, a bin, a ditch. It was by chance that we brought him in, for pickpocketing. When he saw the purse, it was like he'd just remembered that he'd killed somebody. The blood was on a T-shirt under his coat, which didn't have any traces on it. No blood on his filthy hands or anywhere else for that matter. Like he'd cleaned it off the rest of him but forgotten his shirt. Rubbish.'

This is all well and good, but like Carl said, he didn't know who killed Beth then, and he doesn't know now.

'What about the boy who told you Beth had been selling herself for cash? Matthew Riley?'

Carl frowns. 'Yeah, that was another inconsistency. He said it, then took it back almost straight away, the next day I think. We couldn't find anyone to back up his story about Beth soliciting, but the rest of the team took it as read anyway. I always figured he saw wrong, that his girlfriend convinced him to change his statement. Pretty little thing, practically frogmarched him into the station. I can still picture all that bleached blonde hair and her bright red face. Funny what we remember, isn't it?'

Bleached blonde hair . . .

'Do you remember her name?'

Carl smiles. 'Memory like a hawk, me, still sharp after twenty years. It was Kristy.'

So Kristy Riley was at university with my ex-husband when his fiancée died. Funny how she neglected to mention that.

'Lovely name, Kristy. Kristy Travis.'

'Travis?' It has to be a coincidence. There's more than one Travis in Bradford. It doesn't mean that Matthew Riley's wife is connected to Rachael Travis, my lawyer.

'Sounds like a movie star, doesn't it?'

'Did she have a sister, do you know?'

Carl makes a face. 'Do I. Now there's a woman even twenty years can't erase. Kicked up such a fuss about us bringing the university into disrepute that I almost framed her for the murder. I'm happy to say I've never clapped eyes on Rachael Travis again.'

50

'Nick, where are you?' I struggle to catch my breath as I throw my handbag in the car and slam the passenger door. 'I'm on my way to see Kristy Riley, can you meet me there? I've just been with Carl Weston. Kristy lied to us when we spoke to her the other day. She was at Durham with Mark and Matt and she knew all about Beth. I'm going to find out what else she's been lying about. For all we know she's got Dylan in her spare bloody room. And her maiden name was Travis, as in Rachael Travis. Call me the minute you get this message.'

I left Carl with the promise that I will call him if I get any new information about Beth's murder. The information he gave me only backed up what Jennifer had to say yesterday: Beth had found something out about her fiancé that scared her, something he was involved in with the elusive boys Jennifer referred to as the 'Durham elite'. Yet a week later they were still together, playing happy families as though none of it had ever happened. When she'd changed her mind about telling Jennifer, had she given up? Calmed down and gone back to Mark, only to be raped and murdered the following Friday? I don't think so. I think she turned to a new friend, someone whose boyfriend was equally implicated in what Beth had seen. I think she went to Kristy Travis.

The Range Rover is parked on the driveway and I pull in right behind it as close as I can. *No escape,* I think to myself.

I'm going to knock on the front door and demand that Kristy Riley tell me exactly why she didn't tell me about knowing my husband, and exactly what she knows about my son's whereabouts. I'm not going to leave until she tells me everything. Or calls the police.

Despite the car being on the drive, the house looks deserted. There's no answer, no matter how hard I bang on the front door, and a quick look through the front window shows that the TV is off and no lights are on. I'm about to give up and go away – I know, so much for my not leaving until I have the truth – when I notice something that makes my blood run cold. Through the living room window I can see into the dining room beyond, which I know from the last time I was here leads to the conservatory. What is different from the last time I was here is that the beautiful crystal vase that sat in pride of place on the dining room table is now scattered in pieces on the floor. Flowers fan out around it and water seeps around them like blood from a head wound.

I could overlook a smashed vase, dismiss it as an accident, a woman in too much of a rush to clear it up – although I don't think Kristy Riley would be that kind of woman – but that isn't all. Through the doorway of the dining room I see a heeled shoe, cast aside as though dropped carelessly. And next to the shoe is a foot.

I should get back into my car, call the police and go. Before this sensible thought can properly register in my mind, I'm making my way around the back of the house to the conservatory.

Kristy Riley is dead, unrecognisable but for the shock of blonde hair and the designer clothes she is still clad in. Her beautiful face is a mess of blood and bone, not one of her striking features left unharmed.

I stifle a scream. My body spasms and I kneel down in preparation for what I'm sure is going to be a flood of vomit spilling from my throat, but nothing comes. *Call the police,* my mind screams. *Call 999 now.*

But you can't, can you? a more rational part of me says slyly. *How's that going to look? A paranoid convicted murderer, convinced that Kristy Riley knows something about her son's disappearance, heads around to her house and conveniently finds her dead? No Oakdale for you this time, love, this is prison for sure.*

Shit. What do I do? My morals tell me to trust the justice system, do the right thing and report this. I've been brought up knowing right from wrong, and to leave the scene of a crime is wrong. But that was before. That was before I was falsely accused of my son's murder and everyone around me started lying their asses off. Now I know the truth: that the people running our lives are as corruptible as everyone else, and honesty is *not* always the best policy. That's why I do what I do. I run.

I'm in the car and halfway down the road before I consider the implications of this for Rachael. As much as I want to hate her for being a part of what happened to me, I can't forget the help and support she gave me at a difficult time of my life, and this is her sister. I can't tell her that she's dead, but it's hard to go from being grateful to someone to wishing them harm in such a short space of time. I have to warn her she might be in trouble. And as much as I hate to even consider the possibility, it might be my ex-husband she needs to watch out for.

'ZBH Solicitors, Gemma speaking, how can I help?'

'Gemma, it's Susan Webster, could you put me through to Rachael, please.'

'I'll just see if Mrs Travis is availa—'

'No you won't *just* anything, Gemma, this is serious, a matter of life and death, in fact. And you will put. Me. Through. To. Rachael. *Now.*'

Gemma cleverly senses that I am deadly serious and the phone begins to ring again.

'Rachael Travis speaking.'

'Rachael, it's Susan Webster. *Don't* hang up. This is very important.'

'Susan.' Her voice adopts a fake 'so glad to hear from you' tone. 'I wouldn't dream of hanging up. How are you?'

'Have you spoken to Mark today?'

There's a pause, and I can tell she's surprised. I swing the car left on to the dual carriageway and pick up speed. I need to put as much distance between myself and that house as possible, and I need to find Nick.

'Of course not, why would I—'

'Cut the crap, Rachael. This is important. Life or death, mine, my son's and maybe yours, so let's get something straight. I know you are related to Kristy Riley. I know your brother-in-law and my husband were frat brothers or something ridiculously childish like that, and I know you knew I was innocent and you fucked up my case on purpose.'

'I don't know—'

'You don't know what I'm talking about. Of course you don't, and I'm not expecting you to admit you do, so just shut up and listen. If Mark calls you, do not answer. If he shows up at your office, do *not* let him in. Do you understand?'

'Why?' She tries to sound defiant but she just sounds scared.

'I think he's dangerous, Rachael, and I think he might be trying to get to the people who know the truth about Dylan. Just do as I say and stay as far away from him as possible.'

'I spoke to him.' Her confession is panicked now; she's no

274

longer the cool customer I've always seen her as. 'He called about an hour ago demanding to know where Kristy was.' My heart sinks. Even after all that's happened, I'd still hoped my ex wasn't to blame for Kristy's murder.

'What did you tell him?'

'I told him she was at home, as far as I knew. He wanted to know what she'd said to you; he said he knew you'd been there the other day. He went on and on, asking what you'd said to me, what I'd told you. He wanted to know who the guy with you was and where you were staying. Should I call the police?'

'What will you tell them? That you knew I'd been set up for murder and now one of your co-conspirators is after you? You do what you have to, Rachael; I've done my bit by warning you.'

I hang up, hoping I've said enough to save her life. I don't know whether she'll call the police; I suspect she won't. They are going to want to speak to me and I don't have time for questions. I need to find Nick and then get to Mark and find out what he's done with my son.

As I pull into the offices of the *Star*, my eyes sweep the car park for Nick's car. There's no sign of it that I can see, but there are a lot of cars here and he might even have his own spot round the back.

'Hi there, I'm just wondering if Nick Whitely is still about? It's imperative I speak to him,' I tell the pretty young girl on the front desk.

'I'm pretty sure I haven't seen him leave yet.' She frowns, trying to remember. 'Most of us stay until six around here. I'll just buzz up. Who shall I say is calling?'

'Su— Emma,' I correct myself immediately, and wonder uneasily if he will be mad at me coming here. I'm in too much of a state to care. 'He'll know who it is.'

'Sure thing.' The girl picks up the intercom and even in

my panic I wonder briefly if she and Nick have ever got together. I presume most women would fall into his bed given half the chance. It takes me a minute to remind myself that I don't care about Nick's personal life.

'Nick? There's a woman called Emma here to see you.' She replaces the receiver. 'He's on his way down. You can wait over there if you like.' She points to a seating area and smiles.

'Thanks.' I smile back, trying not to convict her of an offence she's only committed in my mind.

My fingers tap nervously against my thigh as I wait. I wonder if Kristy Riley has been found yet. Will Rachael have called the police and told them my fears about Mark? It seems to take a lifetime for the lift to sound, and my head snaps up, but it's only an elderly gentleman who steps out and crosses the foyer. He looks slightly eccentric in his white pinstripe shirt stretched over a portly belly, and his burnt orange bow tie. The top of his head is bald and shiny, with tufts of brown and grey around the sides. He walks over to where I'm sitting and smiles warmly.

'Hello, how can I help you?' he asks.

'Oh, I'm being taken care of, thank you,' I reply. 'I'm waiting for Nick Whitely.'

The man looks confused. 'Yes, that's me. I'm Nick Whitely. And you are . . .?'

51

Beth: 20 November 1992

'If you want to find out if he's telling the truth, you should just follow him.'

She'd dismissed the words as crazy the minute Jen had uttered them so offhandedly, but they had followed her around all week until she couldn't ignore them any longer. Now, though, now that she was crouched behind the rain-soaked bushes staking out the disused building like some kind of secret squirrel, the idea seemed crazy once again.

Beth had seen them turn up one by one, the boys her fiancé called friends, knock four times on the warehouse door and slip inside without a word. All she had to do now was creep up to one of the broken windows and try to sneak a look through, see them playing poker or whatever it was boys did when they had a night of freedom. Then she could make the three-mile trek home in the cold and dark feeling stupid but relieved all the same.

OK then, here goes. She had her story all planned out in case she was caught: her sister had called, her father had been taken ill and she needed to speak to her fiancé. That wasn't so unreasonable, was it? And Mark wouldn't be mad if all he was doing was playing poker. Beth hoped her story wouldn't be tested; she'd worry about explaining Dad's miraculous recovery later. Maybe she should say it was Josh who was ill. They never saw him anyway so it wasn't like he'd drop her in it.

This was crazy. Why did she need to go and look? She'd watched the boys arrive; she knew Mark must be telling the truth. What did she think they were doing in there? She got to her feet, suddenly feeling very stupid. She should go back to her room, get a bottle of wine and take it over to Jen's. They would have a drink and laugh at her temporary insanity. It was about time she spent some quality time with her best friend; she knew she'd been neglecting Jen, choosing to spend all her free time with Mark instead. Maybe it was time to cool things off, build some bridges.

Through the darkness the distant hum of a car approaching made her drop to a crouch once more. The black Vectra, a car she didn't recognise as belonging to any of Mark's friends, drew slowly up to the warehouse and came to a stop less than twelve feet away. Beth held her breath as the driver's door opened and Jack Bratbury stepped out. She let her breath out as slowly as possible and silently prayed that he wouldn't spot her. If Jack saw her crouched there in the bushes, Mark would never hear the last of it.

Beth hated Jack. Loud and brash, he was the leader of the group and a bully. He had taken a shine to Beth and would hit on her at every possible opportunity, whether Mark was watching or not. Especially if Mark was watching, it seemed. 'He's just messing,' he'd say when Beth expressed her discomfort. 'Just a bit of fun because he knows it winds you up.' It wasn't her idea of fun, and Jack wasn't her idea of a friend, but she understood why Mark didn't speak out, even if it infuriated her.

She watched as Jack walked around the front of the unfamiliar car and came to a stop on the passenger side. He opened the door slowly and a pair of long female legs unfolded from within. Beth didn't recognise the girl who followed them, and she knew that if she'd seen this girl before she'd remember. Her long blonde hair

278

skimmed her generous breasts, barely covered by the tiny skin-tight leotard she was wearing. Beth felt a chill just looking at her; God only knew how cold the girl must be feeling. An unsteady falter when she began to walk suggested it was probably alcohol keeping her warm.

Who was she? Beth didn't think she'd heard Jack mention a girlfriend, and anyway this was supposed to be a boys' night, a detail that had apparently eluded this trampy-looking creature. She watched as the pair approached the door, knocked four times then slipped inside, swallowed up by darkness.

There was no way Beth could just leave now. She had to know who this mysterious scantily clad girl was, and what she was doing here tonight. With as much stealth as she could manage on shaking legs, she approached the building.

The windows of the large industrial unit had long been boarded up from the inside, partially rotted boards masking the events unfolding within. It didn't take Beth long to find a fist-sized hole in one of the boards large enough for her to peer through; what took slightly longer was for her to pluck up the courage to press her eye to the hole and peer into the darkness within.

It took her eyes what seemed like an age to process the scene that met them. The absence of light inside the unit had been countered by what looked like a hundred candles, each a different shape and size, casting an eerie glow around the vast space. A large rectangular table covered in black cloth stood in the centre of the room, made visible only by the candles that lined each side, their flickering lights reflecting off goblet-shaped glasses filled with a dark liquid. The ornate oak chairs that sat around the regal looking centrepiece were empty, their intended occupants choosing instead to mill around the edges of the room.

This certainly didn't look anything like a poker night, although what it did look like eluded Beth completely. The boys who had entered the building one by one were now wearing long black robes, black hoods falling forward to create dark holes where their faces *should be. Trying to pick Mark out from the group proved impossible; each figure was a similar height and stature. They stood together in twos and threes, some sipping on glasses of the dark liquid – please God don't let it be blood, she thought for a frantic second – others dragging furiously on cigarettes. Even from outside in the cold Beth could feel the tension in the room; it ran across her skin in waves, radiating from everyone within. Something was going to happen – something more than a game of cards – she could sense that much.*

Where was the girl? She was the one Beth had stayed to see, yet for a moment she seemed almost inconsequential, lost in the strangeness of the scene. Someone spoke, a short, sharp instruction, although Beth couldn't make out the exact words. Some of the covered heads turned towards the corner of the room; others seemed to avert their gaze. Beth strained to see what they were looking at, but billowing robes obscured her view.

The voice spoke again, low and commanding, and Beth knew it must be Jack. The others in the room simply obeyed. Each man took his place at the table and Beth saw what they had been looking at. The girl.

52

'I think there's been some mistake.' Once the shock has worn off, I gather my composure and shake my head. Have I come to the right place? 'I am at the *Star*, right?'

'Indeed you are.' The man who claims to be Nick Whitely nods in reply. 'The one and only.'

Granted I can't see it right at this second, but I know there will be a rational explanation for this.

'I'm looking for a man I've been dealing with who works here. Is there another Nick who works for you? He's about six foot two, short dark hair, bright blue eyes, smartly dressed.' I can see this isn't making any sense to the man in front of me. The girl from behind the desk has come out and is quietly tidying the newspapers on the table near us, probably as a way to find out what's going on – I remember how valuable office gossip is.

'No, I'm sorry, I don't know anyone here who meets that description. Terri?' He turns to the girl, making it clear that he's aware she's eavesdropping.

'Sounds like someone I'd remember.' She shrugs. 'Sorry.'

'What did you say your name is?' he asks, and I realise he knows exactly who I am.

'I didn't. Sorry, I must be at the wrong place. My mistake.' I stand up and flee before either one can ask any more questions.

Back in the car, the shock rises from my stomach to my throat. Nick has lied to me all this time. I've been so stupid, trusting that he is who he says he is, allowing a perfect stranger into my life. I feel as though I've had a one-night stand that I'm too drunk to remember. And now I have no idea where to go or what to do. Should I give up and go to the police? I don't feel like I can do this without Nick. Someone is dead and this is beyond serious.

I drive down the street and park up somewhere that isn't full of journalists to gather my thoughts. If Nick isn't Nick Whitely of the *Star*, then who the hell is he? Is he friends with Mark? God, maybe he went to uni with them, one of the Durham elite even. It would make sense; he could have faked the wine and aspirin episode to make me believe I'm going crazy. Did he break into my house? *Kill a stray cat?* But it's been him who's convinced me there might be some truth in my claims; he's championed my beliefs, made me feel vindicated. Why would he do that just to try and scare me off? To stay close to me, to find out what I know? Then just as we get near to the truth, Kristy Riley is murdered in her own home. *Possibly just minutes after I left a message on Nick's phone telling him I knew who she was.*

My phone buzzes in my pocket. *Nick?* It isn't; the name ROB flashes across the screen: How are you? X I shove the phone back into my pocket. I don't have time for Rob Howe now; all I can think about is what to do about Nick.

I want more than anything to drive to his house and confront him, scream and shout and demand an explanation, but the fact is, he could be dangerous or crazy, probably both. At the very least he is a liar, and a damn good one.

Although saying that I never once questioned who he said he was. In fact looking back at our first meeting I'm not even sure I didn't tell *him* he was a reporter. He could be anyone. Holy shit, what kind of trouble am I in?

No, I decide, I can't go back to his house. I haven't left much there, nothing I can't sacrifice for my own safety, and I still have some toiletries and clothes in the car with me. I have to go somewhere safe, decide whether or not to approach the police with what I know so far. There's no way I can go home. Nick knows where I live, and if he's in this with Mark, he has undoubtedly passed on the information. Dad? I don't think he'd mind, but the thought of putting him in danger, not to mention telling him about Kristy Riley's death and what I've found out about Nick, doesn't sound awfully appealing. I'm not in the mood for a serious discussion about my poor judgement when it comes to pretty men. My only real option is Cassie. I already feel bad that I haven't really kept her in the loop the last few days; everything's been happening so quickly. Can I really ask her if I can stay at her house now?

I think about all the things we've been through together and know she will be OK with it. She is my best friend, and once I tell her about the trouble I've got myself into, she'll know exactly what to do. *Please God let her know what to do.*

53

Beth: 20 November 1992

The girl moved between dark-cloaked figures at the table, refilling their glasses from a bottle of red wine – thank God for that! – and smiling pleasantly at each of them. So she was a waitress. Beth sighed with relief. Trust Jack. He couldn't just hold a poker night; he had to have scantily clad waitresses and ceremonial robes. At least she could make a move now. As soon as she could tear her eyes from the girl.

She moved with the fluidity of a dancer as she brushed lightly against one of the figures and leant over him to fill his glass. A large hand emerged from the robe and brushed against her nearly bare buttocks. His fingers moved lower, pushing aside the small strip of material between the girl's legs, and disappeared. Beth bit her lip. It's not Mark, she told herself firmly. Mark loves you, it's just one of his friends being sleazy.

The stripper – that was how Beth had come to think of her – flinched and moved quickly away from the wandering hands. She glided, slightly more quickly than before, to the top of the table, where the man that Beth presumed was Jack sat, and leant over to fill his glass. Before she could retreat, Jack caught her elbow, pulled her closer and whispered in her ear. Even from a distance, even through this tiny hole, Beth saw the girl's eyes widen. She shook her head firmly and tried to pull away, but Jack's grip was tight. He spoke again, his hooded face closer to hers now, more insistent. The girl's face fell and Jack released her elbow, triumph radiating from his body even while his expression was hidden. The girl stepped to one side, fixed her eyes to the floor and began to slip her arm out of the skin-tight leotard. Every head at the table turned to watch the reluctant striptease. The girl moved slowly, as though she hoped it was a joke, that someone would shout 'Stop, just kidding!' but no one did.

The man at the head of the table stood, pushing his chair roughly aside. He grabbed the girl and pulled at the garment impatiently. Beth saw the flimsy material tear under his powerful hands and he cast it to one side. Underneath the leotard she was wearing only a small pair of briefs, a fact Beth was certain she regretted now. This had gone too far. Should she intervene? Could she just go in there and walk out with the girl, easy as that? She didn't think so. Jack wouldn't let it happen, and anyway, how would she explain why she had been skulking around in the shadows, spying on them?

Maybe she should call the police? No one would ever have to know it was her. But wouldn't Mark get into trouble? Was anything these boys were doing illegal anyway? Beth had seen the girl arrive with Jack. She hadn't looked as though she had been brought there against her will, and even now she had gone back to serving the drinks, albeit with slightly less enthusiasm than before. What if this was all some big game? The police might even charge her with wasting their time.

The atmosphere inside the room seemed to have palpably changed now. The fug of anticipation and trepidation had dissipated, leaving behind a lighter mood. The boys were happy with the naked girl moving among them, getting drunk on it. The girl continued to make sure glasses were full, but now she had taken on a new role, holding cigarettes as the men smoked and lifting glasses to the lips of the *drinkers. The sly, unobtrusive pats on the backside had become more blatant, hands darting out of robes to grab at the girl's bare flesh, pinching and groping as they pleased. She could see the boys were pleased with themselves; behaviour they could never dream of showing in public was positively encouraged around this table.*

As the girl leant over to take one of the glasses from the table, her arm was grabbed roughly by the man next to her. She froze, fear flashing across her pretty face. The hood turned towards the girl's chest and closed around it. When the man pulled away, an angry red mark lingered on the girl's bare breast and her skin was slick with moisture. Was that man Mark? Beth couldn't bear to watch any longer.

The figure at the head of the table spoke again and the room was silent. His words were commanding and must have been aimed at the girl, as she immediately walked over to stand next to him. He took a handful of her thick blonde hair and pushed her face roughly into the table. Beth cringed as she heard the thump of flesh connecting with wood even from where she stood. The figure motioned for the man next to him to stand and approach the girl from behind. Beth saw the dark robes open from the front and close again around the girl's slight frame. She knew what was coming next and she really could watch no more. Gasping for breath, tears streaming down her cheeks, she turned around and ran into the darkness.

54

Cassie's house is much like she is, always spotless and looking its best. I don't know where she got the money from, and I'd never ask – knowing the details will probably only make me an accessory to some crime or other – but somehow she acquired this beautiful house and a car less than a year after her release. She's proud that it's the first place she's ever owned without a man's help – although I seriously doubt she saved up her weekly wages from her canteen job at Oakdale for a deposit.

I spot her car in the drive and feel stupid that I'm so nervous about seeing someone I spend almost every day with. Taking a deep breath, I knock on the door.

'Susan?' Cassie looks suspicious to find me on her doorstep. 'What are you doing here?'

'I'm in trouble, Cass, can I come in?'

She looks reluctant to let me in and I get a fleeting crazy notion that there's someone inside with her. *Is it Nick?* After a couple of seconds she nods and opens the door wider. There's no one there. I'm getting paranoid and crazy. *Crazier.*

'Thanks,' I say gratefully, following her into the front room.

'So what is it?' Cassie's voice is tinged with ice and I instantly regret coming here. Something's changed between us and I know I've caused it.

'It's Nick,' I say almost reluctantly. Should I just leave? Go to my dad's and confess my stupidity? I don't know why I don't tell Cassie about Kristy Riley but for some reason I don't want to. This isn't the Cassie I know and trust.

'What's the matter, did he leave the toilet seat up? Crumbs in the bed, or wait, was it wet socks on the bedroom floor?'

'What are you talking about? I'm not sleeping with him, if that's what you're implying.'

My best friend laughs without humour. 'I'm not implying it, Susan, I'm saying it. You must think I'm so stupid.'

'We're both stupid, Cass,' I inform her wearily. 'We're both really stupid. I'm so sorry.'

Cassie looks confused. 'Don't tell me, he's married.' Her voice still sounds cold, but now she's curious too.

'I have no idea. He could be married, widowed . . . hell, he could be gay for all I know about him.' I tell her about turning up at his office to find the real Nick Whitely, bald and elderly, and when I'm finished she looks just as pissed off as she did before, if not more.

'So when it all falls apart and golden boy turns out to be a dirty rotten liar, you come running to me,' she spits out venomously. 'And I'm expected to pick up the pieces and not say "I told you so".'

I'm genuinely surprised at the anger in her voice. I mean, I can understand her being slightly fed up with me, but this is out of proportion.

'I'm only going to say this once: yes, I'm attracted to him but there has been nothing between me and Nick . . . well, whatever his name is. I'm sorry we took off to Durham without you, and I shouldn't have shut you out. It's just been so crazy, everything's been happening at once. If I'd known you were going to get jealous . . . I didn't even realise you liked him . . .'

Cassie looks at me with pure disgust in her eyes. 'I think you'd better leave,' she says, and I feel like someone has punched me in the stomach. I don't know where else to go.

'What?' I say stupidly.

'Just go, Susan,' Cassie repeats, shaking her head. 'I do really hope you find Dylan and get your happy ending.'

I pick up my bag and leave the house, feeling hurt and bewildered. OK, I made a mistake, but surely it isn't worth ruining three years of friendship over. I'm tired and every muscle in my body aches. All I want to do is collapse on to a bed, any bed, and sleep. But I can't. I'm going to have to go to the police. I'm going to hand myself in; tell them everything I know about Dylan, Mark and even Kristy Riley. At least in prison I'm safe from all the people trying to drive me crazy, or worse. Exhausted and confused, I get back in my car and head for the nearest police station.

I've been driving less than ten minutes when my phone rings. Nick's name flashes across the screen and my heart begins to pound. Barely taking my eyes off the road ahead, I reach over, click the cancel button and the call joins the other three missed calls on the list. My phone responds by ringing again. This time 'Dad' shows up on the screen.

'Dad, hi. I'm driving right now, can I call you back?'

'It's urgent, Susie. I've just had a visit from the police. They, erm, they want to speak to you.'

My heart speeds up again and fear spreads through me, starting with a tightening in my chest. 'What do they want? Is it about Mark?'

'Yes and no. Susan, they said a woman is dead and they want to speak to you and Mark in connection with her murder. They think you killed her.'

Shit. Shit, shit, shit. 'I didn't, Dad. I had nothing to do with that woman's death.'

'Of course you didn't, darling,' he says with absolute conviction. Relief floods through me. If my dad believes me, then everything is going to be OK. 'I just wanted to warn you. Whatever's going on, a woman is dead and I'm worried about you. What are you going to do?'

'I don't know, Dad. I'm scared.' It's good to admit how I feel out loud and I'm so glad to have my father back in my life. Even if I am potentially about to go back to prison for another murder I didn't commit.

'I'll call you in a little while,' I say before my father can speak again. 'I think I'm going to hand myself in and explain, hope they believe my crazy story. I'll call you. I love you.'

'I love you too, Susan. Take care of yourself.'

'I will, Dad.'

I pull into a side road opposite a park full of mothers playing happily with their children. There's a toddler on the slide, laughing gleefully as he slides down into his mother's arms and quickly runs around to the steps to start again. I sit and watch, imagine that I'm that mother, that Dylan is the little boy sliding down towards me. I whisper a silent prayer that I'll find him safe and sound and that I'll be whole once more, no longer a jigsaw without a piece, a snuffed-out candle, a mother without a child.

The shrill sound of my mobile phone ringing for a third time shocks me from my trance. I look down, but it's a number I don't recognise.

'Hello?'

'Is that Susan?' The voice is female and unfamiliar. She doesn't wait for me to answer. 'This is Margaret. Margaret Webster.'

I know who this woman is. Although we've never met, her presence was with me throughout my married life. She was conspicuous by her absence at my wedding, the birth of my son, and then his funeral. Margaret Webster is my ex-mother-in-law.

'Margaret? What are you doing in this country?'

'I live in this country, Susan, in Halifax. I'm not sure what Mark has told you, but I've always lived here. And I'm ringing because Mark is missing.'

'Mark is missing?' I snap angrily. 'You do surprise me. Tell me something I care about.'

So she does. 'He's gone to find Dylan.'

55

Mark: 27 November 1992

What was he doing here?

Mark had asked himself the question over and over on the drive up. He'd only just managed to convince Beth not to go to the police after last week, thanks to Kristy. And she'd threatened to call off the engagement if she ever found him near this place again.

Yet here he was.

He'd been trying to tell the Brotherhood all week that he was leaving, but he'd not yet managed to conjure up the strength.

Tonight. When tonight was over, he'd tell Jack once and for all.

The dark room was slowly filling up with the hooded figures, a ritual he'd become accustomed to over the past few months. He still remembered the night Jack had introduced the robes. That was the night things had begun to change, to twist and distort until nothing but a warped interpretation of the Brotherhood that Jack's great-great-grandfather had been a part of had remained. Eleh Toldot. These are the generations.

Jack was the last to arrive, as always. Mark shuffled uncomfortably, picking up his wine and putting it back down again in between wiping his clammy palms against his floor-length black garb. It was impossible to relax, even more so than usual. Beth thought he was away for the weekend, visiting his parents as a way of escaping the weekly meeting until he could tell them his time was up, yet here he stood, drawn to the disused warehouse like a crack addict to his pipe.

'You OK?' Matty's voice broke into his thoughts, dragging his mind back into the room. Matt was the only one who knew of his intention to leave, and Mark still hoped he would come with him. Matt had gradually become the best friend he had, as he'd come to realise what Jack was really like. He thought Kristy wanted Matt to leave too, but Matty had known Jack longer, plus Kristy wasn't as insistent as Beth. Kristy had known about Eleh all along, although she'd only discovered the depths of the Brotherhood's depravity when Beth had turned up at her room last week and broken down. Even then she'd accepted it. Mark knew that Kristy was the definition of a gold-digger; he'd swear she'd only come to university to find someone who could give her the privileges that came with being associated with the Durham elite. She valued that too much to force Matt to make a choice. She was different to Beth: no morals, no principles.

The air inside the room was saturated with tension, a mixture of excitement and fear. Some of the faces visible to him beneath the hoods were filled with boyish glee; others looked like they were going to be sick. Mark knew he wasn't the only one horrified by what the Brotherhood had become; he also knew none of the others would have the courage to leave with him.

'Mark? I asked if you were OK,' Matty repeated, his voice low.

'I'm fine,' he replied, not trusting his voice enough to elaborate.

'Well you look like shit. Pull yourself together or Jack will see there's something wrong straight away. Just get through tonight and we'll find a way for you to tell him you're out.'

Mark nodded.

Just get through tonight. Easier said than done.

56

The words seem to take an eternity to sink in. 'He's what?' I say stupidly, but there's no way I misheard her. My ex-husband has gone crazy. He's killed an innocent woman and *he knows where my son is*.

'I'm so sorry, Susan, I know this will come as a massive shock but I'd rather not talk about it over the phone, we really don't have time. Richard is out searching for them now.'

'Richard?' I interrupt quickly. 'As in Richard Webster, Mark's father?' I don't add *Mark's dead father*.

'Yes, you sound surprised.' She doesn't wait for me to elaborate. 'Can you come here, Susan? I think we need to talk.'

'Where is here? Where has Mark gone? Where's Dylan been all this time?'

'I don't know where Dylan's been, Susan, Mark doesn't know. There's some explaining I need to do.' She gives me details of their address in Halifax.

I mentally calculate how fast I can get there. It's going to take me over an hour – anything could have happened to my little boy by then. Pictures of Mark sitting in his car, windows closed as exhaust fumes fill the small space, run through my head, but what choice do I have? He could be anywhere by now; there's nothing for me to do here except call the police, and what's the likelihood they are going to believe a murder suspect when she says that her ex-husband has gone to find her dead son, and her dead father-in-law is out searching for them both?

My decision is made. 'I'll be there as soon as I can.'

'Have you found them?' I demand the minute Margaret Webster opens the door to me fifty minutes later. I've broken every speed limit on every road on the journey here, and between speed cameras and congestion charges I'm likely to be bankrupt and banned from driving for life. I don't wait to be asked in. I don't introduce myself. 'How does he know where Dylan is? How does he know he's alive?'

I push past Mark's mother. The house is beautifully kept, a huge detached show home, and normally I would soak in every detail. Right now I wouldn't have cared had the walls been painted in molten gold and a naked footman answered the door.

'No sign of them,' the woman replies. She's biting her lip and her eyes flit to the door every few seconds. 'Oh God, this is such a mess. I'm so sorry.'

She takes my elbow and leads me through to the living room, where a pot of tea and two mugs sit on a glass coffee table. It would seem even the very rich put the kettle on when the going gets tough.

'We hadn't spoken to Mark for years when Dylan was born.' Margaret pours me a mug of tea and passes me the sugar. With shaking hands I add four spoonfuls. The hot sugary drink calms me down slightly, although the intense feeling of dread doesn't dissipate. I try to tell myself that Mark would never hurt Dylan, but the fact that for the past few days I've been telling myself he couldn't have hurt his ex-fiancée only for him to murder his best friend's wife hasn't entirely escaped me.

'Why not?' I ask.

'He didn't want anything to do with us.' She still looks hurt by the memory. I can feel my anger returning but I'm trying to rein it in. Despite what these people have done to me, my son's safety is the only thing that matters now. The rest of the emotional shitstorm can be dealt with later. 'It all started when Beth died.'

'You know about Beth?' It's a stupid question, of course she does. This is Mark's mother, the woman who brought him up, fed him, clothed him, sang him sweet lullabies to get him to sleep and comforted him when he brutally murdered his fiancée.

'Beth was practically part of the family at one time.' Ouch.

'The night she died, Mark turned up here around two a.m. He was crying, absolutely hysterical and babbling something about the Brotherhood. Richard took him into the office where he thought I couldn't hear them, but I could of course. Mark told Richard how he'd killed Beth, he hadn't known, it was an accident. He just kept saying he hadn't *known*. He wanted to go to the police, but Richard put a stop to that idea. He sent him straight back to Durham and promised it would be sorted. The next day, when Beth's body was found, the police were everywhere; they wanted to talk to me, to Richard, to Mark. Then they were gone. Within three weeks the investigation was over and I was left to pick up the pieces.'

'How could you just pretend you didn't know?'

Margaret shrugs. 'It was easier than you'd think. I had a choice. Either pretend I'd heard nothing, or tear my family apart, drag our name through the mud and send my only son to prison.'

Well, when you put it like *that* . . .

Margaret stands and walks to the window, her eyes searching for any sign of her husband and son.

'Mark began to fall apart,' she continues, her voice thick with emotion. 'There was no way he was going to finish his degree, he was having a breakdown. As usual, Richard waded in and used his money to fix everything. Durham allowed him to finish his degree from home, and we got our son back. Except we didn't, did we? The man we got back had changed and he was never the same. He hated Richard, hated everything about the way he'd taken over. It was clear he blamed his father for stopping him going to the police that night. He moved away and told everyone Richard was dead. I came out of it lightly, I just emigrated to Spain.' She laughs, a humourless exhale. 'Richard always hoped he'd come round; he kept sending his monthly allowance until Mark told him that if he didn't stop, he'd tell the world what had happened to Beth.'

The money I'd seen in the savings account; that had been my husband's *monthly* allowance? Holy shit, I'd known Mark's parents were wealthy, but this was money on a scale I hadn't even imagined. *Blood money*, I tell myself, *money that can make dead bodies disappear and steal sons from their mothers without question.*

'How does any of this matter to me and my son?' I demand, feeling my anger rising again. Does this woman expect me to feel sorry for her? I've just found out that the last four years of my life were spent without my son *when he was alive all along*, and she's complaining that her precious Durham scholar wouldn't accept his pocket money?

'We hadn't seen Mark for fifteen years when he turned up on our doorstep four years ago to tell us what had happened to Dylan. *Fifteen whole years.* You think four is hard? Multiply that by four and that's what I went through Susan.

And then one day he's back, clutching a picture of the most beautiful baby I'd ever seen. He practically stormed through the front door and barked at me that he needed to speak to his father. When they came back after an hour, Richard told me never to mention to anyone that he had been here. He said the baby's mother had had a psychotic turn, she was suffering from post-natal depression and had killed her son.'

'I would never threaten my son,' I whisper fiercely. 'I love my son.'

'I suspected as much,' she replies simply. She moves away from the window and comes to sit in front of me again. 'Even after that day, Mark was still furious at his father for whatever had happened at university – more so now, it seemed. Then a week or so ago he turned up here again, shouting and yelling about you, about a photograph you'd been sent. That's when the men started showing up. Private detectives, I'm sure of it. I didn't know what was going on at first, but eventually I overheard enough to figure it out. They've been looking for Dylan.'

'They said I killed him.' Cold tears run down my cheeks, pooling on my collarbone. 'How could they be looking for him?'

Margaret looks at me at last, her eyes full of pity. 'They say money talks, but that's not always true, Susan. Sometimes money buys silence.'

'What does that mean? What kind of people are you? Why didn't you say anything?'

'It was too late. I didn't know the whole truth, certainly not enough to be sure that Dylan was alive and you were innocent. Once again the truth threatened to finish us, and to be entirely honest with you, I was being selfish. I had my son back in my life and he needed me. When your child needs you, Susan, you never give up on them.'

'Who does Mark think has Dylan? Where has he gone?'

Margaret looks like she'd rather tear out her own tongue than carry on talking, but I couldn't care less. So many questions are running through my mind, questions that this woman can't answer. Why did that photo make Mark think Dylan was alive if he'd found him dead in our home? Who does he think took him, and how? *Why would anyone take my baby?*

'I don't know. I'm so sorry. Mark came round here this morning shouting that you were going to find out the truth, that he knew where Dylan was and who had taken him. He got in the car before we could calm him down and sped off. Richard rang him right away but we could get nothing from his mobile. He'd totally disappeared.'

'How did he know all of a sudden where Dylan was? For God's sake, Margaret, who had he spoken to? What had he found out? Where the hell is he?'

Right on cue my mobile phone vibrates in my handbag. I make a grab for it and my blood runs cold at what I see. It's a text from Rob: **Found Mark and know where Dylan is. Come.** There's an address in Durham.

I jump to my feet and grab my bag. *He knows where Dylan is.*

'What is it? Where are you going?' Margaret demands, fear on her face.

'I'm going to get my son back.'

57

The address Rob has given me is another hour and a half away and fear clutches at my heart the entire drive. Margaret wanted me to wait for Richard so that they could come with me, but I can't imagine a scenario where those two people can make this any better. Without Cassie or Nick to fall back on, I'm alone. But that's OK, I can do this alone. For a long time I doubted myself, my sanity, my strength of character. I doubted myself as a woman, a mother and a human being. What kind of person murders their own son and just . . . poof! . . . forgets? Now things are different. I'm no longer the woman who committed that senseless act; I'm a woman whose son was taken from her, a mother who will not give up until her baby is back in her arms. I'm not afraid for myself; I'm afraid I'll be too late for my son.

Too many times on the journey I wonder what I'll do if Mark has found Dylan, if he asks me to run away with him. After everything he's put me through, I wonder if I could do it. Turn back the clock and become a family again, forget the last four years and start afresh with the man I loved. I'm ashamed to admit that I'm considering it. Just like that, he's found our son and life is as it was.

Daylight has given way to a murky darkness by the time I pull up at the disused warehouse Rob has directed me to, and my first instinct is that I've made a big mistake. My sat nav's red pin is flashing, indicating that I've reached my destination, but how can this be where I need to be? Surely Mark hasn't brought our son here?

Moonlight picks out the huge crumbling building. Black squares on the face of the old grey brick hide where the windows once gaped and the door is big enough to get a truck through. Scanning the trees either side of the approach I can't see any sign of anyone else here – no cars, and no lawyer or ex-husband waiting to greet me. Did Rob even say Mark would be here? I pull out my mobile. His text is still on the screen and the postcode is the same as the one I programmed in outside Margaret's house. This is the right place. On impulse, I press 'Forward' and scroll down until I see Cassie's number. She's four hours away and can't stand the sight of me, but something is very wrong about this and I don't want to go in without telling someone. I've seen the movies.

But still, the decision is made. If there's even the smallest chance I will find out what happened to Dylan in there, then there's no way I'm turning back.

The gravel crunches under my feet and the slam of the car door doesn't so much announce my presence as broadcast it to every soul in the area. So you know I'm here, Rob, now it's your turn.

My breath rises like steam and I pull my arms around my chest, rubbing them to try and generate some heat. I wish now I'd given some more thought to what I'm wearing. My jumper is so thin I can see the hairs on my arms poking through.

The weathered sign above the door announces that the building once belonged to G. K. Sankey. I wonder if Mr Sankey believed in under-floor heating – somehow I don't think so.

'Hello? Rob? Mark?' The place is so still, so silent that the sound of my voice seems wrong, like talking out loud in a library.

I lock the car door and move quickly over to the door of the building, not wanting to be out in the open more than I need to. Like I said, I've seen the movies. When I'm close enough to touch the heavy wooden door, I can see that it's only attached to the frame by one of its hinges and is twisted slightly, leaving a gap big enough for a person to climb through. Hands wedged either side of the frame, I hoist my body up into the darkness and drop through.

Shadows dance across the walls of the warehouse, the cavernous space lit only by the orange flame of a fire in a black metal bin in the middle of the floor. Someone's here.

'Rob? Mark?'

My words reverberate against the steel joists in the rafters, against the dusty concrete floors and the darkness beyond the flames.

'Susan.' My heart flies into my throat and I take a step backwards, my heel connecting with the broken door. 'Susan, I'm here.' My ex-husband hurries forward from the darkness. In the flickering light of the flames and smoke he seems thinner, more drawn even than he did just a few days ago.

'Where's Dylan?' I ask. It's hard to reconcile in my mind that Dylan is four years old now. In my head I'm still half expecting Mark to thrust a three-month-old baby into my arms. Will I ever get over that lost time? 'Where is Rob?'

My back is pressed against the damp twisted door. For the first time since I arrived my heart is thumping murderously and my breath has caught on a hard lump in my throat. Smoke from the fire stings my eyes. Oh shit, please don't let this be a panic attack. Not now, not when I'm so close, not when my little boy needs me maybe more now than ever.

'Who's Rob?'

'Rob Howe, Rachael's boss? From ZBH Solicitors. He said you'd found Dylan.'

'Rob Howe?' Mark's face creases into a frown. 'What does he look like?'

'Floppy brown hair, blue eyes, scar on his neck?'

'Fuck.' Mark swears quietly.

'What? What?'

'Fuck, fuck, fuck. That's not Rob Howe, Susan, it's . . . Oh God, no. He said he had Dylan?'

'No, not exactly. If he isn't Rob Howe, then who is he?' Faced with a choice between panic and anger, my brain has chosen anger. Just this once, my faulty wiring has decided to work in my favour. 'Who the fuck is he and what has he done with my son?'

My legs step forward automatically, fuelled by fury, until I'm inches from the man I pledged my life to. 'I swear to God, Mark, you tell me what's going on or I'll—'

'Jack.'

I've never met a Jack. I don't know any Jack.

His eyes drop to the floor, studiously investigating the dusty concrete.

'There are things you don't know, Susan, about me, and Jack, and—'

'I know all about Beth.' He cringes at the sound of her name. 'I know what happened to her.'

'You hear that, Mark? She knows.' The voice is calm and familiar, and my eyes search the room for its owner. Beyond the smoke and flames I can't see a thing. The fire crackles and spits sparks and ash on to the floor.

Mark's eyes mirror my own, scanning the darkness for our host.

'Looks a bit different in here without the tables and chairs, doesn't it? Sorry I couldn't recreate the scene exactly, Shakes. I considered it, but the whole thing felt a bit melodramatic.'

There's movement in the corner of the room, and she steps out of the shadows into the firelight.

'Jennifer?' The word catches in Mark's throat and I struggle to remember where I've seen this woman before. Then I remember. Jennifer . . . the library . . . Bethany's best friend . . .

It's like I'm seeing her for the first time, and like I've known her for years. Her long dishwater hair has been dyed a deep red, and a shaky hand has applied eyeliner in thick black lines around her eyes. But I'm not seeing her standing in the light of the fire, surrounded by smoke and fluttering ash. I'm seeing her in the doorway of the house Mark and I shared, silhouetted against the bright sunshine of the day, hearing her voice say 'Mrs Webster?' on the day my life ended.

· 'You were in my house. That day, you came to my house.'

A thin-lipped smile. 'Bit late to start jogging down memory lane now.'

'What were you doing there? What are you doing *here*? Where's Rob? Where is my son?'

'Rob wasn't Rob. Maybe nothing is as it seems, Susan, did you ever think that? Maybe black is white and down is up. Maybe ZBH stands for Zara, Bratbury and Howe, and maybe the man you met is the puppeteer. Maybe you don't have a son. Maybe you killed him.' Jennifer speaks offhandedly, as though it means nothing to her. She's crazy. Does she have Dylan? She steps closer and I smell a sharp, fresh paint smell. She's holding a small silver object in her fingers. A lighter.

'I think we all know that isn't true.' I'm trying to keep my voice level, not give away the terror that has frozen my legs together. I feel a bead of sweat tickle its way down my spine and into the small of my back. 'You have my attention now, Jennifer, isn't that what this is all about? The photograph, Kristy Riley . . . this?'

Both their faces look confused. Good, let them be confused. I've been confused for four years.

'What photograph?' Jennifer asks at the same time as Mark says, 'What about Kristy?'

'Ha.' My laugh is without the slightest bit of humour. 'Looks like I'm not the only one who isn't completely in the picture.'

'Riley's dead,' Jennifer states. 'Both of them, actually. You thought you were so clever, Billy, helping Matt pull that disappearing act. If only he'd waited patiently for Kristy and the little princesses to join him. Instead he had to have an attack of conscience and try and find me. Jack wasn't going to let that happen.'

'Matty's dead?' Mark's face crumples and he closes his eyes in pain. 'You fucking bitch.' He opens his eyes and charges towards her.

'Whoa, boy.' Jennifer holds up the lighter and flicks the flame, illuminating her face. Mark stops short a foot away from her. 'What's one more, eh? Bethany, Kristy, Dylan, they're all collateral damage. These are the generations, eh? Anything to protect the Brotherhood. Protect your own asses more like. Well not this time. I had your back once upon a time, Mark, but that's not enough.'

'Why didn't you tell me that Matt Riley was your best friend?' I aim my question at Mark but don't take my eyes off Jennifer. 'Why haven't you ever spoken about him to me?'

Mark shakes his head. 'Matty and Kristy are from a time I never wanted you to hear about. I never wanted to get caught up in difficult explanations, or have one of us trip up and mention . . . what happened. I just wanted to protect you, Susan.'

'Aw, bless.' Jennifer's voice cuts between us. 'Maybe there's more to Mark than meets the eye. For example, does it surprise you to know that he and I were lovers at university?'

'No.' It should, but it doesn't. How did I know that?

'No, of course not. I told you once already. I knew you'd remember. Bit late, though, Susan.' She says it the way you'd tell your child they were a bit late for lunch. *What does she mean, she's told me once?*

'We weren't lovers,' Mark spits. 'I made a stupid mistake, once. The biggest mistake of my life. A mistake that ruined everything.'

Jennifer ignores him as easily as if he hasn't spoken. 'She's going to remember it all soon, Mark. Then she'll hate you just like I do. I'd say I'm sorry you won't be around to see it, but I always knew it was coming to this, even if you didn't. I can finally say I hate you.'

'Jennifer, please.' Mark's voice is a squeak, and I try and beg him with my eyes to stay quiet. Quiet so I can think, quiet so he doesn't get us killed.

Jennifer pulls a face at me. 'Seriously, Susan, what did we ever see in this guy? Are you sure *you* don't want to do this? I don't think anyone would blame you. Maybe we could even get the police to invoke the double jeopardy law. I know usually it relates to the same crime twice, but an eye for an eye, eh? You've already done the time . . .' She holds the lighter out to me and I hesitate. She's crazy. She's actually bat-shit crazy. Does she think I'm going to kill him? Would she let me just take it? She laughs and pulls it away again. I've missed my chance. 'No? I don't blame you, to be honest. Killing a person, it changes you. Taking a life, well you have to be a real fucked-up individual. Don't you, Mark?'

Mark groans and puts his hands to his face.

'OK, back up. Good boy.' She picks up something from

the floor by the fire. Handcuffs; she has come prepared. 'Put these on, just one arm. That's it, now over by the wall.'

I can't even properly see the wall, and when Mark hesitates, she takes two strides forward and grabs him roughly by the arm. She's no match for him physically, but either she's stronger than she looks or he's not putting up any fight, because he starts to move. My foot inches backwards. I'm going to run for it, hopefully get help before she hurts him.

'Don't even think about running.' I don't know how she's seen me move through the dark and the layer of smoke. 'I'll set this place off before you can take another step, and I'd like to bet this lighter fluid is faster than you. Over here, and make it fast. When lover boy realises where we are, I'll have more than the pair of you to worry about.'

I realise she's talking about Nick, but I decide not to tell her how unlikely that scenario is. Nick isn't coming to rescue me. I pray to God Cassie has received my text and the police are on the way.

Mark looks at me, something like hope entering his eyes. *He believes her*, I realise. *He really thinks we're going to be rescued.* I can't believe that he's driven us down this path and he thinks I'm going to be the one to get us rescued. Well sorry to disappoint you, darling, but I'm a very bad judge of men, remember . . .?

'Down there.' Jennifer points to the floor next to the bare breeze blocks of the wall. 'There's a pipe. One on you and one on the pipe. There's another set here for the missus.'

Mark does as he's told, kneeling down next to the wall, and with a sickening clarity I know exactly what she's going to do. The smell I noticed when she walked in: not fresh paint. White spirit. She's going to set the place on fire.

'I'm not getting down there.' If I do, we'll both be trapped in a burning building.

Jennifer's eyes harden in anger. 'Get the fuck down.'

'You must be kidding me. You'll have to kill me.'

She pinches her lips together and rolls her eyes upwards, sighs impatiently. 'Fine,' and before I realise what's she's doing, she raises her hand and my head explodes with pain.

58

Mark: 27 November 1992

Four loud blows against the door signalled the arrival of their leader. Mark felt the colour drain from his face and his chest tingle. Was this what a heart attack felt like? The largest boy in the room by a rugby-playing mile, a bulk Mark recognised as Jack Bratbury's right-hand man Adam Harvey, was at the door in seconds and Mark's heart felt like lead as he heard it swing open.

The room began to buzz; as always, Jack was not alone.

'Evening, gents,' he greeted, his voice bouncing around the warehouse. 'You're probably wondering what I've got for you here. Not my usual offering, I'll admit.'

He shoved forward the hunched figure he had been holding up. The girl was clearly out of it and fell to the floor, making no effort to stand. This had never happened before. Usually the girls he arrived with were at the very least lucid; willing participants in Jack's games, at first anyway. This girl was neither willing nor a participant. Her robe was one of theirs; when she hit the floor, it flew up, uncovering bare skin underneath. Her head was covered with a black hood, but unlike theirs her hood hid her face too.

'What's up with her, she a dog?' one of the boys asked. The others began to snigger; Jack laughed.

'OK, I admit this was a last-minute plan. Things fell through and I couldn't let one of my boys leave without a proper send-off, could I?'

The buzz was back. Who was leaving? What was Jack talking about? Mark felt as though his lungs had filled with lead. Did he know?

Relax, he told himself, trying to take deep, unnoticeable breaths. He could be talking about anyone.

Jack stepped over the unconscious girl on the floor, the focus of the room suddenly taken away from her, all eyes on him as he walked over to where Mark was standing, rigid with fear. He clamped a heavy hand on Mark's shoulder, a little harder than necessary, and leaned in, his lips lingering uncomfortably close to Mark's ear.

'Did you think I wouldn't know? Did you really think I was just going to let you go?' he hissed. Blood pounded in Mark's ears; his mouth was too dry to speak. 'You're going nowhere,' Jack continued, louder now. 'Without a proper send-off!' The group around them laughed, tension beginning to fizzle.

'Line up, boys,' Jack instructed. So they were skipping the pleasantries. 'You first.' He handed Mark a small square foil packet and gestured to where the girl lay. 'Someone get her on the table.'

Mark risked a look at Matty, whose eyes were bolted to the floor. His feet walked him to where the girl had been spread-eagled on the long table, her robe and hood still in place.

'How am I meant to get turned on when I can't even see what I'm screwing?' He tried to sound nonchalant but his voice wavered and cracked.

'Don't be so fucking ungrateful,' Jack spat. 'Get on with it. The rest of us want our go. Do this and you can go back to your little woman and forget about us. If you don't – well, Adam's been waiting to kick the smug look off your face since we were fifteen.'

He wanted so desperately to say no, to tell Jack to go to hell. He *wanted to walk out of the warehouse, make the three-mile trek back to Trevelyan, grab Beth and take her as far away from Durham as he could. But he didn't. He stepped up to the table.*

Just one last time. The words sounded hollow even in his own head. He lifted his robe and undid his jeans.

59

There's a pain in my shoulder where I landed on it when I fell that burns white hot and spreads all the way down to my fingers, and a sudden sharp twinge across the right side of my head. The force of her blow sends me staggering backwards against the wall and my head hits the blocks. Jesus, I'd never have imagined such a petite woman could be so strong, though after meeting Cassie I should have known better. My breath comes in ragged spurts, the wind knocked out of me. I close my eyes and slump downwards.

'Susan!' Mark's voice sounds far away, like he's shouting through water. My face lands in a puddle of something wet and sharp-smelling – the white spirit. When she lights that fire, I'm going up like a Guy Fawkes display. 'You've killed her!'

'She's not dead. Are you, Susan? She's just in shock.' Her voice sounds impatient but I can't answer. My mouth doesn't work, none of my body works, and I don't have the energy. I just want to lie here and let my life spill out over the floor.

'She's banged her head, look, she's bleeding! This has gone far enough, Jen, you have to get help. I've learned my lesson, I'm sorry for what I did to you, to Beth. I'm sorry. I'm sorry.'

I can feel hands on my arm; I'm being dragged across the floor. Maybe I lose consciousness, because when I manage to drag my eyelids halfway open, I'm slumped against the wall next to my ex-husband, my right hand cuffed to a gas pipe.

'You awake?' Oh God, she's still here. I'm still here. Where is Cassie? Where are the police? It feels like we've been in this place all night, but it can only be twenty minutes since I first climbed in through the door. 'Susan? You awake? I want you to hear this.'

'I'm awake.' My throat is dry and the words barely make it out. How hard did she hit me? Does she have lead hands? My breath is still ragged and I realise the smoke is thicker now, filling my lungs and chest. No wonder my head feels full of feathers.

'Ah, good to see you. I didn't want you to miss this bit. It's Mark's final speech. He's going to try and save his own life; possibly yours too but mainly his own. Please bear in mind that Shakespeare here spent his life being a spineless bastard and this won't be the first time he's thrown you under a bus to save himself. Right, Shakes?'

Shakes.

I've never heard Mark's old university nickname, and yet now, coming from her lips, it sounds so familiar, like I knew it all along.

'You called him that. You called him that when you came to the house. Why were you there, Jennifer? What did you come to tell me? What was so bad I chose to block it out for four whole years?'

'So now you want to listen?' She spits the words at me. 'Now you want me to tell you? You didn't want to talk before, did you, Susan? When I came to warn you what your husband was like? You *attacked* me.'

An image screams into my head with such clarity it's as

though it happened this morning. I've laid Dylan in his Moses basket and pulled a blanket over myself on the sofa when I hear the doorbell ring. I cringe: please God don't wake the baby. He doesn't murmur and I pad across the floor to the front door.

'Can I help you?' There's a woman at the door, a frizz of dirty blonde hair and wild brown eyes. She's looking past me into the hall as soon as I open the door, her cheeks flushed and her eyes red-rimmed and puffy; she may have been crying. How have I not remembered this before? When I saw her at the library?

But you did remember, a little voice tells me. *Your mind fought so hard against remembering, you had a panic attack rather than have it all come flooding back. Now it's fight or flight if you want to survive.*

'I shouldn't have attacked you. I'm sorry. I didn't want to believe what you were telling me because if it was true it would have ruined my life. My son's life. I'm sorry.'

Jennifer laughs. 'You hear that, Mark? *She's* sorry. Another poor unfortunate soul you charmed into your bed and whose life you ruined and *she's* apologising! Who's the one who should be sorry, Mark?'

'Me.' The word comes out in a sigh; his head is hanging as though he doesn't have the strength to lift it to meet my eyes. My vision swims; I've lost too much blood. I think I'm going to die and I don't have the strength to be hysterical. Goose bumps crawl along the arm that isn't numb and my teeth begin to chatter.

'Him! He's the one who screwed his fiancée's best friend! He's the one who couldn't face up to his responsibilities!'

'Once!' The word exploded from Mark. 'One drunken mistake, Jennifer! Is that why you ruined my life? Because I had to be wasted to give you what you'd been after for bloody years?'

'I thought you two met at uni?'

Mark scoffed. 'Oh no, Jenny and I go way back, don't we, Jen?'

'I loved you,' she spat back at him. 'Always fucking had. Ever since Jack trailed you home looking like a bedraggled little dog, I knew. I knew we were meant to be together, and I thought you'd finally realised it too; I thought that was going to be it – we would be together. Then you woke up the next day and told me you'd made a mistake. That you'd rowed with that stuck-up little bitch and you'd been too drunk to know what you were doing. You made me swear never to tell her, not to ruin your wonderful relationship over one *stupid mistake*. That's what you called me. But that wasn't it, was it, Mark? You had to completely ruin me.'

'He forced you to have an abortion.' I do remember. I remember hearing those words from this stranger's mouth four years ago and thinking, *She's crazy. She's lying and she's crazy.*

'He forced me to kill my child.' There are tears streaming down her cheeks now, and for a moment I feel sorry for the girl she used to be, in love with a man who treated her so callously.

'Then he tells me the two of them are getting married. There was me, fresh out of the clinic, upset, lonely, furious and devastated that he'd murdered our baby, and Lady Muck comes back from dinner with a nineteen-carat iceberg on her finger.'

'You must have been devastated.'

'Devastated? I was *furious*. That's when I decided I was going to have her killed.'

60

The space that was so huge and draughty just a short while ago now feels no bigger than my cell in Oakdale. The smoke from the fire is thicker, cloying at my throat and stinging my eyes. Jennifer seems oblivious, and Mark is practically catatonic. It's as though he's accepted our fate and is staring ahead, his mind in another place altogether.

'Where is Dylan, Jennifer?'

She pretends she hasn't heard me, or maybe she really hasn't.

'Are you remembering yet, Susan? Do you remember what happened next?'

I struggle to focus, to picture the woman sitting in my front room telling me that the father of my baby had murdered hers. I see her lips forming two words.

'Eleh Toldot.'

She smiles, claps her hands together. 'That's it! You're getting there. We're almost done, I promise. Eleh Toldot.'

A noise comes from Mark, low and indistinguishable.

'What was that?' She crosses to him and picks his head up by the hair. 'For the benefit of the audience, please, sir.'

'I said, "These are the generations."'

Oh God, oh God, I remember. I remember it all. The most horrific story I'd ever heard, a story of abuse and ritual humiliation, a story of overprivileged boys who used the university as their playground. I hadn't believed a word, I'd gone mad, called her a liar and pushed her, hit her, shouted at her to get out of my house and leave my family alone. I can see her now, putting up her arms to defend herself against my blows, and then she pushed me. That was the last time I ever saw my son, as I fell towards the ground.

'You hit your head,' she says lightly, as though she can read my mind. 'I thought you were dead. I thought I'd been given a second chance at being a mum. Mark had given me back my child. And so I took your son.'

'You just took him?' I turn my body to look Mark full in the face again. Pain blasts through my arm and side, I can barely breathe through the smoke and I know I don't have long left. I have to find out the truth before I go. 'And when you got home . . .?'

'I didn't come home, Susan. I was at work when I got a phone call . . .'

Jennifer smiles. 'Cousin Jack. I called him to smooth things over for me. He has the best way of fixing, erm, difficult situations.'

'Jack?' I'm confused. 'The boy you said Beth hated? He's the one who pretended to be Rachael's boss? He's your cousin?'

'Every day since I was born. And he is Rachael's boss, just not the one he said he was. He's so clever. He and Rachael have been keeping an eye on you since you got out; he's senior partner at Zara, Bratbury and Howe and she does as she's told. It was his idea for her to take your case. Like I said, always the puppeteer. Well, nearly always. Jack's always been the clever, popular one, but I knew something he didn't want anyone else to know. I knew about the girls

317

they were all drugging just to get laid. Pathetic. And I knew about Lucy.'

'Lucy?' Even Mark sounds surprised. 'Wasn't she the housekeeper Jack was sleeping with when we were fifteen?'

'Don't be such a fucking idiot, Mark! You were supposed to be the clever one when we were growing up, and yet you just blindly believed whatever he told you. Jack wasn't *sleeping* with her! Don't you remember me telling you that girl was a prick tease? Well Jack doesn't like to be teased, does he? So when she told him where to go, he shagged her anyway whether she liked it or not. Turns out she didn't like it, and Uncle George had to pay a fortune to shut her up. There was no way Jack wanted everyone on campus to know what he was really like, and I was the only person who knew what you filthy little boys had been up to.'

'So you blackmailed him to steal my baby?' My voice is as loud as I can make it; there is as much venom in my words as I have the strength to project.

'I'd already taken Dylan and left. Jack just fixed it after the fact. My cousin is a fucked-up little boy indeed. Let me tell you about Beth.'

She cleared her throat. 'Jack wanted Beth from the minute he saw her. He bombarded her constantly with flowers, jewellery, anything you can think of. She said he scared her but she was polite in her refusals, classy until the end. And the end was inevitable as soon as she got together with Mark a few months later. Jack was never going to allow that to continue.'

'Why not? Couldn't he accept defeat gracefully? Couldn't you?' Where is Cassie? Where are the police? *Where is Dylan?*

'I'm going to let that one go, Susan. I knew when Mark dumped me, when he made me kill our child, that if I played my cards right, Jack would do the work for me. He was so easily manipulated. Angry people usually are. The cleverer they think they are, the stupider they turn out to be. He was so arrogant he wouldn't have thought for a second that he wasn't running the show.' She screws up her face. 'It took months of putting up with Beth preening her feathers like a goddamn peacock, flaunting the rock on her finger and simpering about her wonderful Mark before Jack snapped and decided to take things to the next level. With a bit of gentle persuasion, of course. I threatened to tell.'

I imagine Bethany Connors at her happiest, flicking through wedding magazines, phoning her friends and family to gush about her good news, planning her life with Mark, never knowing that all along the person she believed to be her best friend was silently despising her.

'Does Jack have Dylan now? Tell me my son isn't with Bratbury.' Mark sounds like he'd rather Dylan was brought up by Ted Bundy. Jennifer laughs.

'Now that would be good. Cousin Jack bringing up Mark Webster's son, wouldn't that be poetic justice?' She turns back to me.

'What happened at the clubhouse, *this* clubhouse,' she gestures around with her arms, 'you can imagine. When Mark and Matt dumped her body, I followed them just to make sure they'd done the job properly. They drove like lunatics; I could have been *killed*.' She can't contain her cackle at the joke. 'When she was found, I planned to be there for Mark and naturally we would grieve together. He was going to be mine, after all. We could have a baby, a planned one this time. When they left, I took a few pictures for future leverage, borrowed those same handcuffs you're wearing now. When I took them off, I felt her breath and realised she was still alive. Useless idiots had barely scratched her. She would have bled to death *eventually*, but I couldn't take any chances. I had to finish the job myself. It had to be done.'

'How?' I ask her. I don't want to know but it makes her happy when I ask questions. She grins.

'I put my bag over her face and smothered her.' She relishes the words, as though she's been waiting to say them out loud for a long time. 'She was already unconscious so I didn't get to watch the life drain out of her or anything as pleasing as that, but I have to say it was satisfying. I didn't get nearly as much satisfaction when I killed that bitch Riley. Although I did get a little kick out of using a *real* crystal vase, bought from Riley's family fortune no doubt. Mark will be more rewarding. You're an unfortunate by-product, I'm afraid. I like you, I think we could have been friends.'

After everything I've heard, all the pain I'm feeling, it's this that makes me feel like I'm going to be physically sick. That this woman would identify with me, that she would feel we're kindred spirits in this fucked-up little play will haunt me for life, however short my life may be.

'And Beth's brother definitely had a thing for you.'

'Beth's brother?' When did I meet him?

'The guy pretending to be a reporter.' I can't see her expression as realisation dawns on her, but I hear her chuckle in the dark. 'Oh I see, you didn't know! Well, well, Susan, you really should choose the men in your life more carefully.'

Beth's brother. He'd known all along who the redhead in the photo was, known all about her death. I'd just been a means to an end. He hadn't cared about what happened to Dylan; he'd just hoped I'd lead him to the truth about his sister. I don't know whether I blame him or not for that. To get to Dylan I'd lie to anyone I had to, but that doesn't stop me feeling betrayed. Betrayed and stupid.

My thoughts are cut short at the sound of sirens in the distance. Jennifer hesitates and I can see her trying to judge if they're coming this way.

'Luckily I choose my friends much better.'

It only takes her a second to recover. 'This doesn't change anything. Just moves things along a little faster.'

She sinks into the shadows. Mark doesn't look at me, but when she's out of sight he murmurs, 'There's a break in the pipe. Don't look, it's about ten feet to my right.'

And I thought he'd been catatonic, frozen in shock and fear, when this whole time he's been searching for a way out of this mess.

'When I say go, we've got to move as fast as we can to it. If she sees us, we're dead, but we can't just lie here and wait to die anyway.'

'I'm not sure I can make it,' I whisper. 'My head is so heavy, I can barely breathe and I don't think I can lift myself up.'

'You can do it, Susan. You're strong, stronger than me, stronger than I ever thought you could be.' His voice is filled with something that sounds like respect, a respect I've never heard from him before. His fingers link with mine and he squeezes my hand tight.

'I need to know, Mark, if we're going to die. Did you ever love me?'

'I loved you. I loved you more than you'll ever believe now. And when you gave me Dylan, I was so happy, and so afraid it couldn't last.'

'Because of . . .' I can't say her name. 'Because of what you thought you'd done?'

'Because of what I did. Jennifer may have said I didn't do it, but I did. I killed Beth, and I knew that one day someone would come back and take everything from me.'

'Why didn't you tell me?'

He looks away. 'I don't think you need me to answer that.'

He's right. I honestly can't say what I would have done, whether I'd have made him go to the police, or taken our son and left. All I do know is that the last four years of my life would have been so different.

'When Jack called me that day, he told me that Jennifer had been to our house and told you everything. He said you'd gone mad and Jennifer had called him to calm you down but when he got there it was too late. You'd killed Dylan and blacked out, hit your head on the table. I didn't even go to the house; I met Matty in the car park of the hospital and ran with you into A and E. Matt rushed Dylan through, I didn't even see him. I didn't even get to say goodbye.' His voice breaks. 'I really thought you'd done it, Susan. I never should have believed them, I never should have thought you would . . . but you'd been a different person after Dylan was born; it was easy for me to believe you could have hurt him. As far as I knew, all I was hiding was the reason why you flipped out.'

Warm tears roll down my nose on to my lips, but I don't brush them away. Let him see, let him see how he's hurt me. 'How could you not know? How could you just believe him over me?'

'*You* believed you'd done it.' Mark rubs his face with his free hand. 'Susan, I'd thought about telling you about Beth a million times. I'd imagined you hugging me and telling me it was OK, that we'd get through it together and you'd still love me but I knew deep down that could never happen. When Jack said that Jennifer had told you everything, and that you were both dead, I was devastated, but I believed him because I knew you. I knew you couldn't live the rest of your life with a murderer, and I knew you couldn't turn me in to the police. I thought you'd seen no other choice.'

I do feel for him; my heart aches at the thought of him going through his daily life thinking all the time that he was about to lose everything. I wouldn't wish that on my worst enemy. Then I remember how I felt every day thinking I'd killed my son, how that was a direct result of the terrible thing he had done, and I want him to pay.

'I can't tell you how I would have reacted if you'd told me what happened to Beth.' I keep my voice low and he has to lean in to hear me. 'But know this, Mark, I would have killed all four of you before I let anything happen to my boy.'

'Susan, we'll go to the police, I'll tell them everything, we'll find Dylan, I promise. But we have to get out of here first. For Dylan.' He squeezes my hand again. 'Can you do that?'

I nod.

The sirens are louder now, announcing our rescuers. But they're going to be too late. Jennifer is moving back towards us, something in her hand. A small transparent bottle that looks empty but isn't. White spirit.

'I knew it would come to this.' Her voice is level, calm. 'I hope you're happy, Mark. This is for Beth.'

She lifts her foot, then flings it out, connecting with the bin. Flames reach out from the rim like skeletal fingers grappling to catch hold of the fluid on the ground. Mark screams, 'Go!' just as the bin topples over, the entire wall ignites and the door is lost in a forest of flame.

61

Mark: 27 November 1992

It had almost made it easier, the robe, the hood, no movement or sound. OK, when the girls were conscious he could pretend they were enjoying what he was doing to them, just about. But not seeing the fear in her eyes, not knowing if she was feeling pain or shame, in a fucked-up way, it had helped.

Most of the boys were now slumped in their chairs trying desperately to drink themselves into a guiltless stupor. Mark sat at the edge of the group, drinking more than he knew he should. It wasn't helping.

Jack was standing apart from the rest of them, openly watching Mark down glass after glass. His words rang in Mark's ears: Did you really think I was just going to let you go?

Surely this wasn't it? Was he actually going to be allowed to leave?

'Your turn, boss.' Adam clamped a hand on Jack's shoulder. Mark watched Jack shake his head.

'Not this time, mate. We need to move fast. Time for the finale. Gentlemen.' He spoke more loudly now, addressing the group. 'As you all know, one of our number planned to leave us tonight.'

Everyone's attention was piqued, no one's more than Mark's. Jack turned to face him, his features flickering ominously in the candlelight.

'We here,' Jack gestured around him, 'were born of privilege. Every one of you is here because your fathers, your grandfathers decreed it so. These are the generations. Yet one of you doesn't see that as the same honour as the rest. One of you doesn't appreciate the generosity I have shown in bringing you the finest fruits Durham has to offer, week upon week. The power I have bestowed on you. Perhaps this will make you all see.'

Mark's heart felt as though it would burst from his chest as Jack strode towards him, putting a hand inside his robe and drawing out a small silver object. He gestured for Mark to follow him to where the girl lay prone on the table. She was breathing lightly, her chest rising and falling under the black garb, but she hadn't moved in the hour she had been in the room. Although Mark couldn't see her face under the dark hood, it was clear she was out cold.

'What the hell is this?' Mark asked as Jack handed him what he'd taken from his robe. A knife.

'This is your heritage,' Jack announced, waving his hand around the room, indicating each of the other men and coming to rest on the girl. 'You think you can leave us? You are one of us. Our blood flows in your veins. Now it is time for you to swear your allegiance. To prove yourself. Kill her.'

A couple of the followers gasped involuntarily. Jack swung around to face them. 'Do any of you have a problem with our brother showing his loyalty to the group? Perhaps one of you would rather do it for him?'

All around him heads hung. Shock at what he was proposing rendered the group mute. Not one follower spoke out at the atrocity that was being suggested to them. Except Mark.

'No fucking way. No way, Jack. Are you crazy? Do you even understand what you're saying?'

325

'Crazy?' Jack's voice bounced off every wall in the warehouse. 'Crazy? I make sure you walk on water in this fucking place and this is what I get?' He nodded at Adam, who moved to the corner of the room and picked up a small metal bin.

'I can see you need some convincing.' Jack nodded again, this time at two of the other boys, who flanked Mark and took a tight hold of his forearms. 'Ad . . .'

Adam's face was a picture of triumph. As though he was presenting a trophy, he held the bin up to Mark's face and Mark couldn't help but look inside.

'Condoms?' Fear gave way to confusion. Jack looked pleased.

'Condoms. Condoms that prove that each and every one of you fucked this girl. Now either you do as I've told you, or I'll do it. And every person in this room will be implicated in her death.' He turned to the rest of the group. 'Shall we take a vote?'

It didn't need any discussion.

'For God's sake do it, Webster.' One of the boys at the back, Mark couldn't see if it was Turner or Thorpe, spoke out. 'We're all in this balls deep anyway. Don't let that piece of trash bring us all down.'

There was a murmured consensus. Mark's eyes swung wildly about, desperately looking for someone to tell him this was a joke. Even Matty was examining his shoes, starkly refusing to come to his aid.

'You cannot be serious. Does any one of you actually realise what he's asking me to do? Murder! He's asking me to kill her!'

'No one has to know.' Jack spoke softly, holding out the knife again. 'You do this and we're a brotherhood again. We're all in this together, Mark. Together, just like we always wanted it. We'll protect you. You walk away from us and you'll never have that kind of protection again. You walk away from us and you're finished. A rapist. You'll go to prison and lose your glittering career. Your future with Beth? Over.'

Beth. What would she say if she found out? Mark had no doubt Jack was telling the truth: if he didn't do this, his life with Beth was *over. It was what Jack had wanted from the start, and here it was. He had to do as he was told. Keep Jack sweet. For Beth.*

He stepped forward and took the knife. He heard a gasp, looked up just in time to see Matty momentarily glance up and catch his eye. Then his gaze hit the floor again.

'That's a good choice, Mark, a very good choice. For you, for Beth. Here, let me help.'

Jack moved to where the prone body rested on the table. He lifted the hood to expose a creamy white neck and pointed to a spot to the left of her trachea.

'Left to right, clean sweep. Easy.'

Mark's hand squeezed the handle of the knife, trying to make it feel comfortable in his palm. There was no way he could do this.

'Do it, Mark, just do it. For Beth.' Jack's breath was warm on Mark's cheek. Do it. For Beth.

He followed Jack's instructions. Left to right. A clean sweep. Easier than he'd ever thought taking a life would be. The blood that pumped through his hands was warm and sticky; instinctively he wiped it on his robes, but his hands were stained red. Tainted. He knew in that second that they would be red forever.

Jack let out a long breath and Mark knew in that instant that his leader had never actually expected him to do it. The moment hit him full force. The moment he realised what he'd done. He had actually killed a woman. Someone's daughter, maybe someone's sister, a woman just like Beth.

Jack recovered quickly and slammed Mark heartily on the back.

'Well done, my friend!' His voice echoed out over the dead silence of the room. Mark flinched at the touch and sprang backwards, away from him.

'Don't!' he barked. 'Don't touch me. Oh God, oh God,' and turning away from the group, he retched, then vomited warm bile and alcohol out on to the floor.

'I understand.' Jack held up his hands and stepped back. 'It's your first time, a lot to take in.' He turned to the group. 'Give the

man a round of applause, fellas.' The room remained silent. 'I said clap!'

The boys broke into unenthusiastic applause. Mark thought he was going to be sick again. He sank to the floor, rubbing his eyes over and over, as though he could rub the memory away.

'Get up,' Jack instructed. When Mark didn't comply, Jack nodded at Adam, who pulled him roughly to his feet. 'You have proved yourself loyal to the Brotherhood, my friend. Now it's time to clear up your mess.' He gestured to where the girl was still lying on the table, blood pooling around her, dripping slowly to the floor below.

'My . . .' Mark's tongue couldn't quite form the words.

'Don't worry, Matthew will help you. Wrap her in that,' Jack pointed to a black bin bag underneath the table that Mark hadn't even noticed before, 'then dump her. You can use Adam's car.'

Adam automatically reached into his pocket for his keys.

Jack faced the group once more. 'The rest of you can go. But before you do, let us get one thing straight. We are all in this together.' He pointed at each of them in turn. 'Every one of you fucked that girl tonight; it may as well have been any one of your hands on that knife. The Brotherhood must stick together at times like this.' He turned to look Mark square in the eye. 'That's what friends are for. We were together tonight, in the student bar. All night.'

The boys all nodded numbly. No one spoke as they left, just Matthew, Mark, Adam and Jack remaining.

'I'm proud of you, Mark.' Jack spoke quietly, softly. 'When I heard you were planning to leave us, I was hurt, I thought we were brothers. Now I see you are truly one of us.'

'One of you?' He forced the words out painfully. 'Never.'

Jack laughed. 'Says the murderer.' Mark flinched. 'Oh I'm sorry, I forgot, you did it for Beth. Don't pretend you had noble intentions, Mark: you did what I told you to do to save your own skin. For God's sake, you didn't even want to know whose throat you were slitting. You should have at least asked.'

Something in Jack's voice made Mark's heart clench like a fist.

'Who is she?'

Jack's eyes smiled but his mouth didn't move.

'Who is she, Jack?' They were the first words Matthew had spoken, but they were tinged with urgency. In that second, Mark knew, and he thought Matthew knew it too.

'God, no. Jack, tell me it's not . . .' He ran over to where the girl's lifeless body lay as though wading through water. His hand reached out to the black hood that covered her face. He didn't want to do it, the last thing he wanted was to see the face of the woman whose life he had taken, the gaping wound he knew was under the cloth, but he had to know for sure. His fingers shook as he laced them underneath and slowly lifted the hood. Red hair tumbled out over the table and dead green eyes stared back at him.

62

Mark flings himself sideways, away from the wall of heat and fire, still holding my hand. My arm is wrenched with him and I fall sideways, my feet scrabbling wildly trying to connect with the floor.

Jennifer stands in the middle of the room, watching the orange forks snake towards us. She's screaming, her voice echoing above the roar of the fire.

The pipe beneath us is searing with red heat. My arm slips downwards and connects with the copper; blistering pain shoots through my wrist and I smell the sharp stench of my own flesh burning. Mark jerks his arm upwards, pulling my skin away from the pipe. He uses his free hand to pull me to my knees and together we inch towards the flames.

'It's too hot, we'll be killed!' I hear the panic in my voice and feel the terror rising in my chest. He's pulling me towards the wall of fire; neither of us is going to make it.

The flames are snaking their way up the walls, flowing upwards like a horrific reverse flood. My skin feels like it's blistering from the heat and I imagine Mark catching fire, writhing around in a human fireball attached to my arm. I can still smell the white spirit on my face and I know that if I get too close to the flames I'm dead.

'Now!' He throws himself forward, and at the last minute his free hand grasps the end of the pipe and wrenches it towards us. It comes away from the wall with the most satisfying crunch I've heard in my life. Mark yanks me with it and I fall face first on to the dirt-covered floor, but we're free.

I can hear Mark's agonising screams reverberating around my head, and now they're mixed with another sound, a primal roar. Smoke fills my lungs and I can't scream, I can't warn him that Jennifer is running towards us wielding the bottle like a trophy.

'Mark!' I grab his arm and pull him towards me, forcing his eyes away from his injuries and on to the screaming woman heading straight for us. As her body connects with mine I feel cold liquid slosh over my hair and face, soaking me and her both. I hear one more scream, a low, guttural sound, and see Mark's free hand seize her hair. I look into his eyes and hear myself shout 'No!' but he doesn't hear me. Grabbing hold of her with both hands, he uses every ounce of strength to throw them both towards the white-hot flames.

'Mark!' I try to scream, but smoke fills my lungs and I fall to the floor coughing, struggling for breath.

He's dead, and so is she. My ex-husband, and our only hope of finding our son.

Then I see him, dragging himself towards me. *He's alive. He's alive and we are going to find Dylan.*

'Susan.' He's rasping, his arm over his face to shield himself from the smoke. 'The door.'

I turn to look at it. The twisted wood is crawling with flames, our exit concealed in a sea of orange and black.

'Is there another way out?' I lean in towards him, both of us crouched on the floor as low as we can get. The smoke is thick here but nothing compared to standing height. 'Mark? Is there another way out?'

The smoke is cloying at my eyes and mouth, snaking its way in through my nostrils and invading my lungs. I lie down, just for a second, and Mark lies with me.

'I'm so sorry, Susan,' he whispers in my ear. 'So so sorry. I love you so much.'

'Ssshhh,' I tell him. 'Just pretend with me a minute. Pretend we're at home. Dylan's here, he's here with us, and we'll never leave him again. Promise me, Mark, we'll never leave him again.'

I wait for his promise, but no words come. When I open my eyes to look at him, his are closed.

If I just rest my eyes for a minute, just a second, then I'll be fine. There are no more sirens, no shouting or screaming, just the roaring of the flames, and I roll into Mark's arms for the last time.

63

Jack: 23 July 2009

'I can't help it if you keep employing snitches, Tony. What the fuck am I supposed to do, screen your payroll for informants? I'm a lawyer, not a recruitment consultant. What do you pay that prick Donaldson for?'

The phone beeped in his ear, interrupting his rant. He pulled it away to look at the screen, could still hear Tony Wood bleating at the other end.

Jenny. Oh great, what the fuck did she want?

'Tony, I have to go. I'll call tomorrow to make an appointment to visit. Look, there's no need for that kind of language. Wear something that'll make the other inmates jealous.'

He ended the call, ignoring the furious protests of the man on the other end of the line.

'Jennifer, my beautiful cousin, apple of Lucifer's eye, what do you want from me?'

'You need to get over to Webster's house. Now.'

Well, there was a name he hadn't heard in a while.

'What's going on, Jennifer? Are you at Webster's house now? What have you done?'

There was silence at the other end of the line. Then, 'I told his wife.'

Shit. Shit, shit, shit.

'What did you tell her? What did she say?' He did not have time for this mess right now. He was busy enough with the firm as it was without cleaning up his psychotic cousin's fuck-ups.

'She wouldn't listen, Jack! She tried to fight me. I pushed her. She's dead, and just to be sure, I pumped her full of ket.'

Jack swore loudly. 'Well, I can put you in touch with a good lawyer,' he offered sardonically.

Jennifer laughed, a sound that made the hairs on his arms prickle. 'I don't need a lawyer, Jack. I need you to come and sort this out for me. I'm leaving, I'm driving away right now, and you're going to come here and fix this whole mess.'

'And what makes you think I'll get involved in your little screw-up?' He indicated left and pulled sharply into a side street, making a swift turn in the direction of Mark's house.

'Oh you will,' Jennifer replied. 'And you know you will. Because if you don't, I'm gonna make sure I take you, and your little band of brothers down. How is it going to look, one of the most esteemed lawyers in the country on trial for murder?'

Jack sighed. 'Sorry, Jen, you lost your leverage on that one a long time ago. You have no proof; it'll be your word against mine, and my word means a lot more than yours these days. You're on your own with this one.' He punched Mark Webster's home postcode into his built-in sat nav. Thirteen miles and counting.

The line broke for a second and Jack struggled to hear Jennifer's next words, but when he did, he felt the blood leave his face.

'Do you hear me, Jack? I said I was there. I have proof, I have pictures. And I went back, after you'd finished. I have some, let's say, trophies. So you can come and clear this mess up for me, or you can see me in court. And this time you won't be on the defence team. But not to worry, you know some good lawyers, right?'

Jack sighed. 'Fine. Fine, Jen, I'll sort this for you. But that's it then – we're done. You'll have your evidence and I'll have mine. I don't want to hear from you again.'

'Fine by me. But there's something you need to know before you get here.'

'What? What else could there possibly be?'

More silence.

'I have the boy. Mark Webster's son. And I'm keeping him.'

It took Jack less than twenty minutes to get to where Mark Webster had been living for the last six years. Even though Mark had been trying to avoid him ever since they left Durham, he'd ended up living in pissing distance from Jack's office. How ironic.

He'd used ten minutes of his journey calling around to get this whole mess sorted out. It amused him a little that that had been all it had taken. He'd spent longer ordering Chinese takeaway for dinner last night.

Pulling up at Mark Webster's home, he was struck by how well his former friend had done for himself. True, he'd kept an eye on him from a distance, followed his appointments in the papers, seen his wedding in the Durham alumni memorandum, but he'd never actually been to his house. And he'd missed the fact that he'd had a son, something that obviously hadn't escaped Jen. She must have been so pissed off, turning up here and seeing Mark's perfect life, especially when her own situation had deteriorated significantly over the last few years. His parents had let slip, at one of their many drunken dinners with Jack and his wife, that Jennifer had been mentally unstable for years. She'd broken up with her fiancé after finding out she couldn't have children and had gone back to Durham, choosing to live in a crapheap of a flat rather than accept any money from his auntie and uncle. This must have tipped the scales.

He sat in the car on the corner of Mark's road and waited until he saw the other car approach. It pulled up in front of him and the driver's door swung open.

'What's this about, Bratbury?' Even after all these years,

hearing the voice was like going home. Jack felt a small sliver of regret at the way their lives had turned out, how they had all gone their separate ways.

'Matty, good to see you again.' He wound down his window and smiled. 'How are you? How's Krissy?'

'Don't you call her that,' Matt Riley warned him between clenched teeth. 'Don't even speak my wife's name. What do you think you're playing at, dragging me here?'

'We've got a small problem that only you and I can sort,' Jack told him in a low voice. 'Jen's done something a bit stupid. She's gone and told Mark's wife about our little problem with Beth.'

'What? What do you mean, told her? What did Susan say? Has she gone to the police?'

Jack raised his eyebrows. 'Susan, eh? You and Krissy been round for Sunday lunch, then?'

'Don't be fucking stupid. I've never even met the woman, Mark's so scared of anything coming out. We've had to meet in secret for the last ten years. What do you want me to do about this? Convince a woman I've never met not to go to the police?'

'Susan's dead, Matt.'

It took a few seconds for the words to register, but Jack hadn't anticipated the response he was going to get when they did. Matt made a sound something between a strangled cry and a roar, threw himself at Jack's window and tried to drag him through it.

'Hey, cool it.' Jack pulled away out of Matty's reach. 'I didn't do it.' The words this time remained unspoken. 'She and Jen had a fight. It was an accident. But there's something else. She said Susan went mad, tried to harm the baby. So she took him.'

Matty was speechless.

'Say something, Matty. We have to sort this out before we call Mark, or he's going to drop us all in the shit.'

His old friend's face was red, his lips were tight. He closed his eyes, like something out of a crazy therapy session; Jack could practically hear the idiot meditating.

'OK,' Matt said eventually. 'Do you know where she is? We need to get the boy back before Mark comes home. He never has to know we were here.'

Jack shook his head. 'We can't get the boy back, Matt. She's keeping him.'

'Oh no, oh fucking no way, Jack. We can't do that to Mark. He loves that boy more than life. Do you think he's just going to give him away to keep that crazy bitch happy?'

Jack sighed. He'd known this wasn't going to be easy. 'I don't think you understand. She's blackmailing us, she has photographs of that night in Durham. We are all in the shit if Mark goes to the police.'

'I don't think we're going to have much say in that, do you? How exactly are we going to stop him? You going to kill him too?'

He had to admit, it had crossed his mind on the drive over to Mark's place. Overall, though, it would be too messy. The way he was planning was much neater.

'Not exactly. Look, Susan's dead, and nothing we can do will change that. The only way Mark is going to let this go is if we tell him the boy is dead too. He can grieve, then get on with his life.'

'And the small matter of the missing body? And who killed them both?'

'I've taken care of the body. It'll take a few hours, and that's why I need your help. As for who did it, that's simple. We tell Mark that Susan killed the boy and then blacked out, hit her head on the table or something. She's overdosed on ketamine, so it already looks like attempted suicide.'

'You've taken care of the body?' Matty thumped the side of the car. 'For fuck's sake, Jack! What is this, some fucking gangster movie? How do you take care of a body in real life? How can you even be saying this?'

Jack laughed. 'Oh come on! I know half the criminals in

Yorkshire – hell, I work for half the criminals in Yorkshire! You don't think this kind of thing is real life? You need to come out of your little bubble. That kid that went missing two months ago, the one whose body turned up in the river? You think that was the actual kid? The body was identified from dental records while that kid was halfway across Europe! That's your real life, Matthew.'

Matt leaned in close to the window and Jack thought he was going to lash out again. *'I will thank God every day that I don't live in your world.'*

'Well in that case you'd better pray to your God that when we find Jennifer and bring that child home she doesn't go to the police with everything she knows about you. Because if she does, it isn't just going to be my world, it will be your world, Kristy's world and your daughters' world. Can you imagine how those prison officers are going to love frisking little Tori and Terri when they go to visit Daddy in prison?'

Matt's eyes widened at hearing his daughter's name. *'What do you need me to do?'*

Jack tried his best to hide his smirk. *'I want you to go to the hospital and wait in the car park for Mark to turn up. You'll have Susan and a bundle of Dylan's blankets in the car. Let Mark carry Susan into the hospital; you make sure you rush "Dylan" in. Get him straight through to theatre, where I'll have someone waiting with the body you need. Do not hang around in the car park, do not let anyone ask any questions.'* He took satisfaction from seeing Matt cringe when he said the words 'the body'. *Fucking pussy.*

'What are you going to tell Mark to get him to meet me at the hospital?'

'Just what we need him to know. That Jennifer turned up here and told Susan about Beth. Susan went mad and threatened the baby so Jen called me. By the time I got here they were both dead, and I called you because I knew you were a doctor. I'll make sure he tells the police he found them and took them to

the hospital – that way they won't ask any questions about why Jen was here and what she said to make Susan react so badly. We were never here – you ran into Webster in the car park of the hospital and he begged you for help. Clear?'

Matt sighed, rubbed his face. 'Clear. Make the call, I'll go get Susan.'

64

My body heaves fiercely, retching up thick black bile on to the wet grass. My lungs pull in fresh air like a newborn baby, each breath sending my chest into violent spasms.

Grass?

I fight to open my eyes again and take in more of my surroundings but no part of my body is cooperating. Hands lift me upwards and something hard and cold is squashed over my mouth. My eyelids part halfway. I'm being slid into a metal box . . . no, wait, this must be an ambulance. There's a woman standing next to me holding a mask over my face, and fresh air screams into my lungs. Doors slam, and then the ambulance is moving, sirens are screaming.

'Mark?' I say. 'Where's Mark?'

The woman ignores me, stroking my head and filling a syringe with a clear liquid.

'Where's Mark?' On my second attempt I realise why she's not answering. The words aren't coming out as planned; in fact they're not coming out at all. I don't have the energy to keep my eyes open any longer and I feel them fall shut again.

* * *

The first face I see when I open my eyes is my father's. The ground beneath me is no longer cold and wet but soft, and I know at once that I am in hospital and I am alive. My upper body feels as though it's been hit repeatedly by a baseball bat, and my legs feel as useless as two pieces of cardboard, but here I am. 'Dylan,' I gasp. Fragments of the last time I was conscious flash through my mind like an action movie: Jennifer running towards us, Mark grabbing her by the hair and, desperate to save his own life, tossing our last hope into the flames.

'Shush, sweetheart. You have to rest. The police are looking for Dylan, they're looking everywhere Jennifer has been, speaking to everyone she contacted.'

'Only Jennifer knows where,' I manage. And she's dead, I watched her burn.

Dad looks pained. 'They haven't found her yet, but they don't think they're going to find her alive.'

'And Mark?' I croak.

'I'm so sorry, sweetheart, Mark was dead when they arrived. Your friend Josh said he hadn't been able to get to him on time.'

He takes my hand and grasps it tightly. I squeeze my eyes shut to stop the tears that have started to form at the corners. As much as I want to hate Mark for what he's done, I still remember what it was like to love him. He sacrificed himself to save my life – his final few minutes spent trying to undo a lifetime of cowardice.

'Josh?' *Who's Josh?*

'Thank God for him, Susan. He arrived at the same time as the police, before the fire brigade. They told him not to go in but he went in anyway and pulled you both out of the fire.'

Josh Connors. Beth's big brother. *Nick.*

'Dylan, Dad,' I whisper again.

'I know, sweetie. The police have been doing all they can to piece things together. They've been to Jennifer's flat.'

'But no sign of him? Clothes, toys, anything?'

Dad shakes his head. 'I'm sorry, nothing. I'll get the nurse, she'll want to know you're awake and well.'

There is one person they will let me see. Someone who has been waiting in the visitors' lounge since an hour after I was admitted to the hospital. As she's ushered through the door, I realise there is no one in the world I would rather see.

'Susan!' Cassie runs over to my bed and throws her arms around my legs comically, presumably to avoid my injured shoulder. 'I thought you were a goner for sure!'

I try to laugh but it's impossible, so I manage a weak smile.

'Thanks . . . for the confidence . . . You called the police . . . saved my life.'

She looks suddenly serious, her blue eyes darkening. 'After I almost let you get yourself killed. You never should have had to do that alone, Suze. I'm so sorry. I felt awful the minute you left; I should have called you.'

'I'm sorry,' I tell her. 'Crappy friend.'

'You've never been a crappy friend,' she promises quietly. 'I'm the crappy one.'

In my head I'm smiling warmly, though I'm not sure it translates to my face. 'Bless you . . . you thought . . . pretty man took . . . your best friend?' She doesn't smile.

'Shut up.' She smacks my arm and I wince. 'Shit, sorry. But seriously, Suze, you're all I've got and I felt like I was losing you. I was scared you didn't need me any more.'

'Never lose me,' I promise. 'Especially not for a man. Where is he? Dad said . . .'

'He dragged you out. A bit of a hero really. I rang him straight after I rang the police and he told me everything. He's Beth's brother, Susan. He always suspected there was a connection between what happened to his sister and what happened to you, but he wanted to know how much you knew about Mark. I gave him the address; he was there about two seconds after the police. He even called me to tell me where you were.' Christ, she almost sounds fond of him. 'He's waiting to see you.'

'So why did he tell me he was a reporter?'

Cassie laughs. 'He says he didn't. You assumed he was, and then when you wanted to talk to him about the article he wrote, he went along with it.'

Shit. I try to think back to the first conversation we had – well, if you can call me yelling at him while he sat in the car and stuttered a conversation – but it makes my head hurt. Josh Connors, and yet I still can't think of him as anyone but Nick Whitely.

'Rachael?' I ask.

Cassie frowns. 'She's gone. Her, Bratbury, his wife, they all just took off. The police went to see her and half her clothes were missing, no sign of her passport and some make-up and stuff gone too. They're pretty sure she went with him of her own accord. They're still trying to contact the other partners in the firm.'

I nod. 'No surprise.'

Cassie shakes her head. 'I could strangle the bitch. The police found her emails. It was her and Bratbury who had your house broken into and had you followed by some guys Bratbury hired. She had Joss killed. She's had your phone tapped since you left Oakdale and knew about the photo album from when you signed out all your possessions when you left there. When Jack found out you'd gotten the photo, he sent some really pissed off emails about how he couldn't hurt Rebecca so Rachael would have to make you think you'd gone crazy and sent yourself the photo. They were going to try and have you recommitted. That thug they got to trash your house put the photos in there – Jack was mad when you caught him – he was supposed to wait until you were in bed so you'd think you'd done it in the night. That's why he broke into Nick's house himself after he'd seen you together at ZBH, thinking you were both out, saw you on the sofa and ripped up all your stuff, tried to make it look like you'd attempted suicide.'

Oh God. I'd thought Rachael was my friend, on my side. The visits, the gifts, the words of hope and encouragement. Even after I found out what she'd left out at my trial I didn't want to believe she'd been part of this. I'm shocked to find myself hoping that the police catch up with her and she spends the rest of her miserable life in prison, like she'd planned for me. Jack Bratbury I just want dead.

Two hours later, the nurse ushers Cassie from the room amid protests from the both of us. Apparently I need my rest, as if I haven't just slept for eighteen hours straight. Cassie vows to sneak back with fast food as soon as she can and asks if I have any message for Josh. There are a thousand things I want to tell him, but I can't think of the right words. I just say no.

Epilogue

'Are you sure you're ready for this?' Cassie says, placing her hand on my arm. Her nails are bright pink today and she's dyed her brassy blonde hair dark red with blue at the tips. She's still of the opinion that a new hairstyle can heal all ills. I think it suits her.

'Nope.' My hands are shaking slightly and I squish them by my sides to hide the fact from Chief Inspector Harrison.

'Just listen to what she has to say,' the police officer says. 'I'd rather you heard it from her.'

I look at the man sitting on the sofa next to me. Nick – he's still Nick in my head, for now at least – smiles encouragingly.

Mark is gone. He never made it out of the warehouse after saving my life. I've wept plenty of tears since my dad told me: tears of grief for the man I loved and selfish tears of grief for what we could have had together. His final act in the warehouse was to save my life, and I tried to keep that in mind even after the police told me how they had exhumed my son's coffin and found the remains of a child inside, a child who was not my little boy.

A nod from the police officer tells me she's here. My heart takes a short leap into my throat and my face heats up with nerves. I'm glad we're doing this in my place of comfort; that at least is on my terms.

Mrs Matthews looks the same as the last time I saw her, just a few short weeks ago, the day I got the photograph, in Rosie's café and then again outside the library. Her long blonde hair is pulled back but she has the same nervous, fidgety look, like she has the weight of an army on her shoulders. Only this time I know why. I know who she is.

Cassie rises and gestures with her head to Nick; they both smile at me again and leave without a word. Chief Inspector Harrison has promised I can listen to this story alone – he's heard it after all – but still I'm surprised when he turns to leave too.

We sit for a minute in silence, neither of us knowing how to start.

'I lost my daughter,' she says suddenly, surprising me. She doesn't look me directly in the eye, just concentrates on picking at a piece of skin next to her thumbnail as she speaks. 'She was twenty-two when she went missing. She was ill. It never gets any easier, you know? Well, of course you know.' She looks embarrassed.

'I'd come to accept that she was never coming back. My husband was devastated; he couldn't understand why our beautiful little girl would just leave us, without so much as a goodbye. But she was an adult, she could do whatever she liked. She wasn't officially missing, she just didn't want us knowing where she was.' I can see the hurt in her eyes. What she is telling me, a perfect stranger, is something she has put on a brave face about for years, smiling through her pain when her friends talked about their own children's triumphs.

'Go on,' I encourage gently, trying not to sound too eager.

It doesn't seem to help; she looks as though she is in a place I can't reach, a place filled with pain. After a moment, though, she takes a small breath and continues.

'After nearly fourteen years of no contact whatsoever, she turned up on our doorstep as though she'd only been away a week. She told us she'd got married and had a baby, but the baby's daddy had died. She needed our help to look after it. A beautiful three-month-old boy.'

My heart picks up speed; I can feel its beat now.

'You must have been overjoyed,' I say, trying not to push her too much. At this, though, she smiles, a wonderful smile that lights up her whole face.

'I was,' she says. 'He's the most fantastic boy, beautiful and so cheeky. He's four years old now. You know, of course you do. I just wanted to say it to you face to face. To say I'm sorry.'

I do know, of course. The police told me the minute they found Jennifer Matthews' four-year-old 'son', living with his grandparents. Tests have been done; the results are on their way.

'I had no idea there was anything suspicious about the circumstances in which Simon came to live with us,' she says, her voice a monotone, as if she is reading from a court statement. 'I had no reason to believe Jenny was lying to us, no reason to believe Simon wasn't hers. I had no idea.'

'So you've said.' I'm trying my best not to get angry. For a start, any kind of emotion still causes me physical pain; secondly, I really do know what this has cost her.

'Jenny would leave Simon with us for weekends at first,' she continues. 'Then it was long weekends. It got to the point where he was living with us and she would just visit. Eventually even the visits fizzled out. We were lucky to see her once a month.'

She took my child and then gave him away. She took my child and then gave him away.

'A month ago, we had a visit from a man, looking for Jennifer. He said his name was Mark and he knew Jenny at University. Simon was out with my husband, and for some reason I told the man we hadn't seen Jenny for years. I don't know what made me lie; I must have realised then that something was terribly wrong.'

If it's possible for blood to actually run cold, I'm certain mine does. Every hair on my arms stands on end and a chill runs through me. Rebecca Matthews doesn't notice and pushes on, a determined look on her pretty face. Mark had stood within spitting distance of where our son lived; he'd probably been minutes away from meeting the boy we'd lost. If he'd arrived just a short time later, he might still be alive. I might have my son in my arms, now.

'What happened next?' I try and keep the hostility from my voice. If this woman leaves, I might never find her again.

'He said that Jennifer had called him the day before. He needed to speak to her about his wife, that he was worried he'd made a terrible mistake. He seemed so upset, then he ran off.'

She hadn't been able to resist speaking to him again. And Jennifer Matthew's obsession with my husband had cost her her life.

'When he left, I looked Mark up on the internet and saw what had happened to you. I'd been so wrapped up in our new grandchild, I'd never even seen it in the news, and even if I had, I wouldn't have put the two together. I never heard Jennifer mention Mark. Even still, all that seemed strange was the timing – Jenny had shown up the same evening with this little boy, well, you know. But that couldn't have had anything to do with her.'

My mind struggles to take all this in, and I have to clamp

my teeth together to stop myself from screaming questions at her.

'Then I found the photo of Dylan in an old newspaper article online. I should have gone to the police as soon as I knew, but I was so scared of what Jennifer would do, what my husband would do. He loves Simon so much, I couldn't bear to be the one to betray him like that. Then, when Jennifer died, I just couldn't go through with what I'd started. He's our little boy, all we have left of our daughter. I was glad when the police found us.'

'You sent me the photographs,' I state. Rebecca nods.

'I didn't know what to do,' she confesses, wringing her hands. 'I expected the police at any minute, but no one came. My husband would kill me if he knew what I've done, but I couldn't just pretend I didn't know who Simon really was. I'm a mother, Mrs Webster, and there are some things only a mother can understand. That's why I had to try and get you to find out yourself. I had no idea what the boys had done to those girls all those years ago.'

I nod, letting her cry in silence. There will be no happy ending to her story.

'And the hairbrush and blanket?'

'Jennifer brought the blanket with her when she first turned up with him. He never went anywhere without it. He only stopped sleeping with it last year.'

The thought that my son had a little part of me with him all these years fills me with joy.

'I saw you. In the café. And outside the library. You came to find me in Ludlow.' It seems like a lifetime ago now. Rebecca nods.

'I told my husband I'd gone to find Jennifer, to talk her into coming to see Simon. That's when I posted the photo. Put the article in your bag. To make you question the story you'd been given.'

'How did you find me?'

'My father was a detective; some of his colleagues are still alive.'

'If you'd just come clean, your daughter, my ex-husband, they'd still be alive.'

She squeezes her eyes closed, but tears find their way out anyway.

'Oh God, I know. I'm so sorry.'

I run my hands down the front of my jumper for the third time, removing lint that I know doesn't exist. Today is to be arguably the most important day of my life and I have never been more nervous.

'Are you OK?' Josh asks, placing a protective hand on my shoulder. I feel the calm seep through my entire body. I love the effect he has on me, the knowledge that when I'm with him I will be OK. I nod more confidently than I feel.

'Listen,' he says, turning my face to his. 'There's something I need to tell you.'

We're sitting in his car outside the house that might change my entire life and *now* he has something to tell me? As though he can read my mind he says, 'I have to tell you now in case Rebecca mentions it. After all, he's her nephew.'

Jack Bratbury. The puppeteer in the sick show that was my husband's life. I've heard very little about him since he disappeared with Rachael. I know the firm folded under the scandal, but not before he'd cleared out all the company accounts. It seems that once again Jack Bratbury has got away scot-free.

'What about him?' My hands shake at the thought of a man I've barely encountered.

'They got him.' Josh is smiling, he puts his hands on my

350

shoulders. 'They picked him up coming back into the country with a fake passport. Arrogant son of a bitch thought he could return as if nothing had happened.'

'Why? Why was he coming back?'

'For Mark's funeral.'

The words force the air from my lungs. I'd decided not to go – a huge and difficult decision for me to make, but the right one I'm sure. I can hardly believe that the man who was responsible for all this, the man who caused the downfall of my perfect existence, the ruination of God knows how many girls and their families, thought he could just walk in to Mark's funeral and act as though he was completely innocent.

'What's going to happen to him?' I'm shaking and trying my hardest not to cry.

'He's going to go to prison. For a very long time. I promise.' He puts his hands on my shoulders and steadies me. He's done this more than once in the last few weeks. He has such a calming effect on me, but I'm still wondering what I'm going to do if one of these days he leans forward and kisses me. 'Since everything came out about Beth, they've had girls coming forward from as far back as 1990 saying they were attacked by him and his friends.'

Him and his friends. My husband.

Bracing myself, I ring the doorbell. The thundering of small feet sounds on the stairs and I think for a second that Josh or no Josh, I might just turn and run.

It's only been a week since Rebecca's visit but it has felt like a three-year sentence all over again.

The plain, ordinary-looking white envelope that had the potential to change my whole life sat on my dad's kitchen counter for four hours until I finally broke down and called Josh. After an ordeal that almost cost him his life, he'd have been justified in never wanting to see me again. Instead he turned up on my dad's doorstep and sat with me in silence until I was ready to open it. Then he held me close while I sobbed into his arms. I don't know what will happen to us after this is over; all I know is that I'm not ready for him to leave my life.

The Matthewses put up no fight during mediation while social services decided the best way to reunite me with my son. All Rebecca asked was that they be allowed to stay involved in Simon's life. Given that their daughter kidnapped my son and killed my ex-husband, among other people, her request was denied, but I've fought as hard as I can and promised they will have regular contact with their grandson. They have done nothing wrong and my son loves them; it wouldn't be fair to him to push them away. I can't say I'll be as amenable to his paternal grandparents. The CPS are still deciding whether Margaret and Richard will be charged with obstructing the course of justice in Beth's murder and I don't know yet how I'm going to deal with them.

Today I'm going to meet my son for the first time in four years. We all agreed it would be best for him to be in his own home, and that we'll take it as slowly as he needs. When Rebecca opens the front door, I see that our social services adviser, Michelle, is already there.

'Hi.' Rebecca gives me a quick hug and leads me into the living room, where Michelle is waiting with Christopher Matthews. I introduce Josh; Michelle smiles and greets us both and Christopher offers a curt nod. He might not be putting up a fuss but this is breaking his heart. After hearing the news about his nephew, I can only imagine what this family are going through today.

'OK, Susan, are you ready?' Michelle asks me kindly. I'm not. I don't think, however long I had to prepare for this moment, anything would ever make me ready. Still I nod.

Michelle looks at Rebecca, then goes out into the hallway and I hear her speaking in a low voice to a child. My child.

The door opens. I hold my breath as a beautiful little boy appears in the doorway, looking down at his feet. Rebecca gives him a small nod and smiles at him encouragingly. The little boy takes a few steps into the room and looks up at me and Josh.

'Hiya,' he says brightly. A lump forms in my throat. I don't know if I can trust myself to speak, but I force out the words.

'Hello.' I smile down at the little boy I brought into the world, the little boy I held in my arms and rocked to sleep when he cried. 'My name's Susan. What's your name?'

'Simon,' he says, proudly holding up a toy truck for us both to see. 'Do you like my truck?'

'It's perfect,' I reply, fresh tears forming in my eyes. 'It's just absolutely perfect.'

Reading Group Questions

Postnatal depression lies at the heart of this story. Do you think that Susan received the help she needed? Is there adequate support for mothers suffering from postnatal depression?

Although Susan was unable to process the crime she was accused of committing, she learnt to accept the 'fact' of it. Do you think this is a dangerous approach to healing or a necessary part of the process? Why?

So many of the characters in this book are motivated by love or passion in some capacity, does this go any way towards excusing the crimes they have committed?

Jack's manipulation of Mark is quite remarkable. In your opinion, what is it that makes this possible? Is there a point at which Mark could have changed the dynamic of their relationship?

Do you think that 'Nick' was right to conceal his identity? Why?

The hurt and pain that Susan experiences as she realises that she barely knew her husband is palpable. How much do you think we can ever truly know about those closest to us?

Many of the characters in this book do or have done terrible things. What makes one act more or less forgivable than another?

Most readers will sympathise with Susan, but do you sympathise with Mark at all? Why?

How do you think Cassie's influence affects Susan? Are these women empowered or weakened by their friendship and shared experiences?

What do you think the future holds for Susan and baby Simon?

Suggested Further Reading

Just What Kind of Mother Are You? Paula Daly
The Accident C.L. Taylor
Do Me No Harm Julie Corbin
Cuckoo Julia Crouch

The inspiration behind
HOW I LOST YOU
by JENNY BLACKHURST

In 2011 I gave birth to my first child. Until then I'd been selfish with my time, working long hours as a retail manager and spending my weekends having luxurious lie-ins and lunching out with friends.

Overnight I could no longer choose when I ate, slept, or used the bathroom. I wasn't even Jenny any more, I was Connor's Mummy. When I was made redundant 4 weeks after giving birth it felt like the last of my identity had disappeared with my job – now my son was the only thing that defined me.

It was these feelings, this loss of identity, that made me question a person's sense of self – are we defined by who we are, or what we do? If the notion of 'self' is fragile enough to be broken by the loss of a job how easily can it be bent, or even broken, by others? Do we really know who we are, or what we are capable of?

The central theme of *How I Lost You* is that concept of who Susan once believed she was, and how one act can challenge that belief and lead her to redefine her whole sense of self. Who are you? How well do you know yourself?

Someone Else's Skin

Sarah Hilary

A Richard and Judy Book Club title.

Devastating, brilliant and heralding an outstanding new talent in crime fiction, SOMEONE ELSE'S SKIN is the crime debut of the year.

Called to a woman's refuge to take a routine witness statement, DI Marnie Rome instead walks in on an attempted murder.

Trying to uncover the truth from layers of secrets, Marnie finds herself confronting her own demons.

Because she, of all people, knows that it can be those closest to us we should fear the most . . .

Praise for Sarah Hilary:

'Superbly disturbing' *Observer*

'A slick, stylish debut' Sharon Bolton

'Unflinching without ever being gratuitous . . . it deserves to be massive' Erin Kelly

978 1 4722 0769 2

headline

The Long Fall

Julia Crouch

How far would you go to protect your secrets?

Greece, 1980

Emma takes part in a shattering, violent event. An event to which she is anything but an innocent bystander.

She is only eighteen, but this marks her fall from innocence. It will haunt her for the rest of her life.

London, now

Kate has the perfect existence: a glossy image, a glamorous home, a perfect family. But there are cracks. All is not what it seems.

And now the two worlds are about to collide.

Someone's out for revenge. Someone who has been waiting thirty years . . .

Praise for Julia Crouch:

'Once again, Julia Crouch plays on our darkest fears . . . Brilliant' Erin Kelly

'An absolutely brilliant writer, sharp and compassionate and with a great gift for characterisation' *Daily Mail*

'Brilliant, truly chilling' Sophie Hannah

978 1 4722 0723 4

headline

THRILLINGLY GOOD BOOKS
FROM CRIMINALLY
GOOD WRITERS

CRIME FILES BRINGS YOU THE LATEST RELEASES FROM
TOP CRIME AND THRILLER AUTHORS.

SIGN UP ONLINE FOR OUR MONTHLY NEWSLETTER AND BE THE FIRST
TO KNOW ABOUT OUR COMPETITIONS, NEW BOOKS AND MORE.

VISIT OUR WEBSITE: WWW.CRIMEFILES.CO.UK
LIKE US ON FACEBOOK: FACEBOOK.COM/CRIMEFILES
FOLLOW US ON TWITTER: @CRIMEFILESBOOKS